W9-BCC-884

Spellwright

TOR BOOKS BY BLAKE CHARLTON

Spellwright
Spellbound (forthcoming)

Spellwright

BLAKE CHARLTON

A Tom Doherty Associates Book
NEW YORK

This is a work of fiction. All of the characters, organizations, and events portrayed in this novel are either products of the author's imagination or are used fictitiously.

SPELLWRIGHT

Edited by James Frenkel

Map by Rhys Davies

A Tor Book
Published by Tom Doherty Associates, LLC
175 Fifth Avenue
New York, NY 10010

www.tor-forge.com

ISBN 978-0-7653-1727-8

First Edition: March 2010

Printed in the United States of America

0 9 8 7 6 5 4 3 2 1

To the memory of my grandmother,
Jane Bryden Buck (1912–2002),
for long stories and lessons in kindness

ACKNOWLEDGMENTS

Writing a novel is like escaping a cocoon you spun when you were someone less wise.

That being so, a complete list of my gratitude would include everyone who helped me come to terms with my disability. However, listing all the teachers, students, and friends who supported me would make *Spellwright* heavy enough to qualify as exercise equipment. So if you've opened this book because of the name on its spine—rather than its title—know that you are appreciated and loved.

My particular gratitude I dedicate to those who sacrificed for and believed in *Spellwright*: to James Frenkel, for limitless wisdom and gallons of industrial-strength editorial elbow grease; to Matt Bialer, for taking a chance on a young writer and helping him grow; to Todd Lockwood and Irene Gallo, for the stunning cover; to Tom Doherty and everyone at Tor, for their support; to Stanford Medical School and the Medical Scholars Research Program, for making my dual career possible; to Tad Williams, my glabrous, fantasy-writing, YMCA-basketball Jedi Master, whose fingerprints are all over this story; to Daniel Abraham, for lunar physics explanations and inspiring the concept of "quaternary thoughts" with a casual and brilliant comment over lunch; to Terra Chalberg, friend and publication guardian angel during a trying time; to Nina Nuangchamnong and Jessica Weare, foul-weather-friends and manuscript polishers extraordinaire; to Dean Laura King—wherever she might be—for pulling me out of the rabid premed wolf pack and teaching me to write and chase dreams; to Joshua Spanogle, for friendship and advice on the med student–novelist life; to Swaroop Samant and Erin Cashier, for fiery criticism and golden praise; to Asya Agulnik, Deanna Hoak, Kevan Moffett, Julia Manzerova, Mark Dannenberg, Nicole C. Hastings, Tom DuBois, Amy Yu, Ming Cheah, and Christine Chang, for fresh perspectives and wisdom; to Kate Sargent, for slogging though clunky early drafts; to The Wordspinners (Madeleine Robins, Kevin Andrew Murphy, Jaqueline Schumann, Jeff Weitzel, and Elizabeth Gilligan), for fellowship and teaching me how to talk shop; to Andrea Panchok-Berry, for reading the first, very misspelled draft; to Vicky Greenbaum, for early encouragement and inspiration; and, with all of my love, to Genevieve Johansen, Louise Buck, and Randy Charlton, for believing in me and for being such a wonderful family.

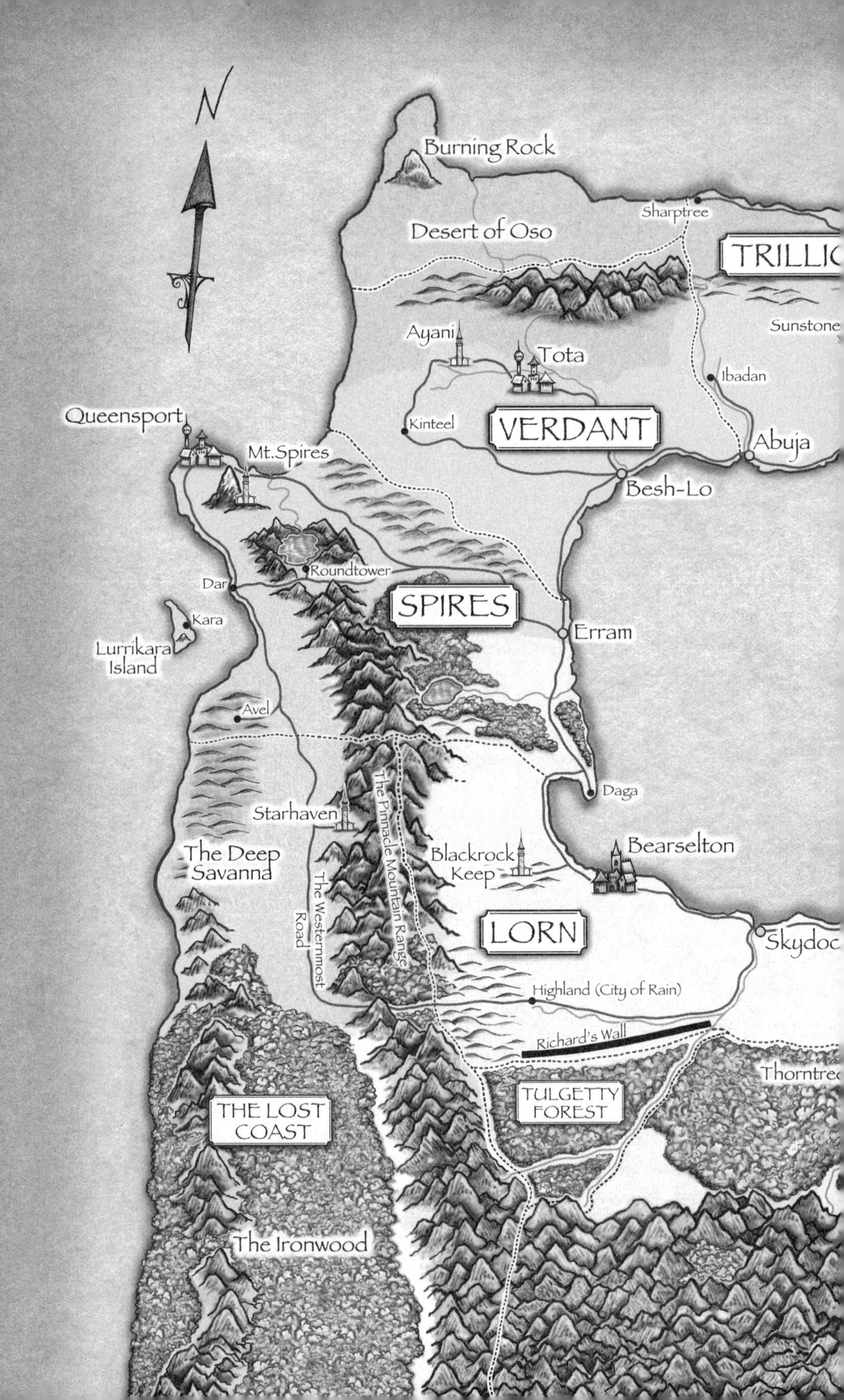
N
Burning Rock
Sharptree
Desert of Oso
TRILLIC
Sunstone
Ayani
Tota
Ibadan
Queensport
Kinteel
VERDANT
Abuja
Mt.Spires
Besh-Lo
Roundtower
Dar
SPIRES
Kara
Erram
Lurrikara
Island
Avel
Daga
Starhaven
The Pinnacle Mountain Range
Bearselton
The Deep
Savanna
Blackrock
Keep
The Westernmost
Road
LORN
Skydoc
Highland (City of Rain)
Richard's Wall
Thorntree
TULGETTY
FOREST
THE LOST
COAST
The Ironwood

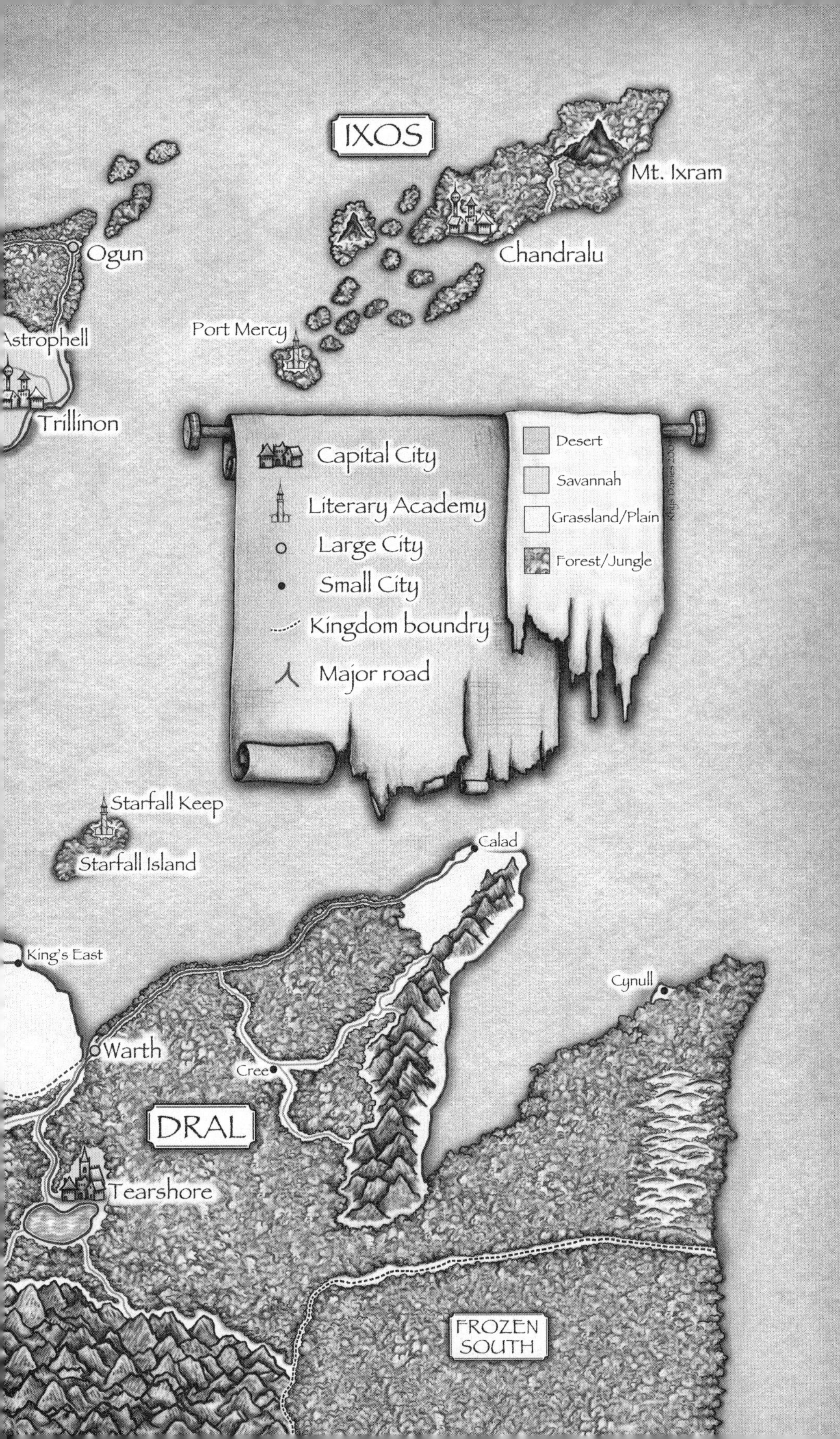
IXOS
Mt. Ixram
Ogun
Chandralu
Port Mercy
Astrophell
Trillinon
Capital City
Literary Academy
Large City
Small City
Kingdom boundry
Major road
Desert
Savannah
Grassland/Plain
Forest/Jungle
Starfall Keep
Starfall Island
Calad
King's East
Cynull
Warth
Cree
DRAL
Tearshore
FROZEN
SOUTH

If one believes that words are acts, as I do, then one must hold writers responsible for what their words do.

—URSULA K. LE GUIN

Dancing at the Edge of the World: Thoughts on Words, Women, Places

Spellwright

Prolog

The grammarian was choking to death on her own words.

And they were long sharp words, written in a magical language and crushed into a small, spiny ball. Her legs faltered. She fell onto her knees.

Cold autumn wind surged across the tower bridge.

The creature standing beside her covered his face with a voluminous white hood. "Censored already?" he rasped. "Disappointing."

The grammarian fought for breath. Her head felt as light as silk; her vision burned with gaudy color. The familiar world became foreign.

She was kneeling on a stone bridge, seven hundred feet above Starhaven's walls. Behind her, the academy's towers stretched into the cold evening sky like a copse of giant trees. At various heights, ribbon-thin bridges spanned the airy gaps between neighboring spires. Before her loomed the dark Pinnacle Mountains.

Dimly, she realized that her confused flight had brought her to the Spindle Bridge.

Her heart began to kick. From here the Spindle Bridge arched a lofty half-mile away from Starhaven to terminate in a mountain's sheer rock face. It led not to a path or a cave, but to blank stone. It was a bridge to nowhere, offering no chance of rescue or escape.

She tried to scream, but gagged on the words caught in her throat.

To the west, above the coastal plain, the setting sun was staining the sky a molten shade of incarnadine.

The creature robed in white sniffed with disgust. "Pitiful what passes for imaginative prose in this age." He lifted a pale arm. Two golden sentences glowed within his wrist.

"You are Magistra Nora Finn, Dean of the Drum Tower," he said. "Do not deny it again, and do not refuse my offer again." He flicked the glowing sentences into Nora's chest.

She could do nothing but choke.

"What's this?" he asked with cold amusement. "Seems my attack stopped that curse in your mouth." He paused before laughing, low and breathy. "I could make you eat your words."

Pain ripped down her throat. She tried to gasp.

The creature cocked his head to one side. "But perhaps you've changed your mind?"

With five small cracks, the sentences in her throat deconstructed and spilled into her mouth. She fell onto her hands and spat out the silver words. They shattered on the cobblestones. Cold air flooded into her greedy lungs.

"And do not renew your fight," the creature warned. "I can censor your every spell with this text."

She looked up and saw that the figure was now holding the golden sentence that ran into her chest. "Which of your students is the one I seek?"

She shook her head.

The creature laughed. "You took our master's coin, played the spy for him."

Again, she shook her head.

"Do you need more than gold?" He stepped closer. "I now possess the emerald and so Language Prime. I could tell you the Creator's first words. You'd find them . . . amusing."

"No payment could buy me for you," Nora said between breaths. "It was different with master; he was a man."

The creature cackled. "Is that what you think? That he was human?"

The monster's arm whipped back, snapping the golden sentence taut. The force of the action yanked Nora forward onto her face. Again pain flared down her throat. "No, you stupid sow," he snarled. "Your former master was not human!"

Something pulled up on Nora's hair, forcing her to look at her tormentor. A breeze was making his hood ruffle and snap. "Which cacographer do I seek?" he asked.

She clenched her fists. "What do you want with him?"

There was a pause. Only the wind dared make noise. Then the creature spoke. "Him?"

Involuntarily, Nora sucked in a breath. "No," she said, fighting to make her voice calm. "No, I said 'with them.' "

The cloaked figure remained silent.

"I said," Nora insisted, " 'What do you want with them?' Not him. With them."

Another pause. "A grammarian does not fault on her pronouns. Let us speak of 'him.' "

"You misheard; I—" The creature disengaged the spell that was holding her head up. She collapsed. "It was different in the dreams," she murmured into the cobblestones.

The creature growled. "Different because I sent you those dreams. Your students will receive the same: visions of a sunset seen from a tower bridge, dreams of a mountain vista. Eventually they will become curious and investigate."

Nora let out a tremulous breath. The prophecy had come to pass. How could she have been so blind? What grotesque forces had she been serving?

"Perhaps you think Starhaven's metaspells will protect your students," the creature said. "They won't. They might keep me from spellwriting within your walls, but I can lure the whelps into the woods or onto these bridges. It won't be hard to do now that the convocation has begun. If I must, I'll snuff out your students one by one. You could prevent all these deaths by speaking one name."

She did not move.

"Tell me his name," the white figure hissed, "and I will let you die quickly."

Nora glanced at the railing. An idea bled across her mind like an ink stain. It might work if she moved quickly enough.

"No answer?" The creature stepped away. "Then yours will be a slow death."

Nora felt a tug on the magical sentence running through her chest.

"I've just infected you with a canker spell. It forces a portion of a spellwright's body to forge misspelled runes. As we speak, the first canker is forming in your lungs. Soon it will spread into your muscles, compelling you to forge dangerous amounts of text. An hour will see your body convulsing, your arteries bleeding, your stomach ruptured."

Nora pressed her palms against the cold cobblestones.

"But the strongest of your cacographers will survive such an infection," the creature sneered. "That's how I'll find him. He'll survive the cankers; the others will die screaming. I'll spare you this torture if you tell me—"

But Nora did not wait to hear the rest. Soundlessly she pushed herself up and leaped over the railing. For a moment, she feared a swarm of silvery paragraphs would wrap about her ankles and hoist her back up to the bridge.

But the force of her fall snapped the golden sentence running through her chest . . . and she was free.

She closed her eyes and discovered that her fear of death had become strange and distant, more like a memory than an emotion.

The prophecy had come to pass. The knowledge would perish with her, but that was the price she had to pay: her death would keep a small, flickering hope alive.

Still falling, she opened her eyes. In the east, the crimson sky shone above the mountain's dark silhouette. The setting sun had shot the peaks full of red-gold light and, by contrast, stained the alpine forests below a deep, hungry black.

CHAPTER One

Nicodemus waited for the library to empty before he suggested committing a crime punishable by expulsion.

"If I edit you, we can both be asleep in an hour," he said to his text in what he hoped was a casual tone.

At twenty-five, Nicodemus Weal was young for a spellwright, old for an apprentice. He stood an inch over six feet and never slouched. His long hair shone jet black, his complexion dark olive—two colors that made his green eyes seem greener.

The text to whom he was speaking was a common library gargoyle. She was a construct, an animated being composed of magical language. And as Starhaven constructs went, she was a very plain spell.

More advanced gargoyles were animalistic mishmashes: the head of a snake on the body of a pig, limbs profuse with talons and tentacles or fangs and feathers. That sort of thing.

But the gargoyle squatting on the table before Nicodemus took the shape of only one animal: an adult snow monkey. Her slender stone torso and limbs were covered with stylized carvings representing fur. Her bare face presented heavy cheeks and weary eyes.

Her author had given her only one augmentation: a short tail from which protruded three hooked paragraphs of silvery prose. As Nicodemus watched the spell, she picked up three books and, using their clasps, hung them on her tail paragraphs.

"You edit me? Not likely," she retorted and then slowly climbed onto a bookshelf. "Besides, I was written so that I can't fall asleep until daylight."

"But you have better things to do than reshelve books all night," Nicodemus countered, smoothing out his black apprentice's robes.

"I might," the spell admitted, now climbing laterally along the shelf.

Nicodemus cradled a large codex in his left arm. "And you've let apprentices edit you before."

"Rarely," she grunted, climbing up two shelves. "And certainly never a cacographer." She pulled a book from her tail and slipped it onto the shelf.

"You are a cacographer, aren't you? You misspell magical texts simply by touching them?" She looked back at him with narrowed stone eyes.

Nicodemus had anticipated such a question; still, it felt like a kick in the stomach. "I am," he said flatly.

The gargoyle climbed another shelf. "Then it's against library rules: constructs aren't to let cacographers touch them. Besides, the wizards might expel you for editing me."

Nicodemus took a slow breath.

To either side of them stretched rows of bookshelves and scrollracks. They were on the tenth and top floor of the library known as the Stacks—a square building that housed many of Starhaven's manuscripts.

Presently the building was empty save for Nicodemus and the gargoyle. Some light came from moonbeams falling on the paper window screens, more from the incandescent flamefly paragraphs flitting about above Nicodemus.

He stepped closer to the gargoyle. "We've been reshelving so long that you've slowed down. So it's only your energetic prose that needs rewriting. I don't have to touch you to do that. All the other apprentices edited their constructs; that's why they and their gargoyles finished hours ago."

"All the other apprentices weren't cacographers," the spell replied, reshelving another book. "Don't cacographers always have to stay this late for Stacks duty?"

Trying not to scowl, Nicodemus laid his books back down on the table. "No, usually we don't need to rejuvenate our gargoyles. It's this damn convocation; the wizards are pulling every manuscript they can think of to impress their guests."

The gargoyle grimaced at their pile of unshelved books. "So that's why we've four times as much work tonight."

Nicodemus gave the construct his most haggard look. "It's worse than you know. I've still got an anatomy text to review and two spelling drills to complete before morning class."

The gargoyle laughed. "You want empathy from a primary construct? Ha! You might be a cacographer, but you can still think freely."

Nicodemus closed his eyes and realized that they stung from lack of sleep. Half an hour had already passed since midnight, and he had to wake with the dawn bell.

He looked at the gargoyle. "If you let me rejuvenate your energetic prose tonight, I'll find you a modification scroll tomorrow. Then you can change yourself however you like—wings, claws, whatever."

The textual construct began to climb back toward the table. "Wonderful, wings from a cacographer. What good would a scroll written by a retarded—"

"No, you pile of clichéd prose!" Nicodemus snapped. "I didn't say 'write.' I said 'find,' which means 'steal.' "

"Ho ho, the boy has some spirit after all." The gargoyle chuckled. She stopped climbing to look back at him. "Steal a scroll from whom?"

Nicodemus pulled a lock of black hair away from his face. Bribing constructs was an illegal but common practice in Starhaven. He disliked it, but he disliked the idea of another sleepless night even more. "I am Magister Shannon's apprentice," he said.

"Magister Agwu Shannon, the famous linguist?" the gargoyle asked excitedly. "The expert on textual intelligence?"

"The same."

A slow stone smile spread across the gargoyle's face. "Then you're the boy who failed to live up to prophecy? The one they thought was the Halcyon until he turned out to be retarded?"

"Do we have a deal or not?" Nicodemus retorted hotly, his hands clenched.

Still smiling, the gargoyle climbed onto the table. "Are the rumors about Shannon true?"

"I wouldn't know; I don't listen to hearsay," Nicodemus growled. "And if you speak one word against Magister, heaven help me but I'll knock you into sentence fragments."

The gargoyle snickered. "Such a loyal apprentice, considering you're offering to steal one of Shannon's scrolls."

Nicodemus clenched his jaw and reminded himself that, at some point, virtually all apprentices bribed constructs with their mentor's work. "Gargoyle, what do you want?"

She answered instantly: "Two stone more weight, so the medium-weight gargoyles can't push me off my sleeping perch. And quaternary cognition."

Nicodemus resisted the urge to roll his eyes. "Don't be ignorant; most humans can't reach quaternary cognition."

The gargoyle frowned and attached a book to her tail. "Tertiary, then."

Nicodemus shook his head. "With your executive text, we can't do better than secondary cognition."

She crossed her arms. "Tertiary."

"You might as well bargain for the white moon. You're asking for something I can't give."

"And you're asking me to be edited by a cacographer. Aren't cacographers incapable of concentrating long enough to finish a spell?"

"No," he said curtly. "Some of us have that problem, but I don't. The only thing that defines a cacographer is a tendency to misspell a complex text when touching it. And I wouldn't have to touch you."

The stone monkey folded her arms. "But you're asking me to deliberately violate library rules."

This time Nicodemus did roll his eyes. "You can't violate library rules, gargoyle; you've only got primary cognition. Your rules only forbid my touching you. All I need do tonight is add more energetic language to your body. I can do that without touching you. I've done this before and the gargoyle didn't lose a single rune."

The spell leaned forward and searched his face with blank stone eyes. "Two stone more weight and secondary cognition."

"Deal," Nicodemus grunted. "Now turn around."

The gargoyle's tail was still attached to a large spellbook. But rather than unfasten it, she stepped on top of the codex and turned to present her back.

Nicodemus's black apprentice robes had slits sewn into the top of the sleeves, near the shoulder. He slipped his arms out of these and looked down at his right elbow.

Magical runes were made not with pen and paper, but within muscle. Nicodemus, like all spellwrights, had been born with the ability to transform his physical strength into runes made of pure magical energy.

By tensing his bicep, he forged several runes within his arm. He could see the silvery language shine through skin and sinew. Tensing his bicep again, he joined the letters into a sentence, which he let spill into his forearm.

With a wrist flick, he cast the simple spell into the air, where it twisted like a tendril of glittering smoke. He extended his arm and cast the sentence onto the nape of the monkey's neck.

The spell contained a disassemble command; therefore, where it touched the construct, she began to shine with a silver glow. Nicodemus wrote a second sentence with his left arm and cast it next to his first. A seam of light ran down to the gargoyle's tail, and the two sides of her back swung open as if on hinges.

A coiling profusion of incandescent prose shone before him.

Different magical languages had different properties, and this gargoyle was made of two: Magnus, a robust silvery language that affected the physical world, and Numinous, an elegant golden language that altered light and other magical text. The gargoyle thought with her Numinous passages, moved with her Magnus.

Nicodemus's task was to add more energetic Magnus sentences. Fortunately, the structure of these energetic sentences was so simple that even a cacographer could compose them without error.

Careful not to touch the gargoyle, Nicodemus began to forge runes in his biceps and cast them into the gargoyle. Soon the Magnus sentences appeared as a thick rope of silvery light that coursed from his arms into the construct.

Though Nicodemus was a horrible speller, he could write faster than many grand wizards. Therefore he decided to provide the gargoyle with extra energetic text now; she might not submit to another edit later.

After moving his hands closer, Nicodemus tensed every muscle in his arms, from the tiny lumbricals between his hand bones to the rounded deltoid atop his shoulder. Within moments, he produced a dazzling flood of spells that flowed into the gargoyle's back.

The blaze grew so bright that he began to worry about bringing unwanted attention to the library. He was standing yards away from the nearest window, but a wizard working late might walk past the Stacks and see the glow. If caught, he would be expelled, perhaps even censored permanently.

Just then a loud thud sounded to Nicodemus's left. Terrified, he stopped writing and turned, expecting to find an enraged librarian bearing down on him.

But he saw only darkened bookshelves and scrollracks. Beyond those was a row of narrow, moonlit windows.

A second thud made Nicodemus jump. It sounded as if it were coming from the library's roof.

He looked up but saw only ceiling. Then the darkness was filled by a repetitive clomping, as if someone were running. The footsteps passed directly over him and then sped away to the opposite side of the library.

Nicodemus turned to follow the sound with his eyes. When the footsteps reached the roof's edge, they ceased. A moon-shadow flickered across two of the paper screens.

Then came a low muttering beside him: "Ba, ball, balloon, ballistic." Something snickered. "Symbolic ballistics. Ha! Symbolic, diabolic. Diabolic, symbolic. Sym . . . bolic is the opposite of dia . . . bolic. Ha ha."

Nicodemus looked down and, to his horror, saw his hand enmeshed in the silver and gold coils of the gargoyle's text. His cacographic touch was causing the once stable sentences to misspell. He must have accidentally laid his hand on the construct when startled by the footsteps.

"Oh, hell!" he whispered, pulling his hand back.

When his fingers left the gargoyle, the two sides of her back snapped shut. Instantly, she was on her feet and staring at him with one eye that blazed golden and another that throbbed with silver light. "Vertex, vortex, university," she muttered and laughed in a way that showed her sharp primate teeth. "Invert, extravert. Ha ha! Aversion, aveeeeersion."

"Ohhhhh hell," a wide-eyed Nicodemus whispered, too shocked and frightened to move.

A sudden nauseating wave of guilt washed through him. He might have irreversibly damaged the gargoyle's executive text.

Then the construct was off, dashing down the aisle. A spellbook was still hooked to her tail. Now, dragging behind her, the book opened and began to lose paragraphs written in several magical languages. Falling from the tortured pages, the paragraphs squirmed as if alive. Two exploded into small clouds of white runes; others slowly deconstructed into nothing.

"Wait!" Nicodemus yelled, sprinting after the misspelled gargoyle. "Gargoyle, stop!"

The construct either did not hear or did not care. She leaped up at a window and exploded through its paper screen.

Nicodemus reached the sill in time to watch her fall down ten stories into a dark courtyard filled with elm trees, grass, and ivy.

As the gargoyle dropped, stray paragraphs continued to fall from the spellbook attached to her tail. Radiant words of gold, green, silver, and white fluttered downward and in so doing formed a comet's tail of radiant language.

"Please, heaven, please don't let Magister Shannon find out about this," Nicodemus prayed. "Please!"

The gargoyle hit the ground and scampered away, but the still-falling coruscation of paragraphs began to illuminate the stone spires, arches, and arcades of the surrounding buildings. Nicodemus turned to sprint after his mistake.

But as he did so, something caught his eye. What exactly, he couldn't say. For when he looked back, it had disappeared, leaving only the vague impression that he had seen—standing atop an ornate stone buttress—a hooded figure cloaked entirely in white.

CHAPTER

Two

The creature, now crouching beside a stone chimney, watched the gargoyle scamper through the courtyard.

The construct's speed implied excessive energetic language; its erratic course, a misspelled executive text. Only a powerful cacographer was likely to produce such a construct.

"Meaning my boy is in that library this very instant," the creature muttered while glaring at the Stacks. He had glimpsed his quarry in the library window, but the rain of paragraphs loosed by the gargoyle had obscured everything but the boy's silhouette.

Suddenly the night resounded with a sharp crack.

The creature turned and saw a silver spell shoot out from behind a stone spire. The spherical text was written in Magnus and so would have a powerful effect on the physical world. Indeed, its blazing sentences seemed designed to blast a human body into a cloud of bone fragments and vaporized blood.

More important, the spell was flying straight for the creature's head.

He dove right, rolling down the slate roof. There was a crash and needles of pain flew down his back. No doubt the Magnus spell had shattered the chimney into stone splinters.

At the roof's edge, the creature came out of its roll and crouched. A flying buttress to another building stood roughly ten feet away. He looked back but there was no sign of the guardian spell that must have cast the Magnus attack.

His body was not in danger; guardian spells were slow on rooftops. But they were lightning quick in courtyards and hallways and so could prevent him from retrieving the boy.

"So the guardians must be removed," he grunted.

With a powerful leap the creature flew into the air, white robes billowing, and landed neatly on the arc of the flying buttress. With care, he ran up the arc to another roof; this one abutted one of the aqueducts that crisscrossed Starhaven. He scaled the aqueduct, and finding it dry, ran eastward.

All three moons were out, gibbous, and gloriously bright. They illuminated Starhaven's many towers and bridges from three different angles, transforming the lower levels into a maze of overlapping shadows.

The wizards, in their arrogance, referred to Starhaven as one of their "academies." In truth, the place was an ancient city, built by the Chthonic people long before any human had laid eyes on this continent. Though the wizards claimed the entirety of Starhaven, they occupied only the westernmost third of the city.

The creature's course led him away from the inhabited buildings. Here stood dark towers, cracked domes, and cobbled streets pocked by weeds.

He waited until the abandoned building echoed with the heavy footfalls of the guardians. Then he raced up a tower's spiral staircase and sprinted north on an upper-level walkway.

Once certain the guardians were far behind, the creature turned westward and focused his every bloody thought on hunting down the cacographic boy.

NICODEMUS PUSHED THE door latch with his elbow, the door itself with his backside. When it swung open, he stepped backward into Magister Shannon's study and fell over sideways.

His arms encircled a tapestry wrapped into a ball and bound by twine. It writhed continuously and in a muffled voice blathered: "Corpulent, encouragement, incorporeal. Ha! Incorporeal encooooouragment!"

Nicodemus rolled away from the tapestry. "Celeste, goddess of the sky, please make her shut up. I'll light a candle for you every night if you just make her shut up."

Unimpressed, Celeste declined to intervene.

"Empathy, apathy, sympathy, hoo hoo!" said the bundled tapestry.

"Two candles?" Nicodemus offered the unseen sky.

"Euphony, cacophony, hoo hoo! Calligraphy, cacography, ha ha!" said the bundle.

Groaning, Nicodemus got to his feet. The study was dark, but both the blue and white moons shone through the open arched windows.

It was a rectangular room lined with oak bookshelves. A broad writing desk sat at one end, a huddle of chairs in the middle.

Nicodemus went to the nearest bookshelf and pulled out a large codex on gargoyle repair and maintenance. The needed spell was on the tenth page. He laid the open book on the desk, slipped his arms from his sleeves, and wrote a short Numinous spell in his right hand. Bending the golden sentence into a hook, he dipped it into the page and peeled off a tangle of Numinous paragraphs that folded into a rectangular crystalline lattice.

Careful not to touch the text, he walked back to the squirming bundle and, with a sharp word, cut the twine cords.

The gargoyle sprang free with a joyful cry.

Nicodemus struck her over the head with the Numinous lattice. The crystalline spell locked around the gargoyle's mind, causing her to freeze in an unlikely pose—one knee and one foot on the floor, both hands reaching skyward. She began to fall forward.

Uttering an oath, Nicodemus extemporized a simple Magnus sentence to catch her. With a few more sentences, he lifted her up and then leaned her against the bookshelf.

As far as he knew, no one had seen him chasing the gargoyle around the courtyard with a tapestry. For that, he said a prayer of thanks to the Creator.

Then he looked at the gargoyle and said in a voice that was soft and sincere, "You stupid, suffering construct. What have I done to you?"

"Fused her Numinous cortices," a rumbling voice replied.

Nicodemus's blood froze. "Magister!" he whispered as a figure moved out of a dark corner.

Grand Wizard Agwu Shannon stepped into a bar of blue moonlight. The glow illuminated white dreadlocks, a short beard and mustache, tawny skin. His nose was large and hooked, his thin lips pressed flat in disapproval.

However, Shannon's eyes commanded the most attention. They presented neither iris nor pupil but were everywhere pure white. These were eyes blind to the mundane world but extraordinarily perceptive of magical text.

Nicodemus sputtered. "Magister, I didn't think you'd be working so late. I was just going—"

The grand wizard stopped him by nodding to the gargoyle. "Who else knows?"

"No one. I was reshelving in the Stacks alone. I was just going to edit her."

Shannon grunted and then looked in Nicodemus's direction. "She shouldn't have let you touch her. What was your bribe?"

Nicodemus felt as if he were breathing through a reed. "Two stone more weight and secondary cognition."

The grand wizard walked to the gargoyle and squatted beside her. "She already has secondary cognition."

"But that's impossible; I never used a modification scroll on her."

"Look at this frontal cortex." The grand wizard pointed.

Nicodemus went to Shannon's side, but lacking his teacher's vision, he saw only the monkey's stone forehead.

"There's some inappropriate fusion, but . . ." Shannon muttered. Using only the muscles in his right hand, the grand wizard produced a tiny storm of golden sentences. Faster than Nicodemus could follow, the spell split the gargoyle's head and began to rearrange her executive subspells.

Nicodemus pursed his lips. "She said she was primary, and the librarians assigned her to reshelving; they only use primary gargoyles for that."

Shannon brought his left hand up to assist his manipulation of the gargoyle's Numinous passages. "How long did you touch her?"

"No more than a few moments," Nicodemus insisted. He was about to say more when Shannon clapped the monkey's head together and pulled the Numinous lattice from her head as if it were a tablecloth.

The gargoyle sank to all fours and looked up at Shannon. Her blank stone eyes searched his face. "I could have a name now," she said in a quick, childlike voice.

Shannon's nod sent his white dreadlocks swaying. "But I wouldn't pick one just yet. Get used to your new thoughts first."

She smiled and then, dreamily, nodded.

Shannon stood and looked toward Nicodemus. "What was it you wrapped her in?"

"A tapestry," Nicodemus said weakly. "From the Stacks."

Shannon sighed and turned back to the gargoyle. "Please re-hang that tapestry and finish reshelving. Use the rest of the night to name yourself."

The energized gargoyle nodded eagerly then scooped up the tapestry and scampered out the door.

"Magister, I—" Nicodemus stopped as Shannon turned to face him.

The old man was dressed in the billowing black robes of a grand wizard. Even in the dim moonlight, the lining of his large hood shone white, indicating that he was a linguist. Silver and gold buttons ran down his sleeves, signifying his fluency in Numinous and Magnus.

Shannon's blind gaze was turned slightly away, but when he spoke, Nicodemus felt as if the old man was staring through his body to his soul.

"My boy, you surprise me. As a younger spellwright, I bribed a few constructs, even got into hot water with overly ambitious texts. But your disability places a special burden on us both. I keenly want you to earn a lesser hood, but if another wizard had seen that misspelled gargoyle . . . well, it would have ended your hopes of escaping apprenticeship and made life harder for the other cacographers."

"Yes, Magister."

Shannon sighed. "I will continue fighting for your hood, but only if there won't be a repetition of such . . . carelessness."

Nicodemus looked at his boots. "There won't be, Magister."

The old man began to walk back to his desk. "And why in the Creator's name did you touch the gargoyle?"

"I didn't mean to. I was editing text into her when there was a crash. Then it sounded like someone was running on the roof. It made me accidentally touch the gargoyle."

Shannon stopped. "When was this?"

"Maybe half an hour ago."

The grand wizard turned to face him. "Tell me everything."

As Nicodemus described the strange sounds, Shannon's lips again pressed into a thin line. "Magister, is something wrong?"

Shannon went to his desk. "Light two of my candles; leave one here, take one yourself. Then run up to Magister Smallwood's study. He always works late. Ask him to join me."

Nicodemus started for the candle drawer.

"Then you're to go straight back to the Drum Tower—no detours, no dillydally." Shannon sat down behind his desk. "I will send Azure to your quarters with a message. Am I clear?"

"Yes, Magister." Nicodemus set up and lit the candles.

Shannon began sorting through the manuscripts on his desk. "You'll spend tomorrow with me. I've received permission to begin casting a primary research spell and will need your assistance. And then there's my new composition class to teach. I'll have you excused from apprentice duty."

"Truly?" Nicodemus smiled in surprise. "Might I teach? I've practiced the introductory lecture."

"Perhaps," Shannon said without looking up from the manuscript he was reading. "Now run up to Magister Smallwood and then straight to the Drum Tower, nowhere else."

"Yes, Magister." Nicodemus eagerly picked up a candle and made his way to the door.

But when he put his hand on the latch, an idea stopped him. "Magister," he asked slowly, "did that gargoyle have secondary cognition all along?"

Shannon paused and then put down his manuscript. "My boy, I don't want to raise false expectations again."

Nicodemus frowned. "Expectations about what?"

"The gargoyle had primary cognition until you misspelled her."

"But how is that possible?"

"It shouldn't be," Shannon said before rubbing his eyes. "Nicodemus, for this convocation we are hosting delegates from the North: Astrophell wizards, some of my former colleagues. Some of them belong to the counter-prophecy faction and so will distrust cacographers even more than other Northerners do. It would be exceedingly dangerous if they learned that your touch both misspelled a gargoyle and elevated her freedom of thought."

"Dangerous because they would want me censored?"

Shannon shook his head. "Dangerous because they would want you killed."

CHAPTER

Three

On the way to Magister Smallwood's study, Nicodemus looked at his candle. It was quavering in time to his hand's fine tremble.

He had never known Shannon to betray even a hint of anxiety. But when the old man had mentioned the Astrophell delegates, his tone had been strained, his words clipped. The danger the Northerners posed must be real indeed.

Worse had been Shannon's statement about not raising "false expectations." Nicodemus shivered; the old man could only have been referring to Nicodemus's lost hope of fulfilling the Erasmine Prophecy.

"Fiery heaven, don't think on it," Nicodemus muttered to himself, as he had done countless times before.

A row of arched windows, all filled with ornate tracery, ran along the hallway. Nicodemus stopped to peer between the flowing stone beams to the starry sky beyond. He slowed his breathing and tried to soothe his frayed nerves.

But his hands still trembled, and it wasn't Northern delegates or unfulfilled prophecies that made them do so.

It was the memory of Shannon's face when the old man had stepped into the moonlight—his white eyebrows knitting together in disapproval, his lips narrowing in disappointment.

The memory made Nicodemus feel as if something were tightening around his heart. "I'll make it up to the old man," he whispered. "I will."

He turned from the window and hurried down the hall to an open door spilling candlelight into the hallway. "Magister Smallwood?" He knocked on the doorjamb. The grand wizard looked up from his desk.

Smallwood was a thin, pale spellwright with a tousled wreath of gray hair. His eyes, though beginning to cloud over, still held black pupils within brown irises.

Nicodemus cleared his throat. "Magister Shannon sends his compliments and asks that you join him in his study."

"Ah, good, good, always happy to see Shannon," Smallwood said with an absent smile. He closed his book. "And who are you?"

"Nicodemus Weal, Magister Shannon's apprentice."

Smallwood leaned forward and squinted. "Ah, Shannon's next cacographic project?"

"I'm sorry?"

"I don't remember the last boy's name. And I've never seen you before."

In fact, Nicodemus had been bringing Smallwood written messages for nearly two years. However, this was the first time Nicodemus had spoken directly to him. "I'm sorry, Magister, but I don't understand about the cacographic project."

Smallwood stretched his arms and adjusted his hood, which like Shannon's was lined with white. "Oh, you know, Shannon takes his work with the Drum Tower boys so seriously. And he's always got a pet cacographer. It's ridiculous the rumors that go round about him; he's so proud when one of you earns a lesser hood."

"Yes, Magister," Nicodemus said, trying not to frown. He had heard rumors about Shannon's former career in Astrophell but never a rumor about the old man's current position as Master of the Drum Tower.

"So, what exactly does Shannon have you doing to earn that hood?" Smallwood asked.

"He's written a spell that allows him to pull my runes into his body. It helps him spellwrite longer texts. We're hoping that if enough linguists feel I'm helpful, they'll give me a lesser hood lined with white."

"Ah, yes, and I'm to be the first who finds you useful." Smallwood's smile seemed genuine. "I believe you'll be assisting Shannon and me tomorrow. Very exciting, very promising research spell we'll be attempting."

"I'm honored to be part of it, Magister."

"And are you teaching yet?"

Nicodemus tried to sound confident. "Anatomy dissections, but not a spellwriting class yet. I'm very much looking forward to it."

"Yes, well, keep pestering Shannon about that; the academy will keep a hood away from you until you're fifty unless you teach composition." The linguist's gaze wandered to the books on his desk. "Did Shannon want me right away?"

"I believe so, Magister."

Smallwood stood. "Very well, very well. Thank you, Nicolas; it is good to meet you. You may go."

"Nicodemus, Magister."

"Yes, yes, Nicodemus, of course." He paused. "Pardon me, but did you say Nicodemus Weal?"

"Yes, Magister."

Smallwood studied Nicodemus with a focused intensity. "Of course," the grand wizard said at last, suddenly earnest. "Foolish of me to forget you, Nicodemus. Thank you for the message. You may go."

Nicodemus bobbed his head and retreated. He hurried to the hallway's end and then ducked into a narrow spiral staircase. Shannon had instructed him to go straight back to the Drum Tower, so he jogged down to the ground level and out into a torch-lit hallway. Walking eastward, he passed Lornish tapestries and gilded stone arcades.

But he was blind to their beauty.

His thoughts were troubled by what Smallwood had said about Shannon. All the apprentices knew that Shannon had suffered some kind of fall from grace back in Astrophell, but Smallwood had implied there were more recent rumors involving Shannon and cacographers.

Nicodemus bit his lip. Smallwood was famously absentminded; it was possible that he was mistaking old rumors for new.

But if that was the case, what exactly had Smallwood been misremembering when he mentioned Shannon's "next cacographic project" and his new "pet cacographer"?

Nicodemus turned to mount a narrow staircase.

Shannon had begun teaching cacographers only fifty years ago, when he arrived at Starhaven. So the source of Smallwood's rumor must have occurred since then.

Reaching the oak doors at the top of the stairs, Nicodemus pushed them open and looked out on the gray slate tiles that paved the yard of the Stone Court.

Centuries ago, the Neosolar Empire had renovated the courtyard after taking Starhaven from the Chthonic people. However, none of the succeeding occupying kingdoms had built over this aspect of the stronghold.

Consequently, the Stone Court demonstrated the classical architecture so common to Starhaven's Imperial Quarter: walls decorated by molded white plaster, arched doorways, wide windows. Each entryway was flanked by a pair of stone obelisks.

However, because of the Stone Court's remote location, the wizards had filled it with several objects too unsightly to reside in Starhaven's more populous quarters.

A forest of Dralish standing stones stood in the courtyard's center. On its eastern edge loitered two marble statues of Erasmus and one of Uriel Bolide. And everywhere—curled up, sprawled out, or lying on any available stone ledge—were sleeping janitorial gargoyles.

Nicodemus started for the Drum Tower, which abutted the court's eastern limit. But as he went, he saw something move within the stone forest.

He stopped.

The movement had been too quick to be that of a janitorial gargoyle. And no neophyte should be awake so late. Perhaps it was a feral cat?

It came again: a pale blur between two standing stones. Apprehension gripped Nicodemus. Wizards wore only black. Cloth of any other color signified an outsider . . . or an intruder.

Starhaven's many towers hid the blue and black moons, but the gibbous white moon hung directly overhead and flooded the court with milky light. As Nicodemus snuck among the standing stones, a crocodile-like gargoyle sleeping on the ground rolled over to regard him with a half-opened eye.

Someone was whispering behind the megalith to Nicodemus's left. "Who's there?" he asked in his boldest voice and stepped around the megalith.

Before him stood a short figure robed in white cloth. It spun around with inhuman speed.

CHAPTER

Four

Magister Shannon, sitting behind his desk, looked in the direction of Smallwood's voice. "Thank you for coming so late, Timothy."

"Quite all right; I'm always up," Smallwood said with his usual warmth. Shannon could not see the other wizard, but judging by his voice, he was standing by the bookshelves.

"But I'm surprised you're awake," Smallwood added. "I didn't think you were a night owl."

Shannon grunted. "I'm not. Two hours ago, I was in bed. A relay text from one of my research projects woke me with a report of unusual guardian activity around the Drum Tower. Seems they've been chasing something around on the roofs."

"Guardian spells," Smallwood said with a disdainful sniff. "Sloppy prose, if you ask me, written with too much sensitivity. Likely they were chasing a feral cat that wandered in from the uninhabited quarters."

"That was my first thought. I came here to look up a few things about editing the guardians' sensitivity. But then my apprentice appeared; seems he heard someone running across the roof of the Stacks."

When Shannon looked at his bookshelf, his eyes saw through the leather bindings to the radiant paragraphs contained within the books. As he watched, a rectangle of green text separated from the rest and unfolded into two smaller rectangles. Smallwood had pulled a book and was browsing through it. "Timothy, are you listening?"

"What? Yes, yes, of course," Smallwood replied and clapped the green rectangles together. "So you think one of the delegates might be sneaking about the roofs?"

Shannon shrugged. "Could be a foreign spellwright. Could be a wizard."

"But spying on the Drum Tower? I know the cacographers are close to your heart, but shouldn't intrigue focus elsewhere? The Main Library, say, or the provost's quarters?"

"Precisely what worries me."

Smallwood coughed. "Agwu, might you be overreacting? I know you were more . . . involved in Astrophell, but this is Starhaven."

Shannon rubbed his mustache to hide his frown.

Smallwood continued. "Perhaps the Astrophell delegates have put you on edge? Brought back the old instincts?"

"Perhaps but unlikely," Shannon insisted. "I've two guardian spells in the linguistics library. I'd like them cast to patrol around the Stone Court. But first I need you to rewrite their protocols to communicate with the gargoyles sleeping there."

It sounded as if Smallwood were shuffling his feet. "Tonight?"

Shannon crossed his arms and looked where he thought his colleague's face might be. "It would help me focus on our research spell tomorrow."

"Tonight it is, then. I am grateful you've included me in this research."

Shannon let out a breath he had not known he was holding.

The rectangle of green prose floated back up to its proper place: Smallwood was reshelving the book. "Is Azure about?"

Shannon shook his head. "She's delivering a message for me." He did not mention that she was also flying about the rooftops searching for anything unusual.

"Pity," Smallwood said, his voice heading for the door. "I wanted to see her Numinous dialect again. Agwu, before I go . . . do I remember correctly that your apprentice was thought to be the Halcyon?"

"You do."

Smallwood continued hesitantly. "Your fear that . . . I mean, perhaps you're jumping to conclusions." He paused. "Let me ask it this way: Do you think Nicodemus is the one of prophecy?"

"Absolutely not."

"Good, good, of course." The door latch clicked. "I'll have the guardian spells cast within an hour. I'll see you tomorrow after midday?"

"Indeed," Shannon said and then waited for the door hinges to creak before adding, "Timothy, truly, thank you."

"Quite welcome, Agwu. Quite welcome." The door clicked shut.

Puffing out his cheeks, Shannon retrieved his research journal from his desk. It was a leather-bound codex about two hands tall. Its spine and face were each embossed with three asterisks, allowing him to identify the book by touch. He opened it and began to write a few notes about the day. He worked for a quarter hour before an unexpected light made him look up.

He could not see his door physically, but he knew exactly where it was. It usually formed a dark rectangle amid the glow of his bookshelves. Where the darkness should have been, there now shone a cloud of golden paragraphs.

Experience told Shannon that he was looking through the door to an incandescent flamefly spell being cast in the hallway.

His first thought was that Smallwood had returned. But Timothy knew the hallways; he rarely cast a single flamefly paragraph, much less a swarm. The author of this spell wanted a good deal of light when navigating Starhaven's hallways.

Most likely a foreigner.

Shannon squinted at the text. It was written with bold words and complex sentences. The author favored compound appositives, an unusual structure.

Shannon grimaced in recognition. It had been a long time since he had seen this spellwright. "Creator save me, what else is going to happen tonight?" he muttered, waiting for the author to knock.

But she did not knock. He closed his research journal. Moments passed. He could see her prose but not her body. Strangely, she let the flamefly paragraphs deconstruct into heatless cinders that snowed down to the floor. What was she waiting for?

Affecting his warmest tone, he called out, "You may come in, Amadi."

Slowly the door hinges squeaked. A woman's calm voice said, "I see that old Magister Shannon isn't as blind as rumor claims." The door clicked shut.

Shannon smiled as he stood. "Old? I'm not so antique as to forget your sharp tongue. Come and embrace your ancient teacher."

Memory guided him around the desk. Amadi's approaching footsteps were light, hesitant. But her embrace was strong and quick. He had forgotten how tall she was. "But the rumors are true," he said while stepping back: "I'm as blind as a cave fish."

She paused. "You don't look old enough to have lost sight."

He chuckled dryly. "Then it's your eyes we should worry about. I'm nearly done with my second century."

"Magister, I'll be sorely disappointed if it's only age that stole your vision," Amadi said in the same teasing tone she had used as a girl. "I've heard stories, legends even, about how you blinded yourself by reading forbidden texts in the Spirish Civil War or by combating twenty mercenary authors while your beard was on fire."

Shannon had been counterfeiting good humor, but now a genuine laugh escaped his lips. "The truth is nothing so scintillating."

"But you don't seem that old."

"You always were a stubborn one." He laughed again and shook his head.

In Astrophell, Shannon had made several powerful enemies who might have planted an agent in the Northern delegation. For this reason, any Astrophell wizard was a potential threat; and yet, despite the danger, he enjoyed talking to his former student and remembering a past life.

"Amadi, I plan to begin ghostwriting in five years," he said in a more playful tone. "So don't bother with flattery about how young I might seem; it only reminds me of your advantage. My familiar is not about to look at you for me. And I'm curious to see you after . . . how long has it been? Fifty years?"

Amadi's leather soles whispered against the floor. "Your fingers may look," she said, suddenly closer.

This was unexpected. "That . . ." His voice died as she took his hands and placed them on her brow.

An uncomfortable pause.

Then his fingertips flowed onto her brief eyebrow ridge; down over her deep-set eyes; up the sharp nasal promontory; softly over the two pursed lips; along the delicate chin.

His memory provided color: ivory for her skin, sable for her hair, watery blue for her eyes. Imagination mixed touch with recollection to produce the image of a pale wizard with fine dreadlocks and an impassive expression.

Shannon swallowed. He hadn't thought seeing an old student would be like this. "Your hair must show a little white by now," he said more quickly than he would have liked.

"More than a little," she said, stepping away. "Will you tell me how you recognized me through your door?"

"With my natural sight gone, my spellwright's vision now pierces the mundane world to see magical text. Through the door, I recognized your compound appositives."

"You still remember my prose style?"

He shrugged. "I also heard your name among the Astrophell delegates; I was expecting to run into you sooner or later. This turns out to be sooner indeed."

"Magister, I want to talk about—"

"Please, call me Agwu," he interrupted. "Or Shannon—it's what my friends use when they have trouble with a Northern first name."

"I don't think I can," she said and then giggled. "Do you remember catching me and the other acolytes out of bed? How can I call you Shannon remembering that?"

He joined his laugh to hers and walked back to his chair. "I had nearly forgotten. What were you little monsters sneaking into the academy? A pair of muddy pigs? Please, take a seat."

"Pigs? In Astrophell?" she asked. Her chair creaked. "It was only one, very clean, goat."

"Whatever it was, you certainly can call me Shannon now that you may carry a grand wizard's staff." He settled into his chair.

"Well then, Shannon, I bring word of your granddaughter."

Shannon's stomach tightened. Her tone was still playful, but her words marked the end of pleasantries, the beginning of politics.

"You do?" he said, forcing his smile to neither broaden nor wilt.

Amadi cleared her throat. "She married a wealthy Ixonian merchant last year."

"Wonderful," he heard himself say. "What else can you tell me?"

"Little more, I'm afraid. I've the merchant's name written down somewhere." She paused. "Forgive me. It must be difficult discussing the life exile took away."

Shannon waved away her comment. "Bah, it was no exile; I accepted this position. Besides, wizards swear off family for a reason. In the beginning, it was difficult getting only fragmented news of my son. But now I've promising research and dedicated students. We are discovering such fascinating things. Just this morning I received permission to begin casting my primary research spell."

Amadi's chair creaked. "And you're content with such a . . . calm life?"

Shannon raised his eyebrows. So she suspected that he still harbored political ambitions? That might be dangerous, especially if she were reporting back to Astrophell.

"Amadi, sometimes it feels as if another author lived that bustling career in the North. Starhaven is a smaller academy, and we're so very far from civilization. But here . . ." He made a show of running his gaze across his books. "Here I enjoy a slower life."

When she did not reply, he changed the subject. "I just moved into new quarters above the Bolide Garden. Janitorial is renovating the gardens; it's not much now, heaps of dirt and clay, but it will be beautiful. I could show you."

Amadi's chair creaked again. "Some Astrophell wizards have been quoting your 'Complaint to the Long Council.'"

His grin faded. "It was my best speech."

"Many still find it inspiring."

"I am glad to hear it, but that life is over. There's no use baiting my appetite for it. I stay clear of Starhaven's intrigue. As a researcher, I can't be completely apolitical. But because of my past, the provost and his officers are happy to leave me out of most entanglements."

Amadi said nothing. The parchment on the table began to crinkle, likely from a breeze coming through the window.

"But never mind me," Shannon said. "How have you spent the past four decades? Studying diplomacy perhaps? Is that where this talk of my past comes from?"

"My hood has a purple lining."

"A sentinel? Yes, you must be wonderful."

She cleared her throat importantly. "I command Astrophell's lead sentinel expeditions. In fact, I led the delegation down here. I even have a personal secretary: a young Ixonian named Kale—only a lesser wizard, but bright and capable."

"Pardon the observation, but it seems odd that Astrophell should send sentinels to our convocation."

"The journey from the North was long. And heaven only knows why our order ever occupied this gargantuan stronghold out in the middle of nowhere. Granted, it makes a fine sight from the Westernmost Road—the highest tower spiring up from the mountainside to dwarf the peaks behind."

Shannon rested his elbows on the table and steepled his fingers. "But Amadi, why should Astrophell send sentinels with its delegation?"

"The diplomats needed protection."

"I see."

"Shannon, is this room safe from prying ears?"

He nodded. "Quite safe. Do you bring news from abroad?"

"News from within."

Shannon leaned forward. "Go on."

Amadi shifted in her seat and half-whispered: "Murder in Starhaven."

Shannon's heart began to strike. "Who?"

"This is a sensitive issue, one that must be hidden until the convocation is over. The delegates must renew the treaties."

"I'm aware of that. Now will you tell me who has been killed?"

"Bear with me, Magister. Five hours ago a janitorial gargoyle working beneath the Spindle Bridge discovered what he thought to be a dying woman."

"What he thought was a dying woman?"

"She was already dead, but her body was still filling itself with a virulent Numinous misspell. The gargoyle, having secondary cognition, assumed she was still alive and took her to the deputy provost of libraries. She, in turn, reported to the provost, who related the information to me."

Shannon paused. "You said this woman fell from the Spindle?"

"So it seems. What can you tell me of the bridge?"

Shannon wondered how much information he should share. Amadi had leaped to the top of the sentinel ranks, and such a feat would be impossible without the support of several factions that despised Shannon. He decided to share only common knowledge until he knew more.

"You seem troubled," Amadi said. "Is it odd that this woman was on the Spindle?"

"Surpassingly odd," he said at last. "According to the historians, the Chthonic people built the bridge not long after they finished Starhaven. But it leads nowhere. Spans nearly a mile of air only to run into a cliff. The Chthonics did cut beautiful designs into the rock. Just north of the bridge's end is a foliate pattern—ivy leaves, I believe—and south is a hexagonal pattern."

"Any explanation for the carvings? Or the bridge itself?"

Shannon shrugged. "Folktales about the Chthonics building a road to a paradise called Heaven Tree Valley. Supposedly when the Neosolar Empire began to massacre the Chthonics, their goddess led them to the Heaven Tree and dropped a mountain on the road. Some say the Spindle once led to that road."

"Any evidence to support such a tale?"

"None. But every so often, the historians probe the mountainside with text, trying to open the way to the Heaven Tree. They've found only rock." He paused. "Do you think the murder is connected to any of this?"

The soft swish of moving cloth told Shannon that Amadi was shifting in her seat again. "Not that I can see," she said and then sighed.

Shannon paused before he spoke again. "Amadi, I am shocked and grieved by this tragedy. And yet . . . please don't think me heartless, but I don't want to become involved. I must think of my research and my students. Helping you might drag me into political situations. As I said, I am a different man than I was in the North. But if you refrain from mentioning my name, I'll give whatever advice I can. But I'd still need to know the victim's name."

A long pause. She spoke: "Nora Finn, the grammarian."

"Sweet heaven!" Shannon whispered in shock. Nora had been the Drum Tower's dean and his fiercest academic rival.

Instantly his mind spun with the possible implications of the murder. It might be an indirect attack by old enemies. It might also be connected to the restless guardian spells and Nicodemus's prowler on top of the Stacks. That would make the Drum Tower the focus of the intrigue.

Shannon fingered the asterisks on the spine of his journal. His enemies might hope to exact revenge by harming his students. His thoughts jumped to Nicodemus. The boy's cacography had proven he was not the Halcyon, but Shannon's enemies in Astrophell might have heard his name and so marked him as their target.

Or, far less likely but more frightening, the boy might have some unknown connection to the Erasmine Prophecy. If that were so, then the fate of all human language would be in jeopardy.

"Did you know Magistra Finn?" Amadi asked.

Shannon started. "I'm sorry?"

"Did you know Finn?" Amadi repeated patiently.

Shannon nodded. "Nora and I both took care of the Drum Tower's students. As the Drum Tower's master, I see to our students' residential matters. As the dean, Nora governed their academics. But these students don't often study. I end up counseling the few who do advance to lesser wizards. Nora had little contact with them. Nora and I were both being considered for the same Chair. Rivals for it, I suppose."

"Go on."

Shannon paused. He dared not share more information with Amadi until he was certain of her allegiances.

So he did what academics do best: he threw his hands in the air and began to whine. "This couldn't come at a worse time, what with the convocation. How can the murderer be caught when everything's in chaos? And my poor research! I can't stop it now; I just sent a message to my apprentice."

Amadi exhaled slowly. "As I said, we hope the investigation will not disrupt the convocation."

"We? Amadi, shouldn't the provost's officers be conducting this investigation?"

She cleared her throat. "Provost Montserrat himself instructed me to lead this investigation."

Shannon fingered the buttons on his sleeves. "Why should the provost appoint an Astrophell wizard to lead a Starhaven investigation?"

"I carry a letter of recommendation from the arch-chancellor."

"I don't doubt your qualification," he said, though he did doubt her intentions.

Amadi continued, "We must conceal this investigation from the delegates. They won't be inclined to renew the treaties if they think a murderer is—"

"Yes, Amadi, as you said. But why come to me? No doubt the provost's officers could have told you about the Spindle Bridge."

A creaking came from Amadi's chair once more. "Do you have a familiar?"

"I already told you that I do."

"I would like to see the creature."

Shannon nodded. "Certainly. She'll soon return from delivering a message to my apprentice. But Amadi, you're investigating a murder; why do you want to see my familiar?"

A long silence stretched out between them. At last the sentinel spoke in a low, controlled tone: "Because you are our primary suspect."

CHAPTER Five

The figure robed in white jumped back nearly five feet and crouched.

The speed with which it moved shocked Nicodemus. He was about to cry out when it stood and lowered its cowl to reveal a woman's tan face.

Her wide eyes gleamed green even in the bleaching white moonlight. Her smooth olive skin and narrow chin resembled those of a twenty-year-old girl, yet she held these youthful features in a calm expression of mature confidence. The waves of her raven hair spilled down around her face to disappear under her pale cloak.

To Nicodemus, she seemed oddly familiar.

"What is the meaning of this?" the woman asked sternly. "I am Deirdre, an independent emissary from the druids of Dral. I was told I had license throughout the fastness during the convocation."

"Your pardon, Magistra Deirdre. I didn't know you were a druid." He bowed.

"Do not call me Magistra. Druids hold no titles." Her voice was calm, but her eyes flicked up and down Nicodemus like flames lapping at a dry log. She walked toward him. "Are you a wizard?"

To her right, the air shimmered. A warm blush spread across Nicodemus's cheeks. "Hoping to become one soon," he replied.

"An apprentice, then. Who is your mentor?"

"Magister Shannon, the well-known linguist."

The druid seemed to consider this. "I have only recently become aware of Shannon."

Nicodemus nodded and then smiled. If he could impress this woman, it might help Shannon's status in the convocation. It was a small thing, but perhaps then Magister would sooner forget the misspelled gargoyle.

"May I assist you?" Nicodemus asked the druid and then bowed to the shadow on the druid's right. "Or your companion?"

Deirdre's full lips rose into a sly half-smile. She examined Nicodemus, then nodded. "Forgive the subtext," she said. "Kyran is my protector."

The shadow beside her welled up out of the ground and coalesced into a human figure whose cloaking subtext fell away, causing the moonlight to shimmer.

Nicodemus nodded to the newcomer. Standing several inches over six feet, the man cut an imposing figure. He had undone the wooden buttons running down his white sleeves to better expose his muscular arms for spellwriting. His complexion was fair, his lips thin, his long hair golden. No wrinkles creased his handsome face; however, among spellwrights, that was not necessarily an indication of youth.

In his right hand, Kyran held a thick oak staff. Nicodemus eyed the object; supposedly the druid's higher languages gained special abilities when cast into wood.

Deirdre was gazing about the Stone Court. "We wish to make devotions to our goddess. A wizard told us there were standing stones here, but these rocks are arranged neither in circle nor grid."

A nearby crocodile-like gargoyle crawled away, perhaps to find a quieter sleeping spot.

"And you wizards have covered the stones with these strange stone lizards."

Nicodemus bowed. "Please excuse the disorder. The standing stones were a gift from a Highland lord. We do not know how they should be arranged. As for the gargoyles, they're not lizards but advanced spells we call textual constructs. You see, Magnus, one of the wizardly high languages, can transform its textual energy into stone."

The druid smiled slightly as if he had just said something amusing.

Unsure what to do, Nicodemus offered more information: "These are janitorial gargoyles. We've written an affection for stone into their minds. So they climb all over the occupied towers, tending to the roofs, searching for crumbling mortar, and keeping the birds away."

Deirdre continued to watch him in smiling silence.

"But if you want to make devotions," Nicodemus added awkwardly, "you might feel more comfortable in one of our gardens. Magister Shannon has just taken quarters above the Bolide Garden, but it's still being renovated."

The male druid spoke. "Why is this place so empty? Where are the other wizards?"

Nicodemus smiled; here was a question he could answer authoritatively. "We're all present. Starhaven only seems empty because it is so large. Once it housed sixty thousand Chthonic people. Now only four thousand wizards and half as many students live here. We are still exploring the uninhabited Chthonic Quarter. There is much to learn. The Neosolar Empire, the Kingdom of Spires, and the Kingdom of Lorn all occupied Starhaven. Each settlement left a distinctive mark on—"

Deirdre interrupted. "What is your name?"

Nicodemus froze. Had he been talking too much? "Nicodemus Weal," he said, bowing.

"Tell me of your parentage."

"My parents?" This was unexpected. Had he offended? "I a-am the bastard son of the late Lord Severn, a minor noble of northern Spires."

The druid nodded. "Your family provides for you still?"

"N-no. Wizards abjure all ties to family and kingdom when they become neophytes. And my younger brother, the new Lord Severn, sees me as something of a threat."

"What of your mother?"

"I never knew her."

"A bastard who doesn't know his mother?" She raised a disbelieving eyebrow.

"One year my father returned from a pilgrimage to Mount Spires with my infant self in his arms. He never spoke of my mother. He died shortly after I came to Starhaven."

The woman nodded. "You are the one who can forge runes in both of the high wizardly languages but can only touch simple spells?"

Nicodemus's mouth went dry. "I am."

"I believe your name was mentioned along with the wizardly prophecy."

"But I am not the one they predict."

Deirdre's mouth went flat as a table edge. "I must ask you an important question. On some people, some wounds do not heal into smooth scars. They form dark, bulging scars called—"

"Keloids," Nicodemus said flinching. "I know what they are. I have one. On my back."

"A congenital keloid?"

Nicodemus blinked.

The druid's expression remained unchanged. "It's congenital if you were born with it.

"My father passed away before the wizards could inquire about it."

Deirdre did not move. "So it might be congenital."

"But the keloid is not in the shape of the Braid," he added nervously, praying that she would not ask to see it. "Or at least, not perfectly. There's another keloid near it. My keloid is not the Braid the Halcyon will wear."

"I see." Deirdre regarded him for another silent moment. Slowly her half-smile crept back across her full lips. "You may go, Nicodemus Weal."

Nicodemus exhaled in relief and bowed. Neither druid moved. "Goodnight, Deirdre, Kyran," he said, and turned for the Drum Tower.

"IRONIC." DEIRDRE LAUGHED as the boy's robe merged with the shadows. "Wrapped in black literally, not metaphorically." She lifted her cowl.

"Why didn't you make him show us the keloid?" Kyran moved to stand beside her. He limped slightly, favoring his left leg and using his walking staff for balance.

She smiled and idly fingered one of the buttons on her sleeve. "Do you have any doubt what we will see?"

"No. No, I don't."

"It is as our goddess said it would be." Deirdre closed her eyes to relish the moment.

"He intrigues you."

She opened her eyes and looked at him. "You were supposed to write some warning magic."

This made him scowl. "You mustn't say 'warning magic.' A spellwright would say 'a warning spell' or use a spell's specific name."

"You're changing the subject."

Kyran continued to scowl. "I did set a warning spell. The boy walked right through it. Wherever he touched the text, the rune sequences reversed or twisted. He corrupted the spell without even knowing it."

"And he gleaned your subtext."

"He did." Kyran glared at her with beautiful brown eyes. "You shouldn't have talked to him for so long. What if you had another seizure?"

She shrugged. "You would have invented an explanation. To him I seem human." She looked at the tower into which Nicodemus had disappeared. "He's been cursed, you know."

"You see it, too?"

"Feel it."

A rook called from high above the fastness. They looked up.

"The boy looks like you," Kyran said.

"Yes. Interesting to find so much Imperial blood in an obscure, minor noble."

"Hiding him from the other druids won't be easy. Nor will be taking him."

"Goddess below, Ky!" Deirdre swore. "Stop thinking like a rabid lycanthrope. We can't 'take' the boy. True, he must go to our goddess's ark without delay, but there are complications. You must think of our escape and how the wizards will react. He must go willingly."

Her protector was silent for a long moment. "He intrigues you," Kyran repeated at last.

"He's a child."

A new subtext was weaving darkness around Kyran's waist, returning him to invisibility. He stared at her silently as the subtext continued up to his shoulders.

She scowled. "You're jealous?"

"Far from it." The subtext covered his chin. "I remember when I intrigued you, so I don't envy the boy." His eyes became soft and then disappeared. "I pity him."

FROM AN EMPTY gargoyle's stoop high up on an abandoned tower, the creature looked down into the moonlit Stone Court. A boy dressed in black was making for the Drum Tower. Two figures robed in white stood among standing stones.

"Druids," the creature muttered. "I hate druids."

The two white-robes below had spoiled his chance to catch the boy. Had he acted immediately, he could have charged into the courtyard, killed them, and censored the boy. But their unexpected presence had delayed him too long; a moment ago he had spotted a wizard in a nearby courtyard casting two new guardian spells. Now was the time for retreat.

Worse than ruining this particular opportunity, the white-robes could create much larger problems. Long ago, on the ancient continent, the creature had faced the druids when their magical school was at the height of its power. The millennia that had passed since then had reduced modern druids to little more than gardeners and carpenters. Even so, the white-robes knew more of the ancient magics than the wizards. Unless handled carefully, the druids could make it all but impossible to reach the boy.

A cold autumn wind whipped about the creature's robes, making them flutter. When he crept away from the ledge, his legs ached and a dull pain throbbed across his forearms.

This body would not last much longer.

"No matter," he muttered, turning away from the Stone Court. Perhaps an important wizard or druid would wander away from the inhabited buildings. In the meantime, he could write a few nightmares.

CHAPTER
Six

Where Amadi sat, Shannon saw only darkness. Now, more than ever before, his blindness both frightened and infuriated him.

"You believe," he said, forcing his voice to be calm, "I pushed Nora Finn from the Spindle Bridge?"

"I seek the truth in all places," Amadi answered evenly.

Shannon grasped the arms of his chair so hard his fingers ached. Was her accusation a disguised attack or an earnest attempt to discover the murderer? There was no way of knowing.

"What you're saying is absurd; I have no connection to Nora's death." He stood and walked to the window. "Wouldn't I have blood on me? Nora's or my own?"

Amadi's chair squeaked in a way that told him she was standing. "Magister, the body was discovered five hours ago. The villain has had ample time to conceal evidence. And you are connected to the murder—twice connected. Four days ago, Astrophell sent a colaboris spell awarding Magistra Finn the Chair for which you two were competing."

"So I killed Nora to steal her honors?" He faced the window. "Fiery blood! Do you think—"

"Secondly," Amadi broke in, "Magistra Finn's body was riddled with a misspell, and you are the academy's authority on misspells."

"I am a linguist researching textual intelligence. Of course I study textual corruption and repair."

He heard Amadi's boot heels click against the floor. She was coming toward him. "I wasn't thinking of your research—although that provides a third connection. I was thinking of your mentally damaged students who misspell texts simply by touching them."

So there it was, the Northern fear of cacographers. He turned his head to show her his profile. "My students aren't damaged," he said in a low tone.

"I believe you're innocent."

He turned back to the window.

"Magister, if you help me, I can clear your name. But I must know everything you know about misspells and misspellers." She paused. "Your reputation makes this a perilous situation. If you're seen as resisting my investigation, it will go poorly."

"My reputation?"

"Every spellwright in this academy knows how important you were in Astrophell. More than a few think you are bitter, perhaps paranoid. Everyone saw how fiercely you competed with Finn for academic appointments."

"I might be competitive, Amadi, but you know I would never murder."

"To prove that, I need your cooperation."

Shannon took a deep breath in through his nose. She was right. Resisting might paint him with shades of guilt.

Now, even more so than before, he had to show that he had become an innocent researcher without political ambition. "If I cooperate, may I continue my research during your investigation?"

"Yes."

"What do you want to know?"

"Let's begin with the misspellers. Why are they here?" Receding footsteps told Shannon she was walking back to her chair. Likely she wanted to sit down again. He didn't follow. As the junior wizard, she could not politely sit while he stood. He remained by the window.

"In Starhaven," he said, "as in other wizardly academies, a spellwright must achieve fluency in one of our higher languages to earn a wizard's hood, fluency in both higher languages to earn a grand wizard's staff. Spellwrights who cannot learn either may still earn a lesser wizard's hood by mastering the common languages. But a few fail even this. Their touch misspells all but simple texts. Here, in the South, we call such unfortunate souls cacographers."

Amadi grunted. "It's the same in the North. We simply do not name dangerous spellwrights so."

"In Starhaven, we do not believe such students are dangerous. We do not permanently censor magical language from cacographers' minds; we permit them to fulfill what roles they can. At present there are maybe fifteen living in the Drum Tower. All but three are under the age of twelve."

"Why so many squeakers?"

"Most of the older ones integrate themselves into the academy as lesser wizards."

"Isn't that dangerous?"

"Dangerous?" Shannon's voice rose. "Dangerous to the cacographers? Possibly. Every so often, a text reacts poorly to their touch. Still, I've never seen an incident result in more than bruises or a misspelled construct. But are cacographers dangerous to wizards? Dangerous to spellwrights fluent in one or both of the world's most powerful magical languages?" He snorted.

Shannon heard Amadi's feet shuffle and guessed that she was shifting her weight and wishing to sit down. "Magister, this goes against what I was taught, against what you taught me."

He planted a hand on either side of the windowsill. "I taught you long ago."

She clicked her tongue in frustration. "But I've read of these misspellers—cacographers, as you call them. Many witches and rogue wizards come from their stock. In fact, one such misspeller was an infamous killer. He was a Southerner, lived in this academy in fact. Now, why can't I think of his name?"

"James Berr," Shannon said softly. "You are thinking of James Berr."

"Yes!"

Shannon turned toward his former student. "Berr died three hundred years ago. You do know at least that, don't you?"

Silence filled the room for a moment, then Amadi's chair creaked a loud complaint as she sat heavily.

Shannon stiffened.

"Please continue, Magister," she said acerbically. "What have I misunderstood? What was so terribly benign about that misspelling murderer?"

Shannon turned away and spoke in short, clipped words. "It was an accident. One of Berr's misspells killed a handful of acolytes. He admitted guilt and they allowed him to stay on as a low-ranking librarian. The boy was only trying to learn. No one would teach him, so he experimented. Unfortunately, two years later, a misspell killed several wizards. Berr fled into the deep Spirish savanna and died."

"So cacographers are dangerous, then?"

"Not once in the three hundred years following James Berr has there been such a dangerous cacographer. It is the Northern fascination with misspelling that makes you suspect that every cacographer is a viper in the bush. A fascination, I might add, that has been championed by the counterprophecy faction, much to the detriment of our academies."

"Magister, I know you have tangled with the counter-prophecy leadership. But I would be careful what you say. Your own provost has spoken sympathetically of their interpretation of prophecy."

Shannon pushed a stray dreadlock from his face. "And you, Amadi, where does your allegiance lie?"

"I am a sentinel," she replied. "We do not play the game of factions."

"Of course you don't," Shannon said coldly.

"I did not come here to be insulted, Magister. I came for information." She paused. "So, tell me, are there any Starhaven cacographers with particular strengths?"

Shannon exhaled through his nose and tried to calm down. "A few."

"And has any cacographer learned to spellwrite in the higher wizardly languages?"

Shannon turned. "What are you implying?"

"The misspell that killed Magistra Finn was written in Numinous."

Shannon stood up straighter. "I'll not have you trying to blame a cacographer simply because you've been frightened by a villain who used a misspell."

"You were never so protective of your students in Astrophell."

He laughed dryly. "You didn't need protection, Amadi. These children are different."

"Different or not, you can't protect them from a just investigation. I ask again: Do you have a cacographer who can write in the higher languages?"

"There is one. But he would never—"

"And who," Amadi interrupted, "is this boy?"

"My apprentice."

CHAPTER
Seven

Before Nicodemus had taken five steps away from the druids, he began forging the Drum Tower's passwords.

Elsewhere in Starhaven stood doors that would not open unless fed hundreds of elaborate sentences. But the Drum Tower's door required only one sentence written in a common language.

Even so, it took Nicodemus an eternity to forge the necessary dim green runes. They had a texture like coarse, stiff cloth. As he worked, he could almost feel Deirdre's stare jabbing into his back.

As soon as the passwords were complete, he dropped them on the black door handles. A tongue of white runes flicked from the keyhole to pull them into the lock. Nicodemus waited impatiently for the tumbler spell to disengage the device. As soon as the iron bolt clicked, he slipped into the entryway and heaved the door shut.

"Bloody awful woman!" he swore. It was a relief to escape the druid's questions about how he had failed to fulfill the Erasmine Prophecy. Hopefully she wouldn't ask any wizards about him. Given what Shannon had said about the Astrophell delegates, renewed wizardly interest in his keloid might be more than embarrassing; it might be dangerous.

He turned and hurried up the stairs.

The Drum Tower had long been used to store the stronghold's emergency grain cache, held against a possible siege. But because Starhaven was too far from civilization to tempt a greedy kingdom, it had never needed this surplus. Therefore no complex security spells lined the Drum Tower's halls, and no complex passwords were needed to open its doors.

For these reasons, the tower's top floors made an ideal home for the academy's most severe cacographers, who could not spell the passwords for the main residential towers.

However, unlike the rest of Starhaven, the Drum Tower had limited space. This forced the tower's master, Magister Shannon, to live elsewhere and required the older misspellers to govern the younger. Nicodemus shared such caretaking duties with his two floormates.

The oldest among them was Simple John, who as far as anyone knew could say only three things: "no," "Simple John," and "splattering splud." This last was John's favorite, which he often used when casting his many soapy janitorial spells.

Most people were terrified when they first encountered John. He stood over seven feet tall and possessed large, meaty hands. His red nose was too bulbous, his brown eyes too beady, his horsey teeth too big. But anyone who looked past John's appearance could not help but love his gentle manner and lopsided smile.

Devin Dorshear, Nicodemus's other cacographic floormate, was less well loved. The acolytes had nicknamed her "Demonscream Devin".

When she was focusing, little separated Devin from a lesser wizard. However, she would often stop spellwriting halfway through a text to contemplate an open window, a creaking board, a handsome wizard. This had gotten her into many unfortunate situations, none helped by her gift for screaming unlikely obscenities—a talent she effectively wielded against leaking inkwells, torn parchments, and the generally rude.

Wizards were less impressed by her effusive obscenities, and so Devin had learned to curb her foul mouth around superiors.

This is how Nicodemus, as he climbed the last few steps, knew no one with authority was present in their common room. "Ooo, you dirty son of a rat-eating butt dog!" Devin screamed. There followed a loud crash.

"Splattering splud!" Simple John called, laughing heartily. Another crash, more obscenities.

Nicodemus looked up to heaven and said, "Not since Los became the first demon has there been so much chaos as now exists on the other side of this door. Celeste, goddess, haven't I had enough tribulations for one night? Perhaps you could put them to sleep. I promise to clean up whatever they've done."

Crash, laughter, crash. "Drink goat piss, you slimy pigeon penis!"

Nicodemus frowned at the closed door. "Dev, do pigeons even have penises?"

Simple John bellowed a battle cry of "SIIIIMPLE JOHN!"

Sighing, Nicodemus opened the door and stepped inside. Immediately, he jumped back to avoid a Jejunus curse that shot past in a pink blur.

Of the common magical languages, Jejunus was the weakest—so weak, in fact, that it was used only for teaching. It had a simple syntax and its large pink runes were identical to mundane letters; this meant that it was almost impossible to misspell and hence safe for cacographers. Perhaps more important, their soft, muddy texture made them safe to handle.

The curse that had missed Nicodemus's nose by inches had read, "*FIND [John's left butt cheek] and LABEL with (I'm a gelatinous poop sucker)*."

Nicodemus groaned.

"Simple John!" trumpeted Simple John. Another crash.

Peering into the room, Nicodemus saw a proud John holding up several sentences that read "*ERASE [Devin's spell]*."

The big man had slipped his arms out of the slits sewn into the tops of his sleeves so as to better see the language forming in his giant muscles. All around John lay overturned chairs and scattered pages.

The big man forged another Jejunus sentence in his bicep and slipped it down into his balled fist. Laughing uncontrollably, he cocked his massive arm and with an overhand throw cast "*FIND and HIT [Devin's right butt cheek]*."

Almost faster than Nicodemus's eyes could follow, the gooey pink ball shot across the room.

Devin dove behind an overturned table, but John's curse flew over the barricade and dropped into a dive attack. Devin screamed something—likely obscene—and popped up from behind the table.

Like John, she had slipped her arms out of her sleeves. From her right hand extended an octopus-like spell, each tentacle of which read, "*Edit [Simple John's incoming spell]*."

John's obscenity was caught among the tentacles and struggled like a minnow. Devin cackled as she began to edit the curse.

As a boy, Nicodemus had loved Jejunus cursing matches. He had hurled handfuls of dirty words with his classmates, had relished flicking obscenities into rivals' faces, had giggled uncontrollably when filthy language had splattered onto another child's back.

But that had been long ago, before the wizards had moved him into the Drum Tower.

"HEY!" he boomed. Both combatants looked at him. "WHAT IN THE BURNING HELLS IS GOING ON HERE?"

Even though Nicodemus was the youngest of the three by thirty years, he had long ago assumed the roles of housekeeper and disciplinarian.

Perhaps mistaking Nicodemus's anger for irritation at being excluded, Simple John cast "*FIND [Nicodemus's ear] and SOUND (a sick donkey farting)*."

Nicodemus quickly wrote "*FIND and ERASE [any spell]*" in the back of his hand and flicked the spell into the air. It careened into John's curse and knocked both texts out of existence with a wet pop. If needed, Nicodemus could flood the room with similar censoring texts.

"What do you think you're doing?" Nicodemus barked. "What if one of the younger cacographers had walked in just now? We'd be in a fine state then. There'd be cursing matches up and down the tower until spring. Or what if a wizard had stopped by? With the convocation on, the repercussions would be horrible."

The other cacographers fell silent. Simple John swallowed his smile and hung his head.

"What's it to you, Nico?" Devin sneered. "Afraid Shannon'll find out? Afraid the old man won't let you teach your precious class?"

"Devin," Nicodemus said, leveling his gaze at the short redhead, "how many penitences do you have left for the flooded privy prank?"

She glared at him.

"Don't you see that our place in Starhaven is not secure? As Magister Shannon just reminded me, our disability puts an extra burden on us. And we all know that in other academies cacographers aren't treated so well. Astrophell censors magical language out of their cacographers."

"As if that would be so bad, to leave this place," Devin groused.

"Well excuse me, my lady. I was unaware of your noble blood." Nicodemus dipped into a mock bow. "Because that's what it'd take to find a life as comfortable and safe as we have here. As an illiterate, you might end up a scullery maid, but think of John. How would he get by?"

"No," Simple John protested softly.

Devin lowered her eyes and dropped her spell. An uncomfortable moment passed.

In the awkward silence, Nicodemus felt a slow sinking sensation. Could he call his floormates reckless when, only an hour ago, he had misspelled a library gargoyle? If caught, his mistake would have damaged the reputation of cacographers far more than the discovery of a simple cursing match.

"Dev, John, I'm sorry," he said in a softer tone. "I had a rough night in the library and disappointed Shannon. He's worried about some of the convocation's delegates. It might even be dangerous for us to be seen misspelling."

Neither of the other cacographers spoke. John was looking at his boots, Devin scowling at the ceiling.

"I'll help clean up," Nicodemus said wearily.

They worked silently. Simple John righted the tables while the other two shifted chairs and retrieved the pages strewn about the floor. Twice Nicodemus saw Devin and Simple John smirking at each other, but when they noticed him watching they jumped back to work.

When finished, Nicodemus snuffed the tapers and trudged into his bedroom. It was cold for the first time since last spring. Autumn was growing old.

He forged the ignition words and tossed them into the small fireplace. A spark spell caught the text and then set the kindling aflame. Light flickered across the modest chamber and Nicodemus's few possessions: a sleeping cot, a desk, two chests, a washstand, a chamber pot.

Under the bed sat a stack of mundane books. Among them was a knightly romance he had bought from a Lornish peddler. The fellow had promised that this particular romance, *The Silver Shield*, was the best one yet.

Nicodemus's love for knightly romances sometimes followed him into his sleep. Since he had arrived in Starhaven, Nicodemus had spent countless hours imagining night terrors to populate the nearby forest. In both his dreams at night and daydreams, he would venture out to vanquish the imagined monsters.

He smiled now, thinking of the strange antagonists his young mind had imagined. Uro was a giant insect with a spiked carapace and scythelike hands. Tamelkan, the sightless dragon, possessed tentacles that grew from his chin. And of course there was Garkex, the firetroll, who spouted flame from his three horns and fiery curses from his mouth.

Dreaming of monsters and battles was a childish pleasure, Nicodemus knew, but it was one of the few he had known.

Looking at the book again, he sighed. His eyes were too weary to read.

He flopped onto his cot and began to untie his robe at the back of his neck. His hair could use brushing.

He was looking around for his comb when the sound of flapping wings came to his window. He turned to regard a large bird with vivid blue plumage. Bright yellow skin shone around her black eyes and hooked beak. "Corn," croaked the bird in her scratchy parrot voice.

"Hello, Azure. I don't keep corn in my room. Did Magister Shannon give you a message for me?"

The bird cocked her head to one side. "Scratch."

"All right, but the message?"

The bird hopped onto the cot and waddled over to Nicodemus. Using her beak to grab onto his robes, the familiar pulled herself onto his lap and presented the top of her head to be scratched; Nicodemus obliged.

"Azure, the message from Magister is important."

The bird whistled two notes before casting a barrage of golden sentences from her head to Nicodemus's.

Languages like Numinous, which could manipulate light and other text, were often used to encode written messages. The spell that Azure had just cast was one such.

The problem was that Numinous had a complex structure, and so a cacographer's touch misspelled all but the simplest Numinous sentences. That is why Nicodemus had to work quickly to translate Shannon's message.

The longer he held the text in his mind, the faster his disability would distort its spelling.

Numinous runes possessed fluid shapes resembling tendrils of smoke or threads of spun glass. Translating them made a spellwright's fingers feel as if they were touching smooth glass. As he worked, Nicodemus's fingers twitched with phantom sensation.

Shannon's message was complicated, and when Nicodemus finished translating, it was garbled:

Nicodemus—

Do n't discuss tonight's conversaton w/ anyone, incldng roomates. V. important to atract littel attn. As planed, come to my study direclty after brecfast. You are excused from aprentice duty four the day.

—Mg. Shannon

Azure presented the back of her head again. "Scratch?"

Nicodemus absently stroked the bird's feathers. Shannon's instruction to avoid attention was worrisome. Nicodemus did not know what was prompting the old man's vigilance, but he had no doubt that it was serious.

"Sweet heaven, the druids," Nicodemus whispered, remembering how his attempt to impress Deirdre had elicited a barrage of questions about prophecy and his disability. "Magister is going to kill me."

"Scratch?" Azure repeated.

Nicodemus looked down and realized that in his distraction he had stopped petting the familiar. "I'm sorry, Azure. I'm exhausted." It was true—his eyes stung, his bones ached, his thoughts seemed slow as pine sap. "I'd better sleep if I'm going to help Magister tomorrow."

"Scratch?"

"Maybe tomorrow."

Finally convinced that she was not going to be petted, Azure hopped over to the window. She made her two-note whistle and flapped away into the night.

Blinking his weary eyes, Nicodemus went to the washstand and, rubbing his hands together, forged the small white runes wizards used for soap. Looking into his polished-metal mirror, he was shocked to see two pink sentences written across his forehead.

At first a scowl darkened his face, but then he laughed.

She must have written some witty prose indeed to sneak the Jejunus curse onto him without his noticing.

Careful not to trip in the dim firelight, Nicodemus stepped through the common room to Devin's door. Muted voices came from the other side. He knocked and walked in.

Simple John and Devin were sitting on her bed playing cat's cradle, John's favorite. They looked up.

"This was well done," Nicodemus said while gesturing to his forehead and the pink words that read:

I Hate Fun.
But I LOVE Donkey Piss!

AFTER DEVIN HAD disspelled the curse from Nicodemus's forehead, the three floormates gossiped about other cacographers and apprentices: who might be promoted, who was sneaking into whose bed, that sort of thing.

Though still exhausted, Nicodemus was happy to stay up with his friends and forget about druids and Astrophell delegates and the other nebulous dangers the night had presented.

As they talked, John and Nicodemus played cat's cradle while Devin brushed out Nicodemus's long raven hair.

"Why in heaven's name," she grumbled, "did the Creator waste such soft, glossy stuff on a man."

Afterward she started to braid her own wiry red hair. "You know," she said, "I've never been sure why all the magical societies have to send delegates to these convocations."

"There's never been one in Starhaven before?" Nicodemus asked without looking up from the game of cat's cradle.

"Not since I've been here. They only happen once every thirty years, and they have to rotate through all the other libraries and monasteries or whatever."

Nicodemus chewed his lip. "Well, I don't know all the details about why the convocations happen, but—"

"—but you've memorized everything Shannon's ever said about them," Devin interjected with a leer.

He stuck his tongue out at her and continued. "So, back during the Dialect Wars—when the Neosolar Empire was falling and the new kingdoms were forming—spellwrights would join the fighting. The result was so bloody that the people couldn't protect themselves from the lycanthropes or kobolds or whatever. For a while, it seemed there might not be any humans left, so all the magical societies signed treaties agreeing never again to take part in the wars that kingdoms fought."

Devin grunted. "And so now all magical societies have to renew their treaties at these conventions or we'll all end up in lycanthrope bellies?"

Nicodemus shrugged. "Something like that. It's complicated. Some societies cheat. I think Magister Shannon was involved in stopping the wizards and hierophants from clashing in the Spirish Civil War. But I'm not sure; he never talks about the war."

Simple John tried to say "Simple John" but yawned instead. Nicodemus ended the game of cat's cradle and sent the big man lumbering off to bed.

Nicodemus started for his own room but then stopped at Devin's door. "Dev, when should I ask Shannon about teaching again? With the convocation happening, things are probably too busy."

She was tapping her chin with the end of her braid. "Actually, the busier wizards are, the more they want to unload their teaching duties onto apprentices. But it's not Magister you need to convince. It's the other wizards who gripe when a cacographer gets in front of a classroom."

Nicodemus nodded and thought about what it would feel like to finally earn a hood. Then he remembered something. "Dev, have you ever worked with Magister Smallwood?"

"That sweet old linguist who's got less common sense than a drunken chicken? Yeah, I used to run Shannon's messages to him back when you were still trying to undress that Amy Hern girl. Do you ever hear from her?"

Nicodemus folded his arms. "I don't, but never mind that. I had a conversation with Smallwood today. Nothing important. But he said I was Shannon's 'new cacographic project' or his new 'pet cacographer.' Do you know if there are current rumors going around about Magister?"

Devin dropped her braid and hopped out of bed. "Ignore it. Smallwood's just being a ninny." She went to her washstand and began to scrub her face. "So what class do you want to teach?"

"Anything to do with composition. But you're avoiding my question. What are the rumors about Shannon and 'pet cacographers'?"

Devin toweled her face. "Just academics gossiping and being petty."

"Dev, not once in the past nine years have I known you to refrain from gossiping."

"So let's gossip. I'd forgotten about Amy Hern. She left for Starfall, right? Why don't you write her on the next colaboris spell?"

Nicodemus waited for Devin to finish drying her face. "Dev, the rumors."

She examined his face. "Not now, Nico; it's late."

"I'm not going to forget."

"No." She sighed. "You won't."

CHAPTER
Eight

The Gimhurst Tower stood at the southern edge of Starhaven's inhabited quarters. Long ago, during the Lornish occupation, it had hosted the Lord Governor's court. Now, save for the scriptorium at its top, the place was abandoned.

With Azure perched on his shoulder, Shannon stole down the tenth floor's outer hallway. Through the parrot's eyes, he regarded the pale moonbeams that slanted through the windows and splashed against the slate floors. The reflected glow lit the hallway's opposite wall and its many sculpted panels. The low-relief carvings presented typical Lornish sensibility—bold and graceful figures without fine detail.

Slowly Shannon passed carved knights, serpents, and seraphs—these last wreathed with tattered gold leaf halos.

A half hour before, Azure had returned to his study after delivering his message to Nicodemus. She had seen nothing unusual on the rooftops. This had only increased Shannon's anxiety for information and so prompted his current expedition.

To his left a space between two panels presented a short, wooden door. Shannon placed Azure on a windowsill opposite and instructed her to send a warning if anyone appeared. A rook's croaking voice came from somewhere out in the night. He turned back to the door. Behind it lay Nora Finn's "private library."

Many academics, rightly distrustful of their peers, hid their most important manuscripts in well-defended secret archives. Maintaining such "private libraries" violated scores of academy bylaws, but the practice was so widespread that no dean or provost dared enforce any of those laws.

Fifty years ago, a newly arrived Shannon had suspected Nora of spying on him for his enemies in the North. He had been brash then, still accustomed to Astrophell's infighting, and so had secretly pried into every aspect of Nora's life. His search had disproved his suspicions and uncovered the location of this private library.

Slowly Shannon ran his finger down the door before him. Blindness prevented him from seeing the pine boards that felt so hard under his fingers.

This was just as well; the boards weren't really there. They were subtexts—prose crafted to elude even the trained eye. Most spellwrights struggled to glean subtexts if only because they believed their eyes. When encountering a door's texture or image, a human mind rarely accepted any conclusion other than that the door existed. Only with knowledge of the author's purpose could a reader hope to see past a subtext's semblance to its true meaning.

Shannon, however, was free of vision's tyranny. He stared into the dark before him and considered how Nora would have written the subtext. First she would have chosen a primary language. Numinous was the obvious choice—it possessed the ability to create illusions by bending light. To the spell's central passages, Nora must have added a few Magnus paragraphs to provide a physical barrier and give texture to the illusion.

After choosing her languages, Nora would have chosen particular sentence structures and diction to help her hide the spell.

Shannon ruminated on Nora's prose style. As he did so, he saw faint golden runes float downward in ordered columns. Now he deduced what must be written between the lines. The faint sentences brightened. Slowly the text's central argument revealed itself, and Shannon gazed upon a door-shaped waterfall of golden prose interlaced with silver sentences.

Out of habit, he undid the silver and gold buttons that ran down his sleeves. His eyes could now see through cloth, but it still felt more natural to spellwrite with arms bare.

Once ready, he wrote a short disspell in his right forearm and slipped it into his hand. This disspell, though composed of powerful Numinous runes, was thin and delicate. Lesser authors would have crafted their most powerful disspell and hacked through the door-subtext like a peasant chopping a tree trunk. Such a crude style would have produced a mangled subtext.

Shannon had spent too many decades sharpening his prose to leave behind such obvious evidence.

With the disspell complete, Shannon drew the text from his palm so it could fold into its proper conformation. This done, he wrote a brief handle onto the blade.

Then, holding the disspell as if it were a paintbrush, he leaned forward and chivvied its cutting edge between two of the door's sentences. With slow, patient pressure he teased apart the subtext's outer sentences to reveal its knotted central passage. Two quick strokes split one of its paragraphs.

With a high grinding whine, the door's golden sentences began to churn as they detected the intrusion and sought to clamp down on Shannon's hand.

But with calm determination, he edited two new Numinous sentences into the split paragraph. The grinding sound died and the subtext quieted.

With steady pinching motions, he darned the central passage. As his hand slowly withdrew, the glassy sentences flowed back into their original conformation.

A smile curled Shannon's lips. The arch-chancellor himself wouldn't know the subtext had been edited. The door clicked softly as it unlocked and swung open. Behind it stood a small space filled with the multichromatic gleam of a magical library.

Shannon cast a quick spell to Azure asking if she had seen anything. The parrot answered negatively and complained of the late hour. Smiling at her snappishness, Shannon left her on the windowsill to keep lookout and then stepped into Nora's private library. He would not need mundane vision in such a textual environment.

It was a small space: five feet wide, ten deep. Though Shannon could not see the bookshelves that lined the walls, he recognized many of the texts they held. Nora had been studying textual exchanges between Starhaven's gargoyles—a subject that provided insight into how magical constructs learned and thought. Shannon's research also focused on textual intelligence; as a result, he possessed many of the same books that Nora had in her private library.

One unfamiliar codex attracted his eye. It lay alone at the back of the room, apparently on a low shelf or chest. Carefully he stepped to the library's end and retrieved the manuscript. It was Nora's personal research journal.

He flipped through the first few pages. Here lay a detailed study of how gargoyles selected information to share with each other. If he could take this book to his study for just one hour, his own research would leap forward. He had made any number of offhand remarks to other wizards about how much he should like to peruse Nora's notes.

Virtue briefly fought ambition in his heart. "I'll regret this tomorrow," he grumbled as morality forced him to continue to flip through the book rather than take it away. Toward its end, he found a personal journal with dated entries.

The majority were complaints about librarians, apprentices, colleagues. Twice he scowled at disparaging remarks about "*that blustering Shannon*."

It wasn't until he reached a date eleven years past that an entry lifted his eyebrows: "*Missive from Spirish noble. Wanted 'to see his sleeping boy.' His father? Boy new to D.Tower. Payment in gold sovereigns.*"

The next winter, Nora had written, "*Spirish master to see sleeping boy in D.Tower.*" Two days later, "*Spirish payment.*"

"Los's fiery blood! Nora was in a noble's purse?" Shannon whispered. The bribing of wizards was rampant in Astrophell and Starfall Keep. But Starhaven, as the only academy removed from the human kingdoms, had known little of such corruption.

Shannon wondered if he'd become soft. Despite competing academically with Nora, he had stopped investigating her private affairs—something he would have found unthinkable in Astrophell.

He reread the journal entries. The "D.Tower" clearly was the Drum Tower. But why would someone pay to see a sleeping boy? It seemed that Nora had supposed the man to be his father.

Shannon frowned at the phrase "Boy new to D.Tower" and thought about which cacographers had moved into the Drum Tower eleven years ago.

A sudden chill ran through his veins. Nicodemus was the only one.

Worse, that was the year the academy had judged Nicodemus's cacography to be proof that he wasn't the Halcyon.

"Creator be merciful," Shannon whispered. Perhaps the academy had misjudged Nicodemus's connection to the Erasmine Prophecy. If so, then these were the last days before the War of Disjunction—the final battle to save human language from demonic corruption.

Shannon continued to flip through the book. Two more entries, each four years apart, read "*Master to see boy*" and were followed by "*Spirish Payment.*" The final entry, dated two days ago, read "*Master's msg confused? No meeting but Strange Dreams about such.*"

Whoever had been bribing Nora had changed how he was to meet her. Had he then pushed her off the Spindle Bridge?

Shannon turned the final page and drew a sudden breath. Written hastily across the page was a sharply worded spell. The dangerous text shone with the brilliant silvery light of Magnus.

On their flat sides, Magnus runes were as hard as steel; on their edges, sharp as razors. Depending on their conformation, a Magnus sentence could become a nearly unbreakable rope or a deadly blade. Even a casual Magnus attack spell could kill, and the one before Shannon was far from casual. He had not seen such linguistic weaponry since the Spirish Civil War.

"Burning heaven, Nora," he swore while closing the journal. "What viper's nest did you wander into?"

He reached down to touch the wood that the research journal had lain upon. It was a bed chest. His hands felt around the object and found it unlocked.

The hinges creaked as the lid opened. His fingers felt for the chest's contents and found coins of an unmistakable weight. There was enough gold to buy a Lornish castle.

After closing the chest, he stood and tried to think systematically. Nora had attached herself to an exceedingly wealthy nonacademic, one who wanted to see a sleeping Drum Tower boy, beginning just when Nicodemus had been declared a cacographer. That implied, but did not prove, that Nicodemus was the one Nora's master wanted.

Shannon also knew that Nora's master was either a Spirish noble or had convinced Nora that he was.

Shannon blinked. The only Drum Tower boy descended from Spirish nobility was Nicodemus.

This still did not prove that Nora had been selling access to Nicodemus, but it made it highly probable. And if the academy had been wrong and Nicodemus was indeed connected to the Erasmine Prophecy . . .

"Heaven defend us all," Shannon whispered and turned to leave the library, but as he moved some instinct stopped him.

As before, the corridor of spellbooks appeared as a wall of multicolored light to his magically sensitive eyes, while the mundane world was black to him. He had received no warning from Azure, nor had he heard anything unusual. But somehow, he knew.

"Who's there?" he whispered.

At first only silence answered him. But then came a slow intake of breath and a low, crackling voice: "Write not a sentence," it rasped before drawing another breath, "or you'll eat your words."

SHANNON DID NOT move. Nora's research journal was still in his hands.

"Lay the book down," the voice said, "slowly."

Shannon bent over to obey, but just before dropping the codex he let his hands slip so that he held only the back cover. He set it on the floor. "You are Nora's murderer?" he asked and straightened.

"The shrew killed herself before I had the chance." A grunt. "It's a recurring problem for me. I killed my master before he named the boy. I won't make the same mistake with you."

Shannon tried to discern where the voice was coming from. "Your master was the noble who paid to see the sleeping cacographer?"

There came another whistling inhalation and a short, dry laugh. "So the old beast replenished the emerald when the boy was asleep? Yes, it was he who had an agreement with Magistra Finn. One she didn't renew with me for . . . squeamish reasons."

Shannon narrowed his eyes. The room's echo made it difficult to guess the murderer's location. "Squeamish because you're not human?"

"How could you tell?"

"You inhale only before speaking," Shannon replied as calmly as he could. "The rest of us find that difficult."

The creature laughed. "Full marks for acumen, Magister. I am not human, nor was master. Though he could fool your kind into thinking so."

"The subtextualization of your prose is impressive. Which faction wrote you?"

The creature laughed louder. "Perhaps I spoke too soon about your acumen. I am not a construct, nor do I care a whit for the wizardly factions."

"You're a demon, then?"

"Not a demon either, but I don't have time for this. What matters now is your name. My guess is that you are Magister Agwu Shannon, Master of the Drum Tower. If so, I have an offer for you."

"I am Magister Shannon," he replied slowly. "And I'm afraid I might share Nora's squeamishness."

"I'd rather the boy lived," the voice croaked. "The stronger he is, the more I gain from the emerald. I'm telling you this so you can understand how . . . lucrative it would be to align yourself with me. Tell me the boy's name and you and I might continue as master and Nora Finn did. Let me visit the boy when he's sleeping—as you put it—and I'll pay you twice Finn's wages. Refuse and I will kill you now. What's more, I'll cripple the boy or be forced to kill him outright."

Shannon swallowed hard. He had not considered that Nicodemus's life, as well as his own, might end tonight.

"You care for the boy," the voice observed wryly. "More than I can say about the grammarian. She cared for what he is, not who."

"And what is he? Is he the one of the Erasmine Prophecy?"

The murderer grunted. "Few things are more annoying than ignorance."

Shannon laughed "And yet you are ignorant of the boy's name."

"I might not know his name, but I will kill every male cacographer in this academy to find him. I can wield dreams as you might wield a net. So unless you want every boy in the Drum Tower murdered, you'll accept my offer."

Shannon glanced down at Nora's research journal. Its back cover lay open. The grammarian's sharply worded spell glowed on the exposed page.

"Do you need more incentive?" the voice asked. "There are rewards brighter than gold. With the emerald, I am master of Language Prime. I could tell you how the Creator made humanity." There was a pause. "You do know what Language Prime is, don't you?"

Shannon responded automatically. "Language Prime is blasphemy."

A dry laugh. "Magister, you lack conviction! You must know that the original language exists. Interesting. What might your connection to the first language be? I could teach you more."

Shannon shook his head. "Villain, you have no spell written, no attack ready. My synaesthetic reaction is very sensitive. I would have felt you forging."

There came a shuffling noise. "True; I haven't a text ready, nor can I spellwrite within Starhaven's walls. The Chthonics filled this place with too many metaspells. But it's not words with which I threaten you; it's a half foot of sharpened iron I'll drive through your skull before you can extemporize two words."

The murderer was right. Shannon could not dash off a spell in time.

"Enough banter," the creature hissed. "You can accept my offer or force me to kill every boy in—"

Shannon dove to the floor. Something whistled above his head and struck the wall behind him with a clang. He grabbed hold of the Magnus spell in Nora's book and pulled.

The wartext leaped from the page into an effulgence of silver runes. Shannon did not know the spell's name or how to wield it, so he blindly threw his arm out toward the voice. The text uncoiled into a long, liquid lash and struck with serpentine quickness.

The murderer cried out with surprise as the silvery text struck a bookshelf. The spell cut through several leather-bound codices with a loud ripping sound.

With a blast of air, each severed spellbook exploded into a blazing nimbus of sentence fragments. Shannon flinched, the brilliance dazzling his text-sensitive eyes.

Then the murderer was on top of him. The universe became a seething blackness of elbows and knees as they rolled over one another. A hand was trying to pull the Magnus spell from Shannon's hand, and then a hard object cut a line of pain across his forehead.

Yawping savagely, Shannon jerked his right hand free and whipped the Magnus spell around. It cut though something with a soft swish.

Instantly the weight lifted from Shannon's chest. The room filled with a high, keening scream. When Shannon sat up, a page of golden text shot toward him. He recognized the page as belonging to Nora's research journal the instant before it smashed into his nose. The murderer must have struck him with the book.

Suddenly he was on his back and struggling to get up. His head felt full of cotton and his ears were ringing. Deconstructing sentence fragments coated every inch of the private library's floor and walls. The fragments were squirming, spinning, and leaping into the air.

Beyond the chaos, Shannon saw Nora's research journal flying away into a patch of darkness that must be the hallway. The inhuman scream began to fade.

Slowly he realized what he was seeing: the murderer had taken Nora's journal and fled.

All around Shannon the deconstructing fragments began to burst. Each small explosion flung phrases across the room. The sharp language cut into his mind and body with hot shards of pain.

Desperately, Shannon felt around the floor for any clue as to why the murderer had fled. His fingers found something long and partially surrounded by cloth. He picked up the strange object and ran out of the library.

Behind him the decomposing sentences began to tear open the other spellbooks. Soon they would spill their contents into the growing textual storm. Shannon pulled the subtextualized door shut.

The hallway went black. Shannon could hear the deconstructing literature crackle and hiss behind the subtext.

But he was safe now. The chaotic language, left in the private library, would deconstruct into nothing.

Something wet and hot was running down his face. Blood.

He was still holding the mysterious cloth-covered object. Perhaps Azure could look at it for him.

Azure!

Fear tore into his gut. What had the murderer done to his familiar?

"Azure!" he called hoarsely. "Azure!" He had turned and was running blindly, arm stretched out. His hand struck a wall and he nearly fell. There came a faint whistle from behind.

He spun around and saw with intense relief a coil of Numinous censoring texts lying on what he assumed to be the windowsill. The murderer had bound the bird magically but had not killed her. The villain must have known hurting Azure would have made recruiting him impossible.

Shannon hurried to pick up the censored bird.

In her fear, Azure bit his pinky hard enough to draw blood. But Shannon wouldn't have cared if she had snapped his finger in two. Cooing softly, he unwound the censoring texts from the bird's head.

Once her mind was free, Azure cast to him a deluge of terrified text: a white-cloaked figure appearing in the hallway and a blazing Numinous spell that came from outside the tower to envelop her mind.

It seemed odd that the murderer had written the censoring text to strike from outside the tower; then Shannon remembered the thing's claim that it could not spellwrite within Starhaven's walls.

"Los damn it, but what could the creature be?" he hissed while scooping Azure up as if she were a loaf of bread.

In his left hand, he still gripped the strange cloth-covered object he had picked up in the private library.

On trembling legs and looking through Azure's eyes, he hurried down the Gimhurst Tower. His breath became ragged as he ran into Starhaven's inhabited quarter.

Twice, mangy cats scattered before him. He did not slow until flickering torches appeared along the walkways. Only then did he take the time to look at himself through Azure's eyes.

The deconstructing sentence fragments had torn holes in his robes and cut small bloody lines into his hands and face. More shocking was the gash that slanted down his left brow. Two of his silvery dreadlocks had been cut by whatever blade had made that wound.

After hurrying through several buildings and across the Grand Courtyard, Shannon reached the Erasmine Spire. Thankfully there were no other wizards about to see him trot up the stairs and into his study.

Still panting, he set Azure on the back of his chair and the strange cloth-covered object on his writing desk. Though she still sent him frightened memories of the attack, Azure was beginning to calm down.

Shannon cast a few flamefly paragraphs above his desk. Once there was enough light, he coaxed Azure into standing on his shoulder. After saying a brief prayer to the Creator, he turned Azure's eyes to the strange object he had taken from Nora's library.

At first he could not understand what he was seeing.

It lay on his desk, wrapped in what was left of a white sleeve. He must have cut it off with the Magnus spell.

Slowly, tentatively, he turned the thing over.

It had been detached just above the elbow joint. There was no blood. Its curled fingers were perfect, down to the hairs growing on the back of the thumb.

"Heaven defend us," Shannon whispered in shock. "The days of prophecy are upon us!"

Patches of the object seemed to be made of pale skin. But even as he watched, these slowly darkened into clay.

Save for this strange fact, the thing was an exact replica of a man's severed forearm.

CHAPTER

Nine

Nicodemus mounted the last few steps to stand panting before a tower door. It was identical to the one he had seen in his dream the previous night.

Contrary to his expectations of danger and intrigue, the day had been long and tiresome, full of busywork for Magister Shannon's research. Moments earlier he had wolfed down his dinner so that he could find a view of the sunset he had seen in his sleep. It had been a strange dream—one that did not fade after waking but grew more vivid.

He pulled the door open to reveal a narrow stone bridge and, beyond, the Erasmine Spire. The sunset bathed the Spire in vermillion light.

Nicodemus smiled and stepped outside; now he would have time to sit on the bridge and read the knightly romance tucked under his arm. A warm breeze picked up as he turned westward.

Starhaven was built halfway up the Pinnacle Mountains. From a distance the stronghold's crenellated walls and massive gatehouse made it look something like a great Lornish castle. But unlike a castle, Starhaven possessed a forest of towers, each an impossibility of height. The mightiest among them—the Erasmine Spire—stood so tall that from its top an observer could peer down on the Pinnacle Mountains.

Even from Nicodemus's present height, halfway up a lesser tower, he could see for miles. Tan patchwork fields of small farms dotted the near landscape. Away from these homesteads, lush oak savanna spread out to the horizon.

To Nicodemus, the long view made the bridge an ideal spot for dreaming and reading.

He smiled again as he opened his knightly romance and heard the familiar creak of a new spine. The pages smelled like childhood.

Nicodemus's smile grew sad. He would like to sit on the bridge all evening. But soon he would have to return to his chores. He looked eastward across Starhaven to the abandoned Chthonic Quarter. Already the evening air above the flat-topped towers was filling with bats.

What a strange sight the Chthonic people must have been, Nicodemus thought. Some stories described them as childlike creatures with bulbous eyes and teeth like needles. Others spoke of clawed monsters with armored plates covering their skin.

Nicodemus looked beyond the Chthonic Quarter. Only a few slivers of sunlight found their way through Starhaven's myriad towers. Most such columns of light landed on the mountains, but just then one illuminated the Spindle Bridge, which arched between the stronghold and the nearest cliff face.

All other Starhaven bridges were wafer-thin testaments to Chthonic stonework. But the Spindle was a thick, round affair, like the bough of an enormous tree. Nicodemus leaned forward.

Even from his present distance, he could see the designs the Chthonic people had scored into the mountain's face. To the left of the Spindle were outlines of ivy leaves; to the right a geometric pattern—three squat hexagons stacked one atop another and flanked by two taller hexagons.

The carvings made him think of the fabled Heaven Tree Valley. Some stories said the Chthonic people had escaped the Neosolar Empire by following the Spindle Bridge to a valley where the flowers bloomed as large as windmills and the mushrooms grew as wide as pavilion tents. With a sigh, Nicodemus looked down at his book.

But he could not find the book.

In his hands sat a lump of bloody clay.

With a cry, Nicodemus dropped the wet mass. It struck the bridge stones with a plop. He tried to step back but his legs wouldn't move, nor would his arms. The blood and clay blackened until it seemed to be made of the night's starry sky.

Slowly, the dark mass crept onto Nicodemus's feet. The oil coated his ankles and made them dissolve. He fell like a toppled statue.

His jaw struck the bridge stones, mashing his molars down on his tongue. Salty blood filled his mouth.

He shrieked as he felt the oil spreading up his legs, his torso, his neck. The sky went black and descended like a sheet. His skin began to rot into large gray scales. The bridge stones trembled and then dissolved into waves that stretched out to the horizon and became the ocean.

Blood seeped from between the patches of Nicodemus's skin. Bones erupted from his back to form wings. His throat convulsed and then stretched out. His rotting skin hardened into rubicund scales.

And then Nicodemus was aloft, pushing his wings down through thick ocean air. Before him flourished the dawn's golden effulgence. But he was something brighter still. If others could see him now, then all would bask in the splendor of his broad chest, golden eyes, ivory teeth. His tail shook like a streamer in the air.

On the horizon, a dark strip of land emerged and became an urban silhouette. Nicodemus had never seen the place before but knew it well. The city encrusted a half-moon bay like a scab around a sore. Further inland stood five hills. Even from this distance, Nicodemus could see the citadel's crumbling marble walls. Behind and above this memory of the ancient world, the Neosolar Palace towered high, its magically polished brass reflecting the red sunrise.

Suddenly the world froze. Nicodemus, wings outstretched, hung perfectly still in the air. Somehow he had become more than one person. He was now an old fisherman looking up from the harbor at the strange flying creature. He was also a beggar girl gazing up from an alley at a cube of solid blackness hovering in the sky. And yet he was also a young wizardly apprentice, far away and asleep in the Drum Tower.

But then a blaze of irrational hatred ignited inside of him. The world unfroze and he was again a glory of claws, wings, teeth.

He dove. The air screamed past as the city rushed up at him. The moment before impact, he flared out his wings and whipped his hind legs around and into the palace. His claws struck the roof, making stone and metal splash into the air like water drops. Working his powerful wings, he exhaled a plume of fire into the palace's open wound.

It took eight more diving passes to topple the central tower. Now the sun was up, but the smoke from his destruction dimmed its brilliance to a burning haze.

The first attackers were insignificant beings, as helpless as the ants they resembled with their metal armor and swarming regiments. They came screaming up from the city. Against his scales, arrows produced only pinpricks of pain. He climbed high into the air, then stooped into a sharp dive. The soldiers bristled with spears and pikes. But at the last moment, he fanned his wings and veered right. With claws extended, he struck a wall.

The falling debris crushed most and sent the others fleeing. Perched atop the crumbling wall, he ended each remaining life with a thin jet of fire.

When he took wing once more, an arc of silvery Magnus leaped up from the citadel and struck him just above his right foreleg. The blow sent him plummeting toward the ground. It was only with a desperate working of wings that he stayed aloft.

Slowly, he regained altitude and turned toward the citadel. As he approached, a second textual blast erupted from the walls. Now prepared, Nicodemus ducked under the spell and dove toward the huddle of wizards who had been casting the attack spells.

A few of the black-robes fled, but most held their ground and cast up a wall of text. A single tail lash shattered the shield, leaving the wizards susceptible to his breath.

In savage celebration, he toppled another wall and loosed a roar that rattled his teeth.

But then the world exploded into strange fire. All around him, gouts of orange-black flame gushed from the toppled stones. Searing pain awoke his instincts. He leaped into the air, but the fire rose with him. The undying flames flickered and snarled in the wind of his wing-beats. What strange magic was this?

Nicodemus bellowed.

Then he saw them peering from behind light-bending subtexts—a whole caucus of pyromancers in their orange robes.

An ambush! He had flown straight into a spell written in the fire-mages' pyrokinetic language. Now the malicious text was burning into his scales, turning his glorious body into ash.

Panicked, Nicodemus worked his wings. To the east, the ocean gleamed in the morning light. The sea! Perhaps it could quench the textual fire.

With a few powerful flaps, he was away from the citadel and high above the city's mercantile heart. But the spellwrights would not let him go so easily. A burning lance of yellow light tore into his right wing. The spell shattered the fourth phalangeal bone and opened a hole in the wing's membrane. A second spell smashed into his belly and sent him faltering down toward the city.

He screamed out terror and flame. Five excruciating wing-strokes stopped his fall and renewed his sprint for the sea.

Slowly he realized that the ocean could no longer save him. Each painful stroke tore a larger hole in his left wing. Once in the sea, he would not be able to regain flight. He would be an easy target for the human warships. Worse, he might not reach the ocean; one more spell would send him crashing down into the city.

But the moments stretched on; each wing-beat flooded his mind with agony. He was not a mile from the estuary now, and still the fire-mages withheld the killing blast.

A realization took shape: the spellwrights would not finish him while he was above their precious city. They knew that his burning carcass would loose a civic wildfire and destroy their gleaming domes, their precious towers.

His broad, serpentine self shook with fury. Why should he die languishing in the waves? Anger cooled his mind and sustained him long enough to turn back toward the buildings.

If he had to die, then so would they.

But then the world froze again. He hung motionless in the air. Again he became more than one person—a beggar girl hiding in an alley, a soldier's wife screaming at the sight of the burning palace, an aged fisherman praying for salvation.

But his anguish and pain grew and the world leaped back into motion.

So down he fell with folded wings to set the city burning. The textual flames roared and then guttered while the city lay quietly in the light of morning. Soon the world would see his terrible beauty in all its glory.

So down he fell and struck with violent fury. His impact shook the earth and set every city bell ringing . . . ringing . . . ringing . . .

CHAPTER
Ten

Ringing . . . ringing . . . ringing . . .

High above the Drum Tower, in the belfry of the Erasmine Spire, an apprentice had spotted the first ray of daylight and begun tolling the massive dawn bell.

Nicodemus, still half-asleep in his cot, came fully awake with a start.

Cold sweat covered his body and made him shiver. His ragged pillow displayed a dark stain. He wiped his mouth and found it encrusted with dry blood. He must have bitten his tongue during the nightmare.

In the wan light he fumbled around on the floor for his clothes. The dream haunted him still; its every image, from bloody clay to the burning city, flickered before his eyes.

After he pulled off his shirt and wiped off the sweat, the crisp autumn air made him hurry to pull on a clean shirt. From outside came the flapping of pigeon wings. Shaking his head, he tried to dislodge the dream as he pulled aside his long hair and tightened his robe's laces at the back of his neck.

"Only a nightmare," he muttered, pulling on his boots. "Only a nightmare," he repeated as he washed his face.

His eyes stung and his body would not quit shivering; the strange dream had prevented his sleep from being restful. Nothing for it but to keep moving.

By the dawn bell's last ring, he was jogging down the Drum Tower's steps toward breakfast.

It was early still and, blessedly, the refectory was nearly empty. Nicodemus never knew where to sit when the hall was crowded. It usually came to a bleak choice: eat with the cacographers and publicize his disability, or eat with the other apprentices and listen to conversations about texts he would never spellwrite. But today he could sit alone and enjoy a breakfast of yogurt and toasted brown bread.

Several seats to his right, a huddle of young lesser wizards sat gossiping. The orange lining of their hoods identified them as librarians. A few were debating how to disspell a bookworm curse, but most were whispering to each other with an urgency that suggested fresh intrigue.

Nicodemus leaned closer and caught a few details: a senior grammarian had failed to attend her evening seminar, and none of her students could find her. Some thought she had been sent to Lorn on a secret quest, another that she had jumped from a tower bridge; a few thought she had gone rogue.

Nicodemus wondered which grammarian they were talking about until one of the gossips noticed his eavesdropping and cleared his throat. He looked away.

To his left, two glassy-eyed apprentices were corresponding in a common magical language. Nicodemus watched the dim green text flit between the sweethearts.

Memories of long-ago breakfasts with Amy Hern drew a thin smile across his face. She hadn't minded his misspelled correspondence. They had often laughed at some of the wilder malapropisms his cacography had produced.

But his smile faded when he thought about finding another woman who would want a lover whose prose was nearly indecipherable.

A moment later, John joined him and began wolfing down the first of his three bowls of oatmeal. "Good morning, John. How do you feel?"

The big man pretended to nod off into his bowl. "You're sleepy?" Nicodemus guessed. John flashed him a lopsided smile. He put a hand on Nicodemus's elbow.

"I'm sleepy, too," the younger man said. "I dreamed I turned into a monster."

"No," Simple John said gently.

Nicodemus nodded. "I hope not." He smiled. "John, does anyone else understand you as well as I do?"

"Simple John!" Simple John piped, brown eyes beaming.

Nicodemus nodded. "Yes, of course they do." He patted his friend's shoulder. "You can say more with your three phrases than I could manage with the grand library's heaviest lexicon."

Laughingly the big man said, "Nooooo-ooo."

With a chuckle, Nicodemus stood up. "I have to hurry off to the old man's study; I'll see you tonight." After returning his plates to the kitchen, Nicodemus left the refectory for the Grand Courtyard. It was a broad, grassy place covered with elm trees and slate-tiled walkways. Everywhere black-robed wizards strolled alone or in pairs. To the west, a horseshoe of blue-clad hydromancers stood around a statue. Nicodemus spotted a gaggle of snowy druid robes in the northeast corner. He hoped Deirdre wasn't among them.

Cutting directly across the courtyard, Nicodemus gazed up at the airy heights of the Erasmine Spire, which at that moment was splitting a hapless cloud in two.

A lance of golden light burst from the tower's peak and shot over the eastern mountains. Nicodemus stifled a yawn and wondered which grand wizard had cast that colaboris spell. Perhaps it had been a communication to some distant monarch or maybe even to a deity.

Nicodemus had nourished so many adolescent dreams of becoming a grand wizard—almost as many dreams as he had of becoming a knight errant. How wonderful it would have been to spend a life counseling monarchs and casting the resplendent colaboris spells that instantly carried information across vast distances. He rubbed his sleep-deprived eyes and wondered if he would ever earn even a lesser wizard's hood.

Another dazzling colaboris spell arced over the northeastern mountains and silently struck the Erasmine Spire. An incoming message, he thought, and wondered where it came from. Abruptly a second colaboris spell flew in from the northeast to strike the Spire. Another golden blast followed on its tail.

Shocked, Nicodemus stopped. An outgoing spell erupted from the tower, this one heading north; it was answered instantly.

"Blood of Los!" he swore. Throughout the courtyard, all those fluent in Numinous stood amazed. Casting a colaboris spell required a vast amount of intricate text and therefore was done only with great justification. Usually that justification was gold; the Order maintained its great wealth by charging monarchs and deities exorbitant fees to cast the spells on their behalf. In fact, the Order had established an academy in Starhaven solely because its soaring towers and location made it an ideal relaying station. But not once had Nicodemus seen so many colaboris spells cast in such a short time. Something important must have happened.

Suddenly a flurry of the Numinous-based spells came raining in from several directions. Nearby wizards cried out in dismay.

The horizontal storm of spells went on and on until Nicodemus thought that every scroll must have been emptied and every grand wizard exhausted. But the golden barrage continued. Moments passed like hours. Then, as abruptly as it had begun, the magic tempest stopped, leaving the morning sky strangely dim.

Nicodemus ran for the Erasmine Spire. Something very, very grave had just happened.

"MAGISTER!" NICODEMUS CALLED, and pushed the study door open. "There's been a colaboris correspondence like you've never seen. There must have been thirty that . . ." His voice died.

Shannon was standing next to two strangers. The first was a tall, fair-skinned woman with blue eyes and dark dreadlocks. Silver and gold buttons ran down the sleeves of her black robe, indicating her rank of grand wizard.

The second stranger was tawny-skinned, green-eyed Deirdre. Her robes were druidic white with wooden buttons on the sleeves.

"Forgive me, Magister. I'll wait in the hall . . ." Nicodemus's words trailed off as he saw the myriad tiny cuts raked across Shannon's face.

"It's all right, my boy," Shannon said calmly. "Come in. We've been waiting for you." He held his research journal and was tracing the asterisks embossed on its face. "Never mind the scrapes; I was working too late and mishandled an ancient spellbook. The blast scuffed me up a bit." He motioned to his face with the journal.

"Yes, Magister," Nicodemus said uncertainly. Each year brought a few reports of ancient codices deconstructing, but for such a thing to happen to a grand wizard was extraordinary.

The old man's blank eyes pointed at Nicodemus's chest. "And you, lad, are you all right? Was there anything amiss in the Drum Tower last night?"

Nicodemus glanced nervously at the strangers. "There was a Jejunus cursing match. I'm sorry if we disturbed anyone."

Shannon's expression softened. "Not to worry about that. Please greet our guests." He gestured in the direction of the wizard. "Magistra Amadi Okeke, a sentinel from Astrophell."

Nicodemus bowed and the woman nodded.

"And Deirdre, a member of the Silent Blight delegation."

"Your pardon, Magister," the druid interrupted. "But I do not speak for Silent Blight concerns. My protector and I provide independent counsel."

Nicodemus had to stop himself from staring. By night Deirdre had seemed handsome. But now that she was standing in the window's sunlight her eyes seemed greener, her skin darker, her loose hair more glossy black. Now she was stunning and looked even more familiar.

Shannon's blind gaze had wandered up to the ceiling. "Well then, Nicodemus, please greet Deirdre, an independent emissary from Dral."

Nicodemus began to worry. Shannon had said that they had been waiting for him. Had his conversation with the druid last night stirred up new interest in his cacography?

He bowed to Deirdre.

"Scratch!" Azure said, and launched herself from Shannon's chair. Nicodemus raised his forearm in time to make a perch for the incoming parrot.

"Tell me again about your bird," an amused Deirdre said. "I thought she was your familiar and couldn't communicate with anyone else."

Shannon turned toward the druid. He was silent a moment before replying. "Sometimes Azure flies a message to Nicodemus, but only I can understand her dialect of Numinous." A golden sentence flew from Shannon's brow to his familiar's. The bird bobbed her head and flapped her way back to Shannon's shoulder.

"For a few wizards, age or literary trauma steals our ability to see anything but magical text." Shannon gestured to his all-white eyes. "Time did so to me. But those like me can rapidly exchange information with animal familiars."

Two Numinous streams rushed between wizard and parrot. Now Shannon pointed his face directly at Deirdre's. "Through this protocol, I can see through Azure's eyes. I'm doing so now."

Deirdre studied man and bird. "Such strange practices you wizards have."

Again Shannon let a silence grow before he responded. "I hear druids also have strange relationships with animals. But hopefully this convocation will do more than renew treaties; hopefully it will make our different societies less strange to one another."

Nicodemus had never heard the old man be so hesitant and so cautious with his words.

Azure, apparently having looked around the room enough for Shannon, broke the Numinous stream and turned to preening one of Shannon's silver dreadlocks.

Magistra Okeke spoke. "We should tell the boy why we are here."

Shannon's mouth tensed, and then he motioned toward three chairs. "Then let us sit. This, Nicodemus, is a fortuitous interview. Deirdre passed me in the halls this morning and inquired about you. And Magistra Okeke appeared at my door only moments ago, quite unexpectedly."

"I would like the boy to talk about the Erasmine Prophecy," the sentinel said, coolly regarding first Shannon and then Deirdre.

Nicodemus felt his cheeks grow hot.

Shannon turned toward the sentinel. "I see you've been busy researching Starhaven rumors."

With a half-smile, the druid looked from one wizard to the other before adding, "I am also interested in this prophecy."

The sentinel narrowed her eyes at the other woman.

Three grand authors in one room, each distrustful of the others—Nicodemus would have felt safer if the study were full of starving lycanthropes.

"Regarding prophecy, there is little to tell," Shannon said. "Nicodemus is not the Halcyon."

"Why so certain?" Deirdre's green eyes fixed on the old man. "Perhaps we should start with what the first wizards foresaw."

Shannon started to reply but then paused. Prophecy, being closely related to religion, was seldom discussed among different magical societies. Doing so was considered impolite at best, blasphemous at worst.

However, Shannon could not refuse a guest's direct request. "Erasmus foresaw the War of Disjunction: the final struggle between demons and humanity that will come when the fiends escape the ancient continent and invade this one. The prophecies predict that Los will be reborn and will lead the Pandemonium—the great demonic army—across the ocean to destroy all human language. Erasmus founded the Numinous Order of Civil Wizardry to repel the Pandemonium. His prophecy predicts that the Order will prevail only if it heeds the teachings of a master spellwright known as 'the Halcyon.' "

Deirdre shifted in her chair. "But how could any force destroy human language?"

Magistra Okeke answered impatiently: "The demons will use special spells called metaspells to decouple the meaning of language from its form."

The druid gave the sentinel a blank look.

"What Magistra Okeke means," Shannon explained, "is that the demons will divorce the signifier from the signified. Phrases and words will take on unexpected meanings. Civilization will crumble into animal brutishness."

"I don't understand your jargon," Deirdre said. "But this interests me. The druids hold to the Prophecy of the Peregrine, which predicts that the Pandemonium will burn our groves and crush our standing stones. Our mundane and magical texts are stored within our sacred trees and megaliths."

"I thought druids believed the War of Disjunction was imminent," Magistra Okeke said. "Something about a fungus killing off Dralish trees."

Still smiling, Deirdre examined the sentinel as if for the first time. "Amadi Okeke, you refer to the Silent Blight. It is a complicated issue. I would prefer not to speak of it here."

The sentinel pursed her lips. "But perhaps you could elucidate some of your order's beliefs, since Magister Shannon was so free with information about wizardly prophecy."

"There's no need to—" Shannon started to say.

"It is all right." Deidre raised an open palm. "The Silent Blight is a . . . 'change,' I suppose I must name it to non-druids. Yes, the Blight is a world change we detected a few decades ago. It is not a disease, but a . . . condition that is affecting all of nature. The evidence comes from the observation that certain kinds of trees are dying in each of the human kingdoms. What is causing the deaths is debated. Some believe the Blight indicates that the War of Disjunction will begin any day now. Others think it is unrelated to prophecy. However, all druids agree on one and only one thing: when the War of Disjunction does begin, a foreign spellwright known as the Peregrine will show us how to protect our sacred places and hence our language."

Shannon nodded. "Some of our scholars report that all magical societies believe the Disjunction will destroy their languages and that only one spellwright might prevent this fate."

Deirdre nodded to Nicodemus without looking at him. "And the wizards once thought he might be the Halcyon?"

Magistra Okeke leaned forward, her eyes flitting between Shannon and Deirdre.

Though Shannon's face remained impassive, he cast a brief sentence to Azure. The parrot lowered her head, allowing the old man to stroke the feathers along her skinny neck. Nicodemus recognized this as a habit comforting for both bird and man.

At last Shannon spoke. "Our prophecy describes the Halcyon as being the child of an unknown mother, as having a birth to magic powerful enough to be felt for hundreds of miles, as forging both Numinous and Magnus before reaching twenty. All of these things describe Nicodemus perfectly."

The pride ringing in the old man's voice made Nicodemus's cheeks grow hot again.

"However," Shannon continued, "Erasmus also described the Halcyon as bearing a congenital keloid scar in the shape of the Braid rune. Nicodemus's mark is ambiguous. More important, the prophecy predicted that the Halcyon would master many styles and wield language with elegance and justice. He foresaw the Halcyon destroying the feral kingdoms and forging a staff powerful enough to slay the reborn Los."

"And that is why I can't be the Halcyon," Nicodemus insisted. "My cacography prevents me from mastering any style or producing anything close to elegant prose. For a while, the wizards thought I would outgrow my difficulty. But when it became apparent that my touch would always misspell, they knew I wasn't the Halcyon."

"Nicodemus," Deirdre said, "how were you born to magic?"

He shifted in his seat. "In my sleep, when I was thirteen."

The druid's mouth curved almost imperceptibly upward. At the same time, the sentinel narrowed her lips.

Deirdre asked, "Do you remember what you were dreaming about the night you were born to magic?"

"No," he lied.

The sentinel spoke. "As a cacographer you cause misspells by handling text, but have you noticed if your touch makes other things more chaotic? For example, do those near you often become sick? Or do the fires you light tend to escape the fireplace?"

Nicodemus was about to say that he had not noticed anything like that when Shannon interrupted in a low tone. "Amadi, Provost Montserrat has personally observed Nicodemus and determined that that is not the case."

An icy sensation—half-thrill, half-fear—spread through Nicodemus. The Provost had observed him? But when and how?

Magistra Okeke stared at Shannon for a long moment. "I will see the boy's keloid now."

Nicodemus touched a lock of his long black hair. "There's really no need, Magistra. The scars are misshapen. And we don't know if I was born with it or not."

The sentinel only stared. He looked at Shannon, but his teacher's expression was as blank as a snow field. No help there. He looked at Deirdre. She only smiled her infuriating half-smile.

So with his heart growing cold, Nicodemus turned his chair to present his back to the sentinel, pulled his hair over one shoulder, and began to unlace his robes.

AS HE UNTIED his collar at the back of his neck, Nicodemus's fingers ran across the keloid.

He had felt the scars countless times before, traced their every inch with his fingertips. Once he had even arranged two bits of polished brass so that he could see their reflection.

Unlike most scars, which were pale and flat, a keloid scar bulged out and darkened. Nicodemus's complexion was a healthy olive hue, but the weals on his neck shone a glossy blue-black—like a colony of parasitic mollusks growing into his flesh.

He fussed over his hair every night so that it would remain long enough to hide the keloids. He hadn't had to reveal them for nearly five years.

His face burned as he pushed his collar back to expose his neck and shoulders.

"Goddess!" the druid swore. "Do they hurt?"

"No, Magistra," he said as evenly as possible.

He heard the sentinel walk over to him. "I can see the shape of the Braid in the scars."

The "Braid" she was referring to was a rune in a common language named Vulgate; it consisted of two vertical lines connected by a serpentine line that wove between them. By itself the Braid could mean "to organize" or "to combine."

Nicodemus had no sensation along the keloid, but he could feel the pressure of Magistra Okeke's finger as she traced the scars down his neck. She spoke. "Druid, is the Peregrine prophesied to bear a keloid in the shape of the Braid?"

"Predicted to be born with such," the druid answered. "There have been false Peregrines who have created such a keloid through branding. And, as I understand it, we do not know if Nicodemus's mark is congenital."

"But, Magistras, there's an error in the middle of it," Nicodemus said, his face still hot.

Magistra Okeke grunted. "Child, you don't know how right you are."

He tried not to flinch as her finger traced the blotch. This second scar took the imperfect shape of a written letter "k" that had been pushed over onto its legs—the same shape as the Inconjunct rune.

By itself an Inconjunct meant either "as far apart as possible" or "as incorrect as possible." Therefore, a Braid paired with an Inconjunct could mean "to disorganize to the furthest extent" or "to deconstruct to the basic components."

Deirdre swore under her breath: "Bridget, damn it!"

Shocked by the druid's blasphemy against her own goddess, Nicodemus turned around. She had lost her half-smile and was frowning at his neck.

"You are distressed, Deirdre?" Magistra Okeke asked. "You thought perhaps Nicodemus was the Peregrine?"

The druid sighed and returned to her chair. "Yes, Amadi Okeke. The answer to both of your questions is yes."

"Well, druid, I agree with your assessment," the sentinel said. "If this scar is fate's work, then it is a clear sign that Nicodemus is not the Halcyon. But I wonder if it might have another meaning."

Shannon snorted. "You're getting carried away, Amadi." His voice softened. "Thank you, Nicodemus. You may cover your neck now."

Dizzy with relief, Nicodemus began to tie his collar's laces.

Deirdre sat back into her chair. "Agwu Shannon, Amadi Okeke, apologies for occupying your time."

Returning to her seat, Magistra Okeke asked, "What does the provost think of the Inconjunct?"

"He does not believe it is a rune," Shannon answered curtly. "He believes it is the result of human error."

Magistra Okeke's eyes narrowed. "I don't understand."

Shannon opened his mouth to speak, but Nicodemus interrupted: "Magister is too kind to say that most likely my parents branded me. It might be shameful, and many may look down on my family because of it. But I'd rather face the shame than have anyone again believe that I'm involved in prophecy."

Shannon frowned. "Nicodemus, who told you that you were branded?"

Nicodemus looked down at his boots. "No one, Magister. It's what I figure people must say."

Deirdre gazed out the window, all sign of interest gone.

Meanwhile the sentinel looked Nicodemus up and down. "You've had the scars all your life?"

Nicodemus forced himself to meet her stare. "When I was an infant, my stepmother gave me my last name because of them."

Magistra Okeke raised her eyebrows.

"The word 'weal' is a synonym for 'welt,'" Nicodemus explained. "Hence Nicodemus-of-the-weals became Nicodemus Weal."

Shannon cleared his throat. "But 'weal' has another meaning. It can mean 'the common good.' It's an antonym of woe."

Nicodemus put on his bravest smile. "I've always said that that makes it a contranym."

Deirdre looked at Nicodemus so abruptly he started. "Why would you say that?" The half-smile returned to her lips.

"Oh-h," Nicodemus stuttered. "W-well, a contranym is a word that means the opposite of itself like 'dust' or 'bound.' If I'm dusting the table, you don't know if I'm sweeping the dust off it or sprinkling some onto it. And the weal is the opposite of woe, but woe to him with a weal."

Shannon laughed softly even though he had heard this attempt at wit before. Nicodemus gave him a grateful glance.

Deirdre was nodding. She seemed about to speak but an urgent knock sounded at the door.

"Enter," Shannon called. The door swung open to reveal Magister Smallwood. "Agwu! It's that astounding colaboris correspondence. News most terrifying from abroad!"

CHAPTER
Eleven

"Nicodemus, please attend our druid guest while I hear this news." Shannon stood. "Deirdre, forgive us a moment." Two Numinous arcs sprang between the old wizard and Azure as he made for the door. The sentinel followed.

Nicodemus stood and watched them go. He would have given anything to avoid being left alone with the druid.

He looked back at Deirdre. Her wide eyes and smooth skin made her seemed no older than twenty, but her slight smile betrayed an ancient, matronly amusement. "I think I handled that rather well," she said. "Let us sit. There's much to discuss."

Frowning in confusion, he retook his seat.

"Nicodemus, do you know that we're distant cousins?" the druid asked, her smile growing. "I consulted Starhaven's genealogy library. We share a pair of great-great-grandparents."

Nicodemus's head bobbed backward. This was unexpected. But then he realized why the druid seemed familiar: save for her eyes, she was a younger and more beautiful copy of his aunt. "Are you Spirish?" he asked.

She shook her head. "Dralish, but of Imperial descent. Do you know what that means? The ancient continent was ruled by an Imperial family who possessed the same black hair, green eyes, and olive skin that you and I have."

Nicodemus felt an old memory stir. "My father once said he could trace his ancestry to the first Spirish Landfall."

Deirdre nodded. "Just so. When humanity fled the ancient continent, each member of the imperial family boarded a different ship. The Maelstrom scattered the human fleet; as a result, our relatives are spread across the land in both powerful and humble families."

She studied him. "I have many Imperial aspects, save for my height, or rather, my lack of height. But you seem to have all the Imperial features."

Nicodemus fought the urge to fidget with his sleeve. "It's flattering to hear you say so."

"It makes one wonder who your mother might be," she said.

He looked away at the window.

"I am sorry," she said, touching his knee. "Forgive my speculation."

"There is nothing to forgive," he said without looking at her.

"Nicodemus, I must tell you something." She paused. "Please carefully consider what I say next." She leaned forward. Paused. "You have been crippled by a horrible curse."

He blinked. "I'm sorry?"

"You are cursed."

"In which language?"

"In no magical language of this land."

"Forgive my skepticism, but if I haven't been cursed in a known magical language, then how can you see it?"

Deirdre folded her dark hands on her white lap. "There are many things that cannot be seen by writers of the new magics."

"New magics?" Nicodemus frowned at her odd diction.

The druid nodded. "When our ancestors crossed the ocean, most ancient magics were lost. Only the Dralish and Verdantians preserved their ancestral ways, which evolved into the old magics. All other magic has been invented since then."

He knew that what she was saying was true. "But what does this have to do with a curse? And shouldn't we speak of old languages, not old magics?"

Deirdre's mouth tensed for a moment but then relaxed into its usual half-smile. "Magics, languages, it's all one. The point is that while the new languages might be more powerful, they restrict their writers' vision; they prevent their writers from knowing the wisdom of the ancient continent."

"And they prevent us from seeing curses?" Nicodemus asked skeptically. "Forgive me, but I did spend last night disspelling a curse from my forehead."

The druid waved his words away. "Wizards call any malevolent text a curse. What infected you is different. It was written in a language from the ancient continent and therefore left an aura dimly visible to those fluent in the old languages but invisible to those fluent only in the new."

"All right, say I have been cursed. What infected me? Is it some disease I've got?"

Deirdre was silent for a moment. Then she leaned forward and said, "Isn't it obvious, my friend, that someone has stolen your ability to spell?"

Nicodemus blinked. "That's impossible. No known spell—"

"This curse comes from the ancient world, where knowledge of how language could affect the body was far greater. The histories describe magic that could regrow a severed arm or restore the memories lost to a blow on the head."

Nicodemus could not deny what she said; the ancients had had an incomprehensibly sophisticated understanding of the mundane world, including medicine.

The druid continued, "Your curse was one such ancient spell. It must have invaded your mind and stolen its growth or altered its development. Whatever the case, it removed the part of your mind needed to spellwrite correctly."

"But who would want to curse me?"

"There are men and women in every human kingdom who worship demons," she replied. "We know little of them other than that they have formed a clandestine order. They call themselves the Disjunction because they wish to initiate the War of Disjunction. Whoever has cursed you must be among their number.

Nicodemus's throat tightened. "You think I'm the Halcyon."

Deirdre eyed the door. "Last spring, my goddess commanded me to travel to Starhaven, where I would find a 'treasure wrapped in black and endangered by the falling night.'" She motioned to Nicodemus's black robe. "The Dralish prophecy predicts that the Peregrine will be an orphaned foreigner—one born to magic in the dreamworld."

"But the keloid," Nicodemus exclaimed. "You saw that it's not a true Braid. You swore, in fact. You agreed with Magistra Okeke that I can't—"

She held up a finger. "Amadi Okeke asked if I were distressed and if I had thought you were the Peregrine. Both of those things were true. She assumed that your keloid disqualifies you from being the Peregrine."

"It doesn't?"

Deirdre's half-smile returned. "We Dralish use a different dialect of the common magical languages; the common runes have different meanings for us."

"And my keloid means something different to you?"

The druid's smile widened. "To us, the Braid means 'to combine' or 'to grow.' More important, the second mark on your neck is an exact copy of a rune called the Crooked Branch."

"And its meaning?"

"It describes something that is wild or unrestricted. So the combination of a Crooked Branch with a Braid would mean 'wild or unrestrained growth.'" The druid laughed. "I swore when I saw your keloid, not because it excludes you from our prophecy, but because it describes you as difficult to govern or contain."

Nicodemus shook his head. "But you still don't know if my keloid is congenital or not."

The druid cocked her head to one side. "You don't like the possibility that you might fulfill our prophecy?"

Nicodemus stammered but couldn't come up with a reply.

She shrugged. "Well, I need no further convincing. Here you are, just as my goddess said you would be—wrapped in black and endangered. Gravely endangered. Someone has maneuvered you into this haven of new magic, where druids almost never come. Our first task is to free you from Starhaven."

"But I'm not imprisoned."

"Nicodemus Weal, think of what your keloid and your curse mean. Someone has stopped you from becoming the Peregrine. It is not safe here."

"But I'm surrounded by wizards. Who could harm me here?"

"Who? The one who cursed you, of course." She shook her head. "Nicodemus, you were not meant to be crippled."

Her words filled Nicodemus with giddiness and confusion. What if she was correct? What if his cacography was a mistake? Everything would change. He would change. His life would begin again.

Deirdre's eyes widened. "Your heart knows I am right. Listen to me. Do you know what an ark is?"

Nicodemus looked away. "Cacographers aren't instructed in theology."

"An ark is a vessel that contains a deity's soul and much of her power. With Kyran and a dozen devotees, I have brought my goddess's ark to this place. If we could bring you to the ark, my goddess may lift your curse."

Nicodemus pursed his lips. Was it possible?

Deirdre continued excitedly. "We could not bring the ark up to Starhaven. This place is filled with ancient Chthonic magic that would damage the artifact. So instead we have placed it under guard in that village . . . the one down on the Westernmost Road. I can't remember the name."

"Gray's Crossing."

The druid smiled. "The same. My party has taken rooms at the inn there. And all of the devotees, two of them druids, now guard the ark. We simply need to slip you free from Starhaven and bring you down to Gray's Crossing so that my goddess can protect you. From there we shall ride to the civil forests of Dral to begin your druidic training."

Something in the way the druid spoke—perhaps the zeal in her eyes, or maybe the urgency in her tone—cooled Nicodemus's excitement. "But why should your goddess want to heal my cacography?"

"Because you're the Peregrine!" she exclaimed, leaning forward. "The defender of our civilization!"

The woman's bright eyes seemed free of deceit; still Nicodemus did not trust her. "I can't go with you." He put his now trembling hands in his lap.

Deirdre's smile faltered. She started as if waking from a dream. "Yes," she said, the excitement draining from her face. "The Braid and the Crooked Branch. I couldn't expect less."

"Even if I trusted you completely, I couldn't leave Starhaven. Numinous and Magnus spellwrights may not forsake the Order. If I left Starhaven, they'd send sentinels to cast a censorship spell on me to snuff out my literacy."

The druid tapped a forefinger against her pursed lips. "It seems your jailer has planned well. You are trapped. We must assume that such a clever enemy has planted conspirators among the wizards."

"Conspirators?" he said with a laugh. "Look, the Creator knows I want what you say to be true, but there's no evidence for it." He stood and walked to the window.

"Nicodemus, unless you trust me now, there will be violence," Deirdre said, her voice suddenly full of fervor. "The one who cursed you will discover my presence and the presence of my goddess. Blood will be shed in Starhaven."

Despite the sunshine coming through the window, Nicodemus shivered. Deirdre's every expression suggested that she sincerely believed what she was saying. However, there was a desperation in her tone, a maniacal excitement in her eye.

Nicodemus had seen such passion before—seen it grow and then wither in every young cacographer that came through the Drum Tower. Like a crippled child, Deirdre must have hung her every desire on one hope.

"My apologies, druid," he said, meeting her eyes, "but I cannot trust you so blindly. I will discuss this with Magister Shannon."

Again the zealous glow melted from the druid's expression and left only the wry half-smile. "Here I was worrying that your keloid marked you as too headstrong to be controlled. I couldn't have been more wrong. It is worse that you are uncontrollable in this way."

Nicodemus turned to the windowsill. "And what way is that?"

"You are frightened. Insecure, dependent on your master, childish."

Nicodemus closed his eyes; her words felt like a punch in the gut. But he kept his thoughts calm. He had had plenty of practice surviving brutal honesty.

"Deirdre, I won't guess your age." He turned his face up to feel the sunshine. "Despite your looks, you must be decades older than I am. No doubt

I'm a child next to you. I haven't even guessed what game you are playing. But at least I see that you are a game-player and would make me a game-piece."

Deirdre spoke in a dry, accusing voice. "I have put myself in great danger by warning you of your curse."

Nicodemus took a long breath. She was still vying for advantage, still trying to convince him. On unsteady legs, he returned to his chair. "Deirdre, I'm a cacographer, a cripple, a mooncalf apprentice. I do not plan; I do not scheme. But twenty-five years of retardation have taught me how to tell the painted from the plain, the guileful from the genuine."

The druid regarded him. "And how to speak masterfully."

"Flattery." He closed his eyes and pressed four trembling fingers to his forehead. "I know that Magister is plain and that you are painted. I will tell him."

She shook her head. "Then listen to me, game-piece Nicodemus. One day you will not have the luxury of hiding behind your disability. One day soon you will have to paint your face and play my game or die."

He said nothing.

"Before you tell Shannon," the druid said coolly, "consider that he might, perhaps unknowingly, serve our enemy."

Nicodemus started to protest, but she held up her hand. "And perhaps he does not. But men speak with loose tongues. Telling Shannon what I told you may start rumors. At present, your jailer doesn't know that you are aware of him. Informing Shannon may alert him to your new knowledge. Informing Shannon may ignite a bloody struggle before Kyran and I are ready to defend you."

Nicodemus frowned. "If Shannon were a demon-worshiper, he never would have left me alone with you."

Deirdre cocked her head to one side. "You care for him."

Nicodemus blinked.

Her infuriating half-smiled returned. "Game-piece Nicodemus, beware of Shannon. He is only a man. If he is your jailer, then he might be an imperfect one. Leaving you alone with me might have been simply a mistake." She paused. "Don't you wonder what caused those unusual cuts across his face?"

Nicodemus opened his mouth to defend the old man, but before the words came, muffled voices sounded at the door.

"They're coming back." Deirdre leaned forward and took his hand. "Nicodemus, if you remember anything, remember that the wizards are more than they seem. Shannon is more than he seems. We must get you to my goddess's ark in Gray's Crossing; you will be safe there. Until then, take this."

From the folds of her robe, she withdrew a small sphere of polished wood and placed it in Nicodemus's palm. A root wound around the object.

"It is called a Seed of Finding," she said softly. "If you need me, break the root that encircles the Seed and I will come. I have another artifact that will allow me to find you so long as you are touching the Seed."

She closed her hands around his and knelt. "By Bridget's love," she said, her green eyes fixed upon him, "I hereby pledge myself to the protection of Nicodemus Weal, our beloved Peregrine."

CHAPTER Twelve

Nicodemus stared down at the wooden orb. It didn't look like any seed he had ever known. A tingling warmth was spreading down his fingers. "Its power is quick," he whispered.

Deirdre released his hand. "Keep it safe. Many wizards would pay their weight in gold for this spell."

Nicodemus met her gaze. "If I gave this to a wizard so that he could study the druidic languages in it, and the other druids learned that you gave it to me—"

"—they would strangle me before our goddess's altar. Just as the wizards jealously guard Numinous and Magnus, the druids guard the higher druidic languages." She stood. "You see how I risk my life for you."

Across the room the door latch chirped. Nicodemus stood and stuffed the druidic artifact into his belt-purse.

Deirdre stepped away from him as the door swung open to reveal an exhausted Shannon. Azure, perched on the wizard's right hand, bobbed her head.

"My esteemed druid," the grand wizard rumbled, "I have just heard a report that will harrow your soul. But might I have a moment with my apprentice first?"

"Of course," Deirdre said with a bow.

"Nicodemus." Shannon gestured to the door.

The younger man followed the grand wizard into the hallway.

When the door clicked shut behind him, Shannon held a gnarled forefinger to his lips and cast a miniature river of Numinous from his brow to Azure's. The bird looked over the old man's shoulder and down the dark hall. A responding sentence flew from bird to wizard.

It was then that Nicodemus noticed the sentinel, Magistra Amadi Okeke, standing partway down the hall. She half faced them while talking to a male sentinel whose long black hair was done up in an Ixonian bun.

Unexpectedly, Azure began to flap and screech. "Help me calm her down," Shannon said. "She's absorbed my anxiety about the news."

Nicodemus stepped forward to stroke Azure's dorsal feathers. Though she submitted to his reassuring fingers, the familiar continued to squawk. Shannon began cooing over the bird. "Ohhh, Azure, old friend, Azzzure . . . there now . . . Azzzure."

Nicodemus frowned; usually Azure quieted when receiving such attention.

Suddenly he realized that Shannon wasn't cooing at all; he was talking under his mother-bird impersonations. "Azure, ohhh . . . Amadi may be listening. No, don't look at me . . . Azzzure, there now . . . that's her private secretary she's talking to; an Ixonian man named Kale."

Azure wasn't agitated; she was deliberately creating enough noise to drown out their conversation.

"If I tell you something shocking," Shannon murmured, "can you keep your face blank?"

Nicodemus nodded slightly.

"Oh, there now, Azure. Did you know Magistra Nora Finn?"

"Yes, but I've spoken to her only a few times," Nicodemus whispered.

"She was murdered last night."

All the air seemed to be pulled out of Nicodemus's lungs.

"There now, Azure, old friend. Don't look surprised. Good. Oh Azzzzure. Keep your expression neutral; it gets worse. The sentinels suspect both you and me of killing Nora. Worse, I encountered the true murderer last night. I am almost certain the villain is hunting you. Oh, Azzzzure. Ohhhh . . . don't breathe so fast; you'll faint."

The ground seemed to be tipping under Nicodemus's boots. He had to work hard to slow his breath.

Shannon continued: "The murderer threatened to harm other cacographic boys. I've doubled the protective language around the Drum Tower and ordered that no cacographer is to leave Starhaven."

The old man's eyes narrowed. "Problem is the sentinels are investigating me for murder; they'll distrust anything I say. If I ask them to protect the Drum Tower boys now, they will think it a ploy and refuse. However, I might be able to find some information that will force Magistra Okeke to . . . Nicodemus, are you all right?"

Nicodemus was breathing slower, but the world seemed to be slowly spinning. "Who's the murderer?" he asked in a whisper.

Shannon pursed his lips. "A creature that is neither human nor construct. But we can't discuss this while being watched. Two hours past midday, before our research, meet me in the compluvium. Do you know where that is?"

"Between the Sataal Landing and the Spindle Bridge."

"Yes, Azure. Yes. That's a good bird," Shannon cooed, then lowered his voice again. "I'll explain more in the compluvium. From now on, the sentinels will be watching you. Their presence will keep the murderer away, but if they decide you're guilty of Nora's murder, they'll instantly conduct a witch trial."

Nicodemus clenched his hands. To wizards, a "witch" was any spellwright who used prose for unlawful or malicious purposes. One of the duties entrusted to the sentinels was the formation of witch hunts and trials to bring such villains to justice. However, because the sentinels judged their own trials, those accused were often condemned to death whether or not they were guilty.

Shannon spoke again. "It will be hard, but you must appear innocent and calm. The sentinels will always be watching."

"Magister, you remind me—when you went away, the druid had strange words for me." He quickly related what Deirdre had told him.

Shannon chewed his lip for a moment. "I can't say if Deirdre is correct about the curse or the keloid, but now I too suspect that you are tied to prophecy."

"B-but the Provost himself thought I was branded."

"We can't discuss this now. Listen, there's another reason you need to appear innocent. Magistra Okeke and other Astrophell delegates may belong to the counter-prophecy faction. All members of that faction believe an anti-Halcyon, a champion of chaos, will arise. If they ever decide that you could be this anti-Halcyon, you and I will be dead within an hour. We must convince them that you are a normal cacographer."

"But how can—"

"Shhhh." Shannon pretended to shush his familiar. "You mustn't tell anyone—not another wizard, not John, and especially not Devin."

Thinking of Devin's tendency to gossip, Nicodemus agreed.

"Now, when Azure quiets, we must discuss the news from Trillinon; it's what Amadi expects."

On cue, the familiar ceased her screeching. Hooking her bill into a fold of Shannon's robe, the bird hoisted herself onto the old man's shoulder and began to preen the down on her back. "That's a good bird," Shannon announced. "Nicodemus, I'm afraid I have distressing news."

The younger man glanced over Shannon's shoulder at the sentinel; she had quit her conversation and now stood studying them.

"It seems a malevolent construct has beset Trillinon," Shannon said. "Fire and death now reign in the city. Part of Astrophell has burned and many of our Northern wizards have died because of this monstrous spell."

"What kind of spell?"

"One we do not comprehend." Shannon frowned. "The reports, they speak of—" Azure plucked a feather from her back, a sign of extreme anxiety. "Azure!" the grand wizard scolded even as he cast several soothing sentences to the bird.

"What do the reports speak of, Magister?"

"Of a massive construct that tore into the Neosolar Palace and set the city aflame. They say the spell took the shape . . ." Shannon shook his head as if already disbelieving the words he was about to utter. "The shape of a red dragon."

"ARE YOU ALL right?" Shannon asked.

Pressing a hand to his mouth, Nicodemus answered faintly. "Magister, last night I dreamed I was a dragon attacking a city. I didn't know which city . . . certainly it was a Northern city . . ."

Shannon coughed. "Nicodemus, your face is very pale. Have you gotten enough sleep?"

"No, but—"

"I see you're exhausted, and this news has clearly given you a fright."

"Magister, I dreamed that I changed into a dra—"

"Nicodemus! It's understandable that you should find this news like a nightmare. But it was only a bad dream, nothing that should excite serious . . ."—his voice lowered meaningfully—". . . investigation."

Nicodemus started again as he took the old man's meaning. A glance down the hall showed him that Amadi Okeke was still watching them. "Magister, I'm sorry. I had a nightmare last night, and I didn't get enough sleep. And this news . . . it's all so confusing."

"Quite understandable," Shannon said, resting a hand on his student's shoulder. Azure let out a low, grating squawk. "Damn it, not again," Shannon complained loudly. "Nicodemus, help me again with Azure."

As soon as he began to preen the bird, the old man mumbled, "Tell me briefly." Nicodemus described his nightmare as quickly as possible. When he had finished, Shannon muttered, "In the dream, were you ever two persons at once?"

"Yes!" he whispered. "Each time, right before the dragon attacked, I was not only the dragon but also an old fisherman or a solder's wife or a beggar girl watching the dragon. But the beggar girl didn't see the dragon; she saw a black cube hanging in the sky."

Shannon grimaced. "You were having quaternary thoughts."

Nicodemus looked at the old man to see if he was serious. "I thought spellwrights could reach quaternary cognition only with powerful texts cast about their minds."

"The murderer claimed he could manipulate dreams. I thought it was an empty boast, but now I remember history texts describing ancient spells that could invest sleeping minds with quaternary thoughts. It seems this nightmare was sent to you."

"So, if it was sent to me, I couldn't have caused the dragon to attack the city?"

"Correct," Shannon said with a slight nod. "Quaternary thoughts change perception, not the world. It's vital that you know you did not cause this."

Nicodemus let out a breath he did not know he had been holding. "But why would he send me such a dream?"

"I don't know. But it does imply there is a connection between the murderer and this dragon. Damn it, what if the creature is sending dreams to the other cacographic boys? How can I protect them from that? Regardless, tell no one of this. We will talk more in the compluvium." He squeezed the younger man's shoulder.

Azure stopped her grating roar, and Nicodemus fidgeted with his sleeve as a thought occurred to him. "Your family, Magister, has the Trillinon fire affected them?"

Shannon smiled. "An old friend sent a message in the last colaboris spell. My relatives are safe. Thank you for your concern. Now then, all of the deans and masters have been called to an emergency council, which is troubling because our lectures must continue. My boy, I need a favor."

Nicodemus's eyes widened. "You want me to teach a class? Magister, I've wanted . . . and I've practiced . . . but I don't know if I can do my best under these circumstances."

Shannon nodded. "I know, you've waited for so long to teach and get the chance now of all times. Today's news might make this seem like a trivial task, but it is vital"—he squeezed Nicodemus's shoulder meaningfully—"vital that you make a good impression. Do you understand me?"

"Yes, Magister," Nicodemus said, remembering what the grand wizard had said about the sentinels watching him.

"Good." Shannon released Nicodemus's shoulder. "Given today's news, no one will object to your teaching. The neophytes are all squeakers; not a one over thirteen. Your disability won't interfere. The classroom is in Bolide Hall, third floor, western side. Outline the basic concepts of composition. After class, go to my quarters and get as much sleep as you can before the midday meal. I keep an hour bell and the passwords for my door in the classroom's closet. Use both. You must be rested for our work this afternoon."

Though the terrifying news had fully awakened Nicodemus, his eyes still stung with exhaustion. "Yes, Magister."

"When you wake, eat your midday meal and find me."

Nicodemus exhaled. He really was going to have to teach a class despite the day's terrifying discoveries.

Shannon laughed softly. "I know it may seem impossible, but you must forget everything happening today and become lost in the lecture. If you enjoy the teaching, they'll enjoy the learning. Are you nervous?"

Nicodemus admitted that he was, though "shocked and overwhelmed," he said, "would be a better description."

Shannon grinned. "Understandably so, but don't let the students know or they'll devour you like a pack of lycanthropes. If anything, you want to err on the side of being cavalier." Shannon was famous for his emphatic lecture style.

Nicodemus decided to emulate his mentor's style. That meant somehow bottling up his growing fears and hopes about the prophecy.

"Well then," Shannon said with a nod. "Off with you, then, or you'll be late."

Nicodemus turned for the stairs.

"Oh, I just remembered," Shannon called after him. "You should know that one boy raises a bit of trouble and . . ." The old wizard's voice died.

Nicodemus stopped and looked back.

Shannon was frowning. "You should know this boy, he may be a cacographer."

CHAPTER
Thirteen

Nicodemus jogged through shafts of sunlight that poured in from rectangular windows. Outside the hallway shone a sky so blue it might have been enameled. The crisp autumn air smelled of smoke from the breakfast fires.

His first composition class and he was going to be late.

He tried to focus on the upcoming lecture but his mind wandered. The real world did not seem real. Northern sentinels were investigating him for murder. An inhuman killer was hunting him for reasons unknown. His lost hope of fulfilling the Erasmine Prophecy was returning. And in response . . .

. . . in response, he was going to teach introductory spellwriting to squeakers.

It all seemed insane.

Magister knew what he was doing, he told himself while turning a corner and dashing up a broad staircase. After all, he was the cacographic apprentice, Shannon the grand wizard. Clearly he should handle the thirteen-year-olds while the old man dealt with the truly fearful forces of zealous sentinels, academic factions, and inhuman murderers.

Just then he reached his classroom door and stepped inside. The room was orderly, square, filled with rows of desks. The walls were white, the arched windows wide.

However, the two dozen students dressed in neophyte robes were in chaos. The boys huddled around the windows. Some were yelling, apparently to another unsupervised class in the next tower over. Others were spitting out of the windows, undoubtedly trying to hit the sleeping gargoyles several floors below.

The girls had congregated on the opposite side of the room. Most sat at their desks, arguing or laughing. A few were playing a game that involved singing and clapping.

"Oh . . ." Nicodemus heard himself say, ". . . hell."

The room fell silent. As one, two dozen childish faces turned toward him.

It was then that Nicodemus realized he had been wrong: Shannon was not dealing with the truly fearful. The terror that sentinels and murderers might induce—great though it might be—was nothing compared to the dread inspired by two dozen prepubescent students.

"You're not Magister Shannon," said a pale boy with a mop of brown hair.

Nicodemus most certainly wasn't. The old man would have marched into the room, blustering with jokes and commands. He would have had the squeakers racing for their seats in anticipation.

"I'm Nicodemus Weal," he announced with a confidence he did not feel. "Magister Shannon's apprentice. I'll be giving your first lecture on composition, so take your seats."

Shockingly, the neophytes went to their desks. The boy with the brown hair raised his hand. When Nicodemus nodded, he asked, "Why don't we have Magister Shannon? Where are all the wizards?"

Nicodemus cleared his throat. "Magister, like the other wizards, has been called to an important council."

"Did he tell you the news from the North?" asked a tall girl with short black hair.

Nicodemus started to reply but then realized he did not know how much information he was supposed to share. He took in a breath and said, "I'm not sure if I'm allowed to tell you."

"Or maybe you don't know," the brown-haired boy said in a tone so earnest it—just barely—diffused his confrontational words.

"Maybe I don't," Nicodemus admitted. "But you bring up an excellent point: I didn't say if I actually had heard the news; my phrase simply suggested I had."

The boy frowned.

"That might seem trivial, but it's a good place to start when talking about spellwriting. Why might that be?"

Silence. More frowns.

"Why would I choose words that make it sound as if I know more than I do? Why might I want to use such self-aggrandizing language?"

"Because you can't be a teacher without it?" the brown-haired boy asked snidely.

Though flushed with embarrassment, Nicodemus laughed. A few other students were smiling.

"Perhaps," he admitted. "I was thinking more that such language encourages you to stop thinking about the news and start thinking about me, which would have helped focus you on the lecture material. Regardless, you must start thinking about such things now; if you are to become wizards, you must question how language is trying to manipulate you. What is it pushing you to assume? How is it distracting you?"

The boy raised his hand.

But this time Nicodemus grinned at him. "Put your hand down, lad. I'm not going to tell you if I actually did hear the news from the North. That was going to be your next question, wasn't it?"

The boy nodded.

"Good lad. Persistence is spellwriting's most important ingredient. What's your name?"

"Derrick, Magister."

Nicodemus widened his eyes. "Derrick Magister? You're a wizard already?" A few of the students laughed.

The boy frowned. "I—"

Nicodemus put his hand to his mouth in mock surprise. "But you're so young!" A few more students laughed.

"I meant you, Magister," Derrick said in a tone heated enough that Nicodemus knew he should stop.

"Well, I'm flattered, Derrick. But as I mentioned, I'm only an apprentice." He turned to the class. "This may be horrible for you, but today you'll have to call someone over twenty by his first name!"

A few amused smiles.

"Let's practice." He pointed to the girl with short black hair. "Your name?"

"Ingrid."

He pointed to himself. "My name?"

She opened her mouth but only blushed. Her neighbor leaned over, but Nicodemus rushed in. "No, no, you're ruining the obnoxious-new-teacher effect."

This won him a few more nervous laughs.

The smiling girl only grew redder.

"Nnnn . . ." he started for her. "Nnnnicooo . . ."

She continued experimentally, "Nicodermis?"

He squawked, "I sound like a skin disease."

Genuine laughter.

"Sorry to pick on you, Ingrid, but it's Nicodemus." He turned to the class. "So, now all of you, my not-a-skin-disease-name is?"

As the class laughingly said his name, Nicodemus noticed the sunlight by the windows began to shimmer. "Well then, let's start properly," he said, moving toward the window. "This is a short lecture, and I'll try to make it lively if . . ."

He paused. The shimmering air moved away from him. Warmth spread across his cheeks. Only with an effort could he stop his smile from wilting.

". . . make it lively if you pay close attention." He kept his tone casual even though he was now certain a subtextualized spellwright, most likely a sentinel, was in the room.

"So, how does one acquire magic language?" he asked, turning to the class. "Really it's no different from learning a verbal or mathematical language. First, we learn the symbols. Verbal languages use letters, mathematical languages numbers, magical languages runes. However, anyone with a quill and an inkhorn can forge mundane text. Anyone with eyes can see mundane text. But to see or forge magical text, one must be born with a magically receptive mind."

The boy with brown hair, Derrick, leaned over and whispered loudly to a friend.

Nicodemus walked toward the boys. "Note that when spellwrights speak of 'literates,' they are speaking of those who might achieve magical literacy. All of us in this room are literate; we are fortunate enough to be among the few born with magically sensitive minds."

He stopped before Derrick, who was now forced to stop his whispering.

"Why are most humans born magically illiterate?" he asked rhetorically. "Some authors—sadly a few wizards among them—believe that the Creator has privileged spellwrights, that we are inherently better than the illiterates. Some authors feel we are meant to rule society. I will remind you—as Magister Shannon reminded me when I was a neophyte—that all of our parents are illiterate. Without illiterates we wouldn't exist. Indeed, we owe them a great debt. We aren't meant to rule, but to serve—"

Derrick spoke up. "I don't understand. Why wouldn't we exist?"

Nicodemus studied him. "Spellwrights can't produce children. Moreover, the illiterate life is harder than ours."

"I'm sorry, Nicodemus, but I still don't understand." Derrick's tone seemed earnest, but the boys around him were snickering.

Nicodemus narrowed his eyes "What don't you understand?"

"Why we can't produce children." This sponsored a wave of nervous tittering.

"Spellwrights are sterile," Nicodemus answered, keeping the embarrassment from his expression only with supreme effort.

"You mean we're clean?" Derrick asked, his voice cracking with amusement. His neighbors broke into open laughter.

"No, Derrick," Nicodemus said, staring straight at the boy. If Derrick was going to force the issue, best to get it over with. "I mean that spellwrights can't conceive children when they have sex."

The room now rang with laughter. Nicodemus wondered if he could ever regain the class.

"Sex?" Derrick said with counterfeit shock and raised his hands to his cheeks. "Oh, my virgin ears!"

"Oh, your virgin everything else," Nicodemus shot back in a deadpan tone.

The laughter rose to a crescendo. Derrick's pale face flushed scarlet.

Nicodemus hurried to the front of the class. "So back to learning magical language. We've established that you all have literate minds. So armed, you can learn to forge runes within your muscles. And, as with any language, you will need to build a vocabulary and understand the grammar governing that vocabulary. After that, you will learn how to move the runes through your bodies, how to string them together in sentences, and finally how to cast them out into the world."

The laughter had died, and now two dozen smiling faces were fixed on him. Encouraged, Nicodemus pressed on: "That is why you have attended anatomy lectures and why you will perform dissections. Learning the muscles and bones is especially important. You might want to wrap one paragraph around your humerus and another around your ulna, and so forth. Any questions?"

Derrick's hand shot up.

Nicodemus rolled his eyes. "Let me rephrase: any questions about spellwriting?"

Smiling, the boy dropped his hand, producing another round of laughter.

Nicodemus nodded. "So then, let's talk about different magical languages. Three are known to all magical societies and hence are known as the common languages. Jejunus is the first such language you will learn. Common languages are relatively weak but still important. Anyone who is fluent in a common language can teach it to another spellwright."

He held up a finger. "However, being future wizards, you will spend much more time worrying about the uncommon languages, what we call 'higher languages.' All higher languages are controlled by specific magical societies. For instance, we wizards control Numinous and Magnus. Unlike common languages, higher languages cannot be taught by just anyone. I can forge both the Numinous and the Magnus alphabets, but I couldn't teach them to you without the aid of a magical artifact called a tome."

Nicodemus began to pace, heading first toward the door. "Tomes are beautiful, massive books. Through contact with them, a powerful author may acquire a higher language. Currently there are only three Magnus tomes and three Numinous tomes. We have a pair of them here in Starhaven. Now, these artifacts are important because . . ."

Heat spread across Nicodemus's cheeks. He stopped. It was only then that he noticed a slight shimmer in the air a few paces from the door.

Another subtextualized spellwright? He felt his stomach knot. A second sentinel? Or was someone else spying on him?

He forced these questions from his mind and turned back to the classroom. "Sorry. As I was saying, tomes are important because they protect a magical society's control of a language. Consider that even if you attain fluency in Numinous or Magnus, you can't sneak off and teach the hierophants or the hydromancers how to write in our high languages. You'd need a tome to do that. However, you might still write wizardly spells for them; that's why the Order would hunt you down if you ran away."

He paused to slip his arms out of his sleeves. "Now for a demonstration. I have begun forging the runes for a simple Magnus sentence. I'm forming the runes here, in my forearm flexor muscles. Now the growing sentence spills into my closed fist. Spells must fold into a proper conformation before they become active. I'm helping the sentence fold now. Who can see the runes? Raise your hands."

A few hands went up; Derrick's was one.

Nicodemus smiled and shook his head. "Tsk tsk tsk. Everyone who has raised a hand is lying. It is impossible to see the runes of a magical language unless you are fluent in that language."

The class laughed, Derrick loudest among them.

When they quieted, Nicodemus began again. "In any case, by flicking my hand open . . . thusly . . . I cast the spell into the air. If you were fluent in Magnus, you would see a glowing line of silver runes floating in the air like a ribbon caught in an upward breeze."

He looked hard at his students. "Now, when I cast the spell, some of you might have heard the ringing of a distant bell or felt slightly sick. Others may feel the room is becoming warmer or brighter. This is not a coincidence. You are sensing my spell but not in any systematic way. This is because the magically sensitive mind displaces perception of unknown or hidden magical text to one of the mundane senses. This phenomenon is known as synaesthesia. It's a difficult word, two terrible trochees. I want everyone to say it with me: SIN-es-THEE-zhaa."

The class echoed him in monotone.

He nodded. "Most synaesthetic reactions go unnoticed unless the spellwright is watching for them. They are also unique, meaning everyone has a different synaesthetic sensation."

The girl with the short hair raised her hand. "What's your reaction?"

Nicodemus glanced at the window. "Around hidden spells, warmth spreads across my cheeks. It's a bit like a blush. Now, it takes most students years to identify their synaesthesias. So don't feel bad if you don't—"

He stopped. Perhaps because he was talking about his synaesthetic reaction, heat spread across his entire face. His heart began to beat faster as his mind filled with thoughts of subtextualized sentinels.

He looked back at the door and jumped when he saw a man dressed in black. The newcomer nodded at Nicodemus. "I'm to take the students back to their towers when your lecture's done."

"Oh," an embarrassed Nicodemus said as he recognized the man as one of the neophyte preceptors. "Of course, we can end now."

The warmth was slowly fading from his cheeks and his heart was slowing. He turned to the class. "Well, I congratulate you on surviving my first lecture. Now please form a line heading out the door for your preceptor. Derrick, I will speak with you privately."

AS THE EXCITEMENT of teaching began to dissipate, Nicodemus rubbed his eyes and again felt the sting of exhaustion. He wondered who had been watching his lecture and what impression he had made.

"Am I in trouble?" a sullen voice asked.

Nicodemus looked up. The classroom was empty except for Derrick, who stood before him staring at the floor, his arms crossed.

"Not in the least." Nicodemus sat and withdrew paper and quill from one of the student desks. On one side of the page he wrote "angel," on the other "angle."

"Have a seat, Derrick, and read this." He held out the paper.

Derrick complied without looking him in the face. "Angel," he said after glancing at the paper.

Nicodemus turned the sheet over. "And this?"

"Angel," Derrick repeated.

Nicodemus handed Derrick a blank piece of paper and the quill. "Now write the word 'angle' on this paper." The boy scrawled out "angel."

Nicodemus exhaled slowly. "Derrick, stop me if I am wrong, but you have not been doing well in your studies, even though you understand everything that's going on."

The boy's face darkened, but he did not speak.

Nicodemus continued in a softer tone. "You're a sharp lad. It was difficult to keep up with you as a teacher, and I'm sorry if I was hard on you."

"You weren't—" the boy started to say.

"My guess is you use your wit, your ability to disrupt a lecture, to distract others from seeing that there is something wrong with you. I say this because I was once in a similar situation. Do you understand?"

The boy's mouth softened. He glanced up. "No."

Nicodemus held up the paper. "This reads 'angle.'" He turned it over. "This reads 'angel.' I can easily distinguish between them only because when I wrote them down, I put a dot on a corner of the angel side. If someone else had written them and asked me to read them, as I did to you, I would have seen the difference only with great concentration. I have tried my whole life to be different and have failed. I still misread and misspell. Do you understand now?"

"A little."

"Good. Now listen to me: there is something wrong with you, just as there is something wrong with me. Half the world will tell you that you're worthless and stupid; the other half will tell you that there's nothing wrong with you at all. A few might even say your disability is a gift."

Nicodemus paused as he considered how all the listeners in the room might interpret his words. "The truth is that you are neither broken nor gifted; you are only what you make yourself into. In that regard, you and I are no different than any other student. No amount of classroom antics will protect you from the world until you realize this."

"I . . . I don't understand, Magister."

"Don't call me Magister. I'm not a wizard, and maybe they'll never let me become one. And it's fine that you don't understand. I didn't understand it myself until just now when I had to express it in words. And at your age, I don't know if I could have understood or cared. But can you remember what I said?"

The boy nodded.

"Repeat it for me."

He repeated Nicodemus's words verbatim.

"The fact that you can remember my speech so precisely means that you are not without certain talents, which some of us have. In any case, promise that you will always keep what I said in your mind."

The boy promised, and suddenly Nicodemus had to stifle a yawn. Silently, he thanked Shannon for ordering him to nap before lunch.

"May I go now?" the boy asked glumly.

Nicodemus nodded. "Yes, yes. Catch up with your classmates. You don't have to mention this conversation. If the preceptor asks, tell him I scolded you for being disrespectful." He smiled at the boy.

Without a word, Derrick leaped up from his seat and hurried away.

Nicodemus yawned again and sat for a moment with his elbows on the desk, resting his exhausted head. He was about to stand when a sound made him look up toward the door.

He expected to see more evidence of subtextualized sentinels. Instead he saw that Derrick hadn't left but was standing in the threshold.

"Is something wrong?" he asked.

"No," the boy said, looking Nicodemus in the eye for the first time. "But . . . thank you, Magister."

CHAPTER
Fourteen

When Deirdre regained consciousness, she was lying on the floor, crying.

Kyran knelt beside her, running his hands through her hair and telling her that everything would be all right.

Above him stretched a blank stone ceiling. They were back in their Starhaven quarters.

Slowly her eyes dried. "What happened?" she asked. Her stomach ached and her mouth and throat burned.

"We were subtextualized and spying on the boy's lesson when another subtexualized spellwright, most likely Amadi Okeke, arrived," Kyran rumbled. "You fell into a seizure and I carried you here."

She sat up. "Did the sentinel detect us?"

He shook his head.

"And do the other druids suspect anything?"

Again a head shake.

"Thank Bridget and Boann both," she mumbled while wiping her mouth. The back of her hand came away covered with soggy bits of bread.

She looked at her protector.

"Vomit. Came up when you were seizing. You inhaled some of it. I had texts on hand to clear your lungs. But I can't promise your safety if the fits grow worse."

"Such is the divine illness," Deirdre said, staring at the filth. "It is the goddess's will."

He sniffed. "Is it the goddess's will that you should die?"

"Fitting punishment for what I did."

Kyran's hand appeared under her chin and turned her face to his. "For what we did."

She looked away. "Ky, let's not argue again about if I'm a fool or if you're a fool or . . ."

He pulled her close. He had undone the wooden buttons of his sleeve to expose his arms for spellwriting, and now she pressed her cheek against his bare skin.

"Ky, I don't know who I am," she mumbled into his shoulder. "When I was seizing this time, I had horrible visions. I was standing on the banks of a Highland river when this wolf with a man's head and red eyes jumped on me. And somehow I was stabbed again and again. I melted like oil and went flowing down the river."

With gentle hands, Kyran smoothed her hair until she was calm again.

They both stood, he favoring his left leg as always. After a tremulous sigh, Deirdre looked around their austere room: a chest, a washstand, a chamber pot, two beds, Kyran's oak walking staff leaning against the wall by the door.

She sat down by her pillow.

As Kyran joined her, a rat scurried within a nearby wall. "Tell me of your interview with the boy before he taught," Kyran said while handing her a clean tunic.

"Frustrating." She wiped her face. "He's frightened and resists manipulation. Likely he'll tell Shannon. But at least he understood what I said. It's a seed that will grow later."

Kyran's eyes narrowed. "Grow when?"

She sighed. "The demon-worshiper who cursed him can't be far. I don't like it, but when the fighting starts he'll see that I was telling the truth."

Kyran shook his head and began to button up his sleeves. "You're courting battle with a demon-worshiper merely to manipulate this boy?"

"I court nothing." She stood. "I'd rather smuggle the boy from the fastness tonight, but he's too frightened by his disability to leave his life here." She began to pace. "Don't look at me like that, Ky. A clash would be good for him. It will strengthen him for the coming struggles."

"It might do that," Kyran agreed. "Or it might kill him."

As Shannon labored up steps of the Alacran Tower, Azure gazed through the stairwell's geometric window screens. Outside lay Starhaven's northwest quarter. Its many Spirish towers boasted pyriform brass domes. They stood as bold intermediates to the gray Lornish steeples to the south and the white hemispheres that topped the towers in the northeastern Imperial Quarter.

At times, Azure could glimpse the Bolide Garden far below. At this height, it seemed only a small brown square. Last summer Shannon had taken new quarters overlooking the garden. Ongoing renovations had filled the place with stone heaps and dirt piles.

Inside the stairwell, Azure examined the indigo wall tiles and the ceiling's geometric mosaics.

Shannon, however, couldn't appreciate what his familiar saw. He was too busy wondering if he had successfully covered his tracks. Earlier, while pretending to research several gargoyles, he had used a knifelike spell to cut into their executive texts. That done, he had written into the constructs memories of talking to him until an hour past midday. Then had come the task of eluding the sentinels Amadi had sent to guard him. Hopefully the two fools were still waiting for him to come out of a privy in the Marfil Tower.

Abruptly, a narrow hallway branched off to the right. When Shannon stopped to regain his breath, Azure wrote teasingly about his age and weakening legs. Shannon affected fatigue and dropped his shoulder so quickly the parrot was left flapping and dashing off laughing accusations of betrayal.

After Azure glanced up and down the stairwell, Shannon crept down the dark hallway and up a ladder to a small metal door. For centuries, Starhaven's janitorial records had listed the door as broken: "Corrupted tumbler spell: unfrangible." Janitorial saw no need to fix the door; it opened onto an insignificant gargoyle perch that overlooked the northern walls.

In truth, the door and the landing beyond were the fiercely guarded secret of Ejindu's Sons—a political faction to which Shannon had once belonged.

Azure bobbed her head. She didn't like the dark, claustrophobic space.

"A moment longer, old friend," Shannon cooed while flicking a glowing mass of Numinous passwords into the door's lock. It sprang open with an iron shriek.

Shannon carefully stepped out onto a narrow landing and beheld the bright landscape. To his left lay the vast, grassy coastal plain. Before him the western slopes of the Pinnacle Mountains stretched away to the horizon. Green alpine forests, spotted with scarlet or gold aspen thickets, covered the steep slopes.

He could make out the skeletons of several dead trees. It made him think of what Deirdre had said about the Silent Blight and trees dying across the continent.

A chill wind tugged at Shannon's robes and set Azure flapping to keep her balance.

The landing itself was a narrow slab of gray stone surrounded by a crenellated barricade. To the right of the door, inside a small stone nook, slept an eyeless gargoyle with a bat's face and a pudgy infant's body. Shannon shook its shoulder.

The spell woke with a twitch. "My father has no ears," it croaked. "My father taught me to hear. My father has no eyes; he taught me to see. My father is covered with cowhide."

"Construct, you were fathered from a spellbook," Shannon answered the verification riddle. "And my wisdom was fathered from a codex of Ejindu's teachings. My name is Agwu Shannon."

The gargoyle reached under its feet, into a stone recess that held its white-marble eyes. Other, heavier gargoyles would steal the eyes if it slept with them in.

The gargoyle inserted each marble sphere into its socket, then studied Shannon. "I siphoned a message for you from the last colaboris." It drew from its belly a glowing, golden rectangle.

Shannon took the paragraph. The Numinous runes felt glassy smooth in his hands. He translated:

> *Ejindu's Sons greet our Brother-in-Exile. We feared he had forsaken us. Since the attack on Trillinon and the horrible fire it unleashed, Astrophell has been in chaos.*
>
> *We gladly accept the information our Brother-in-Exile has offered. We do not know if the events in Starhaven pertain to the Erasmine Prophecies. We think it unlikely that Nicodemus Weal is the Halcyon. However, we gladly provide what answers and assistance we can.*
>
> ANSWER: *We know of no faction wishing our Brother or his students harm.*
>
> ANSWER: *We have no knowledge of Mg. Nora Finn's briber or murderer. No Language Prime revival is known to us.*
>
> ANSWER: *We know little of Mg. Amadi Okeke other than that she has secretly sworn allegiance to the counter-prophecy faction.*
>
> ANSWER: *In exchange for our Brother's public pledge of support, we shall grant him full use of our Starhaven constructs; however, at this time, we are unwilling to endanger any of our few Starhaven spellwrights by assigning them to your cause.*
>
> *We hope this generous support convinces our Brother to rejoin the Sons in our struggle for a united and peaceful Numinous Order.*

Shannon let out a long, relieved breath. This response to his original message, sent earlier that morning, was better than expected. He ripped the sentences apart and began mulling over the answers.

The Sons were always well informed of academic politics. If they did not know of a plot against him, then he was sure none existed. That, taken with their ignorance of Nora Finn's briber and murderer, provided strong evidence that the creature Shannon had encountered was not connected to the academy.

Amadi's allegiance to the counter-prophecy factions was more troubling.

Sentinels were prohibited from wizardly politics: a fact that did not stop many sentinels from covertly advancing a faction's interests.

More important, Amadi's allegiance explained why the provost—a counter-prophecy supporter—had appointed her to lead the investigation. It also explained her interest in Nicodemus's scar shaped like an Inconjunct and why she had wanted to know what the provost had thought of it. Amadi had also asked the boy if he noticed that chaos increased around him. She must suspect that Nicodemus was not the Halcyon, but the Storm Petrel—a destroyer predicted by the counter-prophecy to oppose the Halcyon.

"Magister, how do you answer?" the bat-faced gargoyle croaked.

Shannon started; he had forgotten about the Sons' offer of assistance. "Construct, have you read the message?"

The spell wrinkled its bat nose. "I have, as my author intended me to."

"I do not accuse you, gargoyle, I simply need some answers. How many constructs do the Sons command? Do they still control the compluvium?"

The gargoyle lifted a chubby hand to stroke a long, batlike ear. "We do still hold that portion of the roofworld. As well as two Lornish towers and five Spirish ones. We number fifty-four light- and middle-weight gargoyles; twelve war-weight brutes—only two of quickness. There are also three guardian spells."

Shannon idly scratched Azure's neck and thought about this. "I would require both war-quick gargoyles to reside in the compluvium. There must also be enough middle-weight gargoyles to work the Fool's Ladder."

The bat-faced construct began stroking his other ear. "Your purpose?"

"I may need the war texts to guard and perhaps evacuate nine cacographic boys."

The gargoyle blinked. "Their value?"

"They are living, breathing boys," Shannon snapped.

The bat-faced thing shrugged. "The brutes can be edited immediately, but the Fool's Ladder will take at least three hours to assemble."

Shannon took a long breath. It would have been better if the Sons had committed some of their members. Powerful as war-quick gargoyles were, they were no substitute for living authors. Worse was the asking price. Publicly pledging his support to the Sons would end Shannon's freedom from politics. He would have to commit himself to any cause the faction chose. It would make him, once again, a game piece on a bloody board.

Shannon slowly exhaled as he thought about Nicodemus. Without warning, his memory came alive with the image of his long-dead wife, her dark eyes . . .

"I pledge myself to Ejindu's Sons," Shannon announced as he forged a Numinous proclamation of his allegiance.

The construct struggled up onto its infant feet to formally accept the paragraph with a bow.

"One more thing," the grand wizard said, removing a long cloth-wrapped object from his robes, "do you know of a creature or construct that forms flesh when vital but once deconstructed becomes this?" He unwrapped the object.

The gargoyle made a long, frowning study of the severed clay arm. "No, Magister."

Shannon grunted. "Thank you, gargoyle. You have served me well. I wish you quiet dreams." He bowed.

Clumsily, the construct returned the bow before plucking out its eyes and settling down on the roof to sleep.

Shannon walked back into the tower. He wasn't any closer to discovering who or what the murderer was, but at least he had taken steps to confound the creature's next assault.

THINKING MURDER, THE creature stepped through the aspen thicket and grumbled about Shannon's failure to mount a defense. Already one dire surprise awaited the old goat in Starhaven, and soon the creature would rip another life away from him.

He wondered what could be keeping the fool from responding. True, the murder investigation would prevent Shannon from alerting the sentinels. And true, the old human probably thought he had won time by cutting off the creature's arm.

The memory of silver text slicing through tendon and bone made the creature flex his new hand. Maybe he'd wrench off Shannon's arm and see if it came back.

The creature's task in Starhaven, though of paramount importance, was a dull one. And though he looked forward to killing Shannon, he desired more practice matching wits against a human. His survival might one day depend on understanding the beasts.

All around the creature stood white aspen trees. The chill autumn nights had lacquered their leaves with bright yellow. Above, beyond the brightly colored canopy, stretched a vivid blue sky interrupted only by Starhaven's many dark, incongruous towers.

The creature stopped, shifted his white cloak, and considered the ancient city. Different civilizations had dressed up the towers, but underneath the human frippery stood stones still Chthonic. The flowing of each thin bridge into its towers, the undulation of the walls—they spoke of stone fluidity.

How the humans had slaughtered the Chthonic race was a mystery beyond the creature's comprehension.

Indeed, the creature found human nature itself mystifying. In groups, the beasts delighted in codifying laws, religions, grammars. And yet, the creature had yet to encounter a human who did not daily commit a crime or a sin or both. Worse, humans spoke and wrote carelessly, erratically—violating their own grammars, yet easily understanding their own illogical language.

At times, the creature was amazed he had learned human communication at all. His former master had allowed him little contact with the beasts.

Perhaps more intense observation would help. He had already edited a gargoyle near the top of the Erasmine Spire so that it would monitor the wizard's colaboris spells. Further infiltration of Starhaven's gargoyles might be useful. The creature had thought of writing a small, rat-sized gargoyle with augmented hearing. Such a construct could gather information about how the humans lived.

A scrub jay's cry brought his gaze downward. Twenty feet ahead lay a clearing where the younger wizards went to drink stolen wine or roll together in the grass.

The creature walked to the trees' edge. His white cloak matched the aspen trunks. Below stretched a small clearing of knee-high grass.

As he waited, the creature thought about Shannon. The wizard had disappointed; this next counter-strike might cripple the old man.

The creature did not need to return to Trillinon now that the flawed dragon had flown. The other demon-worshipers had their orders. That left plenty of time to find the boy and replenish the emerald—a task so important, it had to be kept secret from the other demon-worshipers. The creature had wanted something like a challenge, but he couldn't risk losing the cacographer.

To the north, a twig snapped. Moving among the trees was a short human in black robes. The plan had worked; the young were easily swayed by dreams.

But perhaps this boy was not the one he sought. Perhaps Shannon and he would play another round. Perhaps the old fool would put up a fight before the creature tore out his throat.

The black-robed human moved closer to the clearing's edge.

The creature frowned and decided that he shouldn't wish for a prolonged match with Shannon. If the emerald were lost, he would have to start over.

The creature began to forge the long Language Prime sentences necessary to compose a canker curse. The War of Disjunction would come sooner if the text he was writing didn't rip this child's guts into bloody ribbons. The creature's lips stretched into a long, lupine smile.

At the clearing's edge—peering about with curious eyes for the beautiful meadow seen in a dream—was a young cacographic boy.

CHAPTER
Fifteen

Nicodemus stifled a yawn and opened the door to Shannon's quarters. The front room was a wide, sunlit place with an expanse of Trillinonish carpet, a writing desk, two bookcases, and four scroll racks.

Nicodemus removed his boots and socks in the Northern fashion and padded over to the windows. Outside the midday sun poured dazzling light onto the Bolide Garden.

Once the square had been a lush patch of grass lined with trees. Nicodemus had played among them as a neophyte. But two years ago the elms had died of an unknown disease.

Since then janitorial had undertaken a renovation of the entire square. The recent need to prepare for the convocation had stopped all landscaping and left the garden full of pale dirt.

The mounds directly below Shannon's quarters were muddy and dark. A fountain had once stood there. One of Starhaven's underground aqueducts must have a poorly sealed outlet at that spot.

A sudden yawn made Nicodemus's jaw crack. "Heaven, bless Magister for ordering me to nap," he murmured. Fingering the hour bell he had taken from the classroom, he thought about what Shannon had said about the murderer, the dragon, and the possibility that Nicodemus was connected to prophecy. The old man's words filled his heart with wild hope and fear. Then there was the druid. Could he trust her?

He fought another yawn and realized that he was too exhausted to think clearly. He turned for the bedroom.

Shannon was Trillinonish by birth, but his mother had been Dralish. Her influence on Shannon's taste was seen in the four-post feather bed that had been hauled all the way from Highland.

Sitting on the bed's edge, Nicodemus examined the spherical brass hour bell and the rectangular mouth cut into its bottom.

From his belt-purse, Nicodemus drew a folded page that he had taken from Shannon's desk. It contained a one-hour tintinnabulum spell.

Though it was composed in a common language, the text had a complicated structure. Normally, if Nicodemus concentrated on keeping the runes from rearranging, he could briefly touch such spells without mis-spelling them. However, his exhaustion would increase his chances of mis-spelling. So he bit his lip in concentration and peeled the spell's first paragraph from the page.

The white words leaped into the air around his pinched fingers and pulled the sequent sentences up with them. The paragraphs began folding into a rectangular cage.

Nicodemus redoubled his focus. He had only this one tintinnabulum; misspelling it would preclude his nap.

At last, the concluding paragraph jumped up and formed a ball that flew around within the tintinnabulum cage. Each time it struck a textual wall, the ball silently deconstructed a rune segment. The spell's cage could with-stand the ball for one hour; after that, the ball would break free and ring the bell.

Nicodemus inserted the spell into the bell's mouth, set the device on the bedside table, and fell back onto the feather bed.

He felt his head meet the pillow; he felt his breathing slow; he felt his legs jerk as they sometimes did before sleep. But he did not feel as if he were falling asleep. He felt as if he were . . . spinning?

A scrub jay cried.

Nicodemus opened his eyes and found himself lying in a meadow out-side Starhaven. He recognized the place as "the glen"—a clearing where students went to drink lifted wine or to lock lips.

Here he had kissed Amy Hern for the first time. That had been years ago.

It had been a quiet evening after a brief snow shower. Their every foot-step had produced a crunch, their every breath a plume of feathery vapor. Above them the sky glowed a solemn winter lavender that painted all the branches purest black. Her lips felt chapped against his lips; her tongue, hot against his tongue. They had been only acolytes.

Remembering Amy, Nicodemus winced. She was no longer Amy Hern but Magistra Amaryllis Hern—a lesser wizard in Starfall Keep. He had not seen her since her departure four years ago. Nor had he received any reply to his messages other than an impersonal note about her new life in Star-fall.

In a lucid moment, Nicodemus realized that he was dreaming. He sat up expecting to wake on Shannon's feather bed, but instead sat up in the glen.

A neophyte stood to his right. The boy had his back turned and was looking toward the aspen trees.

Something large was moving among the pale trunks. Its footfalls sent vibrations through the ground. Its breath was long, slow, bestial.

Nicodemus tried to stand but his legs were clumsy. He felt intoxicated.

The creature stepped out from the trees. Nicodemus tried to look at it but his eyes would not focus on it. The thing's body billowed up into a mass of blurry pallid flesh. Again he struggled to stand but only fell forward. He tried to look up at the creature but again could not focus on it.

The neophyte turned to run. Drunkenly, Nicodemus got onto his knees. Just then a thin rod of flesh exploded from the monster. It shot across the clearing to impale the boy's lower back. The child kept running.

Nicodemus tried to cry out but fell forward. Dirt filled his eyes. With clumsy hands, he cleared his vision.

Then he was no longer in the glen. He was in an underground cavern.

The ceiling glinted with quartz. The floor shone uniformly gray. Before him stood a black stone table with a body atop it. A pale cloak covered the figure. In its gloved hands lay a small gem that glowed green. The stone was lacriform—tear-shaped.

Something twitched at the light's edge. It was a small creature. Its oily blue back was sleek and armored with hexagonal plates—a nightmarish land turtle. It hissed as it stumped forward. Dark tendrils sprouted from the creature's footsteps and grew into ivy vines with unctuous black leaves.

A lance of red light dropped from the ceiling to strike the turtle's back. With a crack, the beast's shell shattered. It screamed as blue oil flowed out of its broken shell. A second turtle materialized and then a third.

As the turtles approached, they trailed wakes of burgeoning black ivy vines. More and more turtles came in from the blackness. Another lance of red light shattered the hexagonal plates on a creature's back. There came two more blasts of light, then ten more.

On the table, the body still lay covered by a white cloak. Then a wind whipped through the cavern and tossed back the figure's white hood.

The face revealed was Nicodemus's own. For a dizzying instant Nicodemus was not just himself but also the figure lying on the table. He was also the turtles crawling on the floor and a terrified neophyte running through the woods back to Starhaven.

As the figure on the table, he sat up. His cheeks bulged and his lips parted to loose a deafening metallic clanging. A tiny ball was flying around inside his mouth.

Suddenly Nicodemus woke in Shannon's feather bed. He had escaped the nightmare and was staring straight at the vibrating hour bell crying out its earsplitting alarm.

CHAPTER
Sixteen

When Shannon returned to his study, he found Amadi ransacking the place with three of her Northern sentinels. Shannon recognized the first—a slender male Ixonian—as Kale, Amadi's personal secretary. The other two were the fools she had sent to follow him.

Upon seeing him, the strangers began forging censor spells—enmeshing texts that could wrap around his head and prevent him from spellwriting.

Shannon, ignoring them, walked behind his desk and set Azure on his chair. He removed several walnuts from a jar on a bookshelf. "I believe an explanation is due," he said mildly.

Amadi answered tensely: "Magister, you deliberately deceived the sentinels I sent to guard you."

Shannon offered a walnut to Azure's outstretched foot. "I was being guarded? I didn't notice. Your sentinels must write excellent subtexts. I wonder how they lost me." He smiled at the two sentinels who had been following him.

They made a comical pair. One was tall and fat with golden buttons on his sleeve. The other was short and thin with silver buttons.

Azure cracked the walnut in her beak and picked out the meat.

Amadi looked at the short sentinel. "In the Marfil Tower," the man blurted. "He went into a privy and then wrote a text to climb to a bridge above."

Shannon laughed and accepted Azure's empty walnut shells. "You flatter me, Magister, to claim I'm capable of such a feat at my age." He laughed again. "In fact, I left the privy by the balcony so that I could question the gargoyle that empties the latrine. Surely your companion watching the balcony saw me." He raised his eyebrows at the fat sentinel.

The man looked away.

"Oh, how embarrassing," Shannon said through a half-smile. "You didn't consider that the privy might have more than one exit. Well, no matter; you may question the balcony gargoyle. It will recall our conversation." He handed Azure another walnut. "I examined other gargoyles afterward." He listed them.

Amadi eyed her underlings. "Go and verify what Magister says."

With a commotion of bobbing heads, the two hurried from the study.

"And Kale," Amadi said to her secretary, "you may deliver those messages now. Interrupt me only with urgent news."

The young Ixonian nodded and left, closing the door behind him.

Amadi, pushing a dreadlock from her face, turned back to Shannon. "Magister, I thought we had an understanding. I am trying to prove your innocence."

"Amadi, I simply did not know I was being . . . guarded, as you put it."

"Magister, I'm not a child anymore." A hint of pain sounded in her otherwise controlled voice. "You knew you were being watched."

"Amadi, I don't—"

"Very well." Her tone was testy. "So there will be no future misunderstandings, I tell you now that we've placed a watch on your quarters above the Bolide Gardens. We did this after following Nicodemus there. We did not disturb his sleep, but after he left my authors searched the place, taking care not to disturb anything. If you persist in this suspicious behavior, we will have to search it more thoroughly." She paused for effect. "Also we have written robust wards on the doors and windows."

Shannon raised an eyebrow.

"No author or text will be able to enter or leave your quarters without disspelling a ward. I would advise against such an action; anyone attempting to sneak in or out of your quarters will be cut in two at the waist. Of course, the sentinels watching your quarters will disarm the wards when you enter or leave."

Shannon made no attempt to hide his irritation. "Your reaction seems extreme considering that you have no evidence of misconduct on my part."

"None indeed? Do you care to explain why your face looks like a lion's scratching post?"

He rolled his blind eyes. "I told you a spellbook deconstructed when I was working late last night. I can fetch what's left of the book, several books, actually."

"Of course you can. And the men I sent to confirm your story about researching gargoyles, no doubt the constructs will exonerate you. You're a linguist studying textual intelligence. No doubt you edited—"

"Magistra, you go too far! I have answered your every question, allowed you to interrupt my research, even given you access to my students. And how do you repay my good will? By spying on me, by ransacking my library, by accusing me of tampering with academy constructs."

Amadi pursed her lips.

"So I will say again," he continued, his voice calmer, "that you owe me an explanation." He held out another nut for Azure. "Without one, I must complain to—"

"Two of your students have died."

The walnut dropped from his hands. "What did you say?"

"Two of your students have died. Adan of Roundtower and Eric Everson. Adan was found on the smithy roof. It seems he jumped from the Weshurst Bridge. His older brother perished in the Astrophell fire. The other boy, Eric, came running in from the forest with a misspell tearing up his insides. The curse worked him to exhaustion. In his robes, the boy had a Numinous scroll—seems he stole the manuscript and was playing with it in the forest."

"Blood of Los," Shannon whispered and sat heavily in his chair. Azure climbed onto his shoulder and began preening his dreadlocks.

Amadi took the seat in front of his desk. "There's no sign that either death was murder. But in light of what happened to Nora Finn, I believe something is awry. So I will ask you again: Magister, where have you been for the past hour?"

"I speak the truth when I say that I was talking to gargoyles," Shannon said numbly.

The murderer had struck faster than he had thought possible. More terrifying, Shannon had issued orders to all wizards supervising cacographers that their charges were not to leave Starhaven. How could the murderer have induced the boys to disobey and escape their teachers?

The murderer had said he could wield dreams as others might wield a net. The monster must somehow be using dreams to compel the boys to stray out of Starhaven's protective walls. "Creator forgive me!" he whispered to himself. This changed everything.

Amadi began to ask a question about the two poor boys.

He stopped her and withdrew the severed clay arm from his robes. The thing was beginning to lose its shape. Nevertheless, he laid it on the table.

While Amadi stared at the arm, he described Nora Finn's private library and his fight with the murderer.

Amadi stared at him with a neutral expression. "Magister, you expect me to believe this?"

His tone grew more urgent. "Go to the Gimhurst Tower; see Nora's private library for yourself."

"According to your tale, the deconstructing spellbooks will have destroyed everything in the private library—even your attacker's weapon. And you said the creature ran off with Finn's research journal. There would be nothing to find."

Shannon had not thought of this. "But the arm."

Looking at the limb, Amadi took a long breath. "I have never heard of anything, living or magical, that changes from flesh to clay. Perhaps such a transformation was possible on the ancient continent. Perhaps a deity could achieve such a thing with a godspell."

Shannon felt his hands go cold. Godspells were immensely powerful and ornate texts written by deities. They were also exceedingly rare.

Amadi was studying Shannon's face. "Magister, do you believe you confronted a god last night? Surely other authors would have detected the presence of a deity in Starhaven."

She was right. "Perhaps not a god, but a godspell," he said quickly. "Amadi, you must believe me. There are forces acting here beyond anything we've known before."

She paused and then asked her next question in a softer tone: "Magister, have you ever had visions not related to quaternary thoughts?"

He blinked. "No, of course not. You think I'm mad?"

"Tell me about your relationship to the druid Deirdre."

"Druid?" he asked in confusion. "Deirdre? Nothing, nothing. She asked for an interview with Nicodemus, and to help the convocation I agreed to—" He stopped. "You think I'm mad and it has something to do with the druid?"

Amadi shook her head. "With the boy. He has a . . . power about him. Why didn't you tell me of his relationship to prophecy during our first interview?"

"Because there is no proven relationship."

Amadi tilted her head to one side. "It seems the boy unknowingly draws spellwrights—you, possibly the druid—to his cause. Consider that his peers are dying of misspells. Perhaps he is responsible for . . . what you perceived."

"What are you implying?"

"Think of the boy's scar—a Braid broken by an Inconjunct. The counter-prophecy predicts that the Storm Petrel will 'untie the Halcyon's weavings' and that he will 'break the braids the Halcyon ties between the human kingdoms.'"

Shannon stood and began to pace. "Amadi, you question my sanity while believing that a mere cacographic apprentice is the Anti-Halcyon? That's madness. How can you believe that a crippled boy is the Storm Petrel? The champion of the demon-worshipers?"

"I look for theories that can explain the recent deaths. This theory is the only one that can explain them all."

Shannon shook his head vehemently. "But I've spoken to the provost. He agrees that Nicodemus's scars were most likely the result of a fanatical mother who branded him."

"I've since talked to Provost Montserrat. He believes we should reevaluate Nicodemus."

Shannon felt nauseated. "You think Nicodemus killed the other cacographers?"

She shook her head. "Nicodemus was lecturing neophytes when the young ones died. Besides, there is no evidence that either boy was murdered. As I said, the counter-prophecies teach us that turmoil shall follow wherever the Storm Petrel flies. If I am right, Nicodemus is unaware of his true nature but is driving these horrible events by some unknown power."

Shannon stopped pacing. Things would become chaotic indeed if Amadi publicly declared that the counter-prophecy was coming to pass. He needed to stop her. He needed to protect the Drum Tower. If he were free for just another day, he could sneak the cacographic boys to the compluvium, where the gargoyles would protect them.

"Magister," Amadi said, "you must admit that Nicodemus might be the one of counter-prophecy."

Suddenly Shannon saw his opening. It would require a bit of finesse, a bit of a bluff. He walked back to his chair but did not sit. "I suppose your faction will be pleased that you are stirring up excitement about the counter-prophecy."

Amadi's eyes narrowed. "Sentinels may not play in the game of factions."

Time for his bluff. "There are some who could link you to the counter-prophecy faction. And if Nicodemus is dangerous, then it might seem that you are letting him run a little wild, letting the bodies stack up a little higher, collecting a little more blood to bolster your claims about the counter-prophecy."

Amadi's face became blank. "What are you saying, Magister?"

"I am saying that if you intend to make claims about counter-prophecy you had best keep a tight watch on Nicodemus and the rest of the Drum Tower. You had best do all that you can to prevent further deaths. If you don't, maybe a rumor will imply that you shirked your duties so as to breed fear and so build support for your faction."

Amadi grunted. "You are trying to force me to protect the cacographic boys from your imaginary monster?"

He sat down. "We would both get what we want."

"I don't take well to threats, Magister. I'm not your student any longer. You can't possibly connect me to any faction. Besides, I have precious few sentinels available to me as it is. With the convocation in progress, the provost's officers are stealing my every free author to look after our guests. But what you say does make some sense." She paused. "Very well, I'll place two guards before the Drum Tower at night and two to follow Nicodemus. But I'm also assigning two to follow you."

Shannon suppressed a smile. "I shall welcome the protection. But we have to make sure the endangered boys don't leave Starhaven. I'll reemphasize my orders that cacographers are not to be let out of doors. You had best seal the Drum Tower at night and write protective wards on the doors and windows. I'll need passwords in case I have to reach the students."

Amadi nodded slowly. "Very well."

Shannon sighed in relief. "Amadi, you'll be glad you took my advice. Now I must go to my field research in the compluvium. Nicodemus will meet me there; I will lead your sentinels over from here. They can watch over us both. Later we've more research in the Main Library."

Amadi leaned forward and spoke earnestly: "Magister, I will go to the Gimhurst Tower and search for Finn's private library. But, as I have said, there is no direct evidence that either of the boys was murdered. Please keep an open mind about the counter-prophecy. Consider that Nicodemus might be the Storm Petrel." She paused. "I suspect we are dealing with a force far more dire than a simple murderer."

"Magistra," he said, "I suspect the same thing."

DEIRDRE CALMLY REGARDED Amadi. A moment ago, the woman had appeared at her chamber door and demanded an interview.

"What is your interest in Nicodemus Weal?" the sentinel asked, sitting on Kyran's sleeping cot.

Deirdre sat on the opposite cot. She had expected the question. "As you observed, Amadi Okeke, I had hoped the boy might be the Peregrine safely delivered to me. But his keloid dashed my hopes." It was not truly a lie—the keloid had dashed her hopes . . . that Nicodemus would be easily won over.

Amadi nodded distractedly. "Druid, does your Order know of a counter-prophecy?"

"I have never heard of such a thing."

"The Erasmine Counter-Prophecy is not common knowledge, even among wizards. It predicts that a malevolent spellwright will arise to become the Halcyon's opposite, a champion of chaos referred to as the Petrel or the Storm Petrel."

"And this champion," Deirdre asked, "might slay the Halcyon and help the demons invade our land?"

The sentinel nodded. "The counter-prophecy predicts that unless we can stop it, the Petrel will begin a corruption of all language. The demons will complete it."

Deirdre willed her face to be calm. "And Nicodemus's unusual scar and his misspelling makes you suspect that he might be this destroyer?"

Amadi took a slow breath. "Doubtless you've heard rumors about . . . unrest in Starhaven. We have noticed a number of dangerous misspells, a few accidents, but nothing that should concern you as a delegate. As a sentinel, my first concern is maintaining safety throughout the convocation. To that end, I entertain all theories of what might be causing these odd events." She paused. "If the druids also know of a counter-prophecy and could identify Nicodemus as—"

"We do not believe in a counter-prophecy," Deirdre interrupted.

"But perhaps those concerned with the Silent Blight might think differently? Should I speak to the other druidic delegates?"

Deirdre shook her head. "We do not believe in a counter-prophecy of any kind. And the druids are not at all certain the Blight is connected to prophecy. I fear we cannot help you."

"I see. Thank you, druid, for your time." Amadi stood and stepped toward the door.

Deirdre rose with her. "If there is any other way I can help, you have only to ask."

Amadi paused by the threshold. "Perhaps . . ." she said, turning back. "I wonder if you could tell me . . . do the druids know of a construct that appears to be made of flesh, but once deconstructed becomes clay?"

The strength seemed to drain from Deirdre's legs. "Have you encountered such a creature?" she asked in what she hoped was a tone of disbelief, not shock.

The sentinel was studying her face. "I surprise you. Don't think me mad for asking such a question. Magister Shannon and I were debating if such a thing was possible."

Deidre forced her lips to smile. "I do not think it mad to wonder such things. We must always seek new understandings." She paused. "What if Nicodemus truly is the dangerous spellwright of your counter-prophecy?"

The sentinel shook her head. "There is no need to be alarmed. In less than a quarter hour, I will have two guards following the boy night and day. His tower will be textually sealed at night. The moment we have evidence that he is dangerous or connected to the counter-prophecy, we'll censor his mind and lock him up in a cell below the Gate Towers."

"Thank you for telling me." Deirdre bowed.

Amadi returned the gesture and left. Slowly the sentinel's footsteps faded down the hall.

"How much of that did you hear?" Deirdre asked.

"Enough," Kyran said from behind her. "So it seems the black-robes have encountered the demon-worshiper you guessed was nearby. Do I need to explain about the creature turning from flesh to clay?"

She turned and saw his silhouette glimmer as he let the invisibility subtext deconstruct. "No, you bloody don't."

The subtext fell from Kyran's head, revealing a stern expression. "We should take the boy now. Our goddess can protect him once we get him to the ark."

Deirdre rubbed her eyes. "We can't. You heard the sentinel; she's placing guards around the boy." The pressure on her eyelids caused floating orange-black splotches across her vision. "Ky, do you think we could find the author's body, kill the demon-worshiper while the creature is sneaking about?"

"No. The true body could be anywhere."

Deirdre swore. "And if Amadi Okeke gets it into her head that Nicodemus is this Petrel, she'll censor him and send him to his death in that prison cell."

"He wouldn't be safe from the creature when locked up?"

She dropped her hands and gave him an exasperated look. "What would happen if you tied up a lamb and left it in the sheep pen?"

He grimaced. "The lycanthropes would come out of the woods."

CHAPTER
Seventeen

Nicodemus stared at the flecks of stew that spangled his emptied lunch bowl.

Midday sunlight was streaming into the refectory—a wide Lornish hall lined with tapestries and clear-glass windows. Above, broad rafters marched across the ceiling and provided hanging posts for the academy's banners. Farther down the table, several librarians whispered about the horrible news from Trillinon.

Using his spoon, Nicodemus began to flatten the drops of congealing stew on the inside of his bowl. A mash of conflicting emotions seethed within his mind.

Half an hour before, he had hurried into the refectory, heart pounding. The nightmare had been as vivid as the previous night's dragon dream. He had been sure it had also come from the murderer, but he couldn't imagine why the villain would send him such strange visions.

He had mulled over the nightmare's images while fetching his stew and finding a private space to sit. The more he thought about the dream, the more it seemed that the episodes of the neophyte and the turtles were incongruous. That had calmed him somewhat. Mundane nightmares were filled with nonsensical shifts. Perhaps the bizarre sequence meant that the dream was simply a dream.

Whatever the case, Nicodemus had told himself, Shannon would know what to do about it; there was no use in worrying now.

He had tried to think about his successful first composition lecture but ended up fretting about the sentinels who had been spying on him. Did they still think him capable of murder? The question had made him think about James Berr, the murdering cacographer who had lived so long ago. Did the sentinels think he was a second James Berr?

Then he had thought about what the druid had told him. Her words had awakened a dormant longing in his heart. Could he actually be the Halcyon? After all these years of coming to terms with his disability, could his cacography be removed?

Half of him wanted to lose himself in dreams of what life might be like if the druid were correct. But the other half was wary and more than a little frightened. What if he dared to believe that he was not crippled and then, once again, discovered that it was all a lie? Could he survive a second disappointment?

He felt his belt-purse for the magical artifact Deirdre had given him. A Seed of Finding, she had called it. Even through cloth, the object made his fingers tingle.

The artifact's power spoke to the druid's sincerity. However, she was clearly after something more than curing his cacography. The more Nicodemus thought about it, the more he questioned her motives.

"Fiery blood," he grumbled, flattening another drop of stew with extra force.

Then there was the advice he had given to the smart-mouthed cacographic boy in his class: "Accept your disability and you will be free," had been the essence of his message. It had seemed true at the time, but here he was, fervently hoping that his own disability could be erased.

Did that make him a hypocrite? He brought the spoon to his lips and tapped its tip against his front teeth. "Yes," he grunted, "it bloody well does."

Suddenly Nicodemus wished everything would just go away. If only he could crawl back to his room and spend the rest of the day reading the knightly romance stored under his bed.

Abruptly Devin thumped her lunch bowl down on the table and sat next to him. "Heard the news?" she asked. "That why you look like you've seen Erasmus's ghost?"

Nicodemus dropped his spoon with a wooden clatter. "Dev, thank heaven you're here! I need to tell . . ." his voice died as he remembered his promise to Shannon not to trust anyone. ". . . need to tell you that I taught my first class on spellwriting. It went well. But the news was so shocking that . . . I don't know how to feel."

"None of us does," she grumbled, sinking a battered wooden spoon into her stew. "Nico, do you think Starhaven takes care of us?"

"Of course. Most likely we'd have magical literacy permanently censored from our minds if we were in Astrophell."

"But maybe that wouldn't be so bad. Do you think common folk are distressed by a fire in Trillinon? What's foreign news to a pig farmer?"

"But, Dev, you'd be illiterate."

She shrugged. "I don't read anything but janitorial texts. Sometimes I feel like we're just ants in an anthill, crippled ants at that. And here comes King Ant now." She nodded at the raised stage on the far side of the hall. Several deans and foreign spellwrights were standing around a long table.

The provost, sitting in a high-backed wooden chair, floated onstage. Even from his present distance, Nicodemus could make out the muris spell billowing under the arch-wizard's seat. If he had been closer, he would have seen an obscenely old man who had been half folded over by time. He also would have seen the grizzled old raccoon the provost kept as a familiar.

"Behold," Devin intoned, "Provost Ferran Montserrat: the only independent mind in this stone heap. That man doesn't answer to anybody but our god and his avatar. The rest of us are bound, antlike, to his will."

Nicodemus watched the provost float to the table's head. With surprising dexterity, the ancient arch-wizard landed his chair and picked up a fork. The deans and their guests sat and began eating.

"Everything is so damn complicated," Nicodemus grumbled before swearing softly, "blood of Los."

"Piss and blood in a silver bowl!" Devin hissed. "I forgot!"

Nicodemus jumped slightly in his seat. "Forgot what?"

Devin's pale face flushed red as she visibly struggled to contain a salvo of obscenity. "Two days ago Magistra Highsmith caught me napping on duty. The old hussy of a historian is making me give a short lecture about Los to the rest of the girls on janitorial. It's her idea of a penance. The old shrew knows cacographers never study theology. I was supposed to look it up but didn't."

Nicodemus raised his eyebrows. "When do you lecture?"

"In half an hour," Devin said with a glare that dared him to chide her. Fortunately, he knew enough to keep his mouth shut. When she spoke again, it was in a calmer voice. "Nico, tell me everything you know about Los."

"I'm a cacographer too, you know. I never took theology either."

"But you memorize everything Shannon says and fawn—"

"All right, all right. Back on the ancient continent there was a golden age when the Solar Empire . . . and that's not the Neosolar Empire, which formed on this continent. Anyway, the original Solar Empire existed in peace with the gods. But someone committed a grave sin that enabled Los, then a powerful earth god, to become the first demon."

"But what sin—"

Nicodemus shrugged. "Every religion has a different answer. Probably no one's right; probably that knowledge was lost when our ancestors crossed the ocean. As wizards we hold to no belief and so are not bound to a religion or kingdom. All you need to know is that Los took a third of the deities to Mount Calax and turned them into demons. He made an army of all the demons and called it the Pandemonium. That's where the word comes from: Pan, all, demonium, demons. So when we say the class was pandemonium we're using hyperbole to—"

"Blasted pisser—" Devin cut herself short and calmed down. "Nico, I get it. Could you just give me the history without your linguistic ramblings?"

Nicodemus grumbled about history and linguistic ramblings being the same thing before continuing. "So after Los formed the Pandemonium, there was a war between deities and demons called the Apocalypse. When it became clear the demons would win, the human deities built huge Exodus ships to cross the ocean. Somehow—no one's sure how—a group of human heroes turned Los into stone. This bought the ships enough time to get out to sea. The demons, being bound to the ancient continent, couldn't follow. Then a powerful wind called the Maelstrom scattered the Exodus ships. That's why each of the current landfall kingdoms has people of different shapes and colorings."

Devin narrowed her eyes. "In ancient kingdoms everyone looked the same?"

"More or less. Certainly someone like me with black hair and olive skin would not have come from the same kingdom as someone with your red hair and freckles."

"There's no need to be snotty, Nico. Cacographers aren't taught this stuff. And I don't hang on Magister's every miniature lecture like you do. When wizards gossip, I'll listen. But I'd rather chew gravel that listen to most of their academic babble." She sniffed. "Just another reason why it'd be better if I were illiterate."

"I'm sorry, Dev, I didn't mean . . . But don't be so unhappy. Even if they permanently censored you, it's not as if you would be free. You've told me yourself, magical illiterates are bound to the land or their trade. They have to work in the fields for lords or barons or whatnot."

She only shrugged and turned back to her stew. "Couldn't be worse than it is here."

Nicodemus leaned forward. "Dev, you'd have no spells to wash your face or clean your teeth. No constructs to empty the night pot. And you'd be short-lived."

Suddenly her brown eyes burned with their characteristic fire. "Well f—" Again she visibly suppressed an obscenity. "I don't care a fig for that! Not all of us are as strong as you, Nico. I'll barely see a century. And I'm nearly fifty already. I might not look it, but I am. If I were illiterate, at least I wouldn't outlive my family."

Nicodemus started to protest but then stopped. "You'd want to get married?"

"Oh, a bloody donkey's ass-crack on that!" she snapped. "I damned well don't want to get married." She began stirring her stew with trembling hands.

Nicodemus could not think of what to say, so he sat in silence and waited until she appeared calmer.

"Dev," he said at last. "Last night I asked you what Smallwood meant when he called me Shannon's new pet cacographer."

"Forget it. It's nothing important." She scowled. "Though it proves my point about being illiterate."

Nicodemus touched her elbow. "Tell me? Please?"

Devin looked at him. "It's all hearsay."

He nodded.

After laying her spoon down, she scooted a conspiratorial half-inch closer on the bench. "Well, years ago Magister was a rising star in Astrophell, both in research and politics. He was also an oddity because his father came from Dral, but his mother from Trillinon. That's why his names sound so different—Agwu Shannon. Anyway, his faction, The Sons of Ejindu, wanted the wizards to take a more active role in keeping any rogue spellwrights from joining the Spirish Civil War. Shannon was their Long Council speaker. And . . ." Devin lowered her voice. "And . . . he got the provost's grandniece pregnant!"

Nicodemus looked dubious. "But spellwrights can't conceive. We're all sterile."

Devin smiled at him. "Nico, sometimes I forget how young you are. That's what we tell the acolytes. Together we're all barren. No two spellwrights have ever conceived. But every so often, a spellwright and an illiterate produce a child."

"Shannon got an illiterate pregnant!"

"Shhhh!" She swatted his shoulder. "Not so loud. Now you see why we authors swear off families. We would outlive them and have to watch them die. That's why it was a huge scandal when Shannon got the provost's grandniece with child."

Nicodemus could only shake his head.

She continued, "So Shannon tried to hide the baby, but his opponents discovered the boy and started the scandal. The provost of Astrophell was furious and made Shannon Master of the Drum Tower in Starhaven. To get rid of him, you see."

"And then?"

"No one knows exactly. Some say Magister did something desperate with his research, hoping a breakthrough would earn him forgiveness. Some say he's blind because his research spell burned out his mundane vision. But whatever happened Magister ended up here at Starhaven. He couldn't visit Astrophell for twenty years or so. By then his wife had died and his son was married. Magister tried to patch things up, but apparently his son hated him for abandoning the family and denounced Magister in public."

Nicodemus blew out a long breath.

"So Magister came back here and became a champion of cacographers." Her wide eyes darted up for a moment. "He chooses one cacographic boy from every generation and tries to help him earn a hood. Before you it was Tomas Rylan. Tom lived with John and me. Magister helped him become a lesser wizard in Starfall Janitorial."

Nicodemus felt his face burn. Had Shannon chosen him as an apprentice only because he wanted a new pet cripple?

Devin stirred the dregs of her stew. "From the moment you came to the Drum Tower, you were Magister's favorite. We weren't surprised when he moved you into the top floor with John and me years before you had earned it."

"Oh" was all Nicodemus could bring himself to say.

Devin looked at him. "So that's what Smallwood meant."

Nicodemus's mind reeled. Shannon had taken him as an apprentice only out of pity? He felt sick. "Thank you, Dev," he said quietly.

"Nico, you shouldn't hold it against Magister; he only wants to help."

He stood. "I should go."

Devin caught his hand and squeezed. "Nico, everyone loves you in the Drum Tower. John and I . . . Don't feel bad."

"I have to meet the old man in the compluvium." He squeezed her hand in return. "I don't want to be late."

"Okay."

He picked up his bowl and cup. "See you tonight," he said and walked away.

CHAPTER
Eighteen

Six of Starhaven's twenty eastern towers held the Sataal Landing more than four hundred feet above ground. Nicodemus tried not to think about the height as he walked eastward along the thin stone concourse. Every fifty feet or so, he climbed a few broad steps to the next plaza.

The surrounding towers and nearby mountains blocked direct sunlight from the landing for all but a few hours during the day. The Chthonics had once cultivated a shade garden here. Antiquarians wrote of tall mountain laurels and soil beds bursting with angel wings, fetterbush, and barronwort.

Now the soil beds nurtured only weeds and ivy. Moss bristled between the wall stones. Feral cats skulked about the place looking for fresh water. Nicodemus couldn't see anyone following him but guessed a subtextualized sentinel was near.

As he ventured farther east, the towers crowded closer. At each new level, the plaza was smaller, the stairway narrower.

Finally the landing terminated in a small, mossy cloister. Nicodemus found his way blocked by the thirty-foot wall that ran between the abandoned Itan and Karkin Towers. A row of metal rungs climbed halfway up the wall to a narrow walkway. Voices echoed from above.

Nicodemus scaled the ladder and found its rungs spaced too closely for human comfort. The Chthonics must have had small hands, he decided. Or maybe small claws? Or perhaps they had had no claws or hands at all but had gripped the rungs with their teeth.

On top of the walkway stood a smiling Magister Shannon with Azure on his shoulder. The old man was cheerfully lecturing four Northern sentinels: ". . . obvious reasons the compluvium's constructs are written aggressively. So we mustn't—ah, Nicodemus, you're here at last."

The sentinels, three men, one woman, all were roughly sixty years in age and wearing gold or silver buttons on their sleeves. They examined Nicodemus with narrowed eyes. Shannon laughingly introduced them as his personal guards.

Nicodemus bowed. He understood their confused looks. They had been sent to investigate Shannon and were taken aback by the old man's enthusiasm. Nicodemus couldn't blame them.

Shannon grabbed Nicodemus's arm and pulled him through the crowd. The old wizard's grip felt like a vise.

The walkway on which they were standing ran into a crevice where the Karkin Tower met the wall. Here a narrow staircase climbed to the wall's top. A seven-foot-tall gargoyle stood guard on the bottommost step.

Its muscled body would have been humanoid, save for the two extra arms growing under the expected pair. And the stone wings bulging from its back would have resembled bird wings but for the two additional carpal joints that allowed the limbs to fold into tight, fiddlehead spirals. Its giant hawk's head glared at the spellwrights with stony eyes.

Shannon was again lecturing the sentinels. "Those of you who've dealt with a war-weight gargoyle will remember that they are dangerous, valuable, and fractious. So use great care when presenting these passwords." The old man produced a scroll from his sleeve and began pulling off Numinous paragraphs.

Nicodemus watched as Shannon handed a set of passwords to each sentinel. The Northerners, however, were studying the massive gargoyle and glancing at one another.

Suddenly Nicodemus realized that Shannon was allowing the golden paragraphs to fold into pleated and stacked sheets: this conformation stabilized much of its language but strained those sentences that folded the text. Such tension could cause rearrangement or fragmentation.

Sure enough, when Shannon handed a copy of the passwords to the female sentinel, two bending sentences snapped.

Nicodemus spoke up, "Magister, her text has—"

"Don't worry, lad. I'll take you through myself. Excuse me, spellwrights. My apprentice has not yet mastered Numinous."

He grabbed Nicodemus again and dragged him to the massive gargoyle. Nicodemus's stomach knotted until the old man released his arm and held out two password texts.

The gargoyle extended its four arms. Each pair of hands took a paragraph and began to fold them. If written correctly, the spells would fold into a pre-set shape.

When the aquiline gargoyle had creased each paragraph into a small starlike shape, it chirped and moved aside.

Shannon put a hand on Nicodemus's back and guided him onto the stairway between the Karkin Tower and the wall.

Behind them, two sentinels held out their passwords to the gargoyle's many arms.

"Be ready for anything," Shannon muttered.

Confused, Nicodemus turned back just as the war-weight gargoyle began shrieking. Two bulky stone arms struck the wall with percussive force. A wing unfurled to block the passage.

A chorus of shocked sentinel voices came from the other side.

"Magisters," Shannon scolded, "you let the passwords fragment! How could you be so careless with a pleated sheet? Check the other two paragraphs."

An apologetic female voice replied that they too had deconstructed.

"Wonderful," Shannon barked. "I can't cast Numinous past this war-weight gargoyle without exciting it to violence."

A dour male voice replied, "Magister, we've orders not to lose sight of you."

Shannon laughed. "A fine job you've made of that. Now Nicodemus and I lack the protection we were promised. Burning heaven! I've a mind to complain to Amadi of this."

The sentinels were silent.

Shannon instructed them to hurry down to the ground level and then hike back up the Itan Tower. From there they might reach the Spindle Bridge. He and Nicodemus would wait on the bridge. "Make it back in an hour and Amadi needn't know," he said and then turned to hike up the steps toward the top of the wall.

The sentinels set off in the opposite direction. Nicodemus hurried after the old man.

"Now we may speak freely," Shannon said with satisfaction. "Even the subtextualized sentinel following you can't get past that brute."

Nicodemus frowned. "Magister, the passwords were misspelled?"

"Not in the least," Shannon said, turning back long enough to wink a blind eye. "They couldn't have been spelled more correctly."

IN THE ITAN Tower, Deirdre laughed at what she saw through the window bars.

She was standing next to Kyran in an abandoned Chthonic hallway—a dark place with slate floors, cracked walls of deep-blue plaster, a black ceiling shaped like roots or rocks. Everything was coated with centuries of dust.

Bright autumn sunlight slanted in through the barred windows, illuminating clouds of languid dust motes. A hand moving through the chilly air spun a few bright specks; Kyran's body pulled with it a maelstrom of flying, sunlit dirt.

"Shannon's used the hawk-headed construct to fool the Northern wizards," Deirdre said. "The simpletons are hurrying down toward the ground. Ky, go and follow them. I want to know if they report his trick."

"I shouldn't leave you."

She turned to look at her protector. Though stooped and leaning on his thick walking staff, he still had to hold his head at an awkward angle to avoid the low ceiling. It made him seem like a giant.

"Are we having this argument again?" she asked, smiling. "You know I never lose."

"Because you never argue about what matters."

"Ky, this is not the time. I need you to watch those wizards."

"There's not another soul for a half mile. Even the black-robes don't come here."

Her smile wilted.

His dark eyes glared at her. Then, with a barely audible grunt, he nodded. One long stride brought him to the barred window. The sunlight turned his hair to gleaming gold, his robes to solar white. He watched the four sentinels hurrying down the stone platform, then turned and strode away down the hall, his walking staff clicking against the stone floor.

Deirdre looked out the window again. Shannon and Nicodemus were hiking up the steep stairway between the wall and the tower. She would need to climb up a few more floors to keep them in view. She set off in the opposite direction from Kyran.

For once, Deirdre was not irritated by her short stature. She did not need to stoop when stepping through the Chthonic doorways, nor did her small feet slip on the short steps.

A cloud of pigeons shot past a nearby window. Deirdre found herself thinking about Shannon. Was Nicodemus's trust in the old wizard well placed? Dare she approach him?

Because she was preoccupied with these questions, it wasn't until she had completed a circuit around the tower, and so climbed to the next level, that she noticed the footsteps.

She stopped near the top of the staircase. The footsteps ceased as well. "Ky," she called, "you're to follow the sentinels, not follow me around like a mother hen."

At first silence greeted her words. But then the footsteps returned at a sprint.

Deirdre's heart began to pound. The wizards had not allowed her to wear a blade. Instinctively, her eyes searched about for a weapon and fell on the horizontal bars the Chthonics had built into their windows. She rushed over and grabbed two rods that had been drilled into the window frame.

No living man could have pulled them free. But Deirdre needed only to put one foot on the wall and heave. The bars exploded from the frame with small clouds of pulverized stone.

The footsteps were loud and echoing now. She crouched and held the two steel bars up in Spirish fighting fashion.

The figure that came running up the staircase wore a tattered white cloak—more a hastily sewn sheet than a proper garment. A voluminous hood covered his head and face.

As Deirdre raised her crude weapons, the creature ran through a square sunbeam. An object extending from his hand became a blazing rectangle of reflected light.

The glare momentarily dazzled her eyes, so it wasn't until the creature was a few steps away that she identified the steel object as an ancient Lornish greatsword.

"LISTEN CAREFULLY," SHANNON said, stepping onto the wall at the end of the Sataal Landing. "We don't have much time."

Azure was riding on the wizard's shoulder and using her eyes to see for him.

"Of course, Magis—"

A few inches ahead, the wall plummeted roughly seventy feet to the shaded impluvium: a deep rainwater reservoir that provided water to Starhaven's inhabited quarters through a series of aqueducts. Beneath the surface lay massive valves and floodgates. Around them moved what Nicodemus first took to be bulbous gray fish, but then he realized they were the water gargoyles that operated the valves.

Beyond the impluvium stretched a mile-wide half-bowl of roofs, gables, and gutters that funneled rain down to the reservoir. This metastructure, composed of the southeast quarter's many different contiguous buildings, was known as the compluvium; and everywhere on it—squatting, stooping, or crawling—were the gutter gargoyles. The constructs were busy mucking leaves out of the aqueducts, scaring off birds, or mending leaky roofs.

"Amazing," Nicodemus half-whispered.

"All of these gargoyles are controlled by a faction to which I once belonged," Shannon explained, hurrying toward a spiral staircase on the wall's opposite end. "If you or the Drum Tower is ever endangered, you must bring all the male cacographers here. That brute down by the Sataal Landing will obey your commands. You're to bring the boys here to the compluvium and hide them; it's a large place and the gargoyles know many secret nooks."

Nicodemus swallowed. "Endangered by what? The murderer? The sentinels?"

"I'll answer in a moment," Shannon huffed. "First let's be clear about what you are to do. Come." They reached the spiral staircase and hurried down the narrow steps. Azure had to bob her head to keep a clear view of where they were going.

At the bottom of the stairs stood a gated tunnel leading into a building Nicodemus didn't recognize.

Using a few Numinous passwords, Shannon opened the gate and pulled it wide. "If danger finds you even in the compluvium, lead the boys through here." Azure whistled nervously as they stepped into the tunnel. "Watch your head."

The tunnel proved to be both dark and long. But together master and apprentice trudged through ankle-deep water to another gate. Shannon sprang the lock and led Nicodemus onto a short walkway that faced the sheer rock face of the Pinnacle Mountains.

They had come onto Starhaven's easternmost wall.

Shannon hurried along the walkway to the Spindle Bridge's landing. Standing beside the bridge was another of the four-armed, hawk-headed gargoyles.

Shannon stopped before the gargoyle and turned to his apprentice. "You are to bring the boys to this construct. He guards a system of constructs and spells we call the Fool's Ladder. It's the only way out of Starhaven beside the front gate. If need be, you can escape into the forest and then lead the boys down to Gray's Crossing." He withdrew a pouch from his robes and tossed it to Nicodemus.

When the younger man caught the bag, it clinked. "Magister!" he exclaimed while peering inside. "There's enough gold here to buy the whole town of Gray's Crossing."

"Hopefully there's enough to buy escape or protection."

"But shouldn't I just find you if there's danger?"

"There might not be time to find me." He closed his blind eyes and rubbed them. "Besides, if you truly are in danger, it will be because I am dead."

THE BLADE FLASHING toward Deirdre's throat was spotted with rust.

She leaped backward, gracefully finding new footing on the narrow steps. Her opponent's crude white hood still covered his face. She wondered how the creature saw. She also wondered why he had risked an attack inside Starhaven, where he could not use magic.

The thing advanced with a backhand stroke. She met the blade with a parry of her right bar. The force of the creature's blow nearly knocked the bar from her hand. The thing possessed strength that rivaled her own. She threw a quick overhand slash with her left bar.

The creature brought up his left arm in time to save his head.

The steel bar smashed into the thing's forearm with enough force to crack a boulder. But there was no crunch of bone. The rod sank two inches into the arm and stuck.

The creature twisted away. In her shock, Deirdre lost her grip on the bar and it slid from her fingers. The monster lunged at her with another thrust.

Deirdre danced away but caught her heel and toppled backward onto the stairs. The creature raised the sword overhead; her bar was still stuck in his forearm.

Clay! she realized. The damned thing was made out of clay!

The greatsword flew downward. Deirdre rolled right and heard the weapon crash against the step beside her. When she looked up, the blade was again flashing toward her.

With both hands, she threw up her remaining bar. Steel met steel with a deafening clang. She kicked down, slamming her heel into the thing's knee. Any blood-and-bone joint would have snapped, but she felt the creature's flesh give.

The thing collapsed with a whistling shriek, but she could tell that the kick had not done lasting damage.

Somehow the creature had known she had no magic or blade. Being made of clay, the monster faced no danger from blunt weapons no matter how powerfully wielded. Only if she could find the author's true body could she kill the creature.

Wasting no time renewing her attack, Deirdre struggled to her feet and ran up the stairs.

"DEAD?" NICODEMUS SAID. "Magister, why would you be dead?"

"Follow me onto the Spindle Bridge," Shannon said wearily. They walked side by side. The clicking of their boot heels on the bridge echoed loudly.

Far below them stretched the alpine forest; ahead, the sheer mountain face. As they went, Shannon related everything he knew about Nora Finn's murder, his encounter with the inhuman murderer, Amadi's suspicions, the counter-prophecy, and Eric's and Adan's deaths.

"Sweet heaven!" Nicodemus exclaimed, stopping. "Little Eric Everson with the long brown hair, he's dead? Adan too?"

He hadn't known either boy well, but their deaths still came as a shock.

"Magister! During my nap, I dreamt of a monster attacking a neophyte in the glen." He described the pale monster and then the cavern filled with the strange turtles.

Shannon made no immediate reply. A gust of cold wind set Nicodemus's robes flapping and his hair fluttering. They were halfway across the bridge.

At last Shannon spoke: "This new nightmare—when you were both yourself and the figure on the table—also sounds to be a form of quaternary thought. What do you know about the levels of cognition?"

"Only that humans have tertiary cognition," Nicodemus answered. "And that constructs can have secondary or primary cognition, which are like tertiary but with restrictions on what they can think or want or remember."

"And quaternary?" Shannon asked.

Nicodemus hesitated. "Are thoughts that are unthinkable without certain texts cast about one's mind."

"Quite right, but do you know what that means?"

"Haven't the faintest," Nicodemus admitted with a laugh. "An unthinkable thought sounds like a silent noise or illuminating darkness."

Shannon smiled. "But you've already thought unthinkable thoughts. In your nightmares, you thought as both yourself and as other creatures. That phenomenon, what we call shared consciousness, is the simplest form of quaternary cognition. At its most basic level, quaternary cognition involves thinking with at least two minds—one inside your head, another made of magical text."

"So the murderer cast a spell on my sleeping mind that allowed me to think with that spell?"

"Yes, but perhaps it was not the murderer who cast it," Shannon replied slowly. "Given what the villain told me, it's likely he manipulated the dreams of Adan and Eric to lure them out of Starhaven's walls. But your nightmares seem to warn rather than lure. The vision of the glen must have been a vision of poor Eric's fate. The fiend wouldn't want you to know how and where he's attacking cacographers."

"But then where are the dreams coming from?"

"We've no way of knowing," Shannon said, scratching his beard. "But we might ask how the nightmares are related. You dreamed of the dragon attacking Trillinon and the murderer attacking Eric while both events were happening. Whoever or whatever is sending you these dreams wants you to know about these events. The dream-sender must want us to find a connection between them. Perhaps the murderer is connected to the dragon."

"And what of the turtles underground?"

"That one is the strangest of all. Perhaps future dreams will reveal more." Another gust of wind set the old man's white dreadlocks swaying.

"But why send these dreams to me?" Nicodemus asked, his voice growing strained. "And Eric and Adan, what do their deaths . . ."

Shannon placed a hand on his shoulder. "It is horrifying, I know, but we've no time to panic or grieve. We have to think logically."

The old man blew out a breath, his cheeks bulging. "We know the murderer seeks you so that you might replenish some artifact, an emerald. I'm unsure what he meant by 'replenish,' but I'm positive that he will attack the Drum Tower boys in an attempt to find you. We must protect you and the other cacographers. That's why we're here."

"Magister, the druid spoke of a demon-worshiper being nearby. Perhaps we should consult her."

"Not until we know more about her and the murderer." The wizard grimaced. "And we know almost nothing for fact."

Nicodemus blinked. "We know the murderer stole my ability to spell."

"That is the druid's explanation."

A strange heat stirred in Nicodemus's chest. "But you said the creature needs me to replenish some artifact. You said the monster claimed his master has been using a gem on me when I was sleeping. That must be why I'm a cacographer."

Nicodemus's hands began to tremble. That had to be it! He was being crippled by magic; therefore, he might yet be made whole by magic.

"Magister! If I could escape this creature, or maybe recover this gem, I would lose my cacography! Maybe I truly am the Halcyon."

"Nicodemus, I do not like to hear you talk like this."

"You think I'm the one of the counter-prophecy? The Storm Petrel?"

The wizard shook his head. "Given what has happened, you likely are connected to the prophecy in some way, but it is too early to say how you—"

"But in Magistra Finn's library, the monster said the emerald gave him power in Language Prime. Magister, what is Language Prime?"

A golden Numinous arc leaped between Azure and Shannon. The parrot raised her head to examine Nicodemus.

"My boy, listen carefully. Language Prime is a very dangerous, very blasphemous idea. You must never mention it in public hearing."

"But why?" Nicodemus asked. He had to make the old man see that he wasn't supposed to be crippled.

"Only grand wizards may know of it."

"But Magister, given the situation—"

The old man held up a hand. "You don't need to convince me. But promise to keep what I am about to tell you in the strictest secrecy."

Nicodemus swore on every demigod in the Celestial Canon.

With a solemn nod, the wizard began: "Perhaps you've learned that when time began, there was only lifeless dust. Into this barren world the Creator spoke the first words. These words were in Language Prime, the first magical language, the language from which all other languages come."

Another gust of cold wind set Shannon's silvery locks swaying again. "The first words created this living world and every creature upon it. Modern scholars believe that after that point Language Prime ceased to exist. But long ago, immediately after the Exodus, when the deities awoke on the new continent, they had no memory and little sense. Many claimed to know the Creator's own language. Some claimed to speak directly to the Creator. In their efforts to master Language Prime and rule all of humanity, the awoken deities began the Blood Crusades. The resulting chaos and war nearly destroyed humanity. That is why the pursuit of Language Prime is deemed blasphemy."

Shannon paused and took in a long breath. "That is why it is so easy for modern scholars to believe that Language Prime no longer exists. If they thought otherwise, it would spark religious wars that would destroy what peace the landfall kingdoms have known."

Nicodemus nodded eagerly. "But you think differently, Magister? You believe Language Prime exists?"

"I don't believe it exists; I know it does."

"But how?"

Shannon pinched the bridge of his nose. "Because the last sight I ever saw—the image that burned all mundane vision from my eyes—was of two sentences written in Language Prime."

DEIRDRE MADE IT halfway around the tower before something hit her from behind.

Pain exploded across her left shoulder and sent her sprawling onto the dusty floor. Next to her clattered the steel bar she had struck into the creature's forearm. The thing must have thrown it.

She rolled over and regained her feet just in time to meet the creature's overhead slash with her remaining bar. She countered with a quick thrust.

The creature, still wrapped in white, leaped back. His greatsword flicked out in a two-handed slash. Deirdre batted down the blade with the bar and stepped in to slam her elbow into the thing's face.

Something that felt like a nose flattened under her blow.

The thing cried out and fell. A dust cloud exploded from under his back as he hit the floor.

Deirdre dove for the thing's sword.

But the monster was still too quick; he squirmed back and away, holding the weapon above her short reach. With a hiss, the thing slashed with the sword across her side.

As the blade rasped against her rib bones, the world exploded into blackness. Deirdre leaped away onto her back. The creature tried to stand, but she kicked her boot toe into his neck. With a strangled cry, the thing toppled backward. Deirdre regained her feet and slammed the bar down on the creature's shin.

She fled.

NICODEMUS BLINKED. "YOU were blinded by Language Prime?"

The grand wizard rubbed his eyes wearily. "The story starts in Astrophell. I was a player in the game of factions then and a little arrogant. I fell in love with the magically illiterate grandniece of Astrophell's provost. When I got her with child, we married in secret."

Nicodemus nodded mutely.

The old man continued. "My enemies discovered my pregnant wife and used her to create scandal. It became a rallying point for the malcontent factions—mostly those that wanted the Order to exert more influence over the kingdoms. Hoping to hide the scandal, the provost announced his plan to send my wife and child away to different clandestine locations where neither I nor the malcontents could find them. I was terrified. I had to act before my wife gave birth, before the Provost could separate them. And so . . . I sought divine intervention."

"You found our god? You spoke to Hakeem?"

Shannon nodded.

"But no one . . . you . . ." Nicodemus stammered. "How?"

A slight smile stole across the wizard's lips. "It's something of a legend among those that seek to break into literary strongholds. My research into textual intelligence gave me an advantage. I wrote a quaternary cognition spell that allowed me to think as the stronghold."

"As the stronghold?"

The old man tapped his forehead. "Impossible, I know, but remember quaternary cognition allows one to think the unthinkable. I couldn't explain it to you better without casting the spell on you. But regardless, the important part was that armed with this text, I snuck into the stronghold and fought its defensive language. For half a mile, I cut and slashed and edited to reach our god's temple."

Shannon's smile grew. "Hakeem was reading at a desk when I reached him. He manifests himself as a thin, tawny-skinned man with silver hair and a long beard. It was the most mundane scene imaginable, and there I was stumbling into his temple, bristling with attack spells and soaked in my own blood. Without even looking up, Hakeem raises a hand and says, 'A moment, my son, I'm near the end of a chapter.'"

Nicodemus's eyes widened. "And then?"

"Then he finished the chapter, of course." Shannon laughed. "And I threw myself at his feet and begged for mercy. I told him I would do anything for my family—I'd undertake any task, perform any labor; I'd die for them . . . and Hakeem did indeed have a task for me."

The wizard's smile fell into a grim line. "A malicious godspell from one of Hakeem's enemies had penetrated his defenses and burrowed into his ark, the physical seat of his soul. All attempts to disspell this traplike curse had failed. So, because the trap could not be disarmed, it had to be sprung."

"Hakeem made you take on the curse?"

"Made me? I embraced it. It was written to destroy a god, not a man. There was a chance it would do nothing at all to me; there was a chance it would kill me outright. I didn't care. Without my wife or son, I couldn't live."

"And the curse was written in Language Prime? Is that how you know it exists?"

The old wizard grimaced. "The divine curse imbued knowledge into its victim's mind and then tried to use that knowledge to harm the victim. Hakeem told me plainly that if I survived, he would use his godspell to remove all my memories of the text."

Shannon narrowed his white eyes. "I remember walking into a small, dark room. I remember Hakeem's ark—a tall crystal obelisk covered with moving runes. Then the world became a blur; I was moving at a tremendous speed but not moving at all. Two sentences appeared. Each one twisted around the other, like two snakes mating. The runes exploded and pain lanced through my eyes. Then, nothing. No image, no vision, only . . . blindness."

Nicodemus held his breath.

Shannon sighed. "I woke in a caravan wagon headed for Besh-Lo. Hakeem had caused every Astrophell wizard to become terrified by the idea of harming my wife and son. He even compelled the merchants employed by the Order to give my wife a comfortable position in one of their trading houses. However, perhaps threatened by my infiltration of his temple, he did not extend such protection to me. He had allowed the provost to seize my research texts and exile me to Starhaven."

Nicodemus paused for what he hoped was a sympathetic moment before pushing on. "But the divine curse, Magister, it taught you Language Prime?"

"It did, and Hakeem erased all my memories of it, except for the image of the two sentences. Until now, I've never told a single soul, living or textual, about that memory. I was always too afraid of what Hakeem might have to do to remove it."

Nicodemus felt his heart begin to kick. "So it's true then: Language Prime is real. Then there might be some connection between me and it. The monster must be after me because of that. Magister, don't you see? I'm not supposed to be a cacographer."

Shannon held up a hand. "Nicodemus, you're jumping to conclusions. The creature said he needed you to replenish an emerald. He did not connect you to Language Prime. You must understand that no human could comprehend Language Prime."

"But how do you know that?"

"Because," Shannon said, "Language Prime has only four runes."

A GUST OF wind swept across the bridge. It sent Nicodemus's long black hair flying and blew Azure from Shannon's shoulder. The poor bird had to flap hard just to stay over the bridge.

"Four runes!" Nicodemus said while struggling to tame his hair. "The language from which all other languages come has only four runes?"

Shannon held his arm up as a perch for Azure. "Strange but simple geometric runes. Two were hexagons with a few radial strokes; the other two were pentagons attached to similar hexagons."

"But, Magister, that can't be right."

"It's difficult to believe," Shannon said as Azure landed on his arm. "The simplest common language possesses twenty-two runes. And the most complex, the shaman's high language, has over sixty thousand runes."

As the wind relented, Nicodemus tucked his hair into his robes. "But a language with only four runes could have only four single-rune words, sixteen two-rune words, sixty-four three-rune words, and so on."

"Exactly," Shannon said, helping Azure climb back onto his shoulder. "Primal words must be very long. Consider that a common language possesses a hundred thousand words, Numinous three times that. So, assuming Language Prime has a vocabulary of at least three hundred thousand, it would need words up to . . ." He paused to calculate. "Nine runes long to create all those words. But if it had twenty runes, it would need words only . . ." Another pause. "Only five runes long."

Nicodemus closed his eyes and tried to figure out what calculations his teacher had used to discern that.

Shannon let out a long sigh. "And with only four runes, those long words would be nearly indistinguishable. Think of trying to memorize a thousand nine-digit numbers consisting of the numerals one through four. Impossible. And the sentences would be hundreds, maybe thousands of runes long. Utter gibberish."

Nicodemus stopped calculating and laughed. "Imagine trying to spell in that language. Everyone would be a cacographer."

Shannon started to say something and then paused. He frowned. His mouth opened, closed, opened again. "Nicodemus . . . that is a profound idea."

"It is?"

A contrary breeze, this one blowing from Starhaven, flowed over the bridge. It brought with it the autumnal scents of moldy leaves and wood smoke.

Shannon was nodding. "What if cacography is simply a mismatch between a mind and a language? Our languages express meaning in a way your mind has trouble reproducing consistently. But you do not structure them illogically. When I edit your texts, they work without error."

Nicodemus nodded, his ears hot with embarrassment.

"But could we compose a language your mind could easily process? If so, then the reverse should be true: we should also be able to create a language so complex that not even the most powerful mind could spell it consistently."

"Oh," Nicodemus said, realizing what Shannon meant. "And maybe that's what the Creator did when making Language Prime. It could be a language so complex that any human attempting to read or write it would be cacographic."

"More than cacographic, completely incompetent."

Nicodemus's hands again began to tremble with excitement. "Magister, there might be a connection between Language Prime and my cacography. Maybe the druid is right. Maybe the monster stole part of me and put it into the emerald. Maybe I'm not supposed to be cacographic!"

Rather than reply, Shannon began to walk toward the Spindle's end. Before them loomed the mountain's rock face and the Chthonic engravings—ivy leaves to the left and the geometric design to the right.

The old man spoke. "My boy, we may be witnessing the first days of prophecy. This morning's dragon attack on Trillinon could mark the beginning of a conflict that will engulf all kingdoms and threaten human language itself. But what frightens me just now is the change I hear in your voice."

He stopped and turned to Nicodemus. "Do you believe that you are the Halcyon?"

"I—" Nicodemus stammered. "You think I'm being foolish to believe that the druid might be right about prophecy?"

The old wizard shook his head. "Not in the least. Besides the present circumstances linking you to prophecy, I have noted the strange effect you have had on some texts. Just last night when you misspelled a gargoyle, you elevated her freedom of thought. Such a phenomenon is unheard of. Perhaps this happened because you are the Halcyon, perhaps because of another reason tied to prophecy. But you didn't answer my question: Do you believe you are the Halcyon?"

"I haven't . . . I don't know if I am or not. I suppose you're right, we can't jump to conclusions. But my point is about cacography. If the murderer magically stole my ability to spell, perhaps I can magically get it back!"

Shannon folded his arms. "Which matters more, fulfilling your role in prophecy or removing your cacography?"

Nicodemus shook his head. "If a demon-worshiper stole my ability to spell, they must be connected. Magister, don't you see? Perhaps I am not a true cacographer."

"A true cacographer?" Shannon asked, eyebrows rising. "Nicodemus, even if we erased your disability completely, it wouldn't undo what has already happened to you. Regarding who you truly are, regarding what truly matters, ending your cacography wouldn't change anything."

Nicodemus could barely believe what he was hearing. "It would change everything!"

Shannon started walking again. "Perhaps this is not the time."

Nicodemus rushed after the old man. "Magister, would it upset you if I learned to spell?"

Shannon kept walking. "Why would you ask such a question?"

"You squash any hope I might have of completing myself."

"There is no such thing as completing yourself. You have always been complete, and you won't—"

For the first time he could remember, Nicodemus deliberately interrupted his teacher. "If I am already complete, if all I will ever be is your pet cripple, then I don't know why we're bothering to keep me alive!"

Both men stopped.

Suddenly Nicodemus realized that he had nearly shouted his last two words. He turned away.

The bridge's railing stood before him. He put both hands on it and tried to catch his breath.

Far below them, a falcon circled above the scattered pines and boulders. Some of the trees had died and withered into wooden skeletons.

"Pet cripple," Shannon said slowly. "I see."

"I know how you pick a retarded boy out of every generation," Nicodemus answered. "Devin knows too. Fiery heaven, the whole academy knows!"

A silence grew until the breeze picked up enough to make their robes luff.

Finally Shannon spoke in a low, rough tone. "Exile from Astrophell nearly crushed me. I lost everything—my wife, my son, my sight, my research. I could have let the loss rot me from the heart to the skin."

Nicodemus looked back toward his mentor.

Azure had laid her head down near Shannon's chin so the old man could scratch her neck.

"My research became futile," the wizard said solemnly. "I had discovered such wonderful things in Astrophell. But in this academic backwater, I couldn't accomplish a quarter of what I did before. In Astrophell, I had a cadre of brilliant apprentices working to advance my studies. Here I taught cacographic neophytes how to avoid hurting themselves. Politics became a constant reminder of my sins."

The old wizard sniffed in annoyance. "I wasted years longing for what I had lost. Until, one day, a cacographic boy came to me in tears to thank me for all I had done. In truth, I had done little more than what was required. But I saw how moved the child was, how badly he needed kindness. I saw in him a way to live again. His name was Allen, a Lornish boy. He's in Astrophell now. The Northerners don't have the slightest suspicion that he, now a hooded librarian, is a cacographer."

Shannon paused. "You think I made you my apprentice because I pity you? Because I keep a cacographer around to lord my ability over him? To feel as grand as I did when speaking before the Long Council? Well, if you think so, Nicodemus Weal, you're a fool."

The younger man was silent for a long moment. "But why then did you choose me for an apprentice?"

Shannon pointed to his milky-white eyes. "I chose you because in the past I have understood cacographers and they have understood me. I chose you because I thought I could help you the most. Besides, you are a useful apprentice. When you cast wordweave, I can complete spells in a quarter of the usual drafting time." The old man grunted. "Have we talked about this enough for you?"

When Nicodemus did not answer, the old man started off toward the mountainside. "Come then. The sentinels will catch up with us soon."

They walked most of the distance to the rock face without talking. Their footfalls echoed loudly, almost unnaturally so. Nicodemus had to take a deep breath before he could break the silence: "I'm sorry, Magister. It's just . . . with the possibility of ending my cacography—"

"I quite understand," Shannon said curtly as they stopped before the mountain's sheer rock face. "Now let us move on. Do you know why we're walking the Spindle Bridge?"

"Because Magistra Finn was murdered here?" Nicodemus stared at the carved outlines of giant ivy leaves.

"Exactly. I wondered if there was a reason she died on this bridge. I wanted to look at the mountainside with my blind eyes. I thought maybe I could see through the stone to some hidden spell, some clue." He sighed. "And my vision pierces the stone but sees nothing beyond."

He wrote a few Numinous sentences and thrust them into the mountainside. "And it seems that there's nothing but rock before us."

Nicodemus stepped back and looked at the hexagonal design on the bridge's other side. "Magister, you said the Language Prime runes were hexagonal. Do they resemble that Chthonic pattern at all?" He pointed.

Shannon shook his head. "I've examined that carving a thousand times since I first arrived at Starhaven. But I can find no resemblance."

Nicodemus glanced at his teacher. Was the old man still upset? "Magister, do you believe the stories about the Chthonics crossing this bridge to escape the Neosolar armies? Do you think they ran away to the Heaven Tree Valley?"

"No, the historians were correct: our ancestors slaughtered every last Chthonic." He turned back toward Starhaven. "There's nothing here. Let's go."

Nicodemus waited a moment before following the old wizard. "Then what are we going to do?"

"Research our enemy," Shannon said. "We know the murderer's made of flesh until we cut him; then he turns to clay. We need to find a mundane text about such creatures. Normally researching such an obscure topic would take the rest of the autumn. But you and I might modify the research we're to complete this afternoon with Magister Smallwood."

Nicodemus found himself looking back at the carvings. "I don't understand."

"We're researching a powerful artifact called the Index. It allows one to quickly search through many texts. Nothing as powerful as what they have in Astrophell, but still impressive. Your task will be to distract Smallwood and the sentinels at the project's end so that I might secretly peek into the Index."

"But why don't we simply tell them what we need to do?"

Shannon shook his head. "Neither Smallwood nor the sentinels would permit it. You will see. After that we must sleep. This day has been like a bad dream."

"Bad dream," Nicodemus echoed. He stopped and turned to look again at the Chthonic carvings.

The wizard also stopped. "What's the matter?"

Nicodemus opened his mouth, trying to articulate the images flashing through his mind.

"In my dream, the one when I napped," he finally managed to say, "I was in an underground place and there was a white-robed body that held a green gem." He looked at Shannon. "Magister, a green gem! And the murderer said he needed me to replenish an emerald!"

The old man frowned.

Nicodemus pointed to the mountain's ivy carvings. "In the dream, the floor was covered with ivy. And out of the darkness came strange turtles. There were hundreds of them, hissing and dying horribly as their shells cracked."

"I don't understand. Turtles?"

"Look, that hexagonal pattern," Nicodemus said, pointing to the other Chthonic carving, "is the pattern of a turtle shell."

DEIRDRE SPRINTED THROUGH the dark hallway. On her left were dark Chthonic doorways; to her right, the barred windows.

Already she could hear frantic footfalls. The thing was after her again.

She raced around the tower and up the stairs on the other side. Suddenly the ceiling burst into a thousand flapping creatures.

Bats! They had been nesting on the ceiling. The floor was soft with their droppings.

She ran on. The sword wound on her ribs was shallow and mending fast, but still it sent agony lancing down her side with every breath. Her robe was wet with blood.

Behind her the creature shrieked.

Redoubling her efforts, she flew around the tower and charged up the next flight of stairs—only to come to a sliding halt.

Before her stood an opening to a tower bridge. The bright midday sun beat down on the gray stones. "No." She couldn't leave the tower; outside of Starhaven's walls the creature could wield magic. "No!" Frantically she turned around.

Footsteps were echoing up from the stairwell.

She ran to one of the small black doors that lined the hallway's inner wall. It was a thick, metal portal. On top sat a squat barred window.

She pulled, but the door would not budge. She heaved . . . and with a metallic scream the thing swung a quarter way through its arc.

Suddenly Deirdre's head felt light. "Goddess, no!" she whispered, slipping into the dark chamber. "Not now!" Her hands began to tremble.

The room was rectangular; the black mass of an ancient stone bed crouched beside one wall. A chorus of terrified rats chattered in one corner. Deirdre yanked the door shut with another loud screech.

Her hands were shaking now. Her stomach felt distended. "No, no," she whimpered, staggering toward the stone bed. Her heart was pounding out a slow, irregular rhythm.

She was having an aura!

Her face and neck began to tingle as if a summer breeze were blowing across her skin. Her breath came in long, involuntary gulps. The world seemed to be filling with beauty. She wanted to cry out with joy. Her legs faltered and she fell onto the floor.

A low, crackling laugh sounded behind her.

With numb hands, she managed to push herself around.

All was blackness save for the door's small, barred window. Through the opening streamed intense white light. The creature was standing outside.

The door shrieked as the creature pulled upon it. A vertical sliver of light grew along the portal's side. The creature heaved once more. Again the hinges screamed, and the sliver of light grew brighter. He was laughing again. Soon he would work the door all the way open.

Deirdre tried to scream, tried to stand. But she was too far into her aura. Her hands shook violently as an ecstatic warmth spread down her back.

"No, we can negotiate," she heard herself groan. "We can negotiate!"

Through the window she saw the creature pause. His pale hands lifted his hood. She squinted, trying to make out his face.

But the world exploded into light and she fell unconscious—lost to the violence of her seizure.

CHAPTER

Nineteen

Nicodemus and Shannon stared at the Chthonic carvings.

They were now certain that Nicodemus's second nightmare was meant to connect the murderer to the Spindle Bridge; however, neither man could guess how the two were connected. The body wrapped in white, the emerald, the turtles, the ivy—it was all too disjointed.

Their boot heels echoing loudly on the bridge stones, they hurried back to the Chthonic carvings to reexamine the rock face. Shannon fashioned several Numinous texts to search the mountainside for a hidden spell or a magical door that opened into the mountain.

But once again he found nothing but solid rock.

By this time, the sentinels had hiked back up from ground level. All four of them began marching down the Spindle, their feet clacking out a distant tattoo. "Here they come," Shannon said. "We mustn't talk of your dreams or the murderer. They're from Amadi's train and will be looking for evidence of the counter-prophecy."

Nicodemus took a deep breath. If the sentinels interpreted one of his misspells as evidence that he was the Storm Petrel, they would leave him bound and censored in some prison. In a cell, the murderer would find him easily; he'd be as helpless as a caged bird.

"We will pretend to be interested only in research," Shannon whispered. "Follow my lead. We must learn more about the creature made of clay. So when I signal, you're to distract the sentinels and Smallwood long enough for me to use the Index."

"But, Magister, how can I distract five wizards. And what is this Index you—"

Shannon cut him off, calling out to the approaching sentinels. The old man launched into a show of anger and scholarly enthusiasm, scolding the sentinels for dawdling, threatening to complain to Amadi, and rambling about his research.

He hurried the party down to ground level and back into Starhaven's inhabited quarters, all the while griping about his primary research spell and the need to hurry so as not to keep Magister Smallwood waiting.

Sure enough, when the party returned to Shannon's study, Magister Smallwood was standing outside the door, a mass of scrolls in his arms. "Agwu, who are all these people?" Smallwood asked in surprise.

"Timothy, I brought some extra arms." Shannon unlocked his door. "Come, Magisters, we've much to carry." Shannon shooed the sentinels into his study and began piling books into their hands. One tried to protest but was overpowered by Shannon's threat to tell Amadi of their uncooperative attitude.

After a few moments, every sentinel bore a stack of books piled from elbows to eyeballs. Shannon loaded an avalanche of scrolls into Nicodemus's arms. To keep the manuscripts from toppling over, Nicodemus had to clamp his chin down upon the pile.

Meanwhile, Smallwood was gathering a stack of books into his own arms and advising the sentinels on the best way to hold their stacks.

"Well then, we are ready," Shannon announced when he held his own pile of scrolls. "Nicodemus, would you use your young eyes to open the door?"

"Of course, Magister." Nicodemus wrote a simple Magnus sentence along his right forearm and used his index finger—his only free digit—to flick the spell around the door latch. With some shuffling, he worked the latch and pulled. "It's open, Magisters. Where are we going?"

"To the Main Library," Smallwood replied from behind his stack of scrolls. "Shannon, I thought you had told your apprentice about our research spell."

Led by Nicodemus, the two grand wizards stepped out into the hallway. The sentinels followed close behind.

Shannon clicked his tongue in annoyance. "Timothy, it has been an unusual day. I haven't had time."

"There's no need to be defensive, Agwu," Smallwood said. "I was merely asking a question."

The party reached the staircase and began negotiating the narrow steps.

"Well, Nicodemus and visitors from the North, let me explain," Smallwood said with his usual professorial enthusiasm. "Years ago, Magister Shannon and I conceived of a research spell to visualize the texts surrounding the Index, but we didn't receive permission to proceed until the other day, when—"

"Timothy," Shannon interrupted, "Nicodemus doesn't know what that artifact is, and you must remember to speak of it only in secure environments."

"Quite right," Smallwood said. "Forgive my forgetfulness. Nicodemus, would you cast a murmur spell so we may speak freely?"

Traditionally, apprentices cast any commonplace spells their wizards required. Shannon usually excused Nicodemus from this duty. Smallwood, in his typical fashion, had forgotten this fact.

With a deep breath, Nicodemus began forging the needed runes within his right forearm. Though written in a simple common language, the murmur spell called for complex sentence structures and an elaborate conclusion.

When finished, Nicodemus disliked his rendition, but there was nothing to do but cast it with another flick of his index finger.

Rather than expanding into a sound-deadening cloud, the glowing white misspell fell to the ground and shattered. The sentence fragments danced upon the floor stones like water beads on a hot skillet. Nicodemus's cheeks flushed with shame. "My apologies, but I—"

"I believe an issue this sensitive requires a Magnus language text, perhaps a subrosa spell," Shannon said. A grateful Nicodemus glanced back at the old man.

The party continued downward as Shannon wrote. The sentinels murmured among themselves. Then came the wet sound of Shannon spitting out the subrosa spell. Instantly a soundproof sphere of interlocking petals encased the group.

Smallwood cleared his throat. "So, Nicodemus, Magisters, as I was saying, we have many a codex in Starhaven but only one Index. To the naked eye, the Index seems a mundane book of usual size. But the spells coursing within its covers are extraordinary; they connect the Index to every scroll, book, and tome within Starhaven's walls."

Smallwood paused to shift the scrolls in his arms. "To search the Index for mundane text, all one need do is think of a subject and open the book. Simply pick up the codex intending to read about synaesthesia or magical advantage or whatever, and the artifact's spells will reproduce all available information on the subject."

Just then the party entered the Women's Atrium, whose ceiling held mosaic depictions of famous female wizards. Nicodemus regarded the doglike guardian spells that flanked the Main Library's vaulted entrance.

The constructs' Numinous bodies stood eight feet tall and possessed long canine fangs, muscular shoulders, and burning eyes. Thick, curly fur covered the creatures' fearsome heads but not their sleek bodies. Under her gateward paw, each spell controlled a large Magnus ball.

As the party approached, the two constructs pulled back their lips, but Shannon calmly began casting them the necessary passwords.

Smallwood continued his lecture unfazed. "Conversely, to conduct a search for magical text with the Index, you simply lay a hand on any of the illuminated pages, and your mind is brought into contact with the book's spells. Just thinking of what you are looking for will cause the book to list all known spells that fit your criteria. Once you select a spell—and here is the truly fantastic aspect—the book infuses knowledge of that text into your mind. So you see why the Index is so valuable: through it, a search that might have taken weeks is completed in moments."

Appeased by the passwords, each guardian stretched her paws forward into a dog bow, signaling that the wizards could pass.

As they walked in, Nicodemus looked up into the splendor of the Main Library; he had seen it only a few times before. Beside him, a sentinel murmured amazement.

Floor upon floor of ornate wood paneling and leather-bound books stretched up far as the eye could see. On every level, arching windows allowed long shafts of sunlight to fall through the warm and dusty air. Almost impossibly far above them, a few wooden bridges spanned the library's cavernous space.

On the ground floor, a two-story stone structure in the room's center acted as a headquarters to the librarians who tended the books at all hours. A maze of waist-high reference shelves radiated out from this building and surrounded ordered ranks of long study tables. The hundred or so studying wizards filled the air with the sounds of turning pages and hushed conversations.

Smallwood lectured on. "Now, about the Index, there is tremendous demand for the thing. The Council on Artifact Use must approve every query to make sure the book is never endangered. It is a difficult job, especially considering that, even though we know how to use the Index, we don't know what makes it work. Its operative spells are written in an unknown language." The wizard laughed. "There is also the matter of private libraries. Because the Index can search any codex within Starhaven's walls, many grand wizards who illegally keep private libraries worry that their secrets might be discovered by rivals using the Index."

The party continued with Shannon and Smallwood in the lead, Nicodemus in the middle, and the four sentinels trailing behind.

They reached the library's rear wall and ventured into one of the many alcoves. Nicodemus had never noticed this particular inlet before. It stretched on for at least a hundred yards and seemed like a long, book-lined cave.

"You see, Nicodemus," Smallwood said as they walked, "our research spell seeks to learn how the text around the Index works, for clearly the artifact possesses some form of textual intelligence. It might tell us much about quaternary cognition—how certain spells allow us to think with text. Some speculate the Index might be a Chthonic creation."

Just then the party came to the cavern's end and beheld a guardian spell sleeping in front of a wide metal door. The golden construct's massive head rested upon her spherical Magnus passage. Slowly a single canine eyelid rose to reveal a burning eye. Suddenly the construct was on all fours, growling fiercely. Shannon tossed a thick stack of passwords at it.

The guardian snapped the text out of the air as if it were a ham steak. After a long distrustful stare, it bowed. Behind the spell, the door swung open to reveal a windowless room with stone walls. At the chamber's center, a marble podium held the Index.

Polished brown leather covered the book's face. Two brass bands wrapped around its spine, securing themselves to the board with three steel studs apiece. A single brass fore-edge clasp held the book shut, and triangular steel tabs protected its corners. As Nicodemus drew closer, he saw innumerable sunbursts etched into the brass. There was no ornate boss upon the face or jewels encrusted in the metalwork, but still it was one of the handsomest books he had ever seen.

After putting down his stack of manuscripts, Smallwood began to undo the buttons that ran down his sleeves, all the while instructing the sentinels to unload their books onto the empty shelves that lined the walls.

Shannon had already unbuttoned his sleeves to reveal arms that constant spellwriting had kept muscular in spite of his age. "Our research spell is named traseus," he explained to Nicodemus. "It's a Numinous and Magnus hybrid designed to visualize the movement of the artifact's language as it searches for a mundane text. The only problem is that traseus is an expansive spell; that is why we need your assistance."

Nicodemus cringed as he slipped his arms out of his apprentice sleeves. If Shannon and Smallwood required more runes than the two could produce on their own, it was going to be an onerous task indeed. He looked back at the sentinels, who presently were suffering one of Smallwood's lectures. "Might we ask them to help?" Nicodemus asked Shannon softly.

"As fully invested wizards they would be offended. Besides I'd rather have them lounging about. If they become bored they're more likely to be distracted." He cleared his throat meaningfully.

Nicodemus nodded. "And how much of the spell has been written?" Most often grand wizards wrote long research spells over several days, storing subspells in scrolls or books. Then, at casting, they would peel off the subspells and splice them together.

"None," Shannon admitted. "We've only drawn up outlines."

"And how many runes will we require?"

"Several hundred thousand in each language," Shannon said with a sigh. "I'm sorry, my boy, but this might tire you." He stepped closer, a green sentence conspicuously draped across his forearm.

Nicodemus took the common language spell and translated it: "*Don't forget; your to distract Smlwd and wtch-hntrs.*"

Nicodemus whispered, "Yes, Magister. Do you have any ideas how to sidetrack them?"

The old man shook his head slightly. "Do you?"

Nicodemus's heart beat faster. "Not yet."

CHAPTER
Twenty

The traseus spell proved to be epic indeed. But Nicodemus could not help parse or analyze the text. The only thing he could contribute was strength. And to harness his strength, Shannon had composed the wordweave spell: a text he hoped would endear Nicodemus to other wizards.

To cast wordweave, Nicodemus arranged both the Numinous and Magnus alphabets into a grid of common language sentences. The linguists then used the grid to pull Nicodemus's runes into their bodies.

As soon as a wizard withdrew a rune, Nicodemus forged a replacement and maneuvered it into position. Instantly a rune in the opposite alphabet disappeared—Shannon was writing in Magnus, Smallwood in Numinous—and Nicodemus would replace it, and then a rune in the other alphabet would disappear and so on for hours.

The first to tire of this were the sentinels. They paced or inspected the Index or the bookshelves. Two stepped outside to examine the guardian spell standing watch before the door.

During this time, Nicodemus forged in his arms and slipped the runes down to his fingers. But after two hours of dropping runes into place, his wrists began to ache. When he asked if they might break, Smallwood explained that traseus would be volatile until it was nearly complete; interrupting its composition early would make the spell deconstruct. They worked in silence for another hour.

Though he never found time to look away from wordweave, Nicodemus could hear the sentinels pacing. At one point, Shannon cajoled one of them into writing shields around the bookshelves—this to prevent a chain deconstruction if something went wrong with traseus. Toward dinner, a new set of Northern wizards replaced those on duty.

To vary his routine, Nicodemus began forging within his forearm. He rolled the characters down the back of his hand to a cocked index finger and then flicked the runes into the grid. This saw him through another hour. But then, in a moment of inspiration, he began forging within his tongue and spitting the runes into place. Unfortunately, Magister Smallwood found this distracting, so Nicodemus had to return to forging within his arms.

One napping sentinel began to snore.

Occasionally Smallwood or Shannon stood and placed a completed subspell near the Index. But because Nicodemus's task was so demanding, he did not look up until the traseus spell was nearly complete; by then he was lightheaded and famished.

But the sight of the resplendent text filled him with so much wonder that it eased his discomfort.

Thousands of silver and gold sentences had been spun into a seven-foot-tall sphere. Rubbing his sore arm muscles, Nicodemus walked closer to admire its stunning detail: all across the spell's globelike surface, Numinous and Magnus passages formed miniature streams that flowed like ocean currents.

The spell was stable but not yet seamless; in two places the text parted down a vertical slit. Shannon pulled back one of these as if it were a tent flap. Smallwood climbed into the spell and began editing the slits together.

Meanwhile Shannon shooed the sentinels out into the hallway. "Magisters, you are welcome to watch from a distance," the old man said, "but we must have room to work."

Nicodemus admired the traseus spell for a few moments and then the Index. Retreating to a stool, he discovered that his exhaustion and hunger had produced a headache. "Magisters," he said, kneading his temples, "may I ask a question?"

"Of course," Shannon said, now studying a luminescent passage he was forming in his deltoid and bicep.

"What are we going to search the Index for when the traseus spell is active?"

"Something of known location," Shannon explained, sending the finished passage into his balled fist. "Specifically, Bolide's 'Treatise on Staffs, Wands, and Magical Advantage.' All copies of which are resting on that scroll rack."

Nicodemus saw the wisdom in this. "Might we search for something else when it's finished?"

"Such as?" Smallwood asked. He was scrutinizing several Numinous passages he had fused and hung above the spell's surface like a tiny cloud.

Nicodemus paused. "Such as possible remedies for cacography, researched at institutions other than Starhaven."

"An excellent idea," Smallwood said, plucking a sentence from a textual cloud. "But you must put it before the Council of Artifact Use. And they're always busy."

"But might I conduct a quick search once we're done?" Nicodemus replied.

Smallwood changed two runes and looked up. "I'm sorry, what was that?" When Nicodemus repeated his question, Smallwood smiled and shook his head. "Oh dear, no. Rules are rules. And the council might not want a . . ." He paused to consider another sentence. "They might not want a cacographer using the Index."

Nicodemus looked at the floor.

"I will apply for such a search," Shannon said, "if you will search all Starhaven texts on the matter, and of course"—he coughed meaningfully—"after all pressing matters have been resolved."

Nicodemus looked up. Shannon was scrutinizing a passage with his all-white eyes. "Thank you, Magister, I can promise you that I already have scoured the Starhaven libraries a hundred times."

"Then I will apply."

These words made Nicodemus feel giddy and lightheaded.

"Well, Agwu," Smallwood said, while massaging his right hand with his left, "all the Numinous domains are aligned."

Shannon smiled. "That means I'm holding the only two unconnected lines. My friends, let us pray to Hakeem." The three men bowed their heads to the patron god of wizards. Outside the chamber, the sentinels looked on.

"Timothy, begin the search on the Index now," Shannon said. He bound two sentences and dropped them into the globe.

Smallwood unfastened the Index's fore-edge clasp. With a nod to Shannon, he opened the book, paused, then closed it, paused again, opened it again. He repeated this procedure over and over.

Each time he did this, the Index magically retrieved the information Smallwood sought. "Watch carefully," Shannon said, sitting down next to Nicodemus. "The traseus spell should visualize the Index's language."

For a few moments traseus swirled sluggishly. But then the textual currents gained a windlike fluidity and blew around the textual globe in thousands of different currents. Faster and faster the spell spun until Nicodemus could no longer make out individual sentences. When Smallwood next opened the book, faint purple light flashed around the Index. The grand wizard yipped in joy as the traseus spell gained velocity.

But then something caught.

Several sentences became rigid. Lines snagged and split. Currents spun out of control and formed a linguistic hurricane in the spell's lower hemisphere. The textual storm raged with percussive force, sounding miniature thunder cracks as it broke through stiff sentences. The purple glimmers around the Index disappeared.

"The text is deconstructing!" Shannon called to the sentinels. "Shut the vault!"

They needed little convincing; in the next instant the chamber door began to swing closed.

Shannon withdrew a scroll from his belt-purse and peeled a Numinous spell off its parchment. "Whatever happens, stay within this text," the wizard instructed Nicodemus, casting a golden, spherical shield around him. As an afterthought, Shannon placed Azure on his apprentice's shoulder.

A metallic clang reverberated through the room as the vault's door shut. All was silent for a moment and then several traseus lines broke with a deafening crack. A feathery Numinous geyser spewed from the sphere's upper pole, making the spell wrinkle like a winter apple.

With a backhand stroke, Shannon cast a Magnus lash against the spell and cut open a man-sized rift. "Timothy!" he called. "Get out now."

Smallwood didn't need to be told twice; he scooped up the Index and dashed out of the spell.

Together the linguists hurried back and edited themselves into the protective Numinous spell that surrounded Nicodemus.

Outside the shield, traseus collapsed and began to deconstruct violently. Decaying sentences flew about, striking the translucent shielding spell with jarring force. The three men silently watched the resplendent chaos. All were exhausted.

Unfortunately, their protective spell was no larger than a broom closet and they found themselves standing uncomfortably close.

"Nicodemus," Shannon asked, buttoning up his sleeves, "what did you see when the spell was functioning?"

"Purple flashes around the Index."

Shannon nodded. "As did I. What did you see, Timothy?"

"Nothing," said the pale-faced wizard as he crouched on a stool, which was contained within the protective spell's limited space. Both Nicodemus and Shannon stared at the Index lying in the man's lap.

The air was cold, and so Nicodemus drew his arms back into his sleeves.

With a little shuffling, Shannon managed to turn back toward the vault. Ostensibly he was watching the deconstruction, but by patting Nicodemus's shoulder, he furtively cast a common language sentence into the younger man's chest.

Translating the line, Nicodemus read: "*Mst get Index frm Smllwd while valt is closed. Ideas?*"

Nicodemus had been staring out at the deconstruction with unfocused eyes. The message gave him a wild idea.

He handed Shannon a reply: "*Y have an other shield? Like this won?*"

Shannon nodded.

"*Get it redy.*"

Shannon pretended to cough. "When?" he grunted between hacks.

Nicodemus made a show of thumping Shannon's back then grabbed the grand wizard's robes and yanked down hard. Just before the old man fell sideways, Nicodemus cast an answer into his chest: "*Now!*"

CHAPTER

Twenty-one

With a cry, Shannon fell to his left and knocked Nicodemus toward Smallwood's stool. To avoid landing on the sitting wizard, Nicodemus threw his left hand against the Numinous shield. Nevertheless, his hip crashed into Smallwood's face and sent the wizard sprawling back onto the textual shield. As Nicodemus had hoped, the Index fell to the floor.

Everyone was shouting. The spherical shield seemed about to tip and send them tumbling over each other like bugs in a rolling glass bubble.

But Shannon leaned back against the shield's opposite wall, balancing it. Then, faster than Nicodemus thought the old man could move, he bent down and retrieved the Index from the floor.

Nicodemus exhaled with relief. Now came the tricky part: getting Shannon some time alone with the Index so that he could research their enemy.

Since his first day in Starhaven, Nicodemus had worked on preventing his touch from misspelling magical text. He had focused on rune order, memorized complex sentence structures, learned to block out every thought but those of preserving the spell at hand.

Now, heart racing, he did the opposite.

"Magisters!" Nicodemus cried while nodding toward his hand. His fingers were jammed into the shield's golden sentences. "It's misspelling!"

A dark line grew up from Nicodemus's hand as he willed his cacography to misspell the previously smooth sentences into crinkled zig-zags.

Strangely, the complex Numinous sentences misspelled exactly the way he wanted them to. Most of the time, Nicodemus's touch had made magical text dangerously uncontrollable. The opposite now seemed to be true. But he didn't have time to dwell on this phenomenon; he had to get Shannon away from Smallwood.

"I can't let go!" he lied. "I'm stuck!" A second dark line spread down from his hand. Together, the strata of corruption pulled a deep furrow into the spherical shield. "Magister, use the other shield!" Nicodemus hissed to Shannon. "Form another sphere."

Just then a deconstructing Magnus line punched through the furrow.

The silvery fragment struck Nicodemus in the face, cutting him from cheekbone to jaw.

"Nicodemus!" Shannon called as a spray of blood filled the air.

Nicodemus clapped his free hand against the wound. The contracting ring of misspells now encircled the shield and was pinching the text down on top of him. "Magister Smallwood," he called. "Help!"

The shielding spell was now nearly two spheres joined by a furrow. It looked something like two fused soap bubbles.

Smallwood had been tottering to his feet. Now Nicodemus's cries turned his eyes up to where the apprentice's hand was contextualized into the shield. With a squawk, the pale wizard jumped up and began parsing the corrupted Numinous sentences enmeshing Nicodemus's hand.

When Shannon moved to help, Nicodemus shook his head. "Magister, go! Use the other spell."

Reluctantly, Shannon withdrew a small scroll from his belt-purse. With practiced motions, he peeled the Numinous text from the parchment and edited it into the shield's wall closest to him. The increased textual area in Shannon's sphere reduced the restraining tension on the misspelling furrow; it closed into a tight knot, effectively separating the shield's two spheres.

Nicodemus released the text and withdrew the cacographic force he had been exerting on the shield. Smallwood frantically set to cutting out the corrupted sentences.

Shannon, now standing in a separate protective spell, nodded to Nicodemus and rolled his shield toward the chamber's other side. Just before the wizard disappeared into the storm of deconstruction, Nicodemus saw him cradle the Index in his right arm and open its cover.

"Nicodemus, how could you have been so careless?" Smallwood squawked, finishing the seal on their protecting spell.

The shield had shrunk. Nicodemus had to crouch, his head tilting to one side as he pressed a hand to his cheek to stop the bleeding.

"Shannon trusts you cacographers too much," Smallwood said in the harshest tone Nicodemus had ever heard him use. "You could have killed us. Could have killed us and deconstructed the Index!"

Nicodemus mumbled an apology.

"Well . . . show me that cut," Smallwood said, his tone softening. "I'll do what I can until Shannon can stitch you up with Magnus."

Nicodemus dropped his hand and looked away. Spikes of pain lanced into his head as Smallwood scrubbed the wound with his sleeve; nevertheless, Nicodemus couldn't suppress a small, self-satisfied smile.

"THAT STUNT WITH the shield was exceedingly foolish and . . ." Shannon muttered to Nicodemus.

Four sentinels were accompanying them back to the Drum Tower, and one of the Northern spellwrights was now frowning at the old man.

Shannon waited for the Northerner to look away before finishing his sentence. "Exceedingly foolish, Nicodemus, and exceedingly brave."

Nicodemus started to smile but agony lanced across his wounded cheek. Despite being placed with care, Shannon's Magnus stitches were extraordinarily painful. "What did you learn?" he asked.

Sitting on Shannon's shoulder, Azure raised her head to inspect the nearby sentinels. The party was now marching along a wide Spirish arcade in Starhaven's northern quarter. Presently none of the sentinels was close enough to overhear.

"Nothing about a gem or emerald and Language Prime. And nothing about the Chthonics, ivy, or turtle shells." Shannon paused. "I am sorry, Nicodemus; I just realized I forgot to search for remedies for cacography."

A sinking sensation filled Nicodemus. "That's not important right now. What of our enemy?"

A smile formed beneath the wizard's short beard. "I discovered what manner of creature we face."

Nicodemus turned to the grand wizard. "Magister!" he whispered before remembering himself and returning his gaze to the ground. "What is our enemy?" he asked more quietly.

"We face a golem," the wizard whispered. "They are spells of the ancient world. According to the literature, no one has encountered or created one on this side of the ocean."

"Los in hell," Nicodemus quietly swore. "So we face an author with knowledge of the ancient texts. Perhaps a demon-worshiper after all. What else, Magister? What kind of construct is a golem?"

Again Azure examined the sentinels; they were still too far to overhear. "To create a golem text," Shannon whispered, "an ancient spellwright had to convert his mind into complex text called a 'spirit,' which contained all of an author's magical and mental abilities. This spirit was then invested into a golem body made of earth—most were clay, but there was mention of metal or rock. While animate, a golem is not a construct but a living creature. A golem's durability depended on its substance: an iron golem would outlive a brass golem, a brass golem would outlive a mud golem, and so on. But the sturdier the golem, the more text and time it required to form."

Nicodemus held his tongue as a turn in the arcade brought a sentinel within earshot. Only when the man had moved away did he reply: "And that's why cutting off the murderer's arm didn't slow him down?"

Shannon nodded. "The author's spirit simply disengaged from the wounded body and then formed a new one. But from what I understand, any golem entering Starhaven would suffer from the stronghold's Chthonic metaspells. A clay golem shouldn't last five hours in this place. And one couldn't spellwrite within our walls."

Nicodemus eyed the nearest sentinel. "So the malicious author is not in the stronghold. He could be anywhere."

"Anywhere close by," Shannon corrected.

Fear began to cool Nicodemus's excitement. "We must find the author himself. We could slay the man or creature or whatever it is while its spirit is still in the golem."

Shannon shook his head. "If we knew where the author's body was hidden, we could do just that. But we've no way of finding the fiend."

"But then how can we fight it?"

Shannon started to reply but then stopped as the sentinels stepped in close. Ahead of the party stood the entrance to one of the long halls that separated the Spirish Quarter from the Imperial Quarter. The Drum Tower wasn't far off now.

Once inside the hall, the sentinels spread out, giving Nicodemus and Shannon enough room to whisper.

Shannon explained in a murmur: "If a golem deconstructs before its author's spirit can disengage, then the author dies along with the body. Different golems have different vulnerabilities. Clay golems, being malleable, are impervious to all but the most severe crushing and piercing attacks. However, as I discovered, they can be easily cut."

"But a golem made of granite?"

"Would be slower, stronger, and endangered by blunt attacks of sufficient force." The wizard took Azure onto his hand. "Nicodemus," he said loudly, "would you hold my familiar for a moment? I need to readjust my hood."

Nicodemus held out his hand and was not surprised when the parrot pressed a short Numinous sentence into his palm. "Take a good look at that sequence," Shannon murmured while pretending to fuss over his hood. "Do you think you could recognize it?"

Nicodemus shifted Azure to his other hand and squinted down at the line. If translated it would read, "*nsohnannanhosn*." Nicodemus cleared his throat. "It's your name written backward and then interdigitated with your name written forward?"

The old man chuckled. "You can't spell out the ingredients for ham and eggs, but you can glean that?"

Nicodemus shrugged. "Order never mattered to me."

"You may hand Azure back now," Shannon announced for the sentinels' benefit.

When Nicodemus obliged, the wizard whispered. "That will be my cipher for any broadcast I send. If anything should happen we can find each other using . . . what's the matter?"

"I'm sorry, Magister, I know most apprentices can cast broadly, but I've never—"

"It's a ball of short messages that's cast into an ever-expanding sphere. Spellwrights use them to find each other when lost. They're forbidden in Starhaven because of the confusion they'd cause. However, in an emergency, I'll begin casting many of them so you can find me. Some will have the correct cipher, some a decoy cipher. Each one is an expanding sphere. You are to follow only the correct cipher to its source."

The party climbed a short, wide stairway.

"One more thing," the wizard said: "that furrow in my Numinous shield back by the Index, how did you make it?"

Nicodemus explained how he had deliberately used his cacography to misspell the shield's smooth sentences into crinkled conformations. He didn't mention the strange sensation of increased control he had felt when corrupting the text; that still confused and troubled him. So instead, he focused on how his misspelled sentences had pulled the furrow down into the shield and so distracted Smallwood.

Shannon raised his eyebrows. "You did that by misspelling?"

"No, Magister," Nicodemus said, grinning despite the pain. "When I did that, I couldn't have spelled more correctly."

Shannon chuckled. "Well done, my boy."

The party filed out through a door and into the Stone Court. Nicodemus was shocked to see that the Drum Tower's main door and the ground floor windows were covered by blazing Numinous bars.

The old man explained: "The spells blocking the doors and windows are wards. They can be lifted by applying a key, much like a door's passwords. I've convinced Amadi to give me a key. I'd like you to have a copy in case you need to leave the tower. If possible, I will send Azure with a key to your window tonight. Otherwise I'll give you the key tomorrow."

Nicodemus nodded. "The wards are to protect us cacographers from the murderer?"

"I wanted more, but the provost doesn't want the convocation's attendees to know about the murderer. I don't know if the wards will stop an author capable of composing a golem. But there will be two sentinels guarding the tower. There will also be two of them watching my quarters. So at least we will be safe tonight."

Nicodemus glanced at the old man. "But we haven't talked about everything in my last nightmare. There's the cave I saw with the body and the strange turtles and the hexagonal pattern at the end of the Spindle Bridge. Perhaps our enemy has something to do with the Spindle. Some door in the mountainside or something about moving the mountain . . ."

Shannon motioned for Nicodemus to quiet down. "I've thought of that too. But there's nothing we can do tonight. Now we need to rest while it's still possible."

The old man paused. "Tonight I want you to pay special attention to your dreams."

CHAPTER
Twenty-two

As before, Deirdre regained consciousness and found herself on the ground, crying as Kyran kneeled over her. But this time he had no caresses or soft words. This time his eyes were wide with fear. "Los in hell, Deirdre! Why did you send me away? Are you hurt?"

"No," she gasped between sobs. "No, I'm . . . I'm fine."

Magical willowisps floated about the room, shedding a soft blue-green light. She was still in the Chthonic cell where the creature had caught her. "The vision!" she whispered. "The vision returned."

Kyran wrapped his arms around her and murmured that if she was not hurt everything would be all right.

"In the visions," she said tremulously, "I was on the riverbank again, in the Highlands, and the white wolf came. It had a man's head with burning red eyes. He . . ." She gulped down air. "He stabbed me somehow . . . and I came apart and floated down the river."

"It was only a vision," Kyran murmured. "What happened here?"

Haltingly, she told him how the creature had chased her into the cell and how she had fallen into a seizure just as the creature forced the cell's door open. "But, Ky, why am I still alive? How have you found me?"

"I followed the sentinels to the ground level then back up to the Spindle Bridge, where they met Shannon. They reported his trick to no one. Shannon, the boy, and the sentinels went into a library too well guarded for me to follow." He glowered. "Deirdre, you should never have sent me away! I could have—"

"Ky, you're not listening!" She pushed his hands away. "Why am I still alive? Why didn't the beast kill me?"

"Our goddess must have manifested herself directly in you, so you could slay the beast."

Deirdre sat up. "What are you saying? That Boann is controlling me during my seizures? Why would she do . . ."

Her voice died as her eyes fell on the body lying along one wall. It was covered with a ripped white cloak.

"Perhaps," Kyran whispered, "we won't need to find its true body? Perhaps you slew the construct before the author's spirit could disengage?"

From her current angle, Deirdre could see nothing of the creature's head save the clay neck, which a single sword stroke had cleaved in two.

STANDING ON A tower bridge in the Imperial Quarter, the creature looked down at the Stone Court and the wizards standing guard before the Drum Tower.

"Sentinels for guards, Shannon?" he asked the air. "And wards on the doors and windows?" That would stop him from luring the boys out of the academy with dreams.

Now bolder action was needed.

Perhaps a direct attack? In the Stone Court he could spellwrite. That would let him kill the guards, disspell the wards, and move into the Drum Tower with a blade. But the sentinels might raise an alarm, or a guarding construct might attack when he was inside.

It was too risky.

He thought again about rewriting more of Starhaven's constructs. He had already rewritten a gargoyle on the Erasmine Spire to spy on the wizard's colaboris spells. And he had drafted a ratlike gargoyle with a large ear on its back. Perhaps he could corrupt a war-weight construct?

No, that would take too long.

The creature thought again about Shannon and pulled the back of his hand across his lips. The old human had gone to the sentinels, gaining protection but sacrificing freedom; the sentinels would now watch everything Shannon did.

This was not the intriguing counterstroke the creature had hoped for.

He thought about attacking the Drum Tower with his true body; that would be less dangerous than using a golem. Still, it was too risky. He should be able to devise a safer plan, especially now that he had encountered that girl in the druid robes.

Somewhere among the towers, a raven began to cry. The creature remembered that he still had to run down to Gray's Crossing. "Wretched village," he grumbled.

Leaning on the bridge's railing, he narrowed his eyes and began to think. It was time to remove Shannon from play.

DEIRDRE TURNED OVER the clay head with her boot. Its face had been squashed flat against the floor. No distinguishing feature remained. Long fragments of what looked to have been hair lay scattered around on the dusty ground.

Next to her, leaning on his wooden staff, Kyran grunted. "Perhaps you killed the author along with the body?"

She shook her head. "We must assume the fiend lives. We should take the Peregrine to our goddess's ark as soon as possible. The creature is aware of my presence now and may become more desperate."

"We can't reach the boy now with the sentinels guarding him. But they will keep him safe for the night. We should sleep."

Deirdre looked at her protector. "Do you really think he is safe?"

He regarded her for a moment, his brown eyes nearly black in the green light of his spells. "We must sleep."

WHEN THE IDEA came, the creature laughed out loud.

A cold wind was blowing over the tower bridge. Far below, in the Stone Court, several torches fluttered and winked. The two guarding sentinels pulled their black cloaks more tightly about their frail bodies.

The creature laughed again; the plan was brilliant. By enlisting the sentinels, Shannon had forged the tool that would be his undoing.

During the creature's first encounter with Shannon, he had fled with Nora Finn's research journal, hoping to find the boy's name inside. The woman had been prudent enough to avoid that. But the creature still had the journal, and now was the time to use it.

His new plan to trap Shannon would be a challenge; he could not spellwrite within the libraries. However, he could cast texts into the libraries from outside. Entering the old fool's rooms would be more difficult. He would have to sacrifice his present golem to place the book. Worse was the issue of time: the creature had to run down to the miserable village and back.

Still, it would be possible if he cast the curses immediately.

The creature turned and started for the nearest tower. He did not need to remove Shannon; the sentinels would do that for him.

CHAPTER

Twenty-three

When Nicodemus opened his common room door, the tapers were snuffed and the fire smoldering. Since leaving Shannon, his excitement and fear had faded. Now his empty stomach groaned, his wounded cheek throbbed, and his exhausted eyes stung.

"Fiery heaven," he grumbled, picking his way across the darkened common room. What if he were not excused from apprentice duty in the morning? Would he have to avoid a golem while mopping—

His left shin slammed into something hard. Whatever it was clattered on the floor. "Blood of Los!" he swore. By feeling around with his hands, he discovered a chair's square legs. The squeaking of a bed frame came from Simple John's room.

Nicodemus righted the chair. "Bind those idiots for not cleaning up," he growled. "When I—"

A door opened to spill a vertical beam of firelight into the darkness. "Simple John?" Simple John asked.

Nicodemus's anger melted. "It's all right, John. I just tripped." The door swung wide to fill the common room with the shifting light of the big man's fire. "John, I'm fine."

Simple John inspected Nicodemus's face with concern. "No," he said while plodding over to his fellow cacographer. A powerful hand landed on Nicodemus's shoulder.

"Really, John, the cut was just a research accident. There's no need—"

"No," Simple John said before enveloping Nicodemus in a hug. "Simple John," Simple John said while mashing Nicodemus's head into his chest.

At first Nicodemus leaned into the massive wall that was John and let his arms hang limp. But after a moment, he half-heartedly returned the hug. Simple John released him and said, "Splattering splud!"

"Splattering splud," Nicodemus agreed. "That about describes my life: splattering splud."

They exchanged goodnights and Nicodemus stumbled into his chamber. He'd forgotten to put the paper screen in the window and now the room was cold.

"Oh, hang it all," he sighed and tossed the ignition words into the fireplace. Soon a flame danced among the logs and illuminated his room's usual disarray. He untied his belt-purse and tossed it onto his cot.

At the sound of a knock, he turned to see Devin standing in the doorway. She was pinning a cloak about her shoulders and trying on different frowns.

"I heard you come in," she grunted. "I've been put on nighttime janitorial duty. The bloody provost wants the refectory cleaned in the dark so that none of the foreign—blood and fire! What happened to your cheek?"

Nicodemus covered it with his hand. "Nothing. An accident during Shannon's research."

"Nico, don't be stupid about wanting a linguist's hood. If Shannon's giving you work you can't safely handle you should—"

"Dev, I'm fine."

She held her hands up. "All right, all right. No need to be fussy. But it proves what I was saying about how Starhaven treats us. You think illiterates get cut up when doing their chores?"

Nicodemus sat heavily in on his sleeping cot. "And, Dev, I'm sorry about what I said today in the refectory—about your wanting to get married. I just assumed that because you gossip so much about who's fooling around with whom . . . well, that—"

"It proves you've got donkey dung for brains, I agree," Devin retorted. "But you're not entirely worthless; everything you told me about Los becoming the first demon helped with Magistra Highsmith today."

Nicodemus opened his mouth, but before he could make a sound she said, "Anyway, like I said, I have to go to janitorial in the refectory. I'll be back at some unholy hour in the morning. It's just you and John here tonight. The young ones are asleep despite all the excitement the sentinels outside caused."

She ticked off a few obscenities about sentinels writing wards on their door. "I have to call out and wait for the guards to open the door." She looked up. "You know why they're bottling us up or why we're not allowed to leave Starhaven?"

Nicodemus shook his head. He had promised Shannon his silence.

"Well, if any of the cacographic girls get upset tonight they'll be coming to you. Think you can handle that?"

When Nicodemus said that he could, she left without closing the door. Tiredly he rose and shut it himself. When he turned back, he saw his newest knightly romance lying under his cot. A weak smile creased his lips.

After lighting a bedside candle and covering the window with its paper screen, he sat on the bed and retrieved the book. It was *The Silver Shield.*

The peddler had wanted seven Lornish pennies for the romance; Nicodemus had talked him down to four.

It was a plain codex, leather-bound, without metalwork, and clasped with a simple rawhide cord.

Lightly, he ran his fingers down the spine and remembered the many long between-duties hours he had spent reading.

As the logs in the fire began to crackle, Nicodemus opened the cover and stared at the first line. He passed his eyes over it four times, but each time he saw the letters and not the words. His attention wandered to the illuminations drawn in the margins. Two mounted knights charged each other. A spear-wielding soldier battled a black, scaly-tongued monster.

He lay back, propped up his head on a pillow, and he rescanned the first line. But still his mind refused to read. Slowly, carefully, he traced a finger along the illuminations.

In the morning perhaps he would scold himself for sentimentality, but now his chest rose and fell with a slow sigh.

As a boy he had wanted to escape into such a story. In his dreams, he had populated the nearby woods with imaginary monsters that he could venture out to defeat.

He had wanted to don armor and clash with Tamelkan, the eyeless dragon, or Garkex, the horned firetroll, or maybe a neo-demon who distorted magical language for its own purposes. He had wanted to restore the peace, save the kingdom, be the hero.

One of these boyhood longings echoed through his heart now. Slowly he laid the open book on his chest. He closed his eyes and tried to find the dreams of youth.

He wanted to see a flock of birds, white as snow, flying high above bare stone peaks that surrounded a verdant valley. He wanted a sword on his hip and a chance to walk down into that valley at sunset. He wanted to find night resting on the waterfalls, golden firelight half-hidden in the human dwellings.

And so he fell slowly, gently into sleep. At first he dreamed of the things he had longed for, and he knew peace.

But then came the nightmare.

MAGISTRA AMADI OKEKE stifled a yawn as she began another circuit around the Dagan Courtyard with her secretary.

"But what if neither Shannon nor Nicodemus is connected to the recent deaths?" Kale asked, rubbing his eyes.

It was late and they had been discussing their investigation for hours.

As Amadi considered Kale's question, she looked out into the courtyard. The wide rectangular space was illuminated by incandescent prose strewn along the surrounding spires and vaulting arcades.

Walkways divided the yard into quarters, each of which held flower gardens with a few stone benches tucked into shrub-lined alcoves. On some of these sat green-robed hierophants enjoying the crisp air after a night of treaty negotiation in stuffy libraries.

In the courtyard's center stood a copse of aspen trees, their outermost leaves already autumn gold.

Amadi turned back to Kale. "It's exceedingly unlikely that we will discover a delegate or another academic who wished Nora ill. That's why we must focus on Shannon."

Kale shook his head. "Magistra, you've always said a sentinel can't afford to ignore unlikely possibilities. Shouldn't we question more Starhaven wizards and foreign delegates?"

"Kale, you're upset that I withdrew some authors from your investigations. But we are terribly shorthanded, and we must guard the Drum Tower and Shannon." She exhaled in exasperation. "I'm still amazed by his story of a creature turning from flesh into clay."

Kale shrugged. "Maybe the old man's lost his wits."

"Or maybe he only wants us to think he's lost his wits. Or maybe Nicodemus truly is the Storm Petrel and has corrupted the old fool's mind. It's all too dangerous with those two."

Kale looked at her. "And what of the provost's request to post more sentinels around the delegates' sleeping quarters?"

Amadi rubbed her eyes. "Sweet heaven, that's right. If a delegate ends up dead, the provost will have me skinned alive. But how can we come up with any more authors?"

"I've inspected the wards on the Drum Tower," Kale said carefully. "It would take a master spellwright to disspell them. Perhaps the guards are superfluous?"

Amadi chewed her lip as they turned a corner. "Tempting, but no; we'll leave the guards until I know more about Shannon's story. There's a chance he's telling the truth."

Kale said nothing.

Amadi looked back at the courtyard. "Starhaven must be the strangest bit of architecture humans have ever inhabited."

"Why's that?"

She gestured first at the courtyard in general and then at the aspen trees in its center. "Look at these interlacing arches, these brightly tiled fountains. We'd have to ride clear up to Dar for a better example of royal Spirish architecture. And yet at the center of all these minarets are aspens.

Aspens! There should be palm fronds swaying in a sea breeze, not gold leaves quaking in thin mountain air."

Kale smiled. "It is odd to think of the royal Spirish colonizing this place. They must have been miserable when it snowed."

Amadi nodded. "Three kingdoms tried to remake this chunk of Chthonic rock in their image. All failed, and now we wizards play in the ruins."

Kale chuckled. But before he could say what he found funny, the sound of running feet filled the courtyard.

Amadi turned around to see a young Starhaven acolyte skid to a halt. "Magistra Okeke, you're to come to Engineer's library immediately!"

Amadi frowned. "On whose command?"

The boy shook his head. "Don't know her name, Magistra. A grand wizard, she wears a white badge and three stripes on her sleeves."

Amadi swore. Only a deputy provost could wear such marks. "Take us there quickly," she said.

The boy turned and ran. Amadi hiked up her robes and followed.

They pursued the young page through a blur of hallways to an archway large enough to admit seven horses running abreast.

Beyond sat an extraordinarily wide library. Long ago Starhaven engineers had filled the place with a row of limestone bridges that spanned the width of the room.

Along each arch stretched wooden facades decorated in the ornate Spirish style and converted into bookshelves. A labyrinth of traditional bookshelves flowed beneath the bridges like a river's convoluted currents.

The place was alive with yelling librarians. Teams of black-robes rushed across bridges and among the bookshelves. A sudden, golden jet of Numinous prose exploded from one bridge and was quickly followed by a chorus of shouts.

"Mother ocean!" Kale issued the Ixonian curse. "What's happening?"

Suddenly a nearby bookshelf burst into a molten ball of silvery Magnus. Amadi had just enough time to turn away and cover her face before a shockwave of fragmented prose and manuscripts struck.

When Amadi looked back, she saw a pile of rubble where the shelf had stood. "Firey blood of Los!" she swore. Amid the detritus now wriggled four pale-skinned constructs that took the shape of giant worms or grubs.

Each was roughly a foot long, possessing huge eyes and a segmented body. Just below each spell's bulbous head sprouted three pairs of legs that ended in childlike human hands. More distressing were the bulging hind portions; in those segments speckled bits of half-digested text shone through their translucent carapaces.

"Disspell them before they reach a shelf!" Amadi barked and drew her arm back. Within moments she had filled her fist with a lacerate disspell.

Already the nightmare constructs were scurrying for nearby books. Their grasping, childlike hands moved them over the debris with alarming speed.

Beside her, Kale extemporized a spear made of common magical language. With an ululating war cry, he charged.

Amadi cast her disspell with her best overhand throw. The lacerate text—a whirling mass of Magnus shards—shot through the air to slice through a monster's abdomen. The spell wailed as its carapace split open and disgorged its textual viscera.

Kale leaped over the deconstructing monster and gracefully thrust at the next worm. The thing jumped back to avoid the spear's blade.

Kale, like many Ixoanians, was an excellent spearman. The instant his boots touched ground, he leaped and thrust again.

The worm retreated again but too slowly. Kale's spearhead plunged into its abdomen. The thing shrieked and tried to pull away, but Kale had twisted his spear and caught the thing's carapace with the spearhead's barbs.

"Magistra," he called, improvising a club of blunt passages. "By the bridge!" With a powerful club stroke, he split the construct's head with a crack.

Amadi looked beyond the secretary and saw another construct scampering toward the bridge. By this time, she had composed another lacerate disspell. "Where's the fourth?" she shouted. "Find it."

As she had written it to do, her lacerate dispersed midair and bombarded the unfortunate monster with a storm of blades. The thing clicked and squealed as it began to writhe into deconstruction.

"I can't find the fourth!" Kale called. "I can't find it!" He was turning around frantically, looking for the fourth monster.

Amadi's heart went cold. Not eight feet behind him, one of the monsters had reached a bookshelf. It reared up on its abdomen and used its childish hands to pull a heavy codex from the shelves.

"Behind you!" Amadi shouted.

As Kale spun around, the giant worm opened the book. Its head unraveled itself into a cloud of glowing golden prose.

Kale lunged. But even as his spear whistled through the air, the creature jammed its textual head into the book. Instantly, the thing's body textualized and dove into the pages.

Kale's spear swung through empty air as the codex fell to the floor and snapped shut.

"Damn it! Get back from the book!" Amadi ordered. Kale deftly jumped away. She ran in and covered the infected codex in a thick Magnus shield.

"Magister, what's happened?" a frightened voice asked.

Amadi glanced up to see the boy who had led them to the library staring at Kale. She returned to swaddling the book with Magnus sheets.

"What were those things?" the boy asked.

Kale squatted down to look in the boy's eyes. "Are you all right, lad? There's no danger anymore, but we need to stand farther away."

The boy nodded as Kale pulled him back. "What were they?"

"Bookworms," Kale explained gravely. "Malicious language that invades manuscripts. They eat all the prose in a text and use it to make copies of themselves. When there are too many bookworms in a codex, it explodes. They use the explosion to spread themselves to other books."

"And one of them got into that book?" the boy asked.

"That's why Magistra is casting a containing spell around it. That will protect us if it bursts."

Amadi had never encased an infected codex before, and so she was relieved when she glanced up and saw a small train of librarians rushing toward her. At their head strode an ancient grand wizard in a deputy provost's robe.

"Sentinel Amadi Okeke of Astrophell, I presume?" the deputy provost boomed. She was a short, fat woman. A thin halo of white hair wreathed her wrinkled face. Her hood was lined with orange cloth signifying that she was a librarian. Given her rank, she was undoubtedly Starhaven's Dean of Libraries.

"Yes, Magistra," Amadi blurted, silently cursing herself for not learning this woman's name.

The dean wasted no time. "What is this situation?"

"A violent deconstruction produced four class-four bookworm constructs," Amadi reported. "Three curses were deconstructed but the last infected this codex."

The ancient dean nodded to a librarian behind her. "Hand that to Magister Luro here. He'll lift the curse or destroy the book."

Amadi handed the infected codex to the young grand wizard who stepped forward.

The deputy provost studied her for a moment. "Magistra, we are facing a bookworm infection unlike any I have known. Starhaven's protective language is among the most robust in the world, and yet these curses have spread to four libraries. They are rapidly destroying invaluable manuscripts."

The ancient woman shook her head. "They've tertiary cognition and their executive language confounds all but our most direct methods of deconstruction. Whoever wrote them has an astounding understanding of textual intelligence."

"Textual intelligence?" Amadi repeated. That was Shannon's specialty.

"Indeed," the dean continued. "I must have all available sentinels under my command until this infection is contained. We cannot let the foreign delegates see this chaos. It would embarrass the academy."

As if to punctuate her point, a massive silver ball blossomed on the farthest bridge. An instant later, a thunder-like boom shook the library.

Amadi flinched. "Yes, Magistra, right away."

But the other woman was already striding off in the direction of the blast. Her train of librarians hurried after.

Amadi turned to her secretary. "Wake our sleeping authors and fetch those not fulfilling essential duties. They're to report to her immediately."

Kale raised his eyebrows. "Even those guarding the Drum Tower and Magister Shannon?"

Amadi took a deep breath. "Leave the two following Shannon, but pull the guards from Shannon's quarters and the Drum Tower. We'll put them back as soon as the infection's contained."

"Right away, Magistra," Kale said and was off running.

CHAPTER

Twenty-four

Strangely, Nicodemus knew he was dreaming.

Around him seethed a tunnel of gray and black language—an endless, meaningless mash of written words. He was traveling down it. Magister Shannon's voice sounded above him: "I don't understand. Turtles?"

Then his own voice: "Look, that hexagonal pattern . . ."—the words became faint—". . . of a turtle shell."

The voices died and in their place sounded a long series of rhythmic, echoing clacks.

And then Nicodemus stood in the cavern of his previous nightmare—low ceiling, gray floors, a black stone table. The body lying upon it was again covered in white. Again a teardrop emerald lay in its gloved hands.

But new to the cavern was a standing stone, as tall as a man and as broad as a horse. It stood behind the black table. Three undulating lines flowed from the stone's top down to its base.

White, vinelike stalks erupted from the ground and swayed to an unfelt breeze. The stalks sprouted pale ivy leaves and began to intertwine. Within moments, a knee-high snarl of albino ivy covered the floor.

"I was the demon's slave," a low voice rumbled. It came from everywhere. "I cut him in the river." The voice grew louder. "I cut him in the river!"

Nicodemus tried to run, but the pale ivy entangled his legs. He tried to scream, but his throat produced only a long painful hiss. He reached down to pull at the weeds but froze when he saw his hands covered by the hexagonal plates of a turtle's shell.

Suddenly he could not move so much as his eyelid. From toe to top hair he was encased in thick black shell.

"I CUT HIM IN THE RIVER!"

A blinding red light enveloped Nicodemus. Agony lanced through his every fiber as his shell shattered.

Looking up, he saw the emerald produce a sphere of light—wispy and sallow at the edges, but blazing green at its core.

The small emerald's radiance grew until it burned the cavern and everything in it into airy nothingness.

Above stretched a pale-blue sky, below, lush savanna grass. Ancient oak trees dotted a hillside that overlooked the wide, green water of a reservoir. Nicodemus recognized the place as a springtime Spirish meadow near his father's stronghold.

In the meadow's center, a tattered blanket provided seating for a young boy and a woman. She was a rare beauty: pale skin with a light spray of freckles, bright hazel eyes set above a snub nose, thin lips, a delicate chin.

But her most stunning feature was the long bronze hair cascading down her back in slow curls that glinted gold in the sunlight.

A book, a knightly romance, sat in the woman's lap. Her lips moved as she read from it but the dream provided no sound.

The boy had long black hair and a dark olive complexion. He was perhaps eight years old and gazed at the woman with fierce green eyes. This was as much a memory as it was a dream.

The woman's name was April, the boy's Nicodemus.

This was a vision of long ago when Lord Severn—Nicodemus's father—had seen fit to educate his bastard. The lord had brought April into his household ostensibly to educate his son, but most everyone knew the lord visited her chamber at night.

April had been a kind teacher but not a determined one. After Nicodemus's first dozen futile reading lessons, she began reading her favorite books aloud to him. Being Lornish, April had been enamored of knightly romances. And after the first tale of maidens and monsters, so was the young Nicodemus.

The dream became fluid. The vision of April and his young self began to flicker. Now Nicodemus's image was ten years old. There were flashes of Nicodemus reading alone, but more often he was with April, begging her for something.

Memory provided the details the dream left out. In what was perhaps the only shrewd act of her life, April had noticed Nicodemus's interest in knightly romance and began reading to him less and less. When possible, she stopped at a tale's most exciting point, claiming she was too tired to continue.

The young Nicodemus yearned to learn what happened next in each story, but his progress was slow. At times he confused his frustration regarding the text with his frustration regarding his governess's body.

Noticing his improvement, April ceased reading to him entirely but supplied more books. Now the dream showed only images of Nicodemus reading alone.

The dream world shifted. Gone were the meadow and sunshine.

Nicodemus now watched his ten-year-old self lying abed in his small Severn Hold chamber. He was reading a book titled *Sword of Flame*.

The bedside candles danced as several nights flickered by—this was the time when, in three agonizing months, Nicodemus had taught himself to read so that he might find out if Aelfgar, a noble paladin, could mend Cailus, his broken sword, with the Fire Stones of Ta'nak, and then wield it to free the beautiful Shahara from Zade, an evil cleric who commanded the snakelike Zadsernak.

Although the youthful Nicodemus had had trouble remembering the many silly invented names, he was delighted with the story's inevitable course and eager to read the next twenty-seven books in the series, though he doubted that they were all as good.

Time flickered again. Now Nicodemus saw the warm night on which he had finished *Sword of Flame*. His young self laid the book down on his chest and fell asleep to the sound of spring rain and the cries of a full robin's nest outside his window.

"No," the adult Nicodemus moaned. On this night, in a dream about April, he would be born to magic. The resulting magical effulgence would set the entire western wing of Severn Hold on fire, killing a horse and maiming two stable boys.

"Wake!" Nicodemus shouted. "Wake up!" But his boyish self slept on. He tried to move but found his adult legs paralyzed. The window above young Nicodemus creaked open.

A thick arm of ghostly white ivy vines grew with jerky, nightmare speed onto the window frame and surrounded the bed. The adult Nicodemus yelled again, trying to wake himself.

The nightmare ivy hadn't been there when he had been a boy. But now its pale tentacles leaped onto the bed and within moments blanketed the dreaming child with ashen leaves. The world exploded with light. Everywhere flames roared. A horse screamed its death as the rafters came crashing down around Nicodemus. The stone walls tottered and then fell with a deep, grinding growl.

Suddenly nothing hung above Nicodemus but a too-low nightmare sky of seething gray text. Next to him stood April, untouched by flames. "Run, Nicodemus!" she cried. "He has your shadow!" Darkness radiated from her, blotting out the nightmare sky.

"There is no safe place!" Her hair became trains of stars and spread across the growing night sky.

"The white beast will find you unless you fly from Starhaven! Fly with anything you have!"

Her body faded into nothing and her face became the glowing face of the white moon.

"Fly and don't look back!"

There was a deafening crash and then . . . blackness.

"Never look back!"

AMADI WAS SITTING in the hallway, using two Magnus clauses to pick splinters from her forearm, when Kale found her.

"Magistra! What happened?"

She flinched as a clause drew out a half inch of bloody wood. "Bookworms infested both sides of a bridge. We were containing the first blast when the second went off in my ear. The deputy provost was right: these worms have an uncanny intelligence. Every time it seems we've deconstructed the last one, another violent deconstruction pulls us back into a fray."

She looked up at her secretary. He had several scrolls tucked under one arm and a thick codex under the other. Behind him stood the two sentinels who had been guarding Shannon's quarters.

"And what in the burning hells took you so long?" she asked. "The Drum Tower guards were here an hour ago."

Kale smiled. "News most wonderful! We found a wounded bookworm responding to a leftover homing passage."

He held out one of the scrolls. "Six minor libraries are fighting infestation now. But so far the Main Library has remained free of infection, thank Hakeem. And Starhaven is doing a remarkable job of hiding the whole affair. But still, there is fierce fighting in all of the infected libraries. And it seems that in one of them this bookworm was wounded in a very fortuitous way."

"Fortuitous?" Amadi accepted the scroll.

"By chance, a disspell destroyed most of this bookworm's executive text. So the construct resorted to an older, previously disabled protocol about what to do if wounded." He held out another scroll.

Amadi took it and then looked at the two sentinels who had been on guard duty. Kale was only a lesser wizard, and the bookworms were written in Numinous and Magnus. "You two subdued the construct and then parsed its structure?"

They nodded vigorously.

Kale piped up again. "All the other wounded bookworms have been returning to another location. But this one had been wounded in such a way that it couldn't. However, we were able to learn where it should have gone."

Amadi raised her eyebrows.

"The bookworms have been subtextualizing themselves and returning to a private library in a tower near the Bolide Garden," he explained. "There they've been engulfing some text stored there. Once recovered they head back out to infect other libraries."

"So the author of these bookworms set up this private library as a base for the bookworms?"

Kale held out the rest of his scrolls and the codex. "Just so. And the worms can subtextualize themselves well enough that we never would have found it if it weren't for this wounded worm. In any case, when we found the place, we disspelled the worms and then investigated. That's where we found these."

Amadi set the scrolls on the ground and turned her attention to the codex. "And what are they?"

"What you're holding now is Nora Finn's research journal."

Amadi looked up sharply. "The journal Shannon claimed the clay monster ran off with?"

Kale's smile seemed wide enough to split his face in half. "Exactly! It seems that Nora Finn was taking bribes from a Spirish noble to watch a certain student. And seems there still is another spy. That scroll there contains notes about a correspondence with a different Spirish duke and an Ixoanian admiral. We couldn't figure out why, but the nobles seem to be paying the author to disrupt this convocation."

"We had two spies for Spirish nobles in Starhaven?" Amadi half-squawked. "Nora Finn and the owner of the private library? And this second spy took bribes to set these bookworms loose?"

"Worse than that," the secretary added. "The scrolls by your feet are drafts of curses written to infiltrate a spellwright's body and force it to overexert itself!"

Amadi felt her hands go numb. "Like the misspell that killed Nora Finn and the neophyte. Did you find any evidence of the remaining spy's identity?"

Kale shook his head. "Of course not. The author was too intelligent for that. But Magistra, remember the first bookworm we found; it should have returned to this private library, but it was damaged in such a way that it accidentally returned to a previously designated location. Well, we searched that location and found a hidden chest filled with an appalling number of Spirish and Ixonian coins. And Magistra, you forgot to ask where that location was."

Amadi looked at Kale and then at the two sentinels behind him. "No, don't tell me," she said, pressing a hand to her forehead. "I already know."

CHAPTER

Twenty-five

Though Shannon had been sincere when he told Nicodemus to rest while it was still possible, the grand wizard found himself walking not to his quarters, but to his study. Neither of the sentinels following him objected; they would be up all night no matter if he was lying in bed or sitting at a desk.

After leaving the guards outside and locking the door, Shannon put Azure on a perch and assured her she could sleep. He knew his study well enough to move about without mundane vision.

Though he was exhausted, the idea of a golem had roused his curiosity. How could magical language create such a being? As he pondered this question, habit prompted him to retrieve his research journal and absently finger the three asterisks embossed on its face.

As far as he knew, a spell could gain intelligence only from one of two processes: "direction" and "impression."

Authors creating "direct" textual intelligence had to write clever prose. At its simplest level, this required strings of instructions: *if this happens, then do that; if that does not happen, then do this* and so on. More complex methods directed constructs to recognize patterns or develop evolving webs of decision-making sentences.

However, any "directly" intelligent spell fell short of an "impressed" counterpart. Descended from an ancient spell that survived the Exodus, "impression" used two Numinous matrices. The first matrix inhabited a living mind; the second, a spell's executive language. If physically close, an impressing matrix began to mimic the thought processes of a living mind. In this way spellwrights could "impress" aspects of their own intelligence into texts.

Shannon had given Azure fluency in Numinous through impression, and most gargoyles and all ghosts required a living mind after which to model their thoughts.

What excited Shannon about the golem spell was its implicit connection to impression. To animate a golem, a spellwright had to invest his textual "spirit" into earthen body. To form a spirit spell, an author would have to use a radical form of impression that translated his mind into a text. That would leave the author's body an empty husk until its spirit returned.

So before investing his spirit into a golem, a spellwright would have to plan for his spirit's return to his body. Therefore, a golem would need an escape subspell allowing a spirit to eject itself from a wounded golem.

What Shannon wanted to do was write a linguistic attack that would hinder or destroy a golem's escape subspell. If he could do that, he might slay the golem's author without finding the fiend's living body.

Shannon worked with an excitement he had not known for a half century. After skimming the relevant texts, he had an idea of what functions an escape subspell would have to perform. That left him the task of deducing how a text might fulfill those functions and how an attack spell might interrupt those same functions.

In an hour, he had an outline.

Writing the spell proved more difficult. He worked in Numinous and stored the early drafts on older scrolls. The latter drafts he wrote onto his best parchment. At times his hands shook with excitement and made it difficult to place the lines.

After four hours, he had finished a working draft. At nearly eight thousand characters, it occupied twenty-four pages of his research journal. His fingers ached from gripping the smooth runes. He set about putting in a few expository notes so that he wouldn't forget how the trickier passages operated.

"Shannon, you're still a linguist," he congratulated himself when the spell was finished. "But you're getting old." He leaned back and let himself feel the soreness in his arms, the aching in his knees. The only thing keeping him awake was the knowledge that, if he cast his new spell on the golem, it would trap the author's sprit inside the clay body.

Shannon sat back in his chair and listened to its familiar wooden creaking. Just then he realized he had to get a copy of this spell to Nicodemus immediately. Should he take it over to the Drum Tower now? It was vital that the boy have the spell. But how could he get it to him?

Azure made a low, two-note whistle. Shannon cast an inquiring sentence to her and received an instant reply: she had heard something unusual.

Shannon squinted at his door. No one was spellwriting in the hallway, but farther away, in what must have been a stairwell, shone a ten-foot trail of golden text. He had seen such a thing before: it was a train of a half dozen wizards, all casting flamefly spells to illuminate the dark stairs.

Something was wrong. Deadly wrong.

Shannon scooped up Azure and formed with her the textual exchange that allowed him to see through her eyes. Back at his desk, he stared at the spell he had just written.

He had to get the text to Nicodemus; the boy's life depended on it. Even more frightening, Nicodemus's connection to prophecy meant that his survival might be essential for the fight against the Disjunction and hence for the preservation of human language.

"Hakeem, help me!" he whispered.

Glancing up, he saw the train of flamefly spells begin to wink out as their casters came closer.

He looked back at his spell. It was too long for Azure to carry in her body. And he didn't have time to transfer it to a scroll and have Azure to fly it over. He needed something that was already written.

After scanning his desk, his blind eyes fell on familiar Numinous paragraphs. Azure provided a mundane image of the manuscript: it was the scroll that had, just a day and a half ago, granted him permission to begin research on the Index.

Hushed voices sounded in the hallway.

With shaking hands, Shannon found an inkhorn and a serviceable quill. He rarely wrote mundane letters and he did not trust his exhausted fingers to produce anything legible now. So he dipped the quill's feathered end in ink and used it to paint a wide, sticky stripe over the mundane writing which had granted permission for his research.

Quickly he forged the Numinous paragraphs that would lift the ban on the Drum Tower's door. He slapped these onto the head of the scroll along with a common language note which when translated would read "*key for wards*."

Knocking sounded at the door. "Magister Shannon," Amadi's voice called.

"A moment!" Shannon replied. He had to write something more to Nicodemus about the other passages—had to do it before the sentinels could interfere. Amadi would never allow Nicodemus to have such a powerful text.

"Shannon," Amadi called, "you must open this door!"

Shannon went blank with fear. How could he let Nicodemus know what he was thinking?

Suddenly his mind leaped forward with thought. He forged a few phrases that when translated would read "*Research* ***" and slapped it at the top of the scroll. Then he forged what would translate into the single word "*Dogfood*," copied it once, and then thumbed one word above the first paragraph and the other above the second.

A wall of silvery text shown from the other side of the door; doubtless the sentinels were preparing to knock it down.

Shannon rolled up the scroll and bound it with a Magnus sentence. "To Nicodemus," he whispered, binding the Magnus sentence to Azure's foot. "And beware of the sentinels guarding the Drum Tower." He repeated these instructions in Numinous.

Behind him came a crash as a spell ripped his door from its hinges.

He leaped forward and punched the wooden screen out of his window.

"Magister!" Amadi called. "Do not move!"

Azure made her high two-note whistle and with a clatter of wings flew out the window.

SHANNON LET OUT a long, relieved breath. Amadi began shouting and rough hands grabbed his shoulders and turned him around. The room was ablaze with censoring texts. There must have been seven sentinels in the room.

"Amadi," he said coolly, "I hope you can justify this breach of law and custom."

"Magister," she replied from somewhere to his left, "I'm afraid I can."

He looked in her direction. "And how is that?"

She told him about the bookworm infection and the private library filled with incriminating manuscripts. She then explained about a wounded construct that had been trying to return to his quarters.

"You think I would be foolish enough to write a curse that would return to my own quarters?" he asked incredulously.

A different voice responded. It took a moment for Shannon to recognize it as Kale's. "The chances of the bookworm being wounded in just that way—losing its ability to subtextualize and its homing protocol—are very slight. You could have safely assumed you would never be identified. But unfortunately, Magister, chance conspired against you."

Shannon snorted. "Or the true villain has fooled you into accusing me of his crimes."

Amadi responded dryly. "We've searched your quarters more thoroughly than before. We swept the room for subtexts."

Kale spoke. "We found a subtextualized chest strapped to your ceiling. It holds a fortune in Spirish gold."

For a moment Shannon could not understand what he was hearing. How could the golem have gotten that much coin into his room? The thing couldn't spellwrite within Starhaven's walls.

"So who was it, Magister?" Kale asked. "What Spirish noble was paying you to disrupt this convocation and why?"

"Amadi, you're making a grave error," Shannon said hoarsely.

His former student let a moment pass before replying. "Did you know that Nora Finn was also taking bribes from a Spirish noble?"

He nodded. "I read of it in her journal."

"Why did you not tell me?" Amadi asked.

Shannon scowled. "Because I was more concerned with convincing you of the true villain's existence."

Amadi let another silent moment pass. "Or perhaps you were glad to be free of a competing spy. Tell me, Magister, how did the Spirish gold come to be in your quarters?"

"It was put there."

"By your clay monster? Impossible. As I told you: I had a sentinel watching your quarters. What's more, all the doors and windows were warded and then protected by robust, bisecting texts. Even if your monster did sneak past my guards, the thing would have been cut in half at the waist. It would have had to hide the chest and escape with half a body."

Shannon's blind eyes widened. A clay golem could do just such a thing. "Amadi!" he blurted. "The thing must have done its spellwriting in the Bolide Garden and then used prewritten texts to sneak in and hide the chest. Search the surrounding area. Somewhere you'll find a deposit of clay."

"Magister," Amadi said in a low tone, "the Bolide Gardens are being renovated. Do you want me to slop through all that mud for a lump of clay that looks like a monster?"

Shannon took a deep breath. The monster had planned well. After planting the research journal in his quarters, it must have thrown itself down into the garden. There the golem could have deconstructed amid the dirt piles.

But Shannon couldn't convince Amadi of that. Not here at least. "So you suspect I'm a spy," he said, changing tactics. "Do you also believe I killed Eric and Adan, my own students?"

The room grew quiet. "Some remember how vicious a politician you were back in Astrophell; more than one voice has suggested that—"

"That I murdered my own students to disrupt this convocation?" Shannon growled. "That I sold my soul to some illiterate lord? Amadi, I have never heard such a foul suggestion. And I'll swear under any power you like that I—"

"The witch trial hasn't begun yet," her cold voice interrupted. "Do nothing rash. In this room stands every free sentinel under my command."

Shannon began to respond but then stopped. "You mean, every sentinel but those you sent to guard the Drum Tower and Nicodemus?"

"Still trying to convince me that the clay man is after your cacographers?" Amadi asked. "I think you'd better hold your tongue, Magister. We have wards on the tower's doors and windows. No one's getting to a cacographer tonight. Besides, I couldn't spare the spellwrights to guard the place if my life depended on it. The libraries need every free author to contain the bookworm infection. Unless of course, you can tell us how to eradicate the infestation?"

"I have nothing to do with the bookworms!" Shannon exclaimed. "You can't leave the Drum Tower defenseless!"

No one replied.

Shannon was breathing hard. "Amadi, listen to me! When researching the Index today, I learned of an ancient construct called a golem which is made of clay but contains its author's mind—"

"Magister, some of us here will help decide your witch trial," Kale said. "It would help your cause if you refrained from saying anything foolish."

Shannon realized that there would be no reasoning with the sentinels. He leaped for his bookcase, hoping to reach a stun spell he kept in a hidden scroll.

But before he had taken two steps, a wave of censoring language flashed toward him. Netlike texts wrapped around his mind.

The world seemed to spin and then the lines of glowing text disappeared. Everything went black.

CHAPTER Twenty-six

A low, grating screech jolted Nicodemus awake. Sweat had soaked through his robes. "Who's there?" He struggled out of bed. His candle had burnt to a dark stub.

The screech came again along with the flapping of wings. A golden flash made him look at the window. "Azure!" he exclaimed, pulling out the paper screen.

The parrot flew into his chest. Squawking with surprise, man and bird tumbled onto the sleeping cot. "Shannon! Shannon!" Azure called in a terrified, pitiful voice. "Shannon!"

The familiar was standing on his stomach. Her tiny chest heaved; her head bobbed. A small scroll was bound to her leg by a Magnus sentence. "It's all right," Nicodemus cooed, pulling the scroll free.

Azure scrambled onto his shoulder, and he sat up to read the scroll. His brows knitted in confusion. "Azure, this makes no sense. There's a key for the front door ward. Magister said he'd send that. But there's ink all over the mundane text and these other Numinous paragraphs are gibberish."

He translated the common language words above the gibberish: "*Research* ***" and "*Dogfood.*"

"Shannon!" the bird called and cast a Numinous sentence into Nicodemus's head.

Shannon, having impressed his linguistic abilities into the bird, could have made perfect sense of this sentence. But Nicodemus's translation yielded "*My-old-home-ones ate Shannon!*"

Nicodemus's palms began to sweat. Azure had hatched in Trillinon. Those from her "old home" must be Northerners.

Nicodemus went to the window and peered down into the Stone Court. The sentinels who had been guarding its door were gone.

"Ate" to Azure meant consumed, enveloped. The Northern sentinels must have seized Shannon. "Demigods of the Celestial Canon defend us!" Nicodemus whispered.

Azure leaped from his shoulder and flapped into the night. No doubt she was going in search of where the sentinels were holding Shannon.

Nicodemus turned back to his room and shivered as he remembered his most recent nightmare. "Fly from Starhaven!" April had said. "Fly and don't look back!"

He took a clean apprentice robe over to the fireplace's clicking embers. With trembling fingers, he changed out of his sweat-soaked night robe and thought about the nightmare.

Like the others, this dream had made little sense. The cavern and the body, the episodes from his childhood, April's warning—none of it seemed to fit together.

However, unlike the others, this nightmare provided a clear warning: "The white beast has your shadow!" April had said.

No doubt the "white beast" was the pale monster Nicodemus had seen attacking Eric. That monster must have been the murderer's golem. Therefore, it would make sense if the shrouded body in the cavern was their enemy's true, living body.

But that still left the question of the cavern's location.

Nicodemus thought of the nightmare turtles he had seen in his first cavern nightmare. Then he thought about the hexagonal pattern carved at the end of the Spindle Bridge. The hidden body had to have something to do with the Spindle. But what? Shannon's texts had found nothing but rock in the mountain.

And who might be sending him the dreams? Not the murderer: all evidence indicated the fiend did not know Nicodemus's identity, and even if he did, the villain wouldn't want to reveal any hint of his body's location.

But then again, Shannon had said the nightmares came from special spells that ancient authors knew how to write. Who else besides the golem-wielding murderer had knowledge of ancient texts?

Perhaps there was a clue in the dream? April's voice had spoken directly to him. No one had spoken to him in previous dreams.

The wound on Nicodemus's cheek throbbed again as he remembered April's warning: "The white beast will find you unless you fly from Starhaven!"

Normally such an indication of danger would have sent him running to Shannon, but now the old man was locked up.

Nicodemus noticed that the scroll Azure had brought had fallen to the floor. He picked it up. "*Dogfood,*" Shannon had written above each paragraph—and at the top: "*Research* ***."

Had the old man not had time to tell him what to research? Had he meant to come back and edit the phrase? Perhaps Nicodemus was supposed to research three stars. Or something about Starhaven? But where could Nicodemus research anything?

He began to pace. He tried to breathe on his hands but accidentally brushed the Magnus stitches on his cheek. Pain lanced into his skull and brought with it a sudden memory of his nightmare: "Fly and don't look back!" April had warned him. "Never look back!"

Nicodemus looked at the door. He should run, he thought, taking a step forward. But then he realized that even if he ran, the murderer would continue killing male cacographers. He turned back to the fire. He had to stay.

But he couldn't ignore the dreams. He looked back at the door. Perhaps he should take the other male cacographers up to the compluvium? But if Shannon had wanted him to do that, he would have said so on the scroll.

Again Nicodemus raised his hands to breathe on them, and again he brushed the wound on his cheek.

"Fiery blasted blood!" he swore out loud, the pain igniting his frustration and anger. "I was supposed to be the Halcyon! I was supposed to be sure and decisive. And now I'm afraid to do anything!"

He sat before the fire and held his hands toward the coals.

He must have been cursed. He wasn't supposed to be like this. The golem's author must have stolen his strength and his ability to spell.

But if that were true, it would mean that he could restore his ability to spell. It would mean he could end his cacography.

Nicodemus focused all of his attention on the hope of completing himself. He fed it all of his fear and uncertainty. His desire grew and began to radiate heat. He wasn't going to pace about like a dithering boy. The monster had stolen part of his mind. Hatred blazed within him. He would get the missing part of himself back!

He stood up and decided that he would take the male cacographers up to the compluvium; from there he could plan his next move. Perhaps he would seek to free Shannon. Perhaps he would find a way to strike back against the golem.

Again the most recent nightmare returned to him. "The white beast will find you unless you fly from Starhaven," April had said. "Fly with anything you have!"

In a way, he was fleeing out of Starhaven proper to the compluvium. The dream must have predicted this. But what to take with him? He looked around at his cot, his robes, his books, his endless pages of spelling drills. What would help protect the boys or harm the golem? His eyes fell on Shannon's open scroll and its radiant Numinous paragraphs.

Abruptly, he realized he couldn't take the boys to the compluvium.

Not yet.

The meaning of Shannon's words was suddenly clear. The old man was a linguist after all, and linguists studied all aspects of language . . . even metaphor.

Dogfood.

LEAVING THE DRUM Tower proved simple. Shannon's key disspelled the ward on the door and, of course, there were no guards in the Stone Court.

Nicodemus worried about being stopped in the hallways. But as he hurried through the stronghold, he found it mostly empty. Occasionally he spotted teams of wizards rushing through a hallway as if on an urgent errand. Oddly, they were usually led by librarians.

At the Main Library's entrance, Nicodemus reached into Shannon's scroll and pulled out the passwords. Careful not to hold the text too long, he tossed the paragraph to a guardian spell.

The construct snapped it out of the air and glared at Nicodemus. The canine spell would tear his arms off if it discovered a misspelled rune sequence. A long moment passed as it chewed the words. Nicodemus was about to turn and run when the spell stretched into a dog bow.

Filled with dread, Nicodemus stole into the library. Without sunlight streaming through the windows, the place was dark. Rows of tapers produced dim globes of shifting light that stretched up to the ceiling like an ascending column of stars.

Nicodemus found the place unnervingly empty. He had expected at least a dozen wizards to be working by candlelight. But instead he saw only a handful of librarians rushing off to unknown tasks.

Finding the Index's chamber was easy enough. And the guardian standing watch before the chamber let him pass when he fed her Shannon's second paragraph.

As he approached the Index, his hands began to shake. Back in his room he had been so sure—use the Index to discover Shannon's message, then sneak it away to the compluvium where he could use it to research spells that might harm the golem.

But now Nicodemus noticed faint Numinous sentences running through the chamber's door frame that he hadn't seen before. They could only be the sentences of an alarm spell. Removing the Index would trip that spell and summon swarms of sentinels.

He could not steal the Index, but he could still discover why Shannon had sent him there.

With nervous steps, he crept into the chamber and stared at the Index's blank cover. From outside came the grinding vibration of the guardian shifting her Magnus ball. After cradling the book in his arm, Nicodemus undid the clasp.

Magister Smallwood had said that the Index could search the text of any codex within Starhaven's walls. And Magister Shannon's personal research journal had three asterisks embossed on its spine and face, thereby making "***" its title.

Nicodemus opened the Index with the intention of discovering what Shannon had written for him in his research journal.

Warmth bloomed across his cheeks as his body synaesthetically reacted to the Index's magic. He had expected some synaesthesia, but the strength of this reaction was unsettling. Had something gone wrong? He tried to shift his weight.

But he couldn't. His muscles would not respond. Panic thrilled up his body as he remembered the nightmare of only hours ago. Was he still dreaming?

The synaesthetic heat in his cheeks burned scalding hot even as a more disturbing warmth flushed across his stomach and groin. He knew that this—his second synaesthetic reaction—indicated the presence of a dangerously powerful foreign spell. His fear became panic.

Without warning, violet ribbons of light erupted from the Index and wriggled into his hands. A surge of nausea turned his stomach and he convulsed in a dry heave.

The Index blazed brighter, and Nicodemus could only watch, paralyzed as an incandescent cylinder emerged from the page. His legs buckled and he fell to his knees. The spell lunged into his throat.

The room blurred and a strange roaring sound throbbed in his ears. Blood flowed down his nose and filled his mouth. Involuntarily, he turned and vomited.

Without his willing them to, Nicodemus's arms placed the Index back on its marble podium.

The instant the book's spine touched cool stone, its control over him vanished and he collapsed into darkness.

WHEN NICODEMUS OPENED his eyes, a dull pain was striking the opposite ends of his skull the way a clapper rings the inside of a bell. The world was spinning, and the sour taste of vomit curdled in his mouth.

But he felt like laughing.

The bold arches and thick lines of a new alphabet burned before his eyes with a soft and otherworldly beauty. Like Numinous, this powerful violet language affected light and other text.

After wiping his mouth, Nicodemus staggered to his feet and discovered a myriad of purple sentences floating in slow concentric circles around the Index. More astonishing, a miniature river of the text flowed from the book into his chest and then back.

Slowly he realized what this meant: the Index was a tome, a magical artifact capable of teaching its reader a new language. But it had done so in a shocking and mysterious way.

When Nicodemus was sixteen he had used the Numinous and Magnus tomes to learn the wizardly languages. That had been a slow process, involving days of memorizing runes, vocabulary, and grammar. His ability to see the wizardly languages had developed at a tedious pace. It had been anything but exciting or traumatic.

The Index, on the other hand, had quite literally jammed a new language down his throat.

When he wondered how this was possible, the runes emerging from his chest swelled in number and flowed into the Index. In response, the book flipped a few leaves to present a page worked in black ink. Nicodemus stepped closer to read:

From A *Treatis on Lost Spells & Langeuges*, by Geoffrey Lea

The spell of etching is widely regarded as the most mysterious of the lost godspells. Little is known about this ancent text except that it was written by the primortial sun god Sol. Aparently, a diety would use etching to bind a conscious being, not necessarily a human, as an avatar. There is allso mention of the spell's ability to "impress" a langeuge upon its target through direct mental contact. The Neosolar pantheon regarded etching as tabboo. The great goddess Solmay forbid any diety who pratciced this spell to travel across the ocean to our land. We can only assume that, at the time of the Exodus, the spell of soulsplitting was already available as an alternative method for binding avatars.

Because soulsplitting is the only godspell known to requre the consentual participation of its target, many speculate that etching could be cast upon an unwilling subject. However . . .

Nicodemus's mouth worked silently. Somehow, he had conducted a search for mundane text without touching the Index. He inspected the page again.

The words implied that the book had used a godspell to teach him this new language. But that was impossible; only a living being could write magic, and only a deity could cast a godspell.

Nicodemus reread the passage to make sure he had not misunderstood. The text was the same, but this time something about the words bothered him. He read again.

There was something strange about the words "ancent," "langeuge," and "conscious." He studied each one, trying to decide what it was that caught his eye.

A horrible idea filled his mind.

"No!" he whispered, a wild fear tearing loose in his gut. "No! I didn't!" He staggered closer so that there could be no mistake. "Gods of grace, no!"

But there it was.

Los himself could not have inspired a more excruciating fear than that which now possessed him. He knew there should be an "i" somewhere in the word "ancent." And "langeuge" should end in "-age." As for "conscious," only a fool would fail to put a "huss" after the "s"—conshuss. Or maybe it was "cawnshuss," but definitely not "conscious"—that was absurd.

There was only one explanation: contact with his cacographic mind had filled the Index with misspellings.

It didn't matter, Nicodemus told himself, pressing a hand to his chest. He had intended to steal the artifact anyway.

But the fear building in his mind would not be ignored. Stealing an artifact was a serious crime, and wizards despised nothing more than the destruction of a magical artifact. If they discovered him now, they would permanently censor magical literacy from his mind. Worse, their hatred for him and for all cacographers would multiply a hundredfold. He would become the most infamous misspeller since James Berr had killed those wizards so long ago.

"Calm yourself," Nicodemus said slowly. Perhaps only this document was misspelled. It was written nearly four hundred years ago. Maybe the spellings were different then.

Intending to find Magister Shannon's most recent treatise on spell intelligence, Nicodemus reached out and turned a page. With deep trepidation, he read:

> **From *Concatenation's Effects on Secondary Cognition in Semi-Atonomous Nonsense & Antisense Numinous Disspells*, by Agwu Shannon.**
>
> Resent spell inteligence research has focused on the nessesity of imbuing an aspect of the caster's consciousness . . .

As he read the last word, Nicodemus groaned and shut his eyes. How could this be? Maybe, he thought, maybe the magical texts hadn't been affected. Maybe contact with his mind had only misspelled the mundane texts.

Nicodemus pressed his palm to the page and thought of a spell called "touch." He chose touch because it possessed such a simple, straightforward rune sequence that he would be able to tell if the version contained within the Index was misspelled.

Just as a fisherman's hook yanks an unsuspecting trout from the river, the Index plucked Nicodemus's mind from the wetness within his skull and sent it sailing into a vast and airy space.

It took a moment for him to perceive his new surroundings. Here Nicodemus had no eyes, no body. There was no up, no down. Everything was darkness.

Nicodemus's surprise turned to fear. The blackness became heavy and thick, like humid air. He struggled to free himself but could not. He wanted to scream but had no lungs; he wanted to run but had no legs.

At last he forced himself to relax. Slowly, his mind opened to the strange new world. Tiny glimmers moved all around him. They grew brighter and became glowing gems that hung as if suspended from invisible tree limbs.

His vision became sharper and suddenly it was as if he were floating in the night sky. The luminescent orbs had become stars of different shapes and colors. Some blazed with fierce emerald radiation; others glowed indigo or ivory so dimly that they disappeared when he looked directly at them.

At last he realized that this black firmament was the world within the Index. Now he became aware of his body, swaying somewhere far below on the floor. The realization brought on a wave of vertigo and twisted his face into a grimace.

Back inside the Index, stars of silver and gold appeared. Nicodemus's perception of the book's night sky was rapidly improving; within moments he could see for untold miles. The starry array stretched endlessly away.

Suddenly he realized what he was looking at. These were not stars, but spells. His vision confirmed it. He was staring through the Index at every text contained within Starhaven.

He must be thinking through the spells attached to the Index; he was having quaternary thoughts. It was a glorious, dreamlike feeling. But his elation faded as he remembered why he had entered the Index in the first place.

He needed to find the touch spell.

A white star flashed brighter and began to speed toward him like a comet. An instant later, the spell crashed into him with a soundless explosion.

Removing his hand from the Index made Nicodemus's mind drop like a lightning bolt back into his head. He blinked. Returning to the bony confines of his skull was intensely uncomfortable. He shook his head and felt his ideas slosh around like seaweed.

"Oh . . . yuck!" he said.

Gradually his mind molded itself to his skull. And he found that he could think clearly again.

A new knowledge of the simple touch spell was now inside of him. The spell's primary sequence burned before his eyes as clearly as if he had just written it out a thousand times. But some of the runes were out of order—he knew because touch was one of the few spells simple enough that he had memorized its proper spelling.

Now he was sure: contact with his mind had misspelled one of the Order's most prized artifacts.

Nicodemus put his hands to his face. "No . . . no . . ." he whimpered. Shame and guilt throbbed behind his eyes. He would forever be known as the cacographer who had destroyed Starhaven's most valuable artifact.

"Wait!" he sputtered. "Wait." There was one last hope. Perhaps if he could repair his disabled mind, he could repair the Index. "Show me," he ordered the Index, "any mundane documents relating to curing cacography."

As the book began flipping pages, Nicodemus looked up and muttered a prayer to Hakeem. When the Index stopped, he took a deep breath and looked down, ready to read.

But the page was blank.

BREATH SPILLED OUT of Nicodemus. His cacography had destroyed the Index. Maybe he'd vomit again.

"I had better be the Halcyon," he mumbled to himself while pressing a hand to his belly. If he wasn't, he'd never forgive himself for destroying such a beautiful artifact.

His hands began to tremble.

"Los damn it!" he growled. "I will not be like this." He closed his eyes. "I won't be weak. I won't be crippled."

He had to regain his determination to defeat the golem and erase his cacography. He could do it, if he was bold enough, disciplined enough. There was no time for fear or guilt.

He glared at the Index and cleared his mind of everything but the three asterisks of Shannon's research journal. Then he placed his palm on the blank page before him.

His mind shot upward like an arrow into another plane. But rather than a starry night sky, he floated before a massive golden wall that stretched out almost endlessly in either direction. The wall itself was made of Shannon's Numinous prose.

Nicodemus found himself staring at the journal's first page, dated more than twenty years ago.

Simply by thinking of a later entry, Nicodemus sent the wall sliding to his left. Looking at the wall's distant end, he saw that the text bent back to form a massive circle.

The codex-as-ring spun past in a golden blur. Then, without warning, it slammed to a dizzying, soundless stop.

Shannon's last entry glowed before him. It was a long Numinous spell annotated by common language sentences that glowed green.

Nicodemus frowned, trying to glean the text's purpose. The prose seemed to be that of a disspell, but it was not of the typical nonsense or antisense varieties. Its structure was that of a clamp.

That made no sense. Normally disspells sought to pull apart another spell's argument. This disspell looked as if it would try to hold the other text together.

Nicodemus turned to the annotations. As he read, a smile spread across his face. "Magister," he whispered. "It's brilliant!"

It was not a disspell at all, but an attack spell adapted to hold magical prose inside of a golem. If Nicodemus cast this text on the golem, its spirit would be trapped. The author would be vulnerable.

Abruptly Shannon's spell rushed forward to crash into Nicodemus's mind. The rush of golden prose dazzled his eyes and then faded away to reveal the physical world.

Once again Nicodemus stood swaying before the Index.

A vivid knowledge of the anti-golem spell now burned in his brain. Shannon wanted him to have this when he took the boys up to the compluvium, Nicodemus realized. With this spell he could endanger the golem's author without having to find its true body.

A shiver rushed up Nicodemus's back. He needed to return to the Drum Tower.

The Index lay before him. Closing the book made the halo of purple sentences collapse back into its pages. After a long breath, he turned away and started for the door.

"Don't you want the book?" a quick, squeaking voice said.

Nicodemus jumped back. "Who's there?" He began to write a club of simple Magnus sentences in his biceps.

From the corner stepped a lanky gargoyle with a snow monkey's body, a bat's giant ears, and an owl's bulging eyes. Nicodemus recognized the construct he had misspelled in the Stacks. "Gargoyle, did I meet you last night?"

"Petra," she said, nodding vigorously. "Now I'm named Petra." She grinned at him before scampering to the doorway. "Take the book. You misspelled it like me."

"But the alarm spell will—"

"Alarm spell nothing." The gargoyle peeled a chord of faint Numinous sentences from one side of the doorway. "Get the book and step under this." She pulled the alarm spell free of the floor and held it up above her head.

Nicodemus stared at her for a moment, then fetched the Index. "But not even a grand wizard could move those sentences," he said while ducking under the alarm.

She nodded and spoke rapidly. "Since you rewrote me, I can do things other constructs can't. I can trade and bargain. I got these eyes from a night-watch gargoyle, the ears from a grunt who hunts mice. But I think I still only have secondary thoughts." She looked up at him with childish curiosity. "What's the difference between secondary and tertiary cognition?"

He grimaced. "Secondary constructs can't remember anything about mortality. The academy claims they're not fully sentient, so it's not immoral to deconstruct them."

The gargoyle started. One of her batlike ears flicked away and then back. "Mortality?"

Nicodemus nodded. "As in death. Secondary constructs can't remember what it means to die."

"But I think I still only have secondary thoughts. What is the difference between secondary and tertiary cognition?" Her tone was the same tone as before.

Nicodemus hugged the Index to his chest. "I'm sorry, Petra. I don't know how to tell you."

The gargoyle didn't seem to be listening; her ears were flicking about in different directions. "You should go!" she whispered. "I see and hear many things now. There are corrupt gargoyles now. We constructs are all talking about them. No one knows who's written them. They're spying on the wizards."

Nicodemus swallowed. "What about the gargoyles in the compluvium?"

"They're uncorrupted," she said. "You should leave this place now. Something bad is near."

"Thank you, Petra," he said and turned away.

She laughed and called after him, "Thank you, Nicodemus Weal. You are my author who made me my own author."

Unsure of what to say, Nicodemus hurried away though the library's cavernous center. A thousand thoughts raced through his mind. But when he stepped through the main entrance into the Women's Atrium a realization made him stop.

"Los damn it!" he swore. Because the Index was misspelled, so might be his understanding of Shannon's text. There was no telling if he could produce a functional respell. Fear tightened his throat. Writing this attack spell might even be dangerous.

He started to curse his cacography but then thought of Petra the gargoyle. It took him a moment to identify the warm feeling in his chest as pride—he hadn't felt that for a long time.

He drew in a deep breath and looked up at the atrium's ceiling. The mosaic of Uriel Bolide looked back at him. With her left hand, Bolide was pointing a red wand at a scroll she held in her right. Chips of amber had been used to depict her celebrated long hair.

Her smile was amused, as if she had just discovered the properties of magical advantage by applying a little femininity to a problem that had confounded the then all-male wizards.

Nicodemus was struck by how strongly the woman in the mosaic resembled April. In the nightmare, April's image had stretched above him and her hair had become trains of stars. "Fly from Starhaven!" she had said. "Fly with anything you have!"

Again Nicodemus hugged the Index to his chest. It was all he had.

His steps quickened until he was sprinting across the Stone Court. In a few hours someone would notice the missing Index. Before that happened, he had to hide all of the male cacographers in the compluvium.

CHAPTER

Twenty-seven

On his way up the stairwell, Nicodemus found the Drum Tower silent. He burst into the common room. A chair tried to bite his hip and was knocked flat for its trouble. "John!" he called. "John, wake up! We need to leave."

He rushed into his chamber and threw open the chest at the foot of his bed. With focused urgency, he pulled his winter cloak around his shoulders and then spread a blanket on the floor. On top of it he put the Index, the coin purse Shannon had given him, and a few spare clothes.

His belt-purse lay on the foot of his sleeping cot. When he grabbed it, his fingers began to tingle. He frowned at first but then remembered the druidic artifact—the wooden sphere encircled by a root—that Deirdre had given him.

The Seed of Finding. He put the druidic artifact on the blanket. He might need that.

After scooping up the blanket and twisting it into a makeshift satchel, he ran into the common room.

"Simple John?" Simple John asked from his doorway. The big man's candle filled the room with flickering light and long shadows.

"Everything's all right, John," Nicodemus said. "But I need your help gathering all our boys. Has Devin come back from her night-time janitorial?"

"No," the big man said, eyes wide. "No!"

"John, look at me. Something bad has happened. You and I must take all the Drum Tower boys up to the compluvium. We'll be safe there. And if we're not, there's a way we can leave Starhaven altogether."

The other man shook his head. "No!"

Nicodemus cursed himself. "John, I didn't mean to upset you. Everything's going to be fine. But we must go quickly. Get anything you might need out of your room. Warm clothes especially." Nicodemus moved for the door. "I'll wake the boys."

John stepped in front of him. "No!" he again declared, his bulky frame blocking the door.

"John, we have to do this. It's not safe to stay." John shook his head.

When Nicodemus tried to move past him, John pushed him back with enough force to make him stumble.

"John, listen to me!" Nicodemus said, setting down his makeshift satchel. "We must get the boys to safety."

This set the big man's head shaking again.

Nicodemus began to write common language sentences along each of his fingers. Against a normal spellwright, Nicodemus's disability would have rendered him helpless. But now, facing another cacographer, he could use sentences simple enough for him to avoid misspelling. Simple John wouldn't be able to edit or disspell them.

"I'm sorry I have to do this," he said, flicking his hands open and casting glowing white sentences to wrap around John's arms and legs.

The big man's candle fell to the floor and winked out. Fortunately, the white glow from Nicodemus's spells and the moonlight pouring through the windows provided sufficient light.

In an attempt to edit the spells binding his arms, John cast a green sentence from his chin. Nicodemus caught and destroyed it with a disspell. John tried twice more, spitting out the spells like angry words. Even so, he was too slow. Nicodemus censored each sentence with a finger-flicked disspell.

Seeming to realize that he could not compete with Nicodemus magically, John began to flex his massive arms. Two of the binding spells snapped. But even as the big man broke a third line, Nicodemus sent ten more glowing-white sentences, and then ten more.

John made one last, heroic tug, which made him start to fall over. Nicodemus rushed over and grabbed the big man's arm in time to set him down gently.

John stopped struggling. He was bound as surely as if he were in chains.

"I'm sorry to do this, John," Nicodemus said. "I'll untie you when you're calmer. But you must understand that we are in danger. Unless we take the Drum Tower boys away, they may be hurt."

John was desperately shaking his head.

"I'm going to wake the boys now," Nicodemus said. "I'll come back, and we'll get you ready to go too. All right?" He moved for the door.

Simple John made a sound then, a faint rumbling, as if a beehive were humming in his expansive chest. "Nnnn . . . no . . . nnn," he growled. "Nnnn . . . nnn . . . Nico no."

"John, you said something different!"

"Nnnnn . . . Nnnnico not go."

Nicodemus shook his head. "I need to step out quickly. I'll be right back. Don't worry."

John flinched. "Sstsss . . . strange man tells Simple John not let Nico go."

Nicodemus frowned. "Have you been talking to the foreign spellwrights?"

"No! Long before Simple John comes to . . . comes to here, Typhon tells Simple John not to let Nico go."

"Typhon?" Nicodemus asked. "Do you mean typhoon? A storm talked to you?"

John had to work his lips to speak. "Typhon . . . Typhoneus, red hair, shiny black skin . . . old, old, old."

Nicodemus studied John. "I don't know what you're talking about, and I don't know how it is you can say all these different things now. But John, we must hurry!"

Tears ran down the big man's face and caught on his throat's stubble. "Yes!" he suddenly said. "I will help. But I need . . . need to get the big parchments."

"If I release you, you'll gather your belongings so we can go? You won't keep me from waking the boys?"

"Won't," John said, "block door."

Satisfied, Nicodemus pulled his spells into his hands. He could always cast them out again.

John struggled to his feet and lumbered into his room. Meanwhile, Nicodemus retrieved his bedsheet-turned-satchel.

A moment later, the large man reappeared holding two parchments.

"John, how can you say all these things when no one has heard you say anything but your name, 'no,' and 'splattering splud'?"

"Splattering splud," John echoed forlornly. "Long before, Simple John was the son of a tailor in Trilli . . . Trillinon. But John was stupid so father says get out. Simple John lived on streets for years before Typhon comes. Typhon says he make Simple John unstupid. He can fix all brokenpeople. But says that depends on . . . Nico. He says Simple John must look after Nico and make sure he doesn't leave south place . . . here. Typhon brings Simple John here. Tells me to say only three things. Typhon teaches me big alphabets and tells me to watch Nico. Typhon comes back with emerald every four years to visit Nico when he's sleeping. And he says to use these"—he held up the parchments—"if Nico tries to go."

"Emerald?" Nicodemus exclaimed. "John, what are you talking about? You know that someone came to watch me sleep? Did he steal my ability to spell?"

Rather than answer, John reached into his parchment and pulled out a spell that Nicodemus had heard about but never seen.

Written in silvery Magnus, its pumpkin-sized, two-part body resembled that of a spider, but its hundred multi-jointed legs were nothing like the relative tameness of arachnid appendages. These horrific limbs were twice as long as a man was tall and covered with sharp stony barbs. They rasped their tarsals across the floor.

It was a spell, Nicodemus knew, that had been written during the Dialect Wars, when the Numinous Order had entangled itself in the fall of the Neosolar Empire. It was a time when wizard fought wizard, when new magical languages and societies formed, when deceit and bloodspells killed thousands. And on the day the fighting ceased and the new magical societies agreed never to make war again, the aracknus spell—one of which John now held—was forbidden.

Judging from his eyes, Simple John had had no idea what he was about to pull from the parchment. When the bloodspell bloomed in the big man's hand, he cried out and dropped the construct. With a whirl of legs, the bloodspell shot toward Nicodemus faster than an uncoiling snake.

Nicodemus dropped his satchel and instinctively cast the white spells he had previous used to bind Simple John. But a long leg flicked out and snapped the sentences like threads. And then the bloodspell was on him, gripping him with tens of its horrific legs, lifting him up. A sticky Magnus rope emerged from its abdomen.

Like a spider wrapping its victim in silk, the aracknus spell spun Nicodemus around with its claws. Within moments, all but his head and left arm were enclosed in a cocoon.

The bloodspell scampered up the wall onto the ceiling. After reaching down, it hoisted Nicodemus into the air and, with a second length of sticky rope, bound the cocoon to a rafter.

Then the bloodspell spread itself out, its hundred legs securing its grip: a nightmare on the ceiling. Below, Nicodemus swung helplessly imprisoned.

All the while Simple John yelled: "Uh'AAaaa, Uh'AAaaaaa." Tears returned to his eyes and he shifted his large feet. "Uh'Aaaaa." But when he saw Nicodemus hanging upside down and unhurt, he calmed.

Nicodemus was shocked to find himself still alive. "John, what have you done?" he asked with as much calm as he could muster. "Where did you get this construct? This is dangerous. Call the spell back into its parchment."

John shook his head. "Typhon said Nico no go. Said use parchments to stop Nico until Typhon comes or until Typhon sends Fellwroth. Fellwroth is red-eyes-man. Typhon visit with emerald to watch Nico sleep every four autumns. This should be an autumn when Typhon comes to watch Nico sleep. And Typhon promised he'd come when I used big parchments. And if Typhon can't come, he send Fellwroth of the red eyes."

"John, you're not making sense."

John shook his head. "Typhon said Nico no go. He needs to watch Nico sleep every four years. Touches the scar with the emerald. Typhon said he would come, but there must be something stopping him. It's Fellwroth red-eyes-man that's coming, then. Typhon says use parchments to stop Nico until Fellwroth comes."

"John," Nicodemus cried, "you don't know what you're talking about! John, help me!"

The big man shook his head. "Red beard, black shiny skin, that's Typhoneus . . . says also put this"—he held up the other parchment—"until he sends Fellwroth of the red eyes. He says he fix us; he makes Nico not go." With that John reached into the second parchment and pulled out a spell.

At first, only golden Numinous runes could be seen, but then the spell congealed into a brown and green construct. The thing was as large as a man's head. Its fat, mucus-covered body resembled a toad with its stomach torn out. Its bulging eyes shone with animal greed. A foot-long tongue flopped from its toothless mouth. Nicodemus yelled in wordless terror.

John was yelling too, but he did not let go of the spell. "Nico not cry. Simple John has to." He grabbed Nicodemus's free arm to stop him from struggling and held out the slimy text. Like an infant searching for a nipple, the construct reached for Nicodemus's head.

Nicodemus jerked and twisted his neck, but to no avail. The creature slid its cold hind legs around his throat and dug the tiny claws of its forelegs into his scalp. The spell's soft underbelly spread itself across his head like a gruesome hat.

"John!" Nicodemus exclaimed hoarsely. "This is a censorship spell! Get it off me! John, please!"

With a gurgling burp, the toadlike text converted its tongue back into Numinous runes and plunged it into Nicodemus's head, censoring two common language sentences he had been writing. The glowing white runes stiffened and fell from his shoulder to shatter on the floor. "John! Get it off me!" Nicodemus shouted, struggling to free his arm from the big man's grip. "Get it off me!"

"Shhhhh," Simple John pleaded. He patted Nicodemus's arm. "No cry, Nico. Man will fix brokenpeople. Typhon said bad men and monsters will try to get to us. But Simple John protect. Typhon teach John spell for throwing." In his right hand John held a leadshot spell. It was a simple attack spell—a dense ball of common language that weighed no more than a cork when cast, but once free of the caster's body it took on the mass of a large lead shot. "Nico not cry," John cooed, and squeezed his arm.

Suddenly the creaking of door hinges filled the room.

John jumped up and cast the leadshot with a powerful overhand throw and a cry of "Bad men!"

Somewhere something heavy smacked into flesh. A body collapsed and John yelled triumphantly.

With his free arm Nicodemus pulled at the censorship spell, but the construct strengthened its grip around his neck.

Frantically looking for anything that could help him, he caught sight of his bed-sheet satchel lying open on the floor. On the white cloth sat the wooden sphere with the root growing around it, Deirdre's Seed of Finding! He stretched out his hand, but the artifact lay just an inch beyond his reach. He threw his arm back and forth to swing the cocoon.

A few steps away, John lumbered out of Nicodemus's view while making confused "ah . . . ah . . ." sounds. When the cocoon swung toward his satchel, Nicodemus managed to touch the Seed of Finding with the tip of his middle finger. But he could not grasp it and swung away.

As if sensing danger, the censorship tightened its grip on his scalp.

When the cocoon swung back, Nicodemus put his every effort into reaching for the druidic artifact; he would have willed his arm to disjoint from his shoulder if it meant he could reach the artifact.

But there was no need: he caught the wooden sphere between his index and middle fingers. Careful not to drop it, he maneuvered the ball so that his thumb and index finger pressed on either side of the artifact. By pinching hard, he broke the root.

The wooden sphere fell onto the bed sheet and began to change shape. Part of the artifact melted into a puddle of liquefied wood.

Simple John made a monotone wail. "Uh'Aaaaa . . . Uh'Aaaaa!" It was a cry that sounded out not only his great suffering and humanity but also his retardation. "Uh'Aaaaa!"

Nicodemus was so intent upon retrieving the Seed that he barely heard the cries. The magical artifact now lay on the bed sheet even farther away than it had been. He flung his arm back and forth to swing the cocoon, but the Seed was too far away.

Simple John's wail subsided to a moan. When Nicodemus swung in the right direction, he grabbed a corner of the bed sheet. As the cocoon swung away, he dragged the sheet with him. Judging from the footfalls, Simple John was walking toward him. The cocoon swung back, and just as John grabbed his arm, Nicodemus snatched the Seed.

The instant Nicodemus's fingers touched the artifact, the puddle of what seemed to be liquid wood leaped up to cover the back of his hand with a barklike skin.

The large man was still moaning, but between breaths he muttered to himself. Nicodemus made out snatches of lucid speech: "Typhon said bad men and monsters . . . stop bad men . . . wrong, wrong . . . Simple John was stupid and got it wrong . . . but not again . . . until red-eyes-man comes to fix . . . Fellwroth . . . Fellwroth of the red eyes . . . and monsters." He squatted next to Nicodemus.

"John," Nicodemus croaked, "you need to remove this censorship. It will censor magic out of my mind forever."

But Simple John was not listening. He was rocking back and forth, repeating the words "bad men and monsters." Nicodemus tried twice more to get the big man's attention, but it was no use.

Worse, Nicodemus was having difficulty thinking clearly with the censorship spell locked around his mind. His eyelids became heavy. He fought to stay awake. His life depended on holding on to the Seed of Finding. Time passed; Nicodemus couldn't tell how much.

Then a door crashed open. Light spilled in from the stairwell. "Bad men and monsters!" John yelled, and hurled a leadshot spell toward the door. In doing so, his thigh hit the cocoon and sent Nicodemus swinging.

A shrill voice rang out. For a moment, everything was spinning blackness. Then Nicodemus glimpsed Deirdre brandishing a greatsword above her head. Bellowing, Simple John charged at her. But then the cocoon swung away and Nicodemus saw only darkness.

When he swung back, Nicodemus beheld something that made him think he was hallucinating. A brown bear with glowing white claws and green eyes stood before Deirdre. John lunged at the animal. But the bear swatted the man aside with a paw swipe.

Nicodemus's view swung up to the ceiling. He cried out.

The aracknus spell was descending like a nightmare.

Nicodemus turned away into darkness. The bear bellowed as the bloodspell's razor legs rasped across the stone.

Nicodemus swung back and saw the bear slashing its claws at the bloodspell's legs. There was a flash. Something unseen knocked the aracknus into a shadow.

There came a sickening crunch and then endless seconds with only heavy footsteps sounding in the dark. Abruptly, Nicodemus's world stopped swinging. The bear's tremendous muzzle probed his face, periodically sucking in voluminous sniffs.

Something about the animal was wrong, but Nicodemus couldn't tell what it was for long, confusing moments. Then he realized that the bear's face was made not of flesh and fur, but of wood.

Its black nose was a carved nub of jet; its snout, oak panels engraved with shifting runes. Its glowing eyes were lacquered green buttons, and its spiky brown fur was a thick coat of splinters.

"Will disspelling the construct on your head harm you?" The gruff male voice seemed to come from everywhere at once.

Nicodemus croaked, "No."

The bear's gleaming claws flashed before his face, and the censorship spell fell to the floor with a gurgling scream.

Nicodemus gasped. It was as if someone had opened the top of his head and poured in a bucket of ice water. His mind could breathe again.

Suddenly Nicodemus was on his back, looking up at Deirdre and her companion, Kyran.

The male druid had unbuttoned his white sleeves, but Deirdre had not. The cocoon and bear had disappeared.

"Are you all right?" Kyran asked.

Nicodemus tried to speak but everything hurt.

Kyran spoke. "Did the construct poison you?"

When he could not answer, Kyran reached down and laid a hand on his throat. Heat flushed across Nicodemus's body. Suddenly his every inch sang with vitality.

Kyran removed his hand and the warmth subsided. "He'll be fine." He pulled Nicodemus to his feet. Deirdre grabbed his arm to hold him steady. An ancient greatsword, nearly as tall as she, was strapped to her back.

Dazed, Nicodemus looked around. "I can't . . . I don't understand . . ." He tried to take a step toward his bedroom but the floorboards felt pliable, as if his boots were sinking into them.

Deirdre tightened her grip on his arm. "Nicodemus, forgive us," she whispered. "We thought the sentinels were guarding you. So we slept. We came as fast as we could."

"So the giant was a conspirator?" Kyran said from behind them. "I didn't expect that."

The words hit Nicodemus like a hammer. John! With a few lurching steps, he turned around to see Kyran looking down on his friend's body. "Dead?" was all he could say.

"No," Kyran said. "I've a stun spell around his head. It's a dangerous text, might damage his ability to spellwrite. And it's odd; some kind of spell was already around the man's mind. It was written in a strange language. Now my stun spell seems to have removed it."

Nicodemus exhaled in relief. "Someone took advantage of him. Someone he kept calling Typhon or Fellwroth. The spell you dislodged must have been cast by Typhon or Fellwroth. John wasn't a conspirator. He didn't mean to endanger me."

Kyran's expression softened. "I wasn't talking about what he did to you. I didn't see you until after I disspelled the spider."

"Then . . ." Nicodemus asked, "what . . ." He saw the other body.

Deirdre tried to turn him away. "This," she whispered, "is an evil night."

As she moved, Deirdre drew her moonshadow away from the second body. Nicodemus could now clearly see the side of Devin's face that had not been crushed by Simple John's spell.

CHAPTER Twenty-eight

Air was still flowing into Nicodemus's lungs, blood still coursing through his heart. But as he stared at Devin's body, his own body no longer seemed connected to his senses.

He touched his fingers to his lips without feeling his fingers touching his lips. He closed his eyes without seeing the blackness of his eyelids; the image of Devin's body remained.

Deirdre led him to a nearby chair. "Tell me what happened," she said, sitting him down.

Numbly Nicodemus recounted how Shannon had discovered that a golem was killing cacographic boys and how John had tried to stop him from evacuating the Drum Tower.

"But, I don't . . . why . . ." Nicodemus stammered when finished. "I don't understand." He grabbed the druid's arm. "Tell me how to understand."

She squeezed his hand. "The name Fellwroth is a mystery to me. But Typhon, or Typhoneus, was a powerful demon of the ancient world. He commanded the Pandemonium and was second only to Los himself. The word 'typhoon' is derived from his name. He created the Maelstrom that scattered the human ships during the Exodus."

Kyran appeared at Deirdre's shoulder. "We must hurry," he said, and handed her the Seed of Finding. "I've rewritten its texts." An invisibility subtext was wrapping around the druid's legs.

Deirdre took the Seed and stuffed it into Nicodemus's belt-purse. "If anything separates us, pull the root from the artifact as you did before. Do you understand?"

Nicodemus nodded but then shook his head. "But about Typhon . . . I don't . . . I mean John can't have encountered a demon; that would mean that a demon has crossed the ocean."

Deirdre nodded solemnly. "That is exactly what it means. Nicodemus, the power of the Disjunction is growing. Soon the Pandemonium will cross as well. That must be the truth. Think on it: what spell other than demonic godspell could have warped John's mind so?"

From the shadows, a now invisible Kyran whispered, "Deirdre, hurry!"

Nicodemus was breathing hard. An overwhelming desire to make sense of things filled his brain. If he could only understand, he might begin to feel again.

"So," he said, determined not to be put off by Kyran, "a demon used a godspell to distort John's mind and make his disability worse?" He shuddered. "Yes, that must be it. John had only a three-phrase spoken vocabulary but could spellwrite simple texts in the common languages. He even learned to see Numinous and Magnus. I've never heard of another cacographer like that. Someone distorted his mind so that it would display all the stereotypical traits of retardation."

Kyran spoke quickly. "A curse must have been infesting the poor man's mind, forcing him to keep you here in Starhaven. It seems my stun text has removed that curse. But none of this changes the fact that we must hurry."

Nicodemus shook his head. "John said that every four years the demon would visit me when I was sleeping. But why?"

Deirdre answered. "The demon must have made an incomplete theft of your ability to spell. For some reason he needs to renew the curse every four years."

Nicodemus's eyes widened. "The golem told Shannon that his master was replenishing an emerald."

A sudden realization made him pause. "The demon must have used Magistra Finn and John to reach me when I was sleeping. The golem knew about Magistra Finn and tried to recruit her. But the golem must not have known about John."

Abruptly emotion returned to Nicodemus in the form of stomach-twisting fear. "John said Typhon was accompanied by a 'red-eyes-man' named Fellwroth. That must be the golem's author."

"And that is why we must hurry," Deirdre explained, pulling Nicodemus to his feet. "The demon must have tied some summoning magic to the spider creature. You said John was expecting this Fellwroth to come in response to the parchments. We must not be here when the creature arrives."

"You're right; we must flee." Nicodemus pressed his hands to his mouth. "We have to—" He stopped.

Something was wrong.

"Deirdre, why didn't you unbutton your sleeves for spellwriting?" he asked.

"The magic I use is different! No time to explain. Now, tell me, what do you need to bring?"

"The Index! I left it on the—" Nicodemus's voice died as he turned toward the door and saw Devin's body. "Devin," he whispered.

Deirdre took his arm and turned him away. "Not now, Nicodemus. You can't mourn now. Listen to me. We must get you down to Gray's Crossing; there you'll have my goddess's protection. Then we can mourn, but now we must fly."

"No," he said, "we can't, not without the other Drum Tower boys. They're going with us. The golem is killing the male cacographers one by one. He doesn't know that I'm the one he wants."

"I didn't know," a soft, croaking voice said.

Deirdre and Nicodemus turned. Standing in the door frame was a hunched figure draped in white.

The stranger spoke again. "But I do now."

DEIRDRE PULLED NICODEMUS behind her and drew her massive greatsword with one hand.

"There is no need for dramatics," the creature sneered. "I can't stay long."

In the moonlight, Nicodemus could see little of the creature other than the white cloth covering his body. When he spoke, the air beneath his hood had become blurry.

Suddenly remembering the spell Shannon had written against the fiend, Nicodemus looked for his satchel. He wasn't confident enough to extemporize Shannon's new spell. But if he had the Index, he could refresh his knowledge of it. Maybe then he could attempt the spell.

But the book lay sprawled out on the other side of the common room, not seven feet from the golem.

"The promised arrival of Fellwroth," Deirdre growled, raising her sword. "Villain, are you a lesser demon, or simply Typhon's human lapdog?"

The creature laughed softly. "You know what I am, and you know I slew Typhoneus in your land more than a year ago. So let's forgo the blandishments and move on to the exchange. I cannot take the boy now. I was running to that miserable little village. This pathetic golem was all I had available back here. I should have expected Typhon to plant some kind of guard on the boy." The white robes shifted; the figure seemed to look around. "Who was it? The giant oaf or this broken-faced hussy?"

"I'll rip your heart out!" Nicodemus snarled and stepped forward.

But Deirdre caught his hand. "Nicodemus, no," she hissed. "If you have the chance, run."

The golem wheezed a laugh. "Such courage, Nicodemus. It is good to finally learn your name." The air below his pale hood again became blurry as if filled with a fine powder. He turned to Deirdre. "Does this mean you are refusing the exchange? It's hard to imagine that you would be so stupid."

"You make no sense, Fellwroth. The last time we met, I cleaved your head off. I'd be happy to do the same again."

Nicodemus noticed the moonlight shifting along the back wall. Kyran! The subtextualized druid was sneaking up on the golem.

The creature laughed. "You have more audacity than brains, girl. Think about what you are doing. I have your rock, and with this dead hussy lying here"—he nodded to Devin's body—"you can't stay in Starhaven. The sentinels won't hesitate to censor and bind you. They'll leave you in a prison under some tower; reaching you and the boy then would be easier than picking apples."

The golem drew a wheezing breath. "And if you venture outside of Starhaven's walls, where I can spellwrite, you'll face my full strength. You are trapped, so don't be a fool. Give me the boy, and you will be rewarded."

Deirdre shook her head. "Fellwroth, you are in no position to buy me. You should be more worried about your neck. You can't use your magic here."

"Fool," the golem snapped. "You think I'm afraid of your blade or your man creeping behind me." He laughed. "You won't get—"

"Now!" Deirdre screamed as she sprung forward.

Kyran leaped from the shadows, bellowing a wordless war cry.

Deirdre reached the monster first. She slashed downward with her sword, landed a strike to the golem's shoulder, and tore his white garment from chest to floor. Kyran stabbed something unseen into the golem's back.

The white cloth collapsed as if filled with air.

Nicodemus dashed for the Index. But it was over before he picked the book off the ground.

Both druids were waving their hands before their faces and coughing. The air around them was gray.

"He knew he was safe all along," Kyran managed to say between coughs. "With a body made of this, he could disengage almost instantly."

Nicodemus stepped closer. The druids were enveloped by a thick cloud of dust.

"We've an hour," Kyran said, "maybe less before the author can form a more substantial body. We must go!"

"What of the other cacographers?" Nicodemus asked, hugging the Index closer to his chest.

"They're safe," Deirdre replied. "The monster now knows you're the one he wants. Quickly now, our lives and the fate of the Disjunction may depend on it. Tell me why the sentinels aren't guarding the Drum Tower. Tell me everything."

Nicodemus opened his mouth but did not speak. Fear had compelled him to tell Deirdre of the golem and of John's behavior. He had been too shocked to be suspicious. But now that his wits were returning, he began to wonder how much he should trust the druids.

Deirdre took his hand. "Nicodemus, you are alive only because I gave you the Seed of Finding and because we came to your aid. You must trust us."

Nicodemus shook his head. "I don't know that—"

Kyran spoke. "Nicodemus, the enemy knows who you are and is coming for you. And the monster was right when he said we cannot remain in Starhaven. The sentinels will suspect us of murdering your friend." He nodded toward Devin's body. "We're not safe here. Nor can you flee on your own. Outside Starhaven the creature will be powerful beyond your imagining. Your only hope is to come to our goddess's ark in Gray's Crossing. Only she can protect you."

The druid was right. Nicodemus had no choice but to trust them. "We're taking John," he said.

Deirdre shook her head. "He'll slow us down."

"No," he said. "We must take him. The sentinels will think he killed Devin. Leaving him here would be a death sentence."

"Nicodemus," Deirdre said carefully, "the man was cursed by a demon. We don't know if we can trust him."

"He's coming."

Kyran looked at Deirdre. "I could subdue the boy."

"Try it!" Nicodemus replied hotly. "You could censor me, bind me, maybe even knock me unconscious. But you'll never sneak my body through the front gates. Especially at this hour of the night. The guards will search everything."

Deirdre's mouth flattened. "You know another way out of Starhaven?"

"Only if we bring John with us."

Deirdre looked him up and down and then laughed dryly. "Ky, rouse the big man. Now, Nicodemus, tell me why the sentinels stopped guarding you. Tell me everything about our enemy."

As Kyran worked some unknown language over John, Nicodemus told Deirdre about his strange nightmares, about Shannon's arrest, about the Index, and about the attack spell Shannon had written against the golem.

As Kyran finished, Simple John woke with a low moan. In a few moments Kyran had him on his feet. The stun spell seemed to have fogged the big man's memory. He was confused and couldn't seem to recall where he was. However, he did respond to Nicodemus's voice.

Together, the four of them hurried out of the common room and into the stairwell. Nicodemus held the Index in one hand and John's hand in the other.

"Where are we going?" Kyran asked as they hurried down the steps.

"To the Sataal Landing and the compluvium," Nicodemus called back. "We should fetch the other druids. They could help protect us."

"The other druids in Starhaven can't be trusted," Kyran protested.

"Just as there are wizardly factions, there are druidic factions," Deirdre added behind him. "The druids we can trust are down in Gray's Crossing guarding our goddess's ark."

On the ground floor, Kyran pushed open the door and led them into the Stone Court. Above them shone the brilliant but small blue moon.

The party hurried through the standing stones and into a wide arcade that would take them eastward out of Starhaven's Imperial Quarter and into the Chthonic Quarter. Occasionally John made confused, anxious sounds. He seemed to have trouble focusing his eyes. But Nicodemus kept him calm with a few words and the reassuring pressure of his hand.

A shudder ran through Nicodemus as he thought about what the demon had done to John. He wondered if the big man would remember killing Devin.

"Nicodemus," Kyran said. "If there is trouble, you must stay behind Deirdre and me. And if you have the chance to escape, do so."

Thinking back to how quickly the druids had dealt with the bloodspells, Nicodemus nodded. He asked, "Kyran, back in my common room, when you fought the aracknus spell, there was a strange bear." A cold autumn breeze set Nicodemus's black hair fluttering.

Kyran chuckled. "Didn't you recognize me?"

"But that's impossible. Only a godspell could—"

Kyran laughed. The druid's long, blond hair was also stirring in the breeze. "It wasn't truly a bear but a partial construction, made of the druidic languages and oak. It was wrapped around my body like magical armor."

Nicodemus raised his brows. That explained the bear's wooden face and coat of splinters. "But where did you find oak in Starhaven?"

"I'm going to miss that walking staff," the druid said with a sigh and a nod at his limp.

"You had already written a spell on the staff? But how can your languages animate wood? It should be impossible to—"

Kyran cut him off. "The druidic languages come to us from the ancients. Our languages connect to living tissue—especially that of trees—in a way that is difficult to explain." He smiled. "Besides, Nicodemus, there is more possible with language than can be imagined within your rules of spelling."

CHAPTER

Twenty-nine

Sinking fast but still gloriously bright, the nearly full blue moon sat just above the Pinnacle Mountains. The white moon, in the identical phase as her smaller blue sister, hung high in the western sky.

From their different angles, the moons filled the compluvium with half-shadows of ivory and lapis. Nicodemus—still holding the Index in one hand and Simple John's hand in the other—led the druids across the wall overlooking the compluvium. "The way to the Fool's Ladder is just down that stairwell." He motioned across the wall.

Kyran took the lead.

Far below them glistened the impluvium. The aquatic gargoyles that operated the reservoir's valves were still at work despite the hour. Their movement slowly churned the water, transforming its surface into a coruscation of reflected moonlight.

Deirdre spoke. "That hawk-headed construct with the four arms, the one we passed to get into this place, if it obeys your commands, why didn't you have it follow us?"

"So it can guard our backs," Nicodemus replied, giving John's hand an encouraging squeeze. "There are only two ways into the compluvium."

Together the party hurried down the spiral stairs to the tunnel Shannon had opened. The image of Shannon bound and censored in a sentinel prison haunted Nicodemus as they sloshed through the tunnel to the other side.

When they emerged onto a walkway on Starhaven's easternmost wall, John made a few soft noises. On the landing before the Spindle Bridge stood the second hawk-headed gargoyle. Behind it, the Spindle stretched out through the air to the mountainside. Far below them swayed the dark boughs of the forest.

"I am Nicodemus Weal," Nicodemus told the four-armed gargoyle. "You are to obey my commands and the commands of my companions in white." He nodded to the druids. "We must use the Fool's Ladder."

The construct tilted its head first to one side and then to the other. Its multi-jointed wings snapped open. They stretched nearly fifteen feet in either direction, presenting a solid flank of stone feathers.

With four heavy steps, the gargoyle plodded away from the bridge. The thing's crashing footfalls sent rattling echoes running down the Spindle Bridge.

Starhaven's easternmost wall had two massive iron doors that opened onto the landing. The giant gargoyle took a defensive stance facing the doors. "Could Fellwroth have formed another golem yet?" Nicodemus asked, turning to the druids.

Kyran studied the massive gargoyle. "It depends on what earth the monster is using. He could have formed a clay body long ago."

Deirdre moved to stand next to Kyran. Beside her, John squatted down and pressed his hands against his face; it seemed his wits had not yet recovered from Kyran's stun spell. Nicodemus wondered what the big man would be like now that the demonic curse had been dislodged from his mind.

A silvery glow drew Nicodemus's eyes back to the bridge. Beside the railing now stood a Magnus spell in the shape of a straight-backed chair. Nicodemus walked over to inspect the text. Five feet in height and three in width, the thing could comfortably seat even John's girth.

Curious as to how the spell would carry them to the ground, Nicodemus peered over the bridge's railing. "Fiery blood!" he swore.

A foot below him—its stomach growing directly into the bridge's stones—was half a gargoyle, as if someone had bisected the construct and fused the abdomen to the bridge.

The gargoyle wrinkled its porcine snout and stared at Nicodemus with tiny black eyes. Despite its bestial face, the spell's muscular torso was the same shape as a man's. "One at a time," it creaked.

Just behind the construct grew its exact twin. Another such grew behind it, and so on all the way down to the forest.

Nicodemus blinked. "Do we just sit in the chair?" he asked. "You hand it down among yourselves to the ground?"

The pig-faced thing nodded. "Sit down and hold on."

When Nicodemus straightened and looked back, he found the two druids looking at him. "Is the ladder over the side?" Deirdre asked.

"No, we sit in this silver chair; there's a train of gargoyles back there. They'll hand it down."

"Silver chair?" Kyran repeated.

Nicodemus had forgotten. "You can't see it because it's written in Magnus. I'll show you where to sit."

There followed a brief argument about the order in which they should descend.

As the druids talked, Nicodemus glanced at the iron doors that led onto the Spindle Bridge's landing. It was good to see the hawk-headed gargoyle was also watching the doors.

In the end, Deirdre insisted that she go down first. Nicodemus showed her where to sit and where to hold on. The cold autumn breeze smelled of pine resin.

"Are you sure I'm secure?" she asked nervously. "I don't like holding on to something I can't see. How do you know I won't fall when—" She yelped as the chair tipped backward and slowly sank over the bridge.

Nicodemus ran to the railing and anxiously watched as the muscular gargoyle handed the silver chair down to its neighbor. Deirdre had shut her eyes and was squeezing the chair arms with white-knuckled determination. The next gargoyle took the chair and handed it down again.

Kyran appeared at Nicodemus's side and produced a single slow laugh. "She hates high places. But she's got steel in her soul. Anyone else that scared of heights would be shrieking." He paused. "How old are you, boy?"

Nicodemus looked over, but the man was staring down at Deirdre's descent. "Twenty-six on Midwinter's Day."

"Just a weanling. Ever been in love?"

Nicodemus thought of Amy Hern and the things they had said to each other and what little it had come to. "I hope there's more to it than what I've known."

Kyran produced another humorless laugh. "A good answer."

Nicodemus stood in awkward silence as Deirdre finished the descent. The gargoyles brought the chair up faster than they had handed it down.

John was next. Surprisingly, when Nicodemus directed him to sit in the chair, the big man calmly obeyed. "Why isn't he more distressed?" Nicodemus asked.

Kyran sighed. "It was the stun spell. He can't remember anything now. It should wear off in a few hours."

"I'm worried he might get confused halfway down. Is there any spell you can—"

His voice died when Kyran tore a button from his sleeve and pressed it to John's chest. A globe of verdant light bloomed from the druid's hand and then condensed into a many-tendriled vine.

"Wondrous spell!" Nicodemus whispered as synaesthetic warmth flushed across his face.

The leafy vine spread across Simple John, binding his arms to the chair's arms, his legs to the chair's legs. With dazed calmness, the big man watched the magical plant grow until he was completely entwined. At that point, the vine produced several pendulous bunches of blue wisteria blossoms.

"Flowers," the big man said with difficulty.

Nicodemus squinted at Kyran's sleeve. "Those aren't buttons, are they?"

The druid shook his head. "Seeds augmented with druidic texts."

Just then the chair tipped over the railing. John yelled and began to squirm, but Nicodemus called out reassurance and the big man stopped struggling.

As before, the gargoyles handed the Magnus chair down at a controlled pace. "Deirdre will cut him free when he reaches the bottom," Kyran explained.

The uncomfortable silence returned as the two men watched the chair carry John down to the forest. When the gargoyles returned the chair, relief washed over Nicodemus. He told Kyran how to sit in it.

"I'll see you on the ground," the druid said as the spell tipped over the railing and began to descend.

Nicodemus nodded and was about to reply when the world erupted into a blaze of silver light. A roar like that of a landslide filled the night.

Nicodemus spun around in time to see the gargoyle's right wing disintegrate into a roiling Magnus effulgence.

"NICODEMUS!" KYRAN CALLED from beyond the bridge.

Nicodemus looked down and saw the druid on the Magnus chair, already seven feet below. Green bolts of light crackling around his hands, he pulled another seed-button from his sleeve.

Suddenly, a shrill scream drowned out all other sound.

Nicodemus spun around to see the giant gargoyle turning so it could swing its remaining wing forward with deadly force. Before the gargoyle stood a white-robed figure.

Fellwroth in a new golem!

A hood covered the monster's face but his ashen hands were bare and holding a thick spellbook.

As the stone wing whistled forward, Fellwroth calmly peeled a Magnus spell from the book. With a wrist flick, the monster cast the spell onto the ground. It bloomed into a row of thick, silvery poles. The gargoyle's wing struck the shafts with an ear-grating chirp.

Fellwroth ran forward, pulling a whiplike Numinous disspell from the spellbook. With a screech, the gargoyle swung its two right arms. Fellwroth dodged under the blows and flicked out his golden whip. The long, luminous sentences wrapped around the gargoyle's lower right bicep, cutting deep into the construct's Magnus skeleton.

With a backhand jerk, Fellwroth pulled the whip taut. The force ripped the Magnus sentences from the gargoyle's arm and tore them into frayed ends.

Now deprived of its linguistic skeleton, the gargoyle's lower arm froze into immobile stone.

With a scream, the hawk-headed construct struck out with both its left arms. Fellwroth ducked again, but this time the gargoyle's lower fist struck his shoulder.

With a resounding clang, the blow sent Fellwroth skidding across the landing. He slid across the stones, a trail of white sparks spraying behind.

"Celestial Canon!" Nicodemus swore. "It's a golem made of metal."

Remembering the Index, Nicodemus opened it and planted his hand on a page. Instantaneously the book renewed his knowledge of the spell Shannon had written to trap Fellwroth's spirit within the golem.

With a thundering rumble, the giant gargoyle charged. But the golem quickly regained his feet and rewrote his Numinous whip.

Nicodemus started forging Shannon's spell along his left forearm. "No!" a voice cried from behind.

He turned to see Kyran hoisting himself over the railing. The druid must have created some ropelike spell and hauled himself back up. "We don't fight," Kyran growled. "We run!"

There was a sudden crash. Nicodemus looked back. With its three good arms, the gargoyle had grabbed hold of Fellwroth and hoisted the monster over its head. With a scream, the gargoyle hurled its foe against the wall.

The metal golem crashed into the stones with enough force to crack two of them.

"Now! Run!" Kyran commanded, pulling Nicodemus along the landing and back into the tunnel. They sprinted through the darkness to the compluvium.

Kyran stopped at the stairwell and looked up at the wall that could lead them back to Starhaven proper. Then he looked out into the compluvium's myriad gables, gutters, and shadows. "What kind of body?" he asked.

"Metal," Nicodemus panted.

"It will last too long. We can't hide out there in the compluvium. So we run back to the wizards and search for another way down to Gray's Crossing."

Before Nicodemus could agree, the other man turned and sprinted up the stairwell, his blond hair glinting in the double moonlight. Nicodemus followed.

They were halfway up the stairs when a golden flash made Nicodemus look downward. Fellwroth was backing out of the tunnel. The monster was hurling curses back the way he had come. An avian screech echoed out of the tunnel; the war-weight gargoyle wasn't far behind.

Nicodemus and Kyran topped the stairs and dashed along the wall. They had to reach the steps down to the Sataal Landing.

Suddenly the moonlight ahead of them shivered as if it were full of hot air. A horrible idea flashed through Nicodemus's mind. "Kyran, wait!" he called, skidding to a stop. The druid ignored him. Nicodemus peered over the wall's far side. "Kyran, it's a trap!"

The druid stopped. "What?"

Nicodemus pointed over the wall. Below him stood the Sataal Landing's last cloister and the steep stairs nestled between the wall and the Karkin Tower. "The second war-weight gargoyle should be down there. But there's only a pile of rubble. Fellwroth already deconstructed it. And that"—he pointed ahead to the shimmering patch of moonlight—"is a subtextualized spell. A large one. Likely a stasis trap. Fellwroth drove us up here so we'd run into that spell!"

"I see nothing. Can you glean the sentences?"

Behind them the remaining gargoyle screamed.

"No," Nicodemus said. "I can only glean its presence."

"I'll try to disspell or spring it," Kyran said. Synaesthetic warmth flushed across Nicodemus's cheeks as the older man began to spellwrite in a druidic language.

But an explosion made both men turn. Fellwroth had gained the wall and was running toward them. The hawk-headed gargoyle was limping behind. Both its wings were now shattered, and its lower right and upper left arms were frozen.

"Stay behind me," Kyran barked as he pushed Nicodemus aside. The druid tore a seed-button from his sleeve and pulled back his arm. From his fist sprang thousands of thorny branches. Blue flames blossomed from their tips.

Bellowing, Kyran cast the spell with an overhand throw. As it flew, the tangle of thorns and fire burned bright enough to dazzle Nicodemus's eyes.

There was a crash and a scream. When Nicodemus's vision returned, he saw that Kyran's spell had struck Fellwroth's side. The resulting blast had burnt a wide hole in the golem's robe. The creature's maggot-white torso was now covered with gashes that exposed its metal flesh.

With panicked determination, Nicodemus returned to writing Shannon's anti-golem spell along his left forearm. Farther down the wall, the hawk-headed gargoyle screeched as it hobbled toward them.

Kyran pulled his arm back, and again fiery branches bloomed from his fist.

But it was too late. Fellwroth had cracked open a spellbook and now flicked out a net of Numinous and Magnus.

The censoring text enveloped Kyran and knocked him onto his back. The burning branch spell rolled out of his hand and lost its fire.

"Kyran!" Nicodemus cried. Fellwroth's luminescent Numinous passages had intertwined about the druid's head, censoring him completely. He began to thrash.

Fellwroth rushed forward. Nicodemus peeled his rendition of Shannon's spell from his forearm and cast it. A comet-like spell shot through the air but splashed against the golem's chest. Nothing happened.

It had misspelled.

Nicodemus cursed. He had failed Magister Shannon. The old man had worked so hard to get him the anti-golem spell and his cacography had made a mess of it.

The golem laughed. "There's nothing you can do, whelp. This body is solid iron."

Nicodemus ground his teeth. He could not reproduce Shannon's spell, but he'd be damned before he gave up.

He extemporized a Magnus lash along his thigh and pulled it free. But with a turn of his hand, Fellwroth cast a Numinous wave that shattered Nicodemus's text into phrases.

Nicodemus began to write a second lash, but the monster's pale hand flicked out and grabbed his throat.

Fellwroth's touch made the keloid on Nicodemus's neck flare up with scalding pain. It felt as if the scars had caught fire.

The world dissolved into blackness.

BEFORE NICODEMUS BLAZED the image of his last nightmare. He was again in the low cavern, staring at a body shrouded in white. "Fellwroth's true body," a boyish voice said.

A small tear-shaped emerald sat in the monster's hands. The voice spoke again. "I dream your dreams; you dream mine."

With shock, Nicodemus recognized the voice as his own childhood voice. It was coming from the emerald.

And then everything changed and Nicodemus was far away. He was in a dark room looking at his father—a tall man with long black hair and olive skin. An infant lay on a table.

"This was how we were separated," his boyhood voice said as Nicodemus's father pressed an emerald against the back of the infant's neck. The child shrieked as white light erupted from the gem and cut into his neck.

When the light died the child was left with an angry keloid scar shaped like a Braid rune marred by an Inconjunct rune.

Nicodemus inhaled sharply. His father had branded him. He had not been born with a keloid as the Halcyon was prophesied to be. He could not be the Halcyon!

"Think no more on that," the emerald voice said. "Think on this." Suddenly Nicodemus was in a strange land surrounded by rolling highlands. It was night and a wide river stretched before him.

"This is how Fellwroth took possession of us," the emerald said.

A giant was standing thigh-deep in the dark water. He had long red hair and skin that shone glossy black like a raven's wing. From John's description, Nicodemus recognized the demon Typhoneus.

Suddenly Fellwroth appeared behind the demon and brandished a blade of white light. Silently, Fellwroth stabbed Typhon in the side—stabbed him again and again until the demon collapsed and transformed into a ball of glowing red language. Fellwroth hacked the red language into bits that floated down the river.

Again everything dissolved into blackness. "Beware the scar," the emerald's voice said. "It will betray you to Fellwroth."

THE VISION DISAPPEARED and Nicodemus was again standing on the wall before the compluvium.

Fellwroth's golem had pulled back his hand as if burned by Nicodemus's skin. The monster's ragged white hood still concealed his eyes, but the thin bloodless lips had parted in shock.

Suddenly Nicodemus understood. "The emerald is the stolen half of my mind," he said. "It's the one sending me these dreams. Sending me dreams of where your true body is, dreams of your crimes. Before I saw the dragon and what you did to Eric. Now I've seen what you did to Typhon."

Fellwroth's lips worked soundlessly.

"You were the demon's slave!" Nicodemus exclaimed.

Fellwroth struck out with his hand and screamed: "I CUT HIM IN THE RIVER!"

Nicodemus jumped back and caught Fellwroth's blow on his shoulder. Pain exploded through his chest, and the world spun round. His back hit the ground.

When he looked up, Fellwroth was standing over him with clenched fists. A golden Numinous spike jutted out from the monster's right hand, a Magnus spike from his left.

"I'll hew your retarded mind in half!" Fellwroth snarled and drew back his right fist.

Suddenly Kyran was above them both. Blood covered the druid's face. Again the magically burning branches were growing from his hands. With a snarl, he grabbed hold of Fellwroth's raised fist.

The branches snaked down the golem's arm. Their flames flared into a blaze that burnt off the golem's sleeve and began to melt his arm into quicksilver.

With a metallic howl, Fellwroth turned and slammed his right fist, and its long Magnus spike, into Kyran's stomach.

Nicodemus cried out and struggled to find his feet.

Blood spread across Kyran's belly, but the druid only grasped Fellwroth's arm more tightly. The blue flames roared louder as the burning branches spread down the creature's shoulder.

The monster's howl became a gasp as he squirmed away from Kyran and fell backward onto the cobblestones.

Somehow Kyran yanked Nicodemus to his feet. "For Deirdre," he grunted, and cast a common language sentence into Nicodemus's shoulder.

The now writhing golem was trying desperately to pull the burning thorny branches from his flesh. His right arm had melted down to a thin, useless stalk.

"Don't be like me, boy." Kyran pulled Nicodemus away. "Be anything: be wild, be saintly, be wicked. Love all or love none, but don't be like me."

Suddenly the war-weight gargoyle was before Nicodemus. "Get him to safety at any cost," Kyran commanded.

Before Nicodemus could protest, the hawk-headed gargoyle grabbed hold of him and—as if he weighed no more than a kitten—hoisted him into the air. Nicodemus clutched the Index to his chest.

An inhuman scream turned Nicodemus's eyes back to see the metal golem. The monster had extinguished the blue flames and was now on his feet and charging. A long Magnus lash glittered in his waxy hands. Kyran moved to meet the creature, blue fire again blazing from his fists.

"Kyran, no!" Nicodemus yelled.

With a vicious strike, Fellwroth brought his Magnus lash around, tearing through Kyran from shoulder to hip.

Nicodemus cried out.

The golem charged forward and raised his Magnus lash to strike at the gargoyle.

But then Nicodemus was in the air, falling at tremendous speed. His stomach clenched.

The hawk-headed gargoyle had leaped from the wall.

Nicodemus had only a glimpse of the impluvium's glassy surface before they splashed into it. The moment the gargoyle's feet hit water, its arms lifted Nicodemus up over its head to reduce the shock of impact. Even so, the crash of water seemed to jar the wits from Nicodemus's mind.

His first lucid thought, ludicrously, was for the Index's safety. He tightened his grip on the book even though the water was surely destroying its pages.

His next thought was of the golem. He opened his eyes and felt the shock of icy water on his eyeballs.

The gargoyle's weight was fast pulling them down into the impluvium's depths. But after craning his neck around, Nicodemus could see a blurry white column of bubbles created as the golem hit the surface.

Suddenly a stone face covered with fish scales loomed before Nicodemus. The aquatic gargoyle's rough hands grabbed hold of Nicodemus's robes and pulled. Then dozens more of the tiny hands set upon him, pulling him somewhere. He fought the urge to scream.

Above him the metal golem was sinking fast, its white cloak billowing in the water.

A high-pitched whine filled the water and abruptly many gargoyle hands were shoving Nicodemus into a dark hole. He fought to escape but there were too many.

They stuffed him into a small, black space. A sheet of metal closed above him and there followed a second whine.

In complete darkness, Nicodemus prepared to die.

But the whine grew louder and then Nicodemus was falling, tumbling, banging against the sides of some long tube. He shouted and felt the cold water fill his mouth. The tube began to bend and he slid along its algae-coated bottom.

Suddenly he fell into a mixture of air and water. Something was roaring like a waterfall.

He splashed down into what seemed to be a waist-deep underground river. His mouth opened and drew in long gulps of air.

He let the powerful current pull him along. Slowly the waterfall's roar faded and he could hear things moving in the darkness above him—small, rustling things that spoke with creaking voices.

And then, without warning, he was outside. Above him shone a crystalline night sky. Around him stood a forest of dark towers. A few bats flitted about in the chilly air. Nearly two hundred feet below stretched the weed-covered gardens and stone walkways of the Chthonic Quarter.

The gargoyles had dropped him into an aqueduct, Nicodemus realized, as he floated into another tunnel. The icy current carried him northwest through several towers and across the high aqueducts until it dropped him into a massive brass cistern in the Spirish Quarter.

Whispering thanks to every deity and gargoyle he knew, Nicodemus pulled himself out of the water and ran.

At first he fled aimlessly. He feared that Fellwroth might have followed him down the aqueduct. But once sure that he had escaped, Nicodemus snuck into an old janitorial closet to catch his breath and dry off.

To his shock, he discovered that the Index was miraculously dry. He turned the codex over again and again, looking for some reason why it had not so much as a damp page.

He found no clue. But as he turned the book over, the thrill of escape faded. The keloid scars on his neck began to burn, and his hands began to shake.

At first he thought only of Kyran's horrible death. But then he remembered the sentence the druid had cast into his shoulder before dying.

He pulled the line free and translated it.

Reading Kyran's final words made him feel numb for a while. Then he thought of Deirdre and then of Devin. He thought of John and of Magister Shannon. He thought of his father, branding his infant self.

When the tears came, he did not try to stop them.

CHAPTER
Thirty

Hugging the Index to his chest, Nicodemus peered around the tapestry he was hiding behind.

He stood at Starhaven's westernmost point, in the main hall of its gatehouse. The academy's entrance lay beyond. Two guards, both women, paced the drawbridge.

Each woman was casting, from her waist, a white sentence that held a spellbook open beside her. This action, called "floating a spellbook," gave each spellwright quick access to her book's prewritten offensive language.

Slinking back behind the tapestry, Nicodemus closed his eyes and envisioned the emerald he had seen in his dreams. The stone was a small, flawless teardrop. At the gem's center glowed a verdant spark. This was the missing part of himself.

He shuddered.

If not for this gem, he wouldn't be cacographic. More important, Kyran and Devin wouldn't be dead.

In his imagination, the gem shone brighter and his determination to recover the missing part of his mind grew. Summoning this mental image was how he had stopped the tears in the janitorial station. It was how he would prevent them now.

He let the emerald's light burn away all his sorrow, all his doubt, all his weakness. He must find a way to regain the emerald, to complete himself.

He felt his belt-purse for Deirdre's Seed of Finding. Once away from the stronghold, he would tear the root from the artifact to let the druid know where he was.

Again glancing from behind the tapestry, Nicodemus inspected the two guards. The younger one had long black hair and a pale face. She was unknown to him. But the elder guard's silver hair and dark face were vaguely familiar. If he remembered correctly, she was one of Starhaven's foremost Numinous authors.

Biting his lip, Nicodemus leaned back into his hiding place. Perhaps he should chance a return to the Fool's Ladder; he was never going to escape

Starhaven through the front gate. To get past these guards he'd have to be invisible.

An idea grew in his mind.

Perhaps he could find an invisibility subtext so simple that he could repair any misspellings the corrupted Index might introduce into it.

He opened the book. At first he could not make sense of what he saw. It seemed to be the chapter of an old treatise, but why it had appeared was a mystery.

> **From *Towards a Uniform Spelling* by Gaius Rufeus**
> Many today argue that tolorence for alternative spellings encurages creativity. I conseed that for many texts there are a few alternative spellings that are not only functional but also superior to the conventional spelling. But the number of these fortunate mistakes is dwarfed by the number of alternative spellings (or we should call them misspellings) that are nonfunctional and, in certin cases, dangerous. If wizards are to survive as useful members of the Neosolar Empire then a standard for . . .

Nicodemus frowned. He had been thinking of subtexts, not spelling. The Index was supposed to provide information on whatever subject he wanted to find. He reached to turn the page but then stopped.

Maybe the Index was correct: he hadn't been thinking about subtexts themselves; he had been wondering if he could manage to rewrite a subtext.

He reread the page. So what if a few misspells worked? He'd known that for years. He couldn't deliberately misspell a subtext; the text might flay his face off.

Irritated, he flipped the page to shut the book up. The sheet he turned to contained a treatise on self-doubt and its effect on spellwriting. "I'm supposed to be reading you," he half-whispered, half-growled.

The book didn't answer.

Nicodemus planted a palm on the page and sent his mind flying up into the book's starry sky of spells.

From the darkness, three comet-like subtexts approached, each presenting an explanation of its function.

The first glowed green. It was a long and common language spell named madide. According to its description, the subtext blurred the image of those who cast it, making them difficult to see or strike. There was also a warning:

> *Note that madide's inverted structure prevents most spellwriters from seeing this subtext; however, a spellwright posessing mastery of the comon langeuge may glean the rune sequenses and hense visualize the subtext.*

That wouldn't do; the guards had certainly mastered the common languages.

The second spell shone Numinous gold. Nicodemus recognized the latere subtext—a favorite of Magister Shannon, who sometimes demonstrated a love of practical jokes rare for a grand wizard. This spell formed a halo that continuously showered light-bending runes on its wearer. Laterecasters became invisible so long as they remained still. Slow movement made the air shimmer; rapid movement revealed glimpses of the caster's legs or arms. More important, not even a grand wizard could glean its presence.

"This subtext is truly wonderful," Master Shannon had once mockingly lectured. "For when one packs a friend's shoes full of snow, one does want to be there when he puts them on."

Fear and guilt assailed Nicodemus as he thought of Shannon imprisoned.

But with grim determination, he focused on recovering the emerald and forced himself to consider the latere subtext. It might work; he would have to move slowly and be sure not to stand where the guards might walk. However, it was very complex.

The third spell burned with the violet light of the Index's language. It was written in a terse, self-reflexive style and possessed a brief description:

The words of sceaduganga cover the body, allowing our authors to walk unseen in shadow but not bright light. It deadins the sound of footsteps.

This was precisely what Nicodemus needed. With a flash, the sceaduganga spell crashed into his mind.

Having gotten what he sought, Nicodemus removed his hand from the Index and felt his mind drop back into his skull. As before, the transition from book to brain made his thoughts feel strangely confined.

Nicodemus closed the Index. On the gate, the two guards were discussing an ongoing bookworm infection. Apparently there were supposed to be other guards on the front gate, but the provost had pulled them away to help hunt the worms.

One of the stronghold's cats now prowled the other side of the corridor. Nicodemus glared at the feline, willing it not to come his way and by purring reveal his presence. Another breeze set the torches to guttering.

After a long breath, Nicodemus turned his mind to the sceaduganga spell. Because the text had come from the corrupted Index, it was already slightly misspelled. And for that reason, Nicodemus concentrated on keeping his cacographic mind from further distorting the newly learned spell. After another long breath, he set to writing the subtext along his right forearm.

Although each violet rune required a surprising amount of energy, writing the spell took only moments. When finished, the sceaduganga solidified into a transparent cylinder on his palm. He frowned at his first attempt in a new language. Most likely it was misspelled. He cast the text into the air, expecting it to crash onto the floor.

But it did not fall.

It shot upward and smashed against the ceiling. "Fiery blood!" he whispered as violet sentence fragments snowed about him. His second attempt behaved like a proper misspell and plummeted to the ground. The third spell shot across the corridor to strike the cat and render it invisible. The rats wouldn't like that at all.

The fourth spell crashed onto the floor like the second, and the fifth deconstructed before leaving his hand. Nicodemus's face grew hot with frustration. He badly wanted to break something other than another sceaduganga subtext.

Suddenly his keloid came alive with pain. Clapping a hand onto the scars, he discovered that they were almost as hot as boiling water. This had happened twice before when he was making his way to the front gate. It made him worry about the last thing the emerald had said: "Beware the scar; it will betray you to Fellwroth."

What that meant, Nicodemus couldn't imagine. And he couldn't waste time thinking about it now. He needed to get out of Starhaven.

So he took slow breaths and waited for the scar to cool. When it did, he bent down to inspect the decaying halves of his last two subtext attempts. Both spells had split at the same point in their primary sequence. Undoubtedly, he had made the same cacographic error in both.

"Los damn my cacography," he hissed, fighting a fresh wave of self-hatred. "If only I had that emerald!"

He forced himself to think logically. Was there a way to rewrite the spell to avoid the commands that contained difficult spellings?

He grunted. Perhaps there was. But that would mean deliberately respelling, deliberately misspelling. His whole life he had waged war on his cacography. True, intentionally misspelling the shielding spell back in the Index's chamber had increased his control of that text. But now he was considering something more egregious—willfully composing a misspell.

But the present situation afforded few options: he could either try a respell or lurk around Starhaven until the sentinels or the golem discovered him.

So he made another attempt at the subtext, this time deliberately altering the fractious paragraph. When finished, the respelled text glowed deep purple.

Wincing, Nicodemus cast the pale cylinder into the air, where it floated and began to spin faster and faster until it seemed as if it might split apart.

But the misspelled subtext did not break; rather it cast out a sentence from either side of its body. The whirling lines covered Nicodemus's feet and wove a textual sheet up his leg. Within moments, he was enclosed from boot heel to top hair in light-bending prose. The spell left two thin slits open for his eyes so he might see out from the disguising words.

Elation flushed through Nicodemus.

Slowly, he stepped from behind the tapestry. His boots made no sound on the cobblestones. But as he drew near a torch, the sentences nearest the light began to fray and deconstruct.

This was strange; light shouldn't damage magical language. He moved away from the torch and fed more purple sentences to the subtext. The deconstruction stopped and the spell regained its integrity.

Carefully Nicodemus stepped through the gate and past the guards. A nervous smile began to curl his lips. The guards could not see him; they could not hear him.

It was a wonderful feeling. He had respelled the ancient sceaduganga. Perhaps, one day, he would publish his creation and name it the shadowganger subtext.

His smile grew as he slipped across the drawbridge and onto the mountain road. "Dear heaven, I'm free," he whispered as Starhaven's lofty towers came into view, black against the starry sky.

With a laugh, he turned away from the academy of strict wizardly language and knew that he was safe under his disguise—safe under an epic of concealing, respelled prose.

CHAPTER
Thirty-one

Nicodemus walked into the cold autumn night.

Wind rushed through the evergreens and tore leaves of scarlet and yellow from the aspens. The crisp air smelled of damp earth, moldy leaves. Before him a steep mountain road curved down to the hamlet of Gray's Crossing. Behind him rose Starhaven's black silhouette.

Even though Nicodemus had seldom left the academy and never traveled this road at night, he noticed little of the dark beauty; his mind was too distracted by recent memories and new emotions.

At first he felt only exhilaration. His cacography had helped him escape! But then he turned a bend and saw a rotting log that resembled a woman's body, curled up and facing away. A shiver ran down his body. The toppled trunk grew larger in his vision, revealing pale mushrooms scattered like warts across the wood, their roots eating into the rot.

Devin's half-crushed face flashed before his eyes. He tried to think of the emerald, but his fear and grief would not dissipate. Devin and Kyran were dead. The demon Typhon had turned John into an unwitting killer. Far worse, the monstrous Fellwroth was still alive. The damage Kyran had done to the metal golem was of no consequence. Fellwroth might already be forming another body.

Nicodemus closed his eyes and again sought the emerald's image, but again he failed. Fellwroth would keep coming, no matter how many times he escaped, no matter how many golems he deconstructed.

And yet, when the golem had grabbed his throat, he had heard the emerald's voice as his own childhood voice. He had learned that the gem was the missing part of himself. He had learned that his nightmares had contained visions of Fellwroth's living body.

But could that knowledge do him any good? He wasn't the Halcyon. Prophecy dictated that the Halcyon would be born with a Braid-shaped keloid. Nicodemus's keloid had been created after his birth, when his father had branded him with the emerald.

Worse, Nicodemus still had no idea where Fellwroth's true body might be. True, he knew it was lying in a cavern with a standing stone . . . and inhabited by nightmare turtles? It was nonsensical.

His fear grew and the keloid began to burn again. The scars grew so hot he feared they might singe his hair. He paused to fan the back of his neck.

While he waited for the keloid to cool, he pulled the Seed of Finding from his belt-purse and tore off its encircling root. As before, part of the artifact melted and then recongealed on the back of his hand as barklike skin. Now Deirdre could find him.

However, the Fool's Ladder had landed her on Starhaven's eastern side. She would have to make a long hike around Starhaven to the road Nicodemus now traveled. Even if the druid had set out at once, she could not find him before morning. Until then, he needed a safe hiding place.

He started down the road again, hoping to reach Gray's Crossing quickly.

But the night was not the same; he was not the same. The forest loomed larger and blacker. In the blue moon's light, once familiar meadows became otherworldly landscapes. All around him lurked the loneliness of the road. He shook his head and tried to push away thoughts of Kyran and Devin.

But the night was not to be denied; it had his imagination as an ally. Everything changed. A stump took on a lycanthrope's shape; a leafless branch opened gnarled fingers and hung ready to grab; the wind in the trees began to talk of Chthonic footsteps.

For most of his life, Nicodemus had dreamed of venturing into these woods, of battling monsters on this very road. But he never guessed that he could feel so alone, or that it could be so dark.

And then the blue moon slipped behind a cloud, leaving only the white moon in the sky. The world grew darker still.

Every falling leaf made him jump. Every snapping twig conjured images of lurking horrors. He felt as if his heart were beating an inch behind his eyes. The road seemed to shake. He dropped the Index and fell to his knees.

Behind boughs and under bushes, nightblue terrors grew legs and teeth; they slunk through the tall meadow grass and hid in the shadows. They began to chant in croaking voices, telling stories of how they had drifted among the woods as impalpable wraiths for many long years. They chanted about how Nicodemus's long-awaited journey on the night road was making them stronger.

The night creatures congregated at the forest's edge. And when he looked away, they darted across the road to the trees on the other side. They went mostly unseen, but every so often he glimpsed a gnarled elbow or two shining violet eyes. No two were alike, and they were all around him, muttering and spitting their low chant.

Now breathing hard, Nicodemus realized he was in mortal danger. He realized that he could go back to Starhaven. He looked up at the dark towers. If he returned, the sentinels would imprison him. But what of that? Other people would pass him in the halls, and he would know that the world was constant. He could explain about the golems. The academy would protect him. It would give him a place to lay down his language in the tracks of literary convention.

Still on his hands and knees, he turned to face uphill.

All around, the terrors whispered about their fear that he would flee back to Starhaven and deprive them of a feeding.

An endless moment passed as Nicodemus kneeled, adrift in a fantastic universe.

But then the image of the small emerald appeared before his eyes. At that moment, he decided to remain. He would rather die trying to find the missing part of himself.

The nightblue terrors burst onto the road, moaning with rapture. They circled him: a nightmarish jamboree of limbs, bellies, and teeth. He remained on his knees, frozen with fear.

Some of the monsters were strangely familiar—a small eyeless dragon; a giant insect with a human face; a troll's three-horned head.

Others were such phantasmagoric unions of limbs and fins and fangs that they were impossible to perceive in their entirety. Some of the monsters grabbed at his clothes; others ran their claws through his hair.

But as the night terrors touched him, Nicodemus began to sense their thoughts and feelings. Somehow he knew that his choice to stay on the road had affected them in ways they did not realize.

Just then the wind brought rhythmic hoof beats up from the mountainside. The night terrors froze like stone carvings. Some put claws to batlike ears. Now they could hear the four-beat song of a galloping horse.

Every monster shuddered; they knew what was coming up from the town. They had felt the foul thing riding down this same path not an hour previous.

Suddenly and completely, the emotions in their oily hearts transformed. The monsters changed their minds. With split lips and forked tongues, they whispered around fangs and tusks, telling each other what must be done.

Fighting through his paralyzing fear, Nicodemus tried to crawl farther down the road. But dread placed too heavy a weight on his back and he collapsed. The keloid scar on his neck burned.

Having reached a decision, the nightblue terrors scooped up Nicodemus and carried him into a roadside ditch. There they piled on top of him like children rough-housing with their father. They were determined to cover his every inch with their deep-blue skin.

The horsesong slowed to the two-beat rhythm of a trot. Realizing that he had forgotten the Index on the road, a three-horned troll scampered out, picked up the codex with bony claws, and dove back into the pile of monsters just before a horse and rider came into view around the bend.

Still paralyzed, Nicodemus lay under a blanket of phantasms, all of which had become as still as death. Though a webbed hand covered his right eye, he could still see with his left.

Four white horse legs appeared as the animal trotted to within five feet of where he lay. Two tattered boots dropped into view as the rider dismounted.

The newcomer spoke with a low, gruff voice: "I know you are near, Nicodemus Weal. Your keloid calls out to me." The boots took halting steps around the horse.

Through terror's haze, Nicodemus recognized Fellwroth's voice.

"Moments ago the keloid's texts became diffuse. Something is interfering. But still, I knew I'd find you on this road. You took your sweet time, whelp. I had to wait in the miserable town until I felt you coming down the mountainside."

The boots limped up the road as Fellwroth searched. The monster inhaled with a slight whistling sound.

"Impressive, this spell that hides you and masks the keloid's spells," he growled. "It must be in a language I have never encountered. You must have a new protector; we both know your retarded mind could never manage such a subtext."

Fellwroth now stepped into the meadow on the road's opposite side. Nicodemus, numb with terror, could do nothing but watch as the fiend's cloaked back came into view.

The monster had donned a new white shroud, but he limped badly and his right sleeve hung lifelessly at his side.

This was the same iron golem Nicodemus had faced in the compluvium.

Apparently finding nothing in the grass, Fellwroth staggered back to the horse. "This body has known too much abuse. I have only a few moments. Likely this golem will fail before I find you."

The creature took in another whistling breath. "You are out of Starhaven now, so the game has changed. Your power is greater than I'd supposed. Perhaps we can come to an agreement." He paused for another difficult breath. "Whelp, you now have a choice. And it is vital that you make the right one."

The monster stepped straight toward Nicodemus. "If you continue to run from me, you will die."

The boots stopped not a foot from the pile. "I would rather you lived. That is why I will tell you how to recover the missing part of your mind."

FELLWROTH WAS SO close now that Nicodemus could hear something squeaking like a rusty door hinge inside the golem's body. The monster's heart?

"I trust Shannon has told you about Language Prime," Fellwroth said in a slow, metallic voice. "I trust he told you that it is the first language, the source of all magic. But your old teacher might not have known that Language Prime can be used to change a living creature's body and mind."

The monster's boots shifted toward the meadow. "You should know your father was a demon-worshiper. When you were an infant, Typhon gave your father an emerald we brought across the ocean from the ancient kingdom of Aaraheuminest. But that is an archaic name. The fools of this age have contracted the name to Aarahest."

With a gravelly crunch, the boots pivoted back to face Nicodemus. "Your father used the emerald to cut into your mind. It stole a rare talent that you inherited from your Imperial ancestry. It stole your ability to spell correctly in any language, even Language Prime."

The boots turned downhill. "When I touched you, we both saw your father drawing your ability to spell into the emerald. I had not realized until that moment that the emerald had scarred you. If I had, I could have used the keloid to identify you. But no matter. Now anyone holding the emerald gains the Language Prime fluency that you were born with."

Now the boots turned uphill. Apparently the monster had not given up searching for him. "But unfortunately, the gem loses strength over time. So once every four years, Typhon had to replenish the emerald by touching it to you. The gem is losing strength now. I tell you this so you will know how valuable you could be to me. I reward those I value."

The monster paused as if to emphasize this last claim before continuing. "Who you were and how to reach you, the old monster hid from me. And when I killed the demon, I did so before learning how to find you."

An eerie, metallic laugh filled the night as the monster moved out of Nicodemus's view. "And maybe that is what the emerald wanted. The gem looks after itself, Nicodemus. It longs to return to you. It is insidious. It sends dreams to those near it; it tries to deceive its wielders. It betrayed Typhon. It showed me in a dream how to kill the demon when he was trying to infect a minor deity."

Fellwroth's footsteps halted. "The emerald is using me to find its way back to you. But its desire to be near you now betrays you."

The golem laughed again. "The keloid on your neck is a by-product of the stone. It is not truly part of you. It grows out of proportion of your body. It is disobedient like a canker curse, and like a canker it can forge magical language. When I touched you, the scar sensed that my living body now holds the gem. And so the keloid began to forge Language Prime spells. It broadcasts them to reveal your location to the emerald."

Through the haze of his terror, Nicodemus remembered how the keloid had become unbearably hot.

"I had hoped to follow the keloid's signals to you," Fellwroth added. "But this strange spell that is hiding you from my eye is also diffusing the signal."

A few of the night terrors covering Nicodemus shifted uneasily.

"But I can sense your general proximity. I know you're close enough to hear me. And I might find you yet."

Gravelly footsteps sounded again. "But if I don't catch you with this golem, I will with another. No matter where you run, the emerald will find you. It is part of you."

Again came the eerie, echoing laugh. "Fitting that you will always find yourself."

The footsteps were growing louder. "So there is no use running, whelp. You are one of us. Your mother too was a demon-worshiper. Typhon created you by bringing them together. Your family is vital to the Disjunction."

The monster sniffed as if annoyed. "Ah, yes, you must understand about your family. No doubt you know an Imperial clan ruled the ancient continent. No doubt you know you are an Imperial, one who possesses royal characteristics. But you cannot know that the Imperial family mastered Language Prime. Only those of full Imperial blood could comprehend and compose primal texts. So the Imperials bred themselves carefully to keep the talent. When humanity fled across the ocean, your family was scattered. The blood ran thin and the talent was lost."

Fellwroth's boots came back into Nicodemus's view as the golem hobbled back toward his horse. "Since then, there have been a few others like you, gifted in Language Prime. Typhon has been breeding Imperials since he and I crossed the ocean two hundred years ago. You are one of the products of this breeding."

Fellwroth's legs wobbled, causing the nearby horse to shift its feet. "Why are the demons breeding Language Prime spellwrights? Because Typhon discovered how to use Language Prime to compose a dragon. No doubt you've heard what the first dragon has done to Trillinon. Typhon and I wrote that wyrm using your Language Prime fluency via the emerald. It took ten long years."

Fellwroth's feet shuffled as if the golem was having trouble staying balanced. "But that dragon, being my first attempt, was flawed. So I set it loose on Trillinon to weaken humanity. Now I must replenish the emerald so I can compose another dragon to be stronger and more intelligent. When I have a wyrm powerful enough, I will fly across the ocean to the ancient continent. There I will revive Los and help him to initiate the War of Disjunction."

Somewhere an owl hooted.

"When the demons enslave humanity, they will want captains among the men. If you serve me, Nicodemus, they will give back the missing part of your mind. You will be complete. You will know power, wealth, happiness beyond your ability to imagine."

When Fellwroth spoke again, the words came out clipped, as if the creature were in pain. "So you see your choices. You can serve me and know vast reward, or you can run. I won't kill you when I catch you. I've never wanted you dead. If you perish, I cannot replenish the emerald."

The owl hooted again.

"I will distort your mind, make you more disabled than Typhon made that giant oaf. You will be a slobbering fool. The emerald will replenish itself more slowly, but I will not have to worry about your slipping from my grasp. That has been my goal all along—to find you and further cripple your mind. But now that you are free in the world, I am willing to bargain. Your resourcefulness has impressed me. Join me."

Fellwroth drew another long, whistling breath and waited as if for Nicodemus to call out an acceptance.

"No response? Perhaps thoughts of prophecy cloud your thinking. Perhaps you think fate will save you. I must tell you then that the human prophecies are nonsense. After the Exodus, humanity longed for the return of a full-blooded Imperial so profoundly they fabricated these prophecies. They mixed facts about your family with legend and myth."

Fellwroth began to cough—it sounded like someone striking a pot with a metal spoon. When the racket finally ended, the creature spoke again.

"Some prophecies predict only one full-blooded Imperial will arise to become a savior. The druidic nonsense about the Peregrine is an example. In the same way, the highsmiths prophesied the coming of the Oriflamme, the hierophants the coming of the Cynosure. But other magical societies imagine two Imperials will arise, one a savior, one a destroyer. Wizards are this way with their rot about the Halcyon versus the Storm Petrel. But it's all drivel. All prophecies are equally false."

Again Fellwroth made the clanging cough.

"The truth is that full-blood Imperials like you are only tools. Tools that might be used to impede or empower the Disjunction. And you, Nicodemus, are a tool made by demons for the Disjunction."

Nicodemus screwed his eyes shut. He still felt dazed and numb. He could understand everything the monster was saying, but none of it seemed real.

Fellwroth was making a low, echoing growl. "If you run from me, you will face dangers about which you know nothing."

The monster paused as if considering something. "Only a few human deities were aware of Typhon's presence. The great gods and goddesses are too busy governing their kingdoms to notice. But a handful of lesser deities have discovered Typhon's presence and formed an alliance to oppose him. They call themselves the Alliance of Divine Heretics, and they too have been trying to breed a Language Prime spellwright. But none of your relatives have lived past infancy."

Fellwroth laughed once. "The ongoing war between the Disjunction and the Alliance of Heretics is a pathetic one. We slaughter all Imperials born to the Alliance, and they kill every one born to the Disjunction . . . everyone but you, that is. And I must give Typhon his due; it was brilliant to steal your talent rather than raise you to use it for us. And then he disguised you as a cacographer. Not in a thousand years would the Alliance suspect a retarded boy of being our Imperial."

Fellwroth's legs began to quake. "I'm telling you this because the instant the Alliance learns of your existence, they will assassinate you. Think on it: by killing you they would deprive the emerald of its power and hence deprive us of our Language Prime and so our ability to compose a second dragon."

The monster's legs now shook enough to make him stagger. "You are in more danger than you realize. No doubt the Alliance of Heretics is already aware of you. Who do you think sent Deirdre, that would-be-druid of a girl? She will kill you the instant she has the opportunity to do so without ruining the druids' standing at the convocation. Surely you must understand now, whelp. I am your only chance at survival. You must join me."

Suddenly Nicodemus's keloid started to burn.

The golem's legs quit their tremor. "I think . . ." the monster wheezed as he started to limp toward Nicodemus. "I think I feel your presence."

But walking proved too difficult for Fellwroth; a white hand sank to steady the creature against the ground.

"If I could only see you," Fellwroth grunted. "What is this mysterious language that conceals you?"

Slowly Fellwroth managed to stand. The monster's breathing was more labored now. "Perhaps you hate the Disjunction so much, hate those who created you so much, that you would consider suicide to deprive us of the emerald. It won't make a difference. I have already set the wheels in motion to give you a cousin. In time I will breed another Imperial. Do not sacrifice yourself for nothing."

The monster shuffled closer; his boots were now a foot away. One of the nightblue terrors covering Nicodemus whimpered.

"Nicodemus," Fellwroth wheezed, "bind yourself to our cause and you shall be rewarded beyond your imagination. All you need do is return to Starhaven. I will collect you there."

The monster took another faltering half-step. His toe landed an inch from Nicodemus's face. Two night terrors cringed.

Fellwroth started to take another step, but a night terror threw out a tentacle to strike the golem's shin. The murderer faltered, stumbled backward and then fell to his knees.

A hood covered the monster's face, but his scarred left hand came up to press against a maggot-white throat.

"This golem fails," he hissed. "I leave you, Nicodemus, with a choice. Surrender to me in Starhaven and know godlike power, or resist and die."

A violent cough wracked the monster's chest and threw his head back. His hood slid off to reveal a long mane of pallid hair. Where there should have been smooth forehead shone a bar of flowing Numinous text. His skin was as white as paper. The features of his handsome face were delicate—thin lips, a snub nose, wide eyes.

Another violent cough wracked the creature and he fell forward, his chin striking gravel not four inches from Nicodemus's nose.

Patches of the golem's skin began darkening into gray iron. The thing stared straight at Nicodemus with eyes that had neither white sclera nor dark pupil. They were everywhere blood-red flecked with black.

With a violent shudder, the golem pulled his hand up as if to strike out with a spell.

But a night terror leaped off Nicodemus and onto Fellwroth's arm. It was the three-horned troll. The squat creature pinned the golem's arm to the dirt road.

Suddenly Nicodemus realized that he had seen the troll before. Many times before.

Something was wrong. Horribly wrong.

Nicodemus's heart beat frantically. He struggled to escape the pile of night terrors, but now bright orange flecks flew across his vision. The ground seemed to spin. He was going to faint.

All around him, the night terrors began whispering, urging him to stay still so they could keep him hidden. Before him appeared the small, eyeless dragon with tentacles growing from its chin. He recognized this night terror too; it was called Tamelkan. He had given it that name when he was fourteen years old.

Since arriving at Starhaven, Nicodemus had been imagining monsters to infest the nearby forests. Inspired by countless books of knightly romance, he had dreamed of venturing from the academy to confront his invented foes.

Now, as impossible as it seemed, his dreams had become real. The night terrors that had hidden him from Fellwroth, the creatures that now held him down, were the same monsters he had imagined as a boy.

In a confused panic, Nicodemus thrashed harder and threw off two of the blue monsters. He staggered onto his knees, but Tamelkan lunged at him. The dragon's tentacles wound around his head.

Overcome by his own dark fantasy, Nicodemus fell backward into unconsciousness.

CHAPTER

Thirty-two

When Nicodemus awoke, he was floating through the night-shaded forest.

High above, a breeze whispered through the leafy canopy and set the black boughs swaying. A dappled wash of moonlight ebbed and flowed across the forest floor.

Remembering his near capture by Fellwroth, Nicodemus sat up with a cry. He must have fainted after the golem had expired.

His panicked voice seemed to shatter into a hundred pieces. He fell to the ground, his bottom painfully flattening a snowberry bush.

All around him ran the night terrors that had hidden him from Fellwroth. As he remembered, the creatures were the same monsters he had imagined for his boyhood adventure fantasies. Here was Fael, the lycanthropic neo-demon; Tamelkan, the eyeless dragon with a tentacled chin; insect-like Uro with a human face and hooked hands; Garkex, the horned firetroll.

In his dreams, the monsters had been massive creatures. But these blue-skinned renditions were miniature; even the mighty Tamelkan was no larger than a deer.

Nicodemus remembered that the imaginary beasts had pinned him down on the road. In fact just before he had fainted, Tamelkan had wrapped its tentacles around his head. But the night terrors did not seem hostile now. In fact, when he woke, they had been gently carrying him through the forest.

Garkex—a stone-skinned, three-horned firetroll with serrated tusks—scolded the other monsters in an unintelligible, squeaky voice. The troll was holding the Index above his head.

The sight made Nicodemus wonder if he had gone mad. What he remembered seemed like a hallucination or a nightmare. Had he truly met Fellwroth and learned that his parents were demon-worshipers?

As he considered this question, Garkex's cries seemed to calm the other monsters. They stopped their flight to peer back at Nicodemus.

Garkex continued his unintelligible harangue. Slowly, like frightened dogs, the monsters returned. Some were bowing, some lowering their muzzles or eye-stalks.

The firetroll planted himself directly before Nicodemus and presented the Index.

Nicodemus shook himself. No, he wasn't crazy; he truly had encountered Fellwroth, and he truly was staring at Garkex—his fictional childhood nemesis.

He took the Index from the diminutive troll and hugged it to his chest. Garkex began to lecture him—his horns spitting minute orange flames when he squeaked out more vehement syllables.

Nicodemus stared blankly at the monsters as they lifted him up and recommenced their journey through the forest. He wondered if he should try to flee.

But if the night terrors had wanted him dead, they could have torn him to pieces when he fainted. Or they might simply have let Fellwroth find him.

He decided to let the monsters carry him.

As they went among the widely spaced trees, speckled moonlight passed over them. Their course brought the party to a mountainside creek, which the monsters crossed with impressive speed. Then Nicodemus found himself being carried through a wilderness of sword ferns that tickled his legs. Garkex chastised the vegetation for getting in their way.

When they passed into another patch of moonlight, Nicodemus saw the cold turn his breath into pale jets of air.

The monsters marched through meadows, along ponds, and through dense thickets. Scattered through the forest were dead or dying trees. Watching this scenery, Nicodemus thought about what Fellwroth had told him.

Could he believe the golem? Could it be true that a demon had arranged his birth?

Nicodemus's heart beat faster. From the day he had learned that he was a cacographer, everything had seemed to be error. Life wasn't what it was "supposed" to be. He wasn't supposed to be a source of misspelled, dangerous language. He was supposed to be the Halcyon, the wellspring of constructive, healing texts.

But now it seemed that his disability, his monstrosity, was exactly what was meant to have happened. He came from a family of demon-worshipers. He had been bred to be a monster.

It was possible that Fellwroth had lied. But some instinct deep inside Nicodemus knew that the golem had been telling the truth.

"I won't be a demon's puppet!" Nicodemus growled, clenching his hands. The golem had said that those of Imperial blood could be tools used to assist or resist the Disjunction.

Well then, he would become a weapon for the resistance.

He closed his eyes and imagined the Emerald of Arahest. Its brilliant, lacriform shape appeared before him. Here was his salvation. He would focus his every desire on recovering the gem. And when he had it back, his mind would be complete. Then he could oppose the Disjunction.

Suddenly the keloid scars on his neck grew hot. "Fiery heaven!" he swore.

Fellwroth had said that the keloids were betraying his location by broadcasting spells written in a language he couldn't see. But the golem had also said that some force was diffusing these same spells. He supposed the night terrors now carrying him were the force interfering with the keloids' spells. But despite the diffusion, Fellwroth could still approximate his whereabouts.

There was no escape.

And there was the dragon to think of. What if Fellwroth truly had used the emerald to create the dragon that attacked Trillinon? Could Nicodemus continue to live knowing his death would delay another such attack? Did he have a responsibility to kill himself?

No, he silently vowed, he would not be ruled by fear.

He closed his eyes and cleared his mind. The image of the emerald returned, instantly, vividly. A warm tingling spread across his face. Instinctively, he knew then that what Fellwroth had said was true—the gem was seeking to return to him.

The thought of regaining the emerald made his heart race.

"Calm yourself," he whispered, struggling to control his roiling emotions. He needed to think logically. His next step should be to find Deirdre and learn what he could from her.

Just then the monsters carried him into a pine thicket so dense that they were surrounded by complete blackness. Even midday sunlight would not penetrate here.

Garkex puffed small flames from his horns. The resultant light pierced the gloom to reveal a small cliff face that extended in both directions. The night terrors tramped directly toward it as if it weren't there. Nicodemus had just enough time to throw his arms up before they crashed into the rock face.

Nothing happened.

When he lowered his hands, Nicodemus saw that they had passed right through the small cliff face onto a moonlit promontory. He swore and looked back. The rock wall had been a fiction, an ingeniously written subtext.

Garkex let out a screech, and the night terrors gently set Nicodemus down on a patch of moss.

The party now stood on a knoll that overlooked a moonlit clearing scattered with ivy-covered stone arches, low towers, and crumbling walls.

Nicodemus stared. Once this must have had been one of Starhaven's outlying Chthonic villages. He had read of how the Neosolar Legion had destroyed all such settlements during the Siege of Starhaven.

But why had these ruins been hidden by a subtext?

Garkex began talking rapidly and gesticulating at Nicodemus and the Index. The other monsters bowed. Suddenly Garkex's right arm dissolved into a cloud of indigo runes.

"You're constructs!" Nicodemus exclaimed. "Written in the Index's purple language."

The firetroll marched up to Nicodemus and held out his right hand. Tentatively Nicodemus placed his own palm on top of the construct's. Garkex said something softly as he shook his partially deconstructed arm. A glowing sentence fell from the troll's text. The violet words landed on the back of Nicodemus's hand and bore into his skin.

He cried out and jerked his hand back.

But the firetroll was whispering softly and pointing to his arm. In amazement, Nicodemus turned his hand over and saw that the sentence had been tattooed onto his skin.

Nicodemus knew that every magical language could inscribe itself into only one type of medium. The common and wizardly languages took only to paper or parchment. Druids set their higher languages only into wood. The highsmiths etched their spells only on metal. And apparently whoever had created the Index's violet language had tattooed their prose into living skin.

Slowly Garkex disintegrated into prose and wrote himself onto Nicodemus's forearm. It was unsettling, but painless, to watch the spell slip under his skin.

When it was finished, Nicodemus marveled at the flowing script now coiling down his hand and forearm. Next Tamelkan, the eyeless dragon, appeared before him and began to write herself onto Nicodemus's other arm.

And then all of the monsters were on him, disintegrating and tattooing themselves into his skin.

"Wait," Nicodemus said, suddenly afraid. "Not so many; I . . ." His voice died.

It was over. Every last one of the night terrors was gone.

He stared down at his hands. He hiked up his robes to look at his shins. He even peered down his collar at his chest. Everywhere he was inscribed with flowing, violet text.

"I imagined all of you for my boyhood dreams," he said while examining the language on his palms. "So how could I have written you? I learned the Index's purple language a few hours ago, but I dreamed up Garkex when my voice broke, Fael and Tamelkan when I still had pimples."

He shook his head. Maybe he actually had gone mad. "How could I have written you?"

A glow made him look up. Floating before him was a purple spell.

"Who cast that?" Nicodemus called, looking around for the spell's author. "Who's there?"

The night was empty save for the rubble, silent but for the wind in the trees.

The spell floated toward Nicodemus. He raised his hands and stepped back.

But the spell stopped and unfolded into two parts.

Now curious, Nicodemus peered at the first subspell. It was an instructional text describing how the purple language could encode for written language.

Familiar with analogous protocols that allowed wizards to conduct silent conversations in Numinous, Nicodemus quickly grasped how the spell functioned.

The second part of the purple spell seemed to be an encoded sentence. Nicodemus grabbed it and applied the translation protocol. The resulting line read, "*It was Starhaven who wrote them.*"

Nicodemus puzzled over those words until he remembered staring at the tattoos on his hand and asking, "How could I have written you?"

Again fear jolted through him. "Who cast this?" he repeated and again spun around in a frightened attempt to find the mysterious spellwright. "Who's there?"

No sound came, but as Nicodemus turned round again he discovered another purple spell floating in the air.

Tentatively, he caught the paragraph and translated it.

The indigo language you refer to is called Wrixlan. It is our language for manipulating light and text, much like your Numinous. Wrixlan metaspells fill Starhaven. Your mind sought out Wrixlan because it is eugraphic. You dreamed of these creatures, and Starhaven's metaspells sympathetically took the shape of your dreams. When your creatures achieved enough intelligence, the language governing Starhaven perceived them as a threat and so banished them. That is why the constructs hated you so. You had unknowingly exiled them.

"Who are you?" Nicodemus's wide eyes darted about but saw nothing but ruins and ivy vines. "Where are you?"

As before Nicodemus found another Wrixlan paragraph floating behind him. He grabbed and translated it.

I see the products of your adolescent purple prose have forgiven you. They could have stored themselves in your living codex. But they will draw more strength from your skin. I have been trying to convince them to bring you here.

Nicodemus shook his head. "What do you want? Show yourself!"

This time he saw the textual response form in midair. It looked as if the characters were condensing from moonlight. It read,

I want only a small favor. I can offer many answers. You are in no danger; we are weak. We cannot affect the physical world and can affect the textual world only slightly.

Nicodemus swallowed hard, realizing what this meant. "You're dead?"

The construct appeared first as a soft violet glow among the ivy vines. Then tiny indigo sparks formed in the air and began to swarm, slowly coalescing into legs and a torso.

As the construct moved toward Nicodemus, it became more solid and took on shades of white, indigo, and gray. But its prose never congealed completely. Nicodemus could see through the construct to the collapsed buildings on the other side.

At first glance it might have been mistaken for a human child of eight or ten. Its spindly legs presented knobby knees and wide feet. Its slight torso was covered by a white tunic that afforded a short sleeve for the right arm only.

The construct didn't seem to have a left arm. But its right arm was long and graceful, with a large elbow joint and narrow forearm. Its single hand was wide, its fingers long and slender.

The spell was climbing toward Nicodemus on an ivy-covered staircase. As it moved, it leaned forward to use its elongated right hand as an extra foot.

Nicodemus stepped back as it reached the top of the promontory. Its skin was pale gray, its long hair snowy white.

Its eyes were as wide as a man's fist, their pupils slit vertically like a cat's. Its beaklike nose bent over a soft chin.

It smiled to reveal flat teeth and then cast a Wrixlan sentence into the air. "*You are correct: we are dead. Welcome, spellwright, to our final resting place.*" It bowed.

After taking a deep breath, Nicodemus bowed to what could only be a Chthonic ghost.

CHAPTER

Thirty-three

A sharp knock woke Amadi in her cot. For a confused moment she stared at the stark white walls of her Starhaven cell. In her dream she had been wrestling a giant bookworm. Her now bandaged forearm ached.

The knock came again and she struggled up from her pallet. Outside her window the sky was still black. "Who knocks?"

"Kale, Magistra."

"Enter," she called to her secretary and pulled on a night robe.

The young Ixonian slipped into the room.

"Kale, I shudder to see you. I can't have slept more than an hour. Has the bookworm infection returned?"

"No, Magistra." The man's eyes were wide. "Another death, one of the cacographers."

Amadi drew in a sharp breath. "Shannon escaped?"

"No, he's still imprisoned beneath the Summer Tower. Nicodemus's female floormate, Devin Dorshear, is dead. Both Nicodemus and the big man they call Simple John are missing. Near midnight the young cacographers heard shouting. Until a quarter hour ago, they were too frightened to leave their rooms."

Amadi swore. "But the wards. No one should be able to get in or out of that tower."

Kale pressed a hand to his mouth. "I take full responsibility, Magistra. I was the one who suggested we leave the tower unguarded. It seems Shannon somehow slipped Nicodemus a key to lift the wards. I take full responsibility."

"Nonsense," Amadi snapped. "I had the command." She turned to her bed chest. "Rouse the sentinels. Alert all the guards. I want a search begun before I'm fully dressed. I'll personally go to the provost's officers."

Kale nodded and turned to go.

"But Kale, I'll first examine the dead cacographer. I want two of our sentinels on hand. Where did the murder happen?"

The man paused at the door and looked back. "Drum Tower, top floor.

I'll send two spellwrights straight away. Nothing's been touched . . . but the body, Magistra, it's . . . gruesome."

A QUARTER HOUR after being awakened with news of Nicodemus's disappearance, Amadi found herself in the Drum Tower frowning at a dead lesser wizard.

The girl's face had been crushed by blunt words. A puddle of drying blood surrounded her body. "The killer was a clumsy spellwright," Amadi said to the sentinels behind her. "Must have used a leadshot spell or something simple."

Amadi clenched her teeth. She was almost certain Shannon was guilty of some foul play. Surely the old wizard was in the pay of a magically illiterate noble. Why else would he have hidden so much money in his quarters? Why else would he be connected to the bookworm infestation?

However, now it seemed she was dealing with two murderers. "A cacographer did this," she said. "Nicodemus or the big one."

She wondered if Nicodemus had killed Nora Finn at Shannon's behest. "You there," she said to one of sentinels. "Go to the Summer Tower and rouse Shannon. I need some questions answered."

With a nod, the man ducked out of the common room.

"Another strange thing is all this dust," Amadi grumbled, now pacing about. Mostly the powder was scattered across the room, but next to the door lay a pile of the stuff covered by what looked like a white bed sheet. Even stranger, one corner held a small mound of splinters.

"You," Amadi said to the remaining sentinel, a tall woman with gray hair. "Search the other Drum Tower residences. Tell me if you find similar dust or splinters in any other room."

As the woman hurried through the door, Kale appeared. He was chewing his lower lip. A bad sign. "What is it, Kale?"

"Word from the librarians, Magistra. One of Starhaven's most valuable artifacts is missing."

"Destroyed by a bookworm?" she asked.

The secretary shook his head. "It was in a secure chamber and the Main Library was never infested."

Amadi closed her eyes and took a long breath. "Let me guess: either Shannon or Nicodemus was the last one to use this artifact."

Kale nodded. "There's more. The artifact is a reference codex called the Index; it can access all text stored in Starhaven. And whoever has the artifact has looked up the touch spell."

"And how do we know this?"

"Every copy of the touch spell in the academy is now misspelled."

Amadi frowned. "By accessing texts through this artifact the user is misspelling them?"

Kale nodded. "And all the misspelled touch scrolls are infectious. They cause manuscripts touching them to misspell. An entire pedagogical library in the Marfil Tower has been destroyed."

"Nicodemus!" Amadi growled. "If the boy accesses a text in the Stacks or the Main Library, he could destroy all of Starhaven's holdings."

Kale nodded again.

Amadi swore. "First the bookworm infestation, now this. Chaos incarnate has come to Starhaven."

"Magistra . . . are you saying—"

"Do you doubt it, Kale? Think of the disorder that has spread across Starhaven. Think of the murders, the deaths, the corruption. Think of the scar—an Inconjunct breaking the Braid. The boy seems destined to spread chaos."

Kale took a long breath. "We cannot be certain the counter-prophecy is coming to pass."

"Cannot be certain, but we now have enough evidence that we must act."

She made for the door. "I will question the librarians. I want to learn more about this artifact. You will go to the Erasmine Tower and tell the on-duty officers what has happened. If we don't catch the boy, his mind will rot the pages from our books as a tumor rots flesh. They must wake the provost and tell him that most likely we've found the Storm Petrel."

FELLWROTH, MORE COMFORTABLE now in a new clay golem, stole through the forest south of Starhaven. Two hours until dawn. The air was cold, the sky black. The strengthening wind roared through the woods.

Roughly an hour ago, the signaling texts from Nicodemus's keloid had ceased entirely. At the time, Fellwroth had still been forming a new golem and so had missed the chance to determine the boy's location more precisely.

However, it was clear that the last signal had come from somewhere in this forest—hence Fellwroth's current, systematic combing of the mountainside. Presently, he followed a deer trail into an elm thicket. He had hoped the keloid's signal texts would recommence, but now it seemed the boy's new protector was blocking them indefinitely.

Here the wind was producing a continuous snow of falling leaves. Fellwroth scowled; without another keloid signal, his current search was unlikely to reveal anything other than more autumnal foliage.

A few hours ago he had spoken to a subtextualized Nicodemus on the road to Gray's Crossing. Had his words convinced the boy? Likely not. If Nicodemus meant to surrender, the whelp should have returned to Starhaven by now, and none of Fellwroth's rewritten gargoyles had reported such.

Fellwroth snatched a falling leaf out of the air and wondered why Nicodemus had not accepted his offer.

Only two possibilities suggested themselves: first, threats against Nicodemus's life might be insufficient to win the boy's surrender; or second, the whelp might feel safe now that he had a protector to block the keloid's signals.

Fellwroth crushed the leaf and considered who might be concealing Nicodemus. Not a deity; he would have sensed another divine presence by now. Nor could it be the girl druid acting alone.

Perhaps it did not matter who was hiding Nicodemus. Perhaps he could threaten something other than the boy's life.

He looked toward Starhaven. The dark elm trees blocked everything from view but the lofty Erasmine Spire. A slow smile pulled on his pale lips as a plan formed in his mind.

He would need to use his true body, and it would take a day to move everything into place. Even so, the plan was perfect.

The leaves were falling faster now. Fellwroth laughed. He knew of at least one thing Nicodemus valued more than his life.

"YOU GAVE HIM access to the Index?" Amadi squawked.

Shannon was sitting calmly on his prison cell cot. The guards had written a weblike censoring spell around the old man's head, blocking him from all magical language. Now his blindness would be complete.

Though he must have been exhausted, the old wizard wore a calm expression. "Without my anti-golem spell, Nicodemus would have been helpless."

"Magister, the provost himself suspects Nicodemus is the Storm Petrel, the champion of chaotic language. I can have no more stories of your clay—"

Shannon learned forward. Thick Magnus texts kept his wrists and legs spellbound to the wall, but there was enough slack on the fettering spells to make Amadi step backward.

"Do you find anything strange in the Drum Tower?" he asked. "Maybe not clay, but any earthen metal, granite or steel or—"

"Dust," she said automatically. "There was a smaller mound of splinters, but dust was all about the common room and especially in a pile with a torn white sheet."

Shannon's blank eyes widened. "The arm I cut off the clay golem had a white sleeve."

Amadi shook her head. "Magister, this tale of golems is too much to swallow. Texts from the ancient continent?"

"Amadi, by naming him the Storm Petrel, you admit that the bonds holding the demons to the ancient continent are loosening. And yet you refuse to accept the possibility that magic from the ancient continent has already crossed the ocean."

Amadi said nothing.

"If you had guarded the boy properly, none of this would have happened," Shannon said sternly. "The least you can do now is—"

"Enough," Amadi snapped. "I did guard the boy properly given the bookworm infestation. You slipped him the key needed to escape the Drum Tower. It is you who must clear his name. And there's only one way to do that: help us find the boy. Magister, please. Help us recover the Index and capture the Storm Petrel."

He scowled.

Amadi took a long breath. Perhaps the old man was right. Perhaps she should not have withdrawn the guards from the Drum Tower. If the provost discovered that she had wasted the chance to contain Nicodemus, she might soon join Shannon in a prison cell. "Can you find the boy?" she asked patiently. "Do you know where he might be?"

He shook his head. "If I did, I wouldn't take you to him. By invoking the counter-prophecy, you have ensured that he cannot be safe in Starhaven. The provost is likely to censor magical literacy out of the boy the instant he's found."

"But you must have taught him a cipher for a broadcast spell."

"If I did, I should never use it," Shannon snapped. "You could pretend to pardon me or even stage a prison escape. You could watch me then and see if I go to him. But I will never seek him out so long as I have the slightest suspicion that you are following me."

Amadi began to pace the tiny cell. "Why do you protect the boy?"

"Have you considered that he might truly be the Halcyon?"

"What under heaven could suggest that he is the champion of order in language?" she asked. "His cacographic mind that is infecting the entire stronghold with misspells? His keloid that symbolizes increasing chaos? The death and ruin that follow him as a storm follows a petrel at sea?"

"Open your eyes, Amadi! A construct of ancient language was murdering my students one by one to reach him. Who else could bring ancient language to this continent but a demon?"

Amadi pursed her lips.

The old man continued. "Amadi, it is this demonic construct that has led you to suspect me wrongly. A demonic construct that has you worrying about the counter-prophecy when you should be worrying about the true one."

Amadi opened her mouth, but a sharp knock at the cell door interrupted her. "Enter," she called. The door swung wide to reveal one of the guards, a short man with a curly red beard.

"What is it?" Amadi demanded.

"Message from your secretary," the guard replied and looked down at a green paragraph in his hands.

"Magistra," he read, "the druids Deirdre and Kyran cannot be found. The druids of the Silent Blight delegation claim no knowledge of their disappearance." The guard looked up. "It's signed by Magister Kale."

"Los's fiery blood!" Amadi swore. "What else can go wrong?"

CHAPTER
Thirty-four

As Nicodemus followed the ghostly Chthonic down into the ruined village, he reviewed everything he knew about ghostwriting.

He knew it was something powerful spellwrights did when nearing death. He knew the process involved an advanced form of what Shannon had called impressing: a complex Numinous matrix was written within a ghostwriter's head; over time the matrix became a magical copy of the ghostwriter's mind. A textual body was then written around this magical mind and never allowed outside of the author's living body. Eventually, author and text became one being.

Wizards ghostwrote in Numinous, and the few ghostwriters Nicodemus had seen glowed golden from heel to head.

Nicodemus also knew that when ghostwriters died, their ghosts lived on in a text-preserving resting place. Starhaven's ghosts dwelled below the stronghold in the necropolis.

Nicodemus also remembered that there were several types of misspelled ghosts. A "ghast" was a ghost that attacked other texts or the spellwrights who tended the necropolis. A "ghoul" was a ghost that refused to leave its body, often resulting in a half-animated corpse.

Fortunately, the ghost walking ahead of Nicodemus was not misspelled. Though transparent, its image and textual integrity seemed uncorrupted—a shocking feat for prose that had to be nearly a thousand years old.

Presently, Nicodemus was following the ghost down a steep, crumbling stairway to the ruined Chthonic village. Above them a growing wind was blustering through the trees.

"Magister," Nicodemus said to the ghost as they descended, "How should I address you?"

The Chthonic soul stopped to smile at Nicodemus and hand him three purple sentences. They read, "*You may call me Tulki. In our language, 'Tulki' is the masculine form of the word for 'interpreter.' In life, I was an ambassador between our people and your ancestors.*"

When Nicodemus looked up from this message, he saw the ghost studying him with wide amber eyes. Tulki formed another two sentences in his arm and held them out. "*I am assuming your ancestors were of the Neosolar Empire. You wear the black robes.*"

After reading this, Nicodemus hugged the Index closer to his chest. The Neosolar Empire had slaughtered the Chthonics with the help of a young Numinous Order. "I was born Spirish," he said.

Tulki nodded and wrote his reply: "*Yes, I realize the Neosolar Empire collapsed long ago. I heard once that it was modeled after the Solar Empire on your ancient continent. I would like to have learned more. But now, follow me.*"

The ghost's silken ponytail flew over his shoulder as he turned and loped forward on all three limbs. Nicodemus followed the soul into the rubble and ivy.

As they went, the ghost tossed a paragraph over his shoulder. Nicodemus nearly slipped as he hurried to catch and read the passage. "*You should know that our magical languages will be rough on your skin. When those constructs leave your body, they will score welts on you. Nothing permanent. That is why Chimera, our goddess, gave my people such delicate and pale skin. When alive, we could painlessly write and remove spells from our skin. But this made our hides weak. It was one reason why your ancestors eradicated us so easily.*"

Reading this made Nicodemus slow down.

The ghost stopped and looked back at Nicodemus before tossing him a short text. "*Don't be alarmed; I am not angry. I assume you are a scholar as well. Aren't you here for research?*"

After he finished reading, Nicodemus looked up. "Research?"

Tulki quickly offered another paragraph. "*You are a eugrapher researching eugraphic languages, no? Both our languages—Wrixlan and Pithan—are eugraphic. What else would bring you here? You have a living tome there in your hand.*"

Nicodemus looked at the Index. "Living tome?"

The ghost frowned as he produced another reply. "*That Index's parchment is kept alive by its First Language prose. Maybe you don't know: our languages can be written only on living skin. Your constructs chose to store themselves on your body rather than in the Index; they will be much stronger for it. That is the beauty of our languages: we can make our bodies textual.*"

Nicodemus looked from the Index to the ghost. "I don't understand."

The ghost's chest rose and fell in a silent sigh before he held out a reply: "*Your living tome taught you Wrixlan, one of our languages, because you are a eugrapher, yes?*"

"I am a cacographer."

Tulki shook his head as he wrote a response. He flicked it to Nicodemus. "*That is what our last visitor said so long ago. But consider that all eugraphers misspell in the wizardly languages. They try to make the spelling logical. That is why your mind is attracted to Wrixlan; it is logical and therefore eugraphic. Do you not spell more accurately in Wrixlan?*"

"I . . . I did respell a subtext," Nicodemus said and then stopped as something occurred to him. He looked back at his translation of the ghost's message. Surprisingly, it seemed to have no misspellings. True, his disability prevented him from recognizing many misspelled words; however, when he translated in Numinous, he produced so many errors that even his cacographic mind could identify the resulting misspellings.

"Celestial Canon," he swore softly. "Does this mean I'm not a cacographer in your purple language?"

Now smiling, the ghost formed a reply in his arm and held it out. "*That's right. My people have known for a long time that the condition you call 'cacography' is a mismatch between language and mind. Wizardly spelling is arbitrary. Because you are a cacographer, your mind rejects that arbitrariness. In fact, your mind is drawn to languages with logical spellings, such as Wrixlan. That is why your dreams wrote the constructs that now score your skin. And that is why the Index taught you our language. You are sure you did not come here for research?*"

After reading this, Nicodemus looked up nervously. "No, Magister, I'm not a researcher. But I want to learn more about why I'm not a cacographer in . . ." He let his voice trail off as Tulki began to compose a reply.

The ghost forged several sentences within his forearm, stopped, erased two sentences, edited a few others, and then continued forging.

Nicodemus fidgeted impatiently until Tulki held out a completed response. It read, "*Then I must apologize. When I found the delightful night terrors you had written, I was sure their author would one day discover a Wrixlan tome and so learn to see his own dark fantasies. Nearly three hundred years ago we were visited by another eugrapher—a passionate young male. He wanted to learn everything about eugraphy. He looked like you. But, then again, most human males look alike to me. However, returning to my point, maybe ten years ago, I discovered your constructs in the forest and tried to convince them to bring you here if they ever found you. But most were adamant about wanting to—pardon my frankness—eat you.*"

"Eat me?" Nicodemus laughed in surprise.

Tulki nodded and held out another paragraph. "*Thankfully they led you here instead. My apologies for what might now seem like an abduction. But if you're not a researcher . . . that changes everything. Now I fear for the sixty-three other ghosts dwelling here. I had hoped you might help us. Three centuries have passed since that last eugrapher visited. He refreshed our texts in exchange for our teachings. Long before him, we received Chthonic spellwrights from the Heaven Tree. But it seems the mountain homestead has perished.*"

Nicodemus's eyes widened. "The Heaven Tree is real? The Chthonics escaped across the Spindle Bridge? Is that what it is used for?"

The ghost smiled. "*So you are curious! Before I answer, I wonder if you will replenish our spectral codex—the living book that holds our ghostly texts. We simply require the touch of a Wrixlan spellwright. In return, I will answer all the questions you may have.*"

Nicodemus thought for a moment. "A murderous creature called a golem—it is something like a construct—is hunting me. Can you hide me?"

Tulki's smile faded. The ghost formed a sentence in his palm and stared at it for a moment before tossing it to Nicodemus. It read, "*Are you a criminal or a legionary?*"

"Neither," Nicodemus replied.

This time Tulki's response came quickly. "*Then I will not ask why it is chasing you. You may share that when you are ready. However, I must know how this construct is tracking you?*"

Nicodemus touched the back of his neck. "There is a curse laid upon me that broadly casts a signal text."

The ghost smiled again. "*Then we can help. In this place lies our most powerful living tome. Translating its name was difficult. The term the legionaries chose was 'Bestiary.' It is a great book that hides these ruins with a visual subtext, which you surely already saw. The Bestiary also fills this place with an ancient metaspell that deconstructs any magical literature attempting to leave. So your curse's signaling spell will not escape this resting place.*"

Nicodemus took a deep breath in relief.

Tulki nodded vigorously as he presented another paragraph. "*What's more, any non-Wrixlan construct will rapidly deconstruct if it enters here. Likely this golem would suffer the same if it came here. Your night terrors understood how dangerous this place is for constructs; that is why they inscribed themselves on your skin as soon as you arrived. Parts of them are Wrixlan, but mostly they consist of Pithan—our language that affects the mundane world, like your Magnus. If you replenish our spectral codex, we shall happily allow you to stay in this sanctuary.*"

Nicodemus nodded. "Then we have an agreement."

The ghost glowed brighter as he smiled. "*Most wonderful. What shall I call you?*"

"Nicodemus Weal."

"*Nicodemus Weal, you might find it agreeable to dwell with us for a long time. We have much to teach. Would you like to learn about our people?*"

When Nicodemus said he would, the ghost straightened with professorial pride. "*Then follow me as I explain,*" Tulki wrote and then began to lope further into the ruins on all three limbs, pausing only briefly to cast another paragraph: "*I'll start with the Heaven Tree; it does exist deep in the mountains.*

There was a bridge that led to it. But our metaspells and the blueskin constructs have since blocked the way. No human may reach the Heaven Tree Valley now."

Nicodemus had difficulty reading while walking among the stones. The Chthonic, however, had no trouble writing and navigating the rubble. The ghost moved easily with his thin right arm acting as a third leg.

"Did you lose your left arm in the war against the Neosolar Empire?" Nicodemus asked tentatively.

Tulki stood and looked back with an amused expression. "*No, no,*" the ghost wrote. "*All our people have only one 'arm,' as you call it. Indeed, that was a chief reason why our peoples went to war.*"

"But how could such a—" His voice died.

The ghost had unbuttoned his tunic where the garment covered his left shoulder. A long, ashen limb unfolded. A membrane of skin stretched from shoulder to wrist. The four fingers hung two or three feet long, and between them grew the same membranous skin.

Tulki formed a sentence in this sail of skin. Then the ghost peeled the text off and cast the spell to Nicodemus. It read, "*Translating our word for this 'arm' is difficult. Your closest word might be 'palette.'* "

Tulki formed another paragraph within the membranous skin and then cast it to Nicodemus. "*Appreciate that more skin gives a Wrixlan author more writing space. You black-robes carry books to hold more text. But our bodies are our texts. Long ago, our ancestors dwelled under the mountains with the green-skins and blueskins. Then the first Chthonic tribe created our dialects. It was then that the goddess Chimera helped shape our bodies to escape the brutal underworld of the blueskins.*"

"Blueskins?"

Tulki took a moment to compose a reply. "*Your word for them is 'kobolds,' and for greenskins, 'goblins.' They too write on their bodies. But their hides are tough, their dialects savage. They brand themselves. Our dialects require elegance. Our goddess used the First Language to adapt our bodies to our words. Our skin became soft and amenable to Pithan and Wrixlan; we wrote more and more on our left arms, and so we needed more and more skin.*"

The ghost nodded to his palette before casting the next paragraph. "*Through Chimera's First Language, our left arms grew into palettes. You see why our ancestors thought each other monstrous. A Chthonic born with two arms would be like a human born with three.*"

Nicodemus could only nod.

Tulki looked to the sky and then tossed out two quick sentences: "*Dawn is not far. We must go underground.*" With that, he hurried further into the rubble.

Following as quickly as he could, Nicodemus asked, "But what of

Wrixlan being eugraphic? Can it cure my cacography in the wizardly languages?"

Without slowing, Tulki threw a reply over one shoulder. "*No, but I don't see what there is to 'cure,' as you say.*"

By the time Nicodemus had finished reading this, Tulki had ducked inside an ancient building that still had much of its roof. Nicodemus followed and discovered that inside the hovel a set of narrow stairs led down into darkness.

The ghost's body began to shed a soft, indigo light. "*Mind your big feet,*" he warned with a quick spell and then descended the stairs. "*We hope you will stay with us and replenish our codex many times over the years. To remain hidden from the construct, you must stay underground during the day.*"

"Why?" Nicodemus asked while negotiating the tiny steps.

"*Because bright light, especially sunlight, deconstructs Wrixlan. Your ancestors used this to slaughter us. By night, we possessed spells as powerful as any human text. But by day, we were defenseless. How we used to dread the dawn when the blood-hungry legionaries would come.*"

They reached the bottom of the stairs and now stood in a rectangular cellar with a low ceiling and blank stone walls. "You must loathe me," Nicodemus whispered.

Tulki smiled. "*On the contrary, Nicodemus Weal, if you replenish our text, you will become one of the few humans I have ever truly liked.*"

CHAPTER
Thirty-five

The ghost pointed to a small stone vault and then tossed Nicodemus a sentence. "*Our spectral codex is stored in there.*"

Nicodemus lifted the vault's lid and found a book, nearly the Index's twin, lying at the bottom.

A glowing note from Tulki appeared next to Nicodemus's hand. It read, "*You need only place a hand on an open page. It might have a disorienting effect. Several hours may pass without your noticing. You might see flashes from our past—the codex also contains a history of our people.*"

Nicodemus looked up at the ghost. "Will it make me sick?" When the ghost raised his eyebrows, he explained how touching the Index for the first time made him vomit.

The ghost shook his head. "*That was because the Index forced Wrixlan into your mind. That will not be the case here. The Index is a tome; this book is a simple codex. However, when the sky lightens I must return to its pages. We Wrixlan ghosts never express ourselves outside of a manuscript during the day. The risk of exposure is too great.*"

Nicodemus thought for a moment. "Before I begin, perhaps you could explain one more thing: you mentioned something called the First Language."

Tulki wrote several sentences but then scratched his chin and began editing.

Nicodemus tried not to fidget as he waited.

When the response was finished, Tulki held it out while looking Nicodemus in the eye. It read, "*The other eugrapher from long ago also asked about this. But I can't satisfy much of your curiosity. I know the First Language changed our ancestors' bodies. I know First Language prose keeps our living books alive. But that is all I know. Only by engaging a Bestiary could one learn the First Language. And only high priests were allowed to read a Bestiary in life. We ghosts won't violate the old ways; none of us will engage our Bestiary.*"

Nicodemus thought about this and then asked, "And why call it a Bestiary? Does the book describe animals?"

The ghost shook his head and wrote, "*I don't think so. I think it was a problem of translation. The Bestiary contains knowledge of the First Language. In fact, the center of any Chthonic colony is a Bestiary. It has to be that way, because a Bestiary helped us change to survive in a new realm."*

"And so these ruins were to be a new colony? That's how you came here?"

Tulki wrote for a moment and then handed Nicodemus two paragraphs. "*Not quite. This place was only a town, destroyed during the first siege. We ghosts were stranded here when Starhaven finally fell. When the legionaries breached the walls, several Chthonic warriors took our Bestiary and dashed southward. They hoped to reach the Iron Wood or the Grysome Mountains and establish a new colony. They brought with them two spectral codices. One was filled with artistic and priestly ghosts, the other with political and scholarly ghosts. I was stored in the latter.*

"*But the humans caught the escape party at dawn. The ensuing battle destroyed the codex holding the priestly ghosts. The living Chthonics who survived the human attack brought the Bestiary and the remaining spectral codex here to these ruins. After helping the Bestiary to write the protecting subtexts and metaspells, the living ran for the mountains and the Heaven Tree . . . they never made it.*"

Nicodemus paused for a respectful moment before speaking. "And is your First Language related to Language Prime?"

The text gave him a quizzical look.

Nicodemus tried to explain. "Language Prime is the Creator's language, the language of the first words, the source of all magic."

The ghost frowned and held out a few sentences. "*As I said, I am no priest. But I do remember the Neosolar Empire labeled the First Language as blasphemous. They said we were trying to alter the Creator's text or some nonsense. They used the idea that we were distorting holy language to justify their bloodlust.*"

Nicodemus read this and then said, "I must learn whatever I can about Language Prime. Your First Language might be similar to it. Is the Bestiary nearby?"

The ghost licked his lips before nodding.

"Am I capable of reading it?"

Tulki wrote a response and hesitantly held it out. "*Yes . . . one needs only fluency in Wrixlan to engage the tome . . . but I fear I cannot let you do so.*"

"Your religion forbids it? Is it dangerous?"

The Chthonic shook his head. "*There is a little danger, but not much. And the old ways do not prohibit humans from reading it. But, you see, we allowed the last eugrapher to read the Bestiary. After engaging the text, he grew fractious. He soon left and never returned.*"

Now it was Nicodemus's turn to be puzzled. "What did he learn from the book?"

The ghost cast a reply and then looked at his feet. "*He would not say.*"

Nicodemus suddenly understood. "You fear that whatever upset the previous cacographer will upset me and I won't replenish your spectral codex."

"*Please don't be angry. If you do not help us, we will deconstruct.*"

"I see your dilemma. How about a trade? I will replenish your codex now and promise to return in the future. In exchange, you will let me engage the Bestiary."

The ghost peered into Nicodemus's face and then composed his script. "*Yes, that could work. Let us talk more after you refresh our text. But remember, if it is after sunrise when you wake, I will not be here. Wait for night and do not build a fire or cast any harsh illuminating text. I will return.*"

"Agreed," Nicodemus said, and turned to regard the spectral codex that lay within its stone vault. Its brasswork gleamed dully.

"I do this to demonstrate my good faith." He opened the book and planted his hand on the open page.

EVERYTHING BLAZED WHITE and then faded into black. Suddenly Nicodemus was not himself. Nor was he in his own time.

He was a young Chthonic male pausing from his early evening spell work. His bare feet stood on the newly built tower bridge. Its stones were still warm from the summer sunlight. He looked east. Before him stretched the dusty expanse of felled trees and rock piles.

Soon they would build towers there as well, and the city would grow even larger. Farther away stood the moonlit mountains. In the middle of the sheer rock face gaped a wide tunnel that ran into the mountain.

He remembered that long ago his ancestors had built that tunnel to escape the underworld. But sometimes, blueskin raiders had come screaming out of the tunnel to steal food, tools, and females. His people had led counterstrikes down the tunnel to kill the offending blueskins and take others as slaves.

But now a truce had been made. Wards had been written within the cave mouth to restrict passage. His people had filled the entrance with their metaspells, and the blueskins had matched this with thousands of their digging tortoise constructs. Now only official delegations could pass between the upperworld and the underworld.

In celebration of this truce, his people were decorating the rockface. A carving of ivy leaves was to represent his people's metaspells because ivy, like his kind, grew from stony soil and could climb to great heights. A carving of a tortoise shell was to represent the blueskin's war constructs.

The truce required both his people and the blueskins to meet at the cave mouth every year to renew the agreements of the peace. Some of his people were displeased with the truce; they wanted easier access to the Heaven Tree homestead.

But most were content, and the yearly renewal of the truce was a celebrated holiday. Some even spoke of building a bridge out to the tunnel.

However, a growing number of elders—remembering the horrors they had seen before they left the underworld—argued that they should abandon the Heaven Tree and collapse the tunnel. Only this, they said, would end all contact with the blueskins and so permanently stop the raids.

Without warning the world again dissolved into blinding white light. For a moment Nicodemus was himself again . . . but then everything changed.

He was now a Chthonic elder standing on a sunlit bridge in a completed Starhaven. Many years had passed. Before him stretched the Spindle Bridge. It reached out from Starhaven to land against the solid cliff face. He could see the ivy pattern and the tortoise pattern carved into the rock.

But the tunnel was gone. The bridge ran into solid stone. He tried to remember what had happened to the tunnel but found his mind was filled with terror. He shifted his palette limb underneath his tunic and looked westward. Moving across the oak savanna were two red squares, each a mile in width and length.

Sunlight glinted off helmets and spear points. These were the Fifth and the Ninth Neosolar Legions. They had come to lay siege to Starhaven.

He pulled his palette closer and cursed the sunlight. The hour had come at last. In a matter of days, he and all his people would die.

"Nicodemus!" someone called faintly. "Niiicooodeeemus!"

Abruptly Nicodemus was himself again, standing in the small Chthonic cellar. His hand was hovering above the living codex that held the Wrixlan ghosts. Tulki was gone. Looking back, he saw sunlight shining on the steps that led up to the ruined Chthonic outpost. It was morning.

"Niiicooodeeemus!" His name came again from a distant female voice.

His heart tightened. How had she found him? He was supposed to be hidden.

Then he remembered the Seed of Finding. The last signal text it would have cast would have been from just outside the ruins. She must have reached that spot and started calling out.

"Niiicooodeeeeeemus!" she yelled again.

Deirdre!

CHAPTER

Thirty-six

Nicodemus woke to see Deirdre padding down the cellar stairs. A lone sunbeam had slipped through the tattered ceiling to land on the steps. As the druid walked through the light, the sword strapped to her back glinted solar white. She was holding up the front of her robes to make a basket; on the pale cloth rested small pieces of darkness. Nicodemus picked up the Index and went to her.

"Clear sky, cold and windy," she whispered as they squatted by the nearby wall. "Reminds me of the bright autumn days in the Highlands." She had folded her legs so the nest of blackberries sat in her lap.

Nicodemus set down the Index and watched with single-minded anticipation as her dark fingers extracted a mound of berries and overturned them into his cupped hands.

"John will need some too," he said.

On the other side of the cellar, the big man was curled up on Nicodemus's cloak. Getting him to sleep that morning had been a struggle.

Shortly after Nicodemus had brought Deirdre and John back to the ruins, the big man's wits had returned with a squall of terror and tears. At first, he had screamed every time Nicodemus had touched him. But eventually he let the younger man pull him into an embrace. Then John had begun to repeat the name "Devin . . . Devin . . . Devin . . ." over and over.

Nicodemus had wept with him until exhaustion pulled them both into sleep.

"I set several rabbit snares," Deirdre whispered, feeding herself a berry between words. "With luck, evening will see us with dinner." She searched Nicodemus's face. "Now that we know more about the Chthonics, have you discovered anything about that dream you told me of—the one of Fellwroth surrounded by ivy and turtles? Any clue where the monster's true body is now?"

Nicodemus shook his head. "I thought the body must be in a cave where the Spindle Bridge meets the mountain. There must be some connection to the ivy and hexagon patterns carved into the mountain face. But in the Chthonic visions, I saw that the cave into the mountain had disappeared after the Spindle Bridge was built. And Shannon probed the rock before the bridge and found nothing. There must be some other connection. It's frustrating. I can't consult the ghosts again until tonight."

He popped a blackberry into his mouth and stared down at the tattoos that covered his hands and forearms. It was strange to think about Garkex and the other night terrors being written across his body.

Deirdre was still studying him. "The dreams might not matter. We'll be safe when we reach my goddess's ark. When will you be ready to run to Gray's Crossing?"

Nicodemus paused, a berry at his lips. "When I met the golem, it was coming up from Gray's Crossing."

He had told Deirdre about his strange dreams, his encounter with Fellwroth, and his dealings with the Chthonic ghost. But he had not told her what Fellwroth had said about the struggle between two factions—one demonic, one divine—to breed a Language Prime spellwright.

"Fellwroth must be watching Gray's Crossing," he continued. "He might anticipate our trying to reach your goddess's ark."

Deirdre shook her head; her raven hair gleamed even in the half-light. "A dozen armed devotees—two of them druids—guard the stone. And it's well hidden; Fellwroth wouldn't know where to find it."

Her wide eyes widened; her dark cheeks flushed darker. "Nicodemus, we are so close now. My goddess can sense you nearing. She longs to protect you."

Nicodemus put the blackberry in his mouth and chewed it slowly. "Deirdre, who is your goddess?"

A soft smile curled her lips. "She is Boann of the Highlands, not a powerful deity, but a water goddess of unsurpassed beauty, a dweller of the secret brooks and streams that flow among the boulders and the heather."

Nicodemus thought about what Fellwroth had told him. "Does she have many Imperials—those that look like us—in her service?"

"A few," she said, eating another berry. "My family has done so for time out of mind. In the Lowlands, my cousins serve her. But you must understand that she is a Dralish deity. The Lornish occupy the Highlands still. Those of us holding to the old ways must hide—"

Nicodemus interrupted. "Does she direct your family as to whom they might marry?"

This made Deirdre's eyebrows sink. "We never marry without her blessing."

"Is she trying to produce a Language Prime spellwright?"

"Language Prime?"

"Maybe she called it the First Language. Have you heard of that?"

Deirdre only frowned.

"No, you haven't. But did your goddess know that Typhon had crossed the ocean? Has she been struggling against him for long?"

"Nicodemus, what are you driving at?"

He looked down. "Nothing. Only thinking aloud."

Fellwroth had said that those opposing the Disjunction—the Alliance of Divine Heretics—would kill Nicodemus on sight. But Nicodemus distrusted the monster. If the Alliance wanted a Language Prime spellwright so badly, they might be willing to help Nicodemus recover the missing part of himself in return for his service.

For this reason, Nicodemus hoped that Deirdre's goddess was a member of the Alliance. Clearly Deirdre did not want him dead; she could have broken his neck long ago.

The problem was that Deirdre didn't seem to know about Language Prime or whether her goddess was a member of this Alliance.

But then again, she might know more than she was letting on. Nicodemus needed a way to learn more about her.

Suddenly the blackberry in his mouth became sour. He knew what he had to do. "Deirdre," he said softly, "Kyran is dead."

She looked away. "I know." The room's faint light glowed on her smooth cheeks and accentuated her youthful appearance.

Nicodemus continued, "He died fighting Fellwroth in the compluvium . . . saved my life. He gave me this script." Holding out his empty right hand, Nicodemus pulled Kyran's final spell from his chest with his left. "He asked that I give it to you."

Deirdre looked down at his right hand and then away. "Read it to me," she whispered.

Nicodemus's heart began to strike. "I'd rather you take it."

Again she looked at his right hand and shook her head. "Please, read it to me."

A silent pause.

"Deirdre," Nicodemus said gently, "you're illiterate."

She looked at him as if he had turned into a frog. "I learned to read fifty years before you were born."

"Not mundane language, magical language. You can't read even the common magical languages. You're not a druid."

She started to say one thing and then stopped. Started to say another, stopped. "How did you know?" she managed at last.

"When I told you of Kyran's spell, you looked at my right hand." He nodded to the hand in question, which he had stretched out as if offering something.

She frowned "And?"

"I'm holding the text in my left."

"THERE WERE OTHER clues," Nicodemus added. "Your diction is wrong. You refer to spells and text as 'magic'—no spellwright would use such a general term. You never unbuttoned your sleeves when we were fleeing Starhaven. You claimed to wield a different kind of magic, but any kind of spellwriting would require you to look at your arms. And then there's your greatsword. A man of six feet would need both hands just to lift that weapon. You toss it about as if it were a feather."

Deirdre closed her eyes and pressed a slender hand to her cheek. "Only the druids were called to the convocation. I couldn't get into Starhaven without the disguise."

Nicodemus said nothing.

She looked at the stairwell. The sunbeam was moving up the steps. Maybe three hours had passed since midday. "I am Boann's avatar. Do you know what that means?"

"Theology was thought to be wasted on cacographers. I only know what they say in the stories."

She nodded. "Deities sometimes invest worthy devotees with portions of their souls. Just as golems carry the spirits of their authors, we avatars carry the souls of our deities. If we die before our divine souls can disengage, then part of the divinity dies with us. And those who carry souls of the high gods and goddesses become the heroes of your stories—warriors with impenetrable skin, bards with hypnotic voices, and so on."

She smiled sadly. "Boann is nothing so powerful. My gifts are simple: I do not age, I heal with extraordinary speed, and for a brief time I may possess the strength of ten or eleven men."

Nicodemus was confused. "Why did you come looking for me?"

"What I said before is true. Last spring, Boann ordered me to attend the Starhaven convocation where I would find a 'treasure wrapped in black.' You asked if she knew of Typhon. Perhaps she did and didn't tell me. Now that I think on it, she must have known the demon had hidden you here. Why else send me?"

Nicodemus glanced back to make sure the Index still lay behind him. "Deirdre, I didn't tell you everything Fellwroth told me." He explained what he knew about Language Prime and the monster's claim about two factions striving to breed a Language Prime spellwright.

Deirdre listened with her head resting against the wall. When he finished, she spoke in a flat, exhausted voice. "If they do exist, the Alliance of Divine Heretics is well named. The belief that there is no savior—no

Halcyon for the wizards, no Peregrine for the druids, no Cynosure for the hierophants—is perilously heretical. It denies all prophecies, and the high deities use those prophecies to justify their rule over their kingdoms. The heretical gods would need to remain hidden and wage their war against the Disjunction in secret."

She closed her eyes. "I can't say if any of this is true or not; nor can I say if Boann is a party to this Alliance." She paused. "Though her sending me here to rescue you makes it seem probable."

"But you're her avatar; shouldn't you know her intentions?"

Deirdre produced a quavering sigh. "I am indeed Boann's avatar. Her only one. But . . . a year ago, I lost her love."

Nicodemus hugged his knees to his chest and said nothing.

She took a long breath. "The savage Lornish Kingdom occupies my native Highlands. But there are many among us who fight to restore our homelands to the civil forests of Dral. Nearly forty years ago, I became Boann's avatar in this struggle."

She was breathing faster now, her cheeks flushing. "I was married when she called. I had two sons I loved dearly. But when the goddess commanded me to go, I left without hesitation. Years later, my husband died with nothing but hatred for me. But you must understand how perfect Boann's love is."

The woman's face had grown tense. Her eyes shone with a light that Nicodemus had once mistaken for simple excitement.

She took the greatsword from her back and set it on the ground. "From time to time, Dralish druids sneak into the Highlands to fight for our independence. Kyran came to me two years ago. His nephew was a famous Highland brigand who ceaselessly attacked the Lornish. The Highlanders called him the White Fox. The Lowlanders had worse names for him and marked his wife and sons for death. So Kyran came across the border to smuggle his nephew's family into Dral. My goddess, hating Lornish rule, was more than happy to help."

Deirdre looked at the steps again. "But the Paladin of Garwyn attacked during our crossing into Dral. I managed to save Kyran and his nephew, but not the rest of the family. The paladin slaughtered them."

She shook her head. "I took Kyran and the Fox back to one of my clan's secret holdings. I managed to sneak the brigand back into Dral, but Kyran was too badly wounded. He stayed with us for a year. Boann knew but . . ." She swallowed. "Boann had forbidden me to take a lover, and . . ."

Nicodemus made a soft sound.

"She discovered my infidelity. Some part of me must have known she would. She withdrew much of her soul from me. For an agonizing season,

I was mortal again. And though Kyran and I ceased to be lovers, Boann stayed away. He and I dedicated ourselves to winning her forgiveness."

Nicodemus touched her knee. "But he didn't love Boann; he loved you."

She laughed humorlessly. "Was it so obvious? Yes, he dedicated himself to helping me recover Boann's affection even though it meant helping me forget my love for him. It was a selfless, stupid thing to do. In a way, I was unfaithful to him as well. I tried to explain that the love he and I shared was flawed, human."

The avatar wiped her eyes with a sleeve. "How we used to argue. Tortured circles, around and around. He claimed that he—unlike Boann—would never punish me or withhold his love. The poor fool. Likely, he was right. It was frightening how wildly he loved me. But . . . he couldn't understand that perfect love does exist."

Nicodemus withdrew his hand as he remembered Kyran's death. The man's eyes had burned with agony. Nicodemus had thought the pain was born of the stomach wound. Now he saw what had truly tortured the druid. "Don't be like me, boy," Kyran had growled. "Be anything; be wild, be saintly, be wicked. Love all or love none, but don't be like me."

Deirdre was still talking. "After Kyran and I prayed and fasted, Boann called me back to her ark and invested nearly all of her soul into me. But it has never again been like it once was. Now she no longer trusts me. Now when our wills diverge she . . . sends me into seizures and takes control of my body."

The woman wiped her eyes again. "I should be grateful. Back in Starhaven, Fellwroth's golem trapped me. The monster would have killed me if Boann hadn't controlled my body through a seizure. And I am grateful . . . but sometimes I don't know who I am. Sometimes I feel as if my heart is not my own, as if I am only a vessel for the desires of others."

Nicodemus leaned toward her. "And you believe that if you bring me to Boann's ark, she will trust you again?"

The lines around Deirdre's eyes smoothed. "Yes."

In her gaze Nicodemus saw a desire so strong that it had become emptiness. She had lost part of herself. She was disabled in love. Just as he would be incomplete until he regained his ability to spell, she would be incomplete until she regained her perfect love.

"And so Kyran and I came to Starhaven to atone," she said. "Last spring, Boann ordered us to join the druidic delegation that was passing through the Highlands. We brought many of Boann's devotees and her ark. The other druids, the ones we couldn't go to when fleeing Starhaven, are the true diplomats who came with concerns about the Silent Blight.

They do not trust us; they tolerated us only because they could not refuse a goddess's request."

The woman's fingers clenched into fists. "We must go to Boann as soon as possible."

Nicodemus frowned. "But I have questions for the Chthonics. I might learn something more of Language Prime. Besides, Fellwroth must be watching Gray's Crossing. We have to wait—"

"No!" Deirdre's sharp retort made Simple John stir in his sleep.

"No," she continued in a lowered voice. "If you don't come, Boann may send me into another seizure. She may force me to do things I don't want to." She was looking at him now with eyes wide with fear.

Nicodemus felt his hands go cold. "You haven't abducted me yet, Deirdre. You could have easily done so. Your goddess must know it would be foolish. Fellwroth would find us."

Deirdre pressed a trembling hand to her chin. "Before I met Kyran, I was sure of everything. 'Deirdre wry-smile' they called me. You must have seen it sometime. I used to wear that smile like armor. My love for Boann was so true that I found mortals—with their dithering uncertainties—somehow amusing. But now the half-smile runs off my face like water."

"You wore that smile when I met you."

"I have embraced every sacrifice Boann required," she continued, "leaving my husband, my sons, the society of other mortals. I did not miss them so long as I basked in her love. But now . . . now that Kyran has died because I . . ."

She squeezed her eyes shut. "And such horrible dreams I have—dreams of standing on a riverbank and being stabbed somehow by a wolf with a man's head and glowing red eyes."

Nicodemus's head bobbed back. "In a Highland river?"

She nodded.

Nicodemus spoke excitedly. "Fellwroth killed Typhon in a Highland river, cut the demon into fragments with some kind of disspelling wand. I saw it happen when the golem touched me. And on the road, Fellwroth said Typhon was trying to infect a minor deity. Perhaps it was your goddess."

Deirdre looked at him. "Then that must be how my goddess knew of you. She is the sovereign of Highland rivers; she must have seen Fellwroth betray his master. Somehow she must have extracted knowledge of you from the dead demon. That must be why she sends the visions to me. She has invested so much of her soul in me that she cannot express herself outside of her ark. She has no direct way of communicating with me, except by controlling"—she looked down at her lap—"this body."

Again Nicodemus thought about how she had been disabled by love. He thought about John who, out of love, had sought to protect Nicodemus and who now suffered unimaginably because he had loved Devin. He thought also about what Deirdre had done to Kyran and what Kyran had done to himself.

Gently, he placed a hand on Deirdre's shoulder. "What you did, you did out of love."

She laughed cruelly. "Don't be a romantic fool. There's no force more savage. My love for Boann destroyed my love for Kyran, then destroyed the man himself."

"He chose his path."

Again, the hard laugh. "In that, then, he and I were alike; we loved too well. We all love too well." She closed her eyes. "Will you read me Kyran's last message now?"

He looked down at the dim green sentence in his left hand. It was so simple that even his cacographic mind had not misspelled the translation: "*I loved you always; I love you still.*"

He read it aloud.

Deirdre bent forward, her chin on her chest. Again she wore the half-smile, but it no longer held wry amusement. It pulled her face down into a gruesome mask. She shook silently.

When Nicodemus squeezed her hand, she pulled him into an embrace.

HOURS LATER NICODEMUS woke to find the sunbeam gone from the steps. Only the fading light of dusk came down the stairs.

They were—all three of them—sleeping against the far wall. The Index lay beside Nicodemus, and John was looking at him with frightened eyes.

"Nico," the big man whispered, "you know it was what Typhon made me do?"

When Nicodemus said that he did, the big man closed his eyes and let out a long breath.

"Are you all right, John?"

The other man pressed his lips together and shook his head. "No," he said as tears came to his eyes. Nicodemus reached out and took his hand. John said nothing.

In the silence, Nicodemus could hear the wind whistling through the trees. Somewhere far away, a rook called.

John studied him with wet brown eyes. "Are you all right, Nico?"

Nicodemus didn't look away when his own tears came. "No," he said. "No."

CHAPTER

Thirty-seven

Outside Shannon's cell, a man cried out as if dying.

The old wizard tried to hurry out of his bed but the Magnus chains wrapped around his wrists jerked him back.

He was still spellbound.

Worse, the censoring text locked around his mind kept him from seeing magical language and made the resulting blackness seem to spin.

He was truly blind now.

The cry came again. Moving more slowly, Shannon put his legs over the side of the bed and arranged his robes. He would face the end with dignity.

A thud sounded from the direction of the door. He did not flinch. The thud came again, accompanied by the crack of breaking Magnus sentences.

Shannon straightened his dreadlocks, smoothed his beard. Another thud and the door gave way with a metallic squeal.

Silence, then the clicking of leather boot heels on stone.

"Rash of you to come in your true body," Shannon said as calmly as he could. "The sentinels will know of your existence after you kill me."

"Kill you?" Fellwroth asked with amusement. Something stirred the air beside Shannon. "Nothing so simple, Magister. Come."

Suddenly Shannon was on his feet, hands stretched out before him as Fellwroth pulled him along by his chains.

"I'm no use to you," Shannon called. "The boy's gone. You'll never find out who he is now that—"

"Nicodemus Weal is in the forest south of here," Fellwroth rasped. "Yes, I know his name. And, yes, I could flush him out of hiding. But at best that would start a time-consuming chase; at worst, it would kill the whelp." They were hurrying down a long hallway. "You will carry a message to him."

They turned and suddenly Shannon was stumbling up stairs. "I don't know how to find him," the old wizard said, fighting the dizziness caused by the censoring text.

"Magister, you're a miserable liar," Fellwroth rasped. "I'm going to release you, and you're going to carry my message to the boy."

Shannon shook his head. "Even if I could find him, I would never do so." The stairs ended and again Shannon was walking down a hallway.

Fellwroth snorted. "You insult my understanding of human motivation. I know you'd never go to him if I tracked you. I will not follow. Double back five times over. Romp around in the forests all night looking for a subtextual tracker. You'll find nothing. When you're satisfied, take my message to the boy."

Cold wind blew across Shannon's face. They had left the hallway and were walking in the open air.

"The end game begins," Fellwroth croaked. "It doesn't matter that the sentinels know of me. We play on a field outside of Starhaven now. Should the wizards catch Nicodemus and bring him back here, I would have no trouble pulling him from their prisons. In fact, that's my message to the boy: you and he are to return to Starhaven and place yourselves in the sentinels' custody. I will use a sand golem to retrieve both of you the instant the black-robes have you."

"What makes you think we would do such a thing?"

Fellwroth's footsteps began to produce wooden thuds. Shannon frowned. Could they be walking across the drawbridge?

"You can't feel it yet, Magister," Fellwroth hissed, "but I have laced the muscles around your stomach with a Language Prime curse named canker. It forces the muscles to forge dangerous amounts of text. But I've edited this version to slow its progress. I call it logorrhea. It won't kill you in an hour or even a day. It will grow stronger and stronger until it bursts your stomach. If fortunate, you'll succumb to fever. If unlucky, you will digest your own entrails."

Shannon could hear the wind rushing through the trees. Somehow they were on the dirt road outside Starhaven. What had happened to the guards?

"I will die screaming before I see Nicodemus submit to you," Shannon growled.

"Tell the boy that only the Emerald of Arahest can cure the canker growing in your gut."

"I'll tell him to run as fast as he can."

Fellwroth grunted. "If the boy runs, I will find him or he will die." The monster pulled him hard to the right.

Shannon's boots left the dirt road and began to swish though knee-high grass.

"Tell Nicodemus that if he submits to me, I will grant him partial use of the emerald. Tell him I will cure your canker."

Shannon shook his head. "You're a fool."

The footsteps in front of him stopped. "Twenty paces ahead is a meadow where a horse is tethered to a low branch. I've spellbound your blue parrot to your saddle."

"Azure," Shannon said involuntarily.

Fellwroth laughed. "The sentinels had caged the bird in the stables with childish prose. Now go and tell the whelp what I have told you."

"I'll never—"

Two cold hands yanked Shannon forward by the wrists and peeled the fetters from his arms and legs. The old wizard gasped as the hands tore the censoring text from his head. His mind, restored to magic, reeled with shock. It felt as if icy needles were scraping across every inch of his skin.

"Tell the boy!" Fellwroth snarled, giving Shannon a shove.

The old wizard stumbled backward. His foot caught and he fell onto his back.

The only sound was that of footfalls on pine needles.

"I'll die before I tell him!" Shannon shouted after the monster.

No reply.

"IT'S JUST IN here," the elderly sentinel said.

Amadi was standing in the hallway of a small storage tower. Outside the evening sky was bruising purple.

The gray-haired woman standing before Amadi was a Starhaven sentinel, not one of her trusted Astrophell authors. "Magistra," Amadi said, "I haven't much time. The provost has demanded I prepare a report—"

"One of my younger riders found it on the road up from Gray's Crossing," the woman interrupted. "It was in the ditch, so it's not surprising no one else saw it. Unfortunately, when the rider reported it, the guards didn't believe him." The old woman cast a short Numinous password into the door before her.

A frown creased Amadi's brow. "Didn't believe him about what?"

The old sentinel shook her head. "Best if I show you. I put it in here to prevent rumors."

They walked into a room lit by candles. A young male lesser wizard was staring wide-eyed at something large and dark on the floor.

At first Amadi thought the object was a body. It was lying stomach down. Its left arm had been melted into a thin rod. Small pools of metallic blood had frozen around the thing's shoulder and chest.

"Los in hell!" Amadi approached it. The thing's face was human but for the rectangular window opening into its brow. She bent closer. The head was hollow.

"Pure iron," the woman behind her said. "Took two wizards and a mule-drawn cart to haul it up here."

"Shannon, it seems I owe you an apology," Amadi murmured. "Monsters made of clay and metal."

"Magistra Okeke!" Amadi turned back to the door. "Magistra!" It was Kale.

Amadi groaned. "Every time I see you, Kale, I get more horrible news. So before you tell me something else, let's take care of this." She nodded to the iron carcass. "I need three trusted sentinels to carry it up to the provost's grand hall. And I want Shannon awake and ready to answer more questions."

"That's just it," Kale panted. "Shannon's gone."

"Gone?"

"Someone took him. The guard is dead. The text about the cell was dispelled and the door was knocked down from the outside."

Amadi's mind came alive with questions. Who would want to take Shannon from her? The golem monster? How was she going to explain this to the provost? "Do we know where his captor took him? What direction they went?"

Again Kale nodded. "Out the front gate."

"How is that possible?" the gray-haired sentinel asked. "The front gate is too well guarded."

Kale's frightened eyes turned to the woman. "Many sentinels and guards were wounded fighting the bookworm infestation. The rest were spread out across the stronghold, searching for Nicodemus. There were no guards in the gate house and only two before the drawbridge. Both are dead."

"Raise the alarm," Amadi commanded. "Call the searchers up from Gray's Crossing and in from the forests. No one is to leave Starhaven's occupied towers and halls. And see that the slain guards are prepared for a proper burial."

Kale nodded.

"And tell the digger to make another grave," Amadi added. "After I tell all this to the provost, you'll have to put me in it."

CHAPTER Thirty-eight

Raindrops cut icy flecks of life into Deirdre's wind-numbed face. Billowing clouds blanketed the sky save for a few rents that poured city-sized sunbeams onto the Highlands.

Deirdre was laughing as she galloped down the Highridge Road. To either side, the mountains dropped into deep valleys. Some dells were crisscrossed with stone walls and speckled with Highland sheep. Ravens there were too, clouds of them flapping through the dark sky or filling the few trees like a harvest of noisy, black-feathered fruit.

Topping the next ridge, Deirdre looked down the road to the watchtowers guarding the entrance to Glengorm: one of her clan's fortified homesteads.

As she galloped, sunlight swept across the road and glinted on her armor. The guards cheered as she tore through the open gates.

Down into the glen she flew, barely noticing the fortified houses or the wooden barricades meant to keep livestock in and lycanthropes out. At the bottom of the glen lay a narrow lake. A small stone fort stood on a jetty that extended into the gray water.

Deirdre did not rein in her mare until she was in the fort's stable yard. Her clansmen in the stalls shouted joyously. Others appeared at the windows.

Deirdre swung down and threw her reins to the nearest boy. "Treat her well," she said through a wry smile. "She's had a bit of a run."

The men within earshot laughed at her understatement.

She raised a fist and yelled, "The White Fox has escaped to Dral! Confusion to the Lornish Crown!" The men echoed her cry at near deafening volume.

She led another cheer and then hurried into the fort and up three flights of narrow wooden stairs. When she pushed the door open, Kyran was pacing by the window.

His limp was less pronounced now, but still he favored his left leg, probably would for the rest of his life. His long hair hung across his shoulders in a golden curtain.

Her wry smile renewed itself. "Only half a year ago Paladin Garwyn nearly cut that limb off." She nodded to his bandaged right leg. "Perhaps you shouldn't be troubling it so."

Kyran turned around, his brown eyes alight with expectation. "Great Soul," he said, sinking to his left knee.

She closed the door and went to him. His freshly shaven face turned up toward her. The scar below his ear was little more than a red line now. "My cousin?" he asked. "Did he make it safely to Dral?"

Deirdre suppressed a laugh. "Always so serious, Kyran. The White Fox runs in feral woods tonight. A fist of rangers met us at the river. If they can avoid the lycanthropes, they shall reach Kerreac in less than a fortnight."

Relief drew Kyran's thin lips into a dimpled smile. He took her hand and bent over it. "I swear on Bridget's name that you have my undying love."

His touch made Deirdre's head feel as light as smoke.

There was nothing to indicate it, but she knew that he had meant "you" to be plural, to include her goddess. Her hands trembled as she turned his chin up. "And you shall have ours."

He stood and pressed his lips to hers. Her heart throbbed to an irregular rhythm. She felt as if she were having an aura.

She had thought of this for so long, known how forbidden it was. "From the first," he whispered, "I loved you always."

Laughing, she pulled him closer and stopped his words with her tongue.

She could tell by his kiss that this time he had meant the word "you" to be singular; his love was for her only.

His arms closed around her.

"Do you love me still?" she murmured into his neck. "Love me only?"

"Yes." His voice the briefest susurration by her ear. "I loved you always; I love you still."

Her face tingled with warmth as she pulled back far enough to kiss him again.

Slowly the world tilted so that they lay facing each other. The room dimmed. Her hands trembled badly. His face lost its bristles and became as smooth as a boy's. His long golden hair, flowing all about them, darkened until it was as black as her own. Her hands clenched as an ecstatic warmth flushed down her back. Silently, she prayed she would not fall into a seizure now.

Her lover's eyes lightened from dark brown to deep green. They were not Kyran's eyes.

She was not falling into a seizure but waking from one.

Kyran was dead.

With a shriek, she threw out her arms and turned away from Nicodemus.

DEIRDRE'S SHOVE TOSSED Nicodemus into the air.

Arms flailing, he turned a half-flip and landed on his back. All the air rushed from his lungs.

He tried to inhale but couldn't. Suddenly Deirdre, her druid robes streaked with dirt, was kneeling over him and apologizing.

Long airless moments passed, each one an agonizing eternity. Deirdre took his tattooed hands. "Are you hurt? Why did you do that?"

At last Nicodemus's lungs expanded. "I didn't do anything!" he panted. "You were the one who—"

He stopped.

Only the faint light of dusk came down the cellar stairs, but it was enough to illuminate her tears.

"What did I do?" she asked in a shaky voice. "It was a seizure, Nicodemus; my goddess took control of me. I don't remember a thing."

Nicodemus's throat tightened. He glanced over and saw that John had slept through their exchange so far. Nervously, he turned back to Deirdre. "You . . . you and I were talking about what we should do next. You argued that we need to run to Gray's Crossing and find Boann's ark. I thought it was too dangerous. By now the sentinels will be looking for me."

Deirdre shook her head. "The ark sits in an inn at the town's edge. It won't be difficult to reach undetected."

Nicodemus sat up. His head throbbed where it had struck ground. "Deirdre, I've stolen the Index. Every wizard south of Astrophell must be editing their attack spells and forming witch hunts to find me. Listen, Shannon gave me more than enough gold to see us to Dar or the City of Rain. You must have allies in the Highlands who can help us."

Deirdre was shaking her head. "Nicodemus, it doesn't matter where you run; without divine protection Fellwroth will find you."

Nicodemus winced as his hand brushed his cheek. Shannon's Magnus stitches were holding, but the wound was still tender. "This is where the argument stopped before. But you began to speak of your goddess's beauty and then . . ." He looked away. "And you told me . . ."

"Nicodemus," she whispered, squeezing his hand, "whatever flattery came from my mouth, it was Boann's. She knows how important you are; she wants to protect you."

Nicodemus looked her in the eye. "So she uses your body to manipulate me? That hardly sounds like a . . . Deirdre, I'm sorry. I didn't mean to . . ."

She dried her eyes. "Nicodemus, don't oppose her will. My desires are not my own. She'll control me again. She'll make me overpower you and drag you to her ark."

Nicodemus let go of the woman's hand. "Don't threaten me, Deirdre. I am no wizard, but I am a spellwright."

She retook his hand. "Nicodemus, you might cut me to pieces with your words, but Boann—"

"Let go of me." He tried to pry off her fingers.

Her other hand clamped around his tattooed wrist. "Don't do this; you will lose."

Nicodemus extemporized a common language constricting spell along his tongue and spat the sentences around her elbows.

Surprised, Deirdre weakened her grip just enough for Nicodemus to slip his right hand free. He threw his arm back and wrote along it a short Magnus club. The text most likely was misspelled and would break after a single stroke, but he could deliver at least one blow.

Meanwhile, Deirdre heaved with her great strength and snapped the sentences wrapped around her elbow.

"Deirdre, stop, I've a spell in my—" He fell silent.

She now held the greatsword in her right hand. They locked eyes.

"Please," she whispered, her eyes full of fear, "I cannot yield."

"Then you will have to—" He stopped as a wall of faint golden light washed through the cellar. He jumped.

"What is it?"

A second wall of light flew through the cellar. Nicodemus dropped his Magnus club and caught one of the tiny Numinous words that made up the strange light.

Realization came with a surge of excitement. "It's a broadly cast spell!" He began to translate the golden text. "It's like a magical beacon."

Deirdre lowered the greatsword. "But who would send a beacon to us?"

Nicodemus struggled to his feet. "We have to go. Let go of me." When she did, he ran to pick up the Index.

"What happened?"

He grabbed her forearm as if to pull her along. "I'll explain as we go. Now hurry!"

As they ran up the stairs, Nicodemus looked down at the translated word that glowed faintly gold on his palm. It read "*nsohnannanhosn*."

DEIRDRE FROWNED. AGAIN Shannon doubled over and vomited nothing. Again Nicodemus went to his side and held the old man's dreadlocks back from his face. The Index lay beside them. Azure, perched on a nearby rock pile, bobbed her head nervously.

Deirdre was sitting with Simple John in front of their campfire. Around them stretched the nighttime Chthonic ruins. The horse that Shannon had been riding was grazing somewhere out in the dark.

Above them, the forest's branches tossed in the cold autumn wind; they made a soft rushing sound that was in sharp contrast to Shannon's violent retching.

"What's happening?" she whispered to Simple John.

The big man's face paled. "Magister's throwing up bywords. Bad words. Too many small, repeated words."

They had found Shannon in the forest not an hour ago; he had seemed healthy then. In fact, the old linguist had launched into a story about his escape from the sentinels. He kept urging Nicodemus to turn and flee from Starhaven and travel to another wizardly academy called Starfall Keep.

Apparently, the Starhaven wizards thought Nicodemus was the Storm Petrel destroyer. Shannon thought he could convince the Starfall wizards otherwise. Nicodemus, overjoyed to recover his teacher, had agreed.

As they trekked back to the Chthonic ruins, the boy had told Shannon of everything that had happened since they were separated. Deirdre had argued that before setting out for Starfall, they should first go to Gray's Crossing to seek her goddess's protection.

Her thinking was simple: Nicodemus's keloid would allow Fellwroth to track them. As a result, they would never reach Starfall Keep alive unless they removed the curse from Nicodemus's scar. Deirdre had no doubt that Boann could do exactly that. Therefore, they had to go to Gray's Crossing. However, despite the logic of this reasoning, neither man had heeded her advice.

But now things had changed.

After returning to the Chthonic ruins, they had found Simple John roasting skinned rabbits over a fire. The moment Shannon had touched food to his lips, he had keeled over to vomit out nothing—just as he was doing now.

Deirdre turned to John. "How is it that you can talk now when before you only knew three phrases?"

The big man looked down at his hands. "It was Typhon's curse. The demon tied sentences around parts of my mind that use language, restricted them to the three phrases."

"Forgive me, I didn't—" Her apology was cut short by Shannon's renewed retching. "Nicodemus," she asked, grateful for the excuse to change subjects, "what's wrong with Shannon?"

"Nothing's wrong," the grand wizard panted while sitting up. "It's only a consequence of having a censoring spell peeled off my head too quickly."

"No," Nicodemus said without taking his eyes from the old man. "It's the nonsensical words coming out of his mouth that's the problem."

The old wizard narrowed his blind eyes. His tone became ironic. "So witty with your double meaning."

Deirdre coughed. "I don't understand."

"His story doesn't make sense," Nicodemus answered with irritation. "No censoring spell placed on his head could make his stomach fill with Magnus bywords."

Shannon closed his eyes. Deirdre could see how frail he was. The old man sighed. "I shouldn't have come. I agonized over it for hours, backtracked again and again to make sure the monster wasn't following me. I hoped the monster had lied about Language Prime and the infecting curse. It wasn't a lie."

The old man shook his head. "In the end, I sought you out, Nicodemus, because I feared you might try to rescue me. I only wanted to send you away from that creature; I never guessed the logorrhea would set in so quickly."

Nicodemus touched the wizard's shoulder. "Tell me what happened," he said firmly. "I deserve the truth."

The old man reached out with his knobby hand. Nicodemus took it with his own. "Nicodemus, it seems as if you've aged fifty years since last evening."

"Magister," John said, "we all have."

"Perhaps you're right, John," Shannon said. "Very well, Nicodemus, I will tell you. But promise to run with me to Starfall Keep. We cannot go back. We cannot submit to that monster."

When Nicodemus agreed, Shannon explained how Fellwroth—not in a golem, but in a living body—had pulled him from his cell, and how the monster had used the Emerald of Arahest to infect him with a Language Prime curse called logorrhea, which made him vomit words.

"Magister!" Nicodemus said when the wizard finished. "You made me promise something I didn't understand. No, we will not run to Starfall. That would take until spring; you'd die before we got there."

The old man sat up straighter. "Perhaps Fellwroth was lying when he told you that all human prophecies are false. It is still possible that you are the Halcyon; that possibility forbids you from forfeiting your life for mine. Besides, we dare not trust Fellwroth. If we submit, the monster is likely to kill me anyway."

Nicodemus shook his head. "I won't watch you die."

"Selfishness," the wizard huffed. "Surrender and you empower the demons. Your duty is to confound the Disjunction. And if that means watching me contend with the canker growing in my stomach you—"

An idea bloomed in Deirdre's mind. "This magical canker, is it like the mundane cankers that clerics remove from elderly bodies?"

All faces turned toward her. Shannon spoke. "Clerics are spellwrights that study medicine. We wizards wouldn't know."

A giddy warmth spread across Deirdre's face. "Boann found a canker once on my back. She said they happen often to avatars because we live so long. She said deities routinely cut such growths off their avatars."

Shannon scowled. "But what ails me is not one growth. I can see the runes coming from the cursed muscles around my stomach. The canker is laced all around the organ. Boann could cut my guts into bloody rags and there'd still be more curse to cut out."

Deirdre was shaking her head. "But she is a goddess! You can't—"

Nicodemus interrupted. "Are you sure Boann would heal Magister?"

"If you accept her protection, she would do anything."

Shannon objected. "She can't help me, Nicodemus. Look at the runes appearing in my gut; you can see how diffuse the canker is. Gray's Crossing is far too dangerous; we can't risk the life of a possible Halcyon for that of an old man."

"We can, Magister, and if it comes to that we will." Nicodemus stood up. "First, I need to research something here in these ruins. I might yet learn something about Language Prime. But if I can't find a way to remove your curse, we will go to Gray's Crossing."

The old man scowled again. "Don't be foolish. You have no right to risk yourself for me."

"Magister, I do," Nicodemus retorted. "I'm a cacographer, not a child." He turned toward the ruins.

"Los damn it," Shannon grumbled, and struggled to his feet. "Nicodemus, where are you going?"

The boy didn't look back. "Into the Bestiary."

CHAPTER
Thirty-nine

Nicodemus frowned at Tulki's spell. It read, "*The last eugrapher was furious after engaging the Bestiary. His words became angry and illogical. He claimed the Bestiary's knowledge was a curse to him.*"

When Nicodemus looked up from this note, he found the ghost fidgeting with his long white ponytail.

They were standing outside a dome-shaped ruin overgrown by vines that bristled with leathery brown leaves. Elsewhere the expanse of half-collapsed walls stretched out into the dark.

Behind Nicodemus stood his confused companions. "What's the ghost writing now?" Shannon asked.

Because they lacked fluency in the Chthonic languages, neither Shannon nor John nor Deirdre could see the Wrixlan text.

"The ghost is trying to change my mind," Nicodemus replied, still staring at Tulki. "He's afraid the book will upset me and I won't return to replenish their spectral texts."

"Tell him," John announced haltingly, "you keep your word."

Nicodemus nodded. "The ghost can hear you."

Tulki stopped fidgeting to cast a reply: "*But there might be danger. It was traumatic when the Index engaged you, true? The Bestiary is a more powerful tome.*"

"How did the ghost respond?" Shannon asked.

Tulki studied the old wizard and gave Nicodemus two more sentences: "*Tell the older one about the danger. He will help you see.*"

Nicodemus sniffed in annoyance. "He's exaggerating the danger the tome might pose, to discourage me."

Tulki's eyes widened. "*!*" he flicked at Nicodemus before adding, "*I am not!*"

Nicodemus raised a single, incredulous eyebrow.

Tulki threw his hands up in exasperation. "*I forgot how infuriating young male humans can be. Very well, Nicodemus Weal, I have no evidence of great danger. I am only concerned for your well-being.*"

The cold wind slipped down into the ruins and stirred Nicodemus's long hair. "And concerned for your own well-being," he said, pulling a black lock away from his eyes.

The ghost folded his arms. "*The last eugrapher was also this adamant. Are you sure you are not his descendant?*"

"Now what's happening?" Deirdre asked.

"He's telling me about the last cacographer who came through here about three hundred years ago."

"Good," Shannon said. "Learn as much about that as you can."

Tulki studied Shannon and then cast a sentence: "*Something is wrong with the elder's belly?*"

Nicodemus changed the subject. "Tell me more about the previous eugrapher."

The ghost scratched his chin as he forged an answer. "*The boy was curious and insistent. He looked like you and was thrilled to discover he did not misspell in our languages. A whole autumn and winter he stayed, sleeping through day and studying at night. He became pale and beautifully tattooed. He wrote wonderful constructs, like yours.*"

Nicodemus nodded. "But then he learned about the Bestiary?"

The ghost's shoulders rose and fell in a noiseless sigh. "*And then there was nothing that would please him but to engage it. The reading didn't take more than a moment. He touched the pages and then fell to the ground. We asked what had happened and he began to laugh. 'Gibberish!' he said. 'She showed me that I'm the error. She showed me what cacography truly is.'* "

"What did he mean by that?" Nicodemus said, his heart beginning to kick.

Tulki shrugged. "*We asked him, but the boy only shouted at us. He said that the book had cursed him with the knowledge of what cacography truly was and what the Chthonic people truly were. 'Gibberish!' he kept yelling. 'It's all gibberish!' We tried to reason with him but he wouldn't speak. He left the next evening and never returned.*"

Nicodemus swallowed when he finished reading. "What's this about what cacography truly is? What did he learn?"

"What's the ghost writing now?" Shannon asked.

"Magister," Nicodemus snapped. "I'm trying to read."

The old linguist mumbled an apology.

"Go on," Nicodemus insisted. "What did the other boy learn about cacography?"

Again the ghost shrugged. "*He didn't say.*"

Nicodemus pressed his cold right hand to his mouth and took a steadying breath. "Do you remember his name?"

The ghost seemed to ponder this. "*I believe . . .*" he cast before pausing. "*I believe his name was James Berr.*"

"Los in hell," Nicodemus swore under his breath. James Berr—the very incarnation of malignant cacography!

Tulki's amber eyes studied Nicodemus. "*He did look much like you—black hair, olive skin, green eyes. Was James Berr indeed one of your ancestors?*"

"No!"

The ghost jumped. "*Forgive me. Have I offended?*"

Nicodemus ignored the ghost's questions. "Did he tell you why he left Starhaven?"

The ghost shook his head. "*I've told you everything.*"

"Nicodemus, why are you upset?" Deirdre asked.

Ignoring her, Nicodemus kept his eyes on Tulki. "But what did the Bestiary teach him about cacography? What did he mean, 'It's all gibberish'?"

Again, the ghost shook its head. "*This is upsetting you already. Nothing good will come of engaging the Bestiary.*"

Nicodemus shut his eyes and took a long, quavering breath.

"Nicodemus, tell us what's the matter." Shannon said.

Nicodemus answered without opening his eyes. "The ghost says reading the Bestiary might be dangerous. How dangerous, he doesn't know. I was hiding this from you. I tell you now only because Los himself couldn't stop me from reading the book."

All three of his friends exploded into questions.

Nicodemus went on. "The last human to read the Bestiary was a cacographer like me. He learned the Chthonic languages like me. He even looked like me. And by reading this tome, he discovered something about the nature of cacography."

Nicodemus turned to face his friends. The dappled moonlight revealed three worried figures.

"I'm terrified," he said bluntly. "I have much in common with this ancient cacographer. I must know who he truly was and what he discovered in the Bestiary."

"But why?" Deirdre asked.

"Because I might be just like him."

Shannon spoke. "And who was this other boy?"

"James Berr."

Both Shannon and John flinched. A confused Deirdre looked from one to the other. No one spoke for a moment. Then Shannon said, "Nicodemus, if there is even a slight danger, you mustn't—"

"No, Magister," John interrupted. "He must."

Tulki led Nicodemus to the vine-covered dome. The thick brown leaves barely swayed in the cold wind. To Nicodemus's shock, he saw that they were not leaves at all, but thick medallions of leather.

A curtain of the strange foliage parted to reveal a miniature doorway. "*I appeal to you again*," Tulki wrote, stepping through. "*Reconsider.*"

Nicodemus ducked through the doorway into a small, dark space. "I cannot," he said.

A rectangle of dull amber light glowed in the darkness. As Nicodemus approached, the light grew to reveal that he was standing not in a room, but in a bower of leathery vines. The thick stems and leaves had wound themselves into a tentlike roof around the crumbling building.

The floor was uneven and rough. On closer inspection, Nicodemus realized that it was made of thousands of roots. All of them ran to the room's center and then grew into something resembling a tree stump—"resembling" because after rising two feet into the air, it grew into a massive codex. Its brown leather cover was textured like ash bark. A braid of branches grew from each face to form a clasp. The diffuse amber light was coming from the many pages.

The sound of shuffling feet filled the bower as Shannon, John, and Deirdre entered behind him.

Tulki handed Nicodemus a note: "*Move slowly*."

The Bestiary's glow brightened as Nicodemus approached. Silently, the fore-edge clasp unwove and the book opened with a creak. Shafts of amber light spilled upward from the yellowing pages. Incandescent specks flew up from the spine like embers from a fire.

"Be careful, Nico," John said. Shannon said something too, but Nicodemus could not hear what over the rush of blood in his ears. He pressed his palm against one of the Bestiary's warm, luminous pages.

There was a pause. Nicodemus held his breath and waited for the sensation of flying upward into a night sky that he had known in the Index.

But it did not come. Another pause. "I don't—" he started to say before the ground below him dissolved.

A cry escaped his throat as he plummeted down into blackness.

CHAPTER
Forty

Nicodemus fell into the Bestiary, his mouth filling with what felt like warm, thin oil. He gagged and then accidentally inhaled the slippery blackness. He was drowning. Panic flooding through his mind, he began to thrash.

But his mind could not disengage from the book.

The liquid around him thickened, slowing his fall. With a heave, he pushed the fluid from his lungs and fought the urge to inhale. But instinct soon forced him to draw the thin oil back into his chest.

Slowly his thrashing stopped. He wasn't drowning; he was breathing darkness. His limbs felt weightless. His long hair floated around him.

Nearby, some swimming thing made small waves of force. "Another child of error? A second chance?" said a rough, feminine voice.

Nicodemus's heart beat faster. "Who are you?" He was surprised that he could speak while breathing the liquid dark.

The thing replied with a low, purr-like laugh. It sounded as if it was now circling him.

Nicodemus turned about, trying to see what he was addressing. "I've come to learn about Language Prime. And to learn about the one who came before me."

Again the feline laugh. "I know what you seek, Nicodemus Weal. As long as you are within this tome, I know all you know."

He reached out in the direction of the voice. "Who are you?"

A slippery something wound around his head and slid away so quickly that he did not have time to flinch.

"I am the beast. I am the Bestiary. I am the test-maker, the word-taker, the one who gives the trial before the rule, the power before the purpose. I am a sliver of Chimera, who was the goddess of all Chimerical peoples."

"You're a spell?"

Low laughter replied. "You might call me a spell. You might also call me a fractional soul. When I was myself complete, I made this book one of my avatars and placed myself incomplete into it. You may call me Chimera."

Nicodemus paused to gather his fortitude. "Can you teach me what I want to know?"

Again something silky wrapped around Nicodemus—this time his left arm—and slipped away. "I can," Chimera rumbled. "But only if you accept the price. For if you learn Language Prime, you can never unlearn it."

"And why would that be bad? Will I go blind?"

A current pushed against Nicodemus's back and sent him floating forward. After a moment, Chimera spoke. "Quite the opposite from going blind, you will see more. You will see the truth about the Creator's language."

"Is that what happened to James Berr? You taught him Language Prime, and he learned what cacography really is?"

Chimera's next word came from directly above. "Yes."

Some of Nicodemus's hair floated into his eyes. He pulled it away. "And what of Magister Shannon's curse? Will learning Language Prime allow me to cure him?"

"It would show you how Shannon's curse might be removed. Whether you have the skill to remove it, I cannot say."

Nicodemus could feel Chimera swimming about him more quickly. "My enemies would keep knowledge from you," she rumbled. "If you do learn Language Prime, you will gain the ability to confound Fellwroth and his demon masters. But as in all things, there must be an exchange. I would give you knowledge; you would give me your happiness."

Nicodemus laughed. "That's the trade: my happiness for your knowledge?"

Chimera hissed, "Yes."

"You wouldn't be getting much of a bargain. I haven't much happiness to give."

"Is that supposed be profound or cynical?"

Nicodemus shook his head. "If I ignore an opportunity to remove Shannon's curse, I will never know happiness again."

"You will trade your happiness for the chance, not the certainty, of healing your teacher?"

"I would."

Chimera made no response.

Nicodemus pursed his lips. Was this a mistake? "How will you or Language Prime remove my happiness?"

"By making you completely into the man you are becoming."

His head bobbed back. "Who could be harmed by becoming more thoroughly himself?"

"Who wouldn't be?"

Nicodemus snorted blackness through his nose. "Is that supposed to be profound or cynical?"

Chimera did not answer.

Nicodemus changed the subject. "How will you teach me Language Prime? Will it be like when the Index thrust its purple language down my throat?"

Chimera chuckled. "No, Fellwroth spoke truthfully about your family. The Solar Empire bred an understanding of the Creator's language into Imperials. Your ancestry has provided you with an uncanny and unconscious knowledge of how to read and write Language Prime. James Berr also possessed Imperial ancestors."

Nicodemus's throat tightened. "I am related to him?"

Chimera made a sound like a yawn. "Berr would be your distant cousin. He paid the price and it broke him. Perhaps you are stronger. Will you learn the first language?"

Nicodemus took a long breath of liquid black. "I will."

THE DARKNESS LIT up with four aquamarine characters.

"These are the four runes of Language Prime," Chimera said behind him.

Nicodemus glanced over his shoulder to try to glimpse Chimera but saw only blackness. So he turned back to the complex cyan characters. All were three-dimensional. Two had hexagonal structures; the other two, pentagonal structures. As the runes rotated slowly, Nicodemus realized that he had instantly memorized their every detail. He could already see how they would fit together into long, spiraling sentences.

"I've never learned anything so quickly," he remarked in amazement.

Chimera spoke. "You are not learning; you are awakening an ancestral knowledge. And now that I have shown you the runes, your education is nearly complete."

Nicodemus laughed, but when the hidden creature did not reply, he realized that she was serious. "But I have no Language Prime vocabulary, no grammar." He laughed again. "I don't even know what kind of spells are written in Language Prime."

Chimera's reply came in a whisper. "Look at your hands."

Nicodemus did as he was told and then jumped. An aquamarine glow now suffused his fingers and palms.

"Fiery blood! I'm casting in Language Prime!" He brought his hands closer to be sure. "But the runes are impossibly small," he said in amazement. "There must be . . . I don't know a number large enough to describe how many runes there must be in my pinky alone."

He pulled back his sleeves and then peered down the collar of his robes. His entire body was saturated with Language Prime. "It doesn't make sense," he said. "The other magical languages we forge in our muscles, but these runes are forming in every bit of my body."

The darkness around Nicodemus undulated as Chimera's voice drew closer. "That is because Language Prime runes are not controlled by your body. They are your body."

"That makes no sense. And what is this place, anyway? Is this my real, physical body? Are you showing me illusion?"

"Only your mind is within my book. But the magical body I have given you here will behave just as your physical body does. When you leave the book, you will see that I am not deceiving you." Suddenly her voice was whispering an inch from his left ear. "Now look into nature."

Nicodemus turned to see a square window cut into the darkness. On the other side was an image of the nearby nighttime forest. Much was familiar: pine trees, sword ferns, a young buck picking his way among the vegetation and rocks.

But most wondrously, the deer glowed faintly with cyan light. "He's casting Language Prime!" Nicodemus said. "But that's impossible. Only humans can . . . unless he's a familiar and . . ." His voice died as he realized that the ferns too glowed with Language Prime spells. Only the rocks were devoid of text.

"This must be fantasy!" he whispered.

"No, Nicodemus Weal, what you saw before you learned Language Prime was illusion. Now see the world with new eyes."

Just then a pale emperor moth fluttered before the window. A dark tentacle shot out to encircle the moth and drew it into the blackness.

Nicodemus jerked back in surprise. The liquid darkness around him became as thin as air. The window into the forest winked out of existence.

The large moth fluttered about in a panic. Because of the dark, Nicodemus could not see the insect's body; rather, he saw the Language Prime texts that saturated the creature.

"I have pulled this moth's mind into the Bestiary and given it a magical body that will behave exactly as its physical counterpart would. Now hold out your hand, Nicodemus Weal, and see into the life of things."

Nicodemus reached out and the moth fluttered about his arm for a moment before alighting on his thumb.

As the insect's legs grabbed hold of Nicodemus's skin, an ecstatic heat rushed through his body. He felt dizzy, almost intoxicated. His thoughts became as light and far ranging as smoke tendrils caught in the wind. Time slowed; even the movement of his blood seemed suspended.

Shining in his mind was a text longer than any he previously could have imagined. All the books in Starhaven could not have held half its length.

The spell—though consisting of only four runes—contained innumerable twists, turns, and self-referential passages.

But what shocked Nicodemus most, what spawned a mystical sense of wonder, was the certainty that this text was the same thing as the moth.

Nicodemus would have thought the spell beyond human comprehension if not for the perfect knowledge of it now shining in his mind.

It was true, then. He was an Imperial. He had been born with the gift to read and comprehend Language Prime.

The moth flapped its wings once. Nicodemus looked again at the pale, delicate creature and felt its endless, intricate beauty so keenly that his heart ached.

To him the moth was both a living animal and a poem.

He tried to speak, tried to explain the awe coursing through his veins like a drug, but all he could manage was a rapturous whisper, "She's the most beautiful spell."

"Touch any living thing and you will find the same language," Chimera said in a voice that had become almost sing-song. "I could provide for you the prose within an oak leaf or a trout's belly. I could show you the miniature creatures that infect wounds. In each you would find Language Prime. That is why this tome is called the Bestiary. It reveals that every beast and every plant is made from the Creator's language, from the Creator's godspell."

Nicodemus understood. "Life is magical language."

SLOWLY NICODEMUS'S TRANCE began to dissipate. He put his free hand to his brow as the implications of his revelation unfolded. "So, if life is language . . . then Language Prime spellwrights could edit diseases from the sick, or close wounds by coordinating a body's healing, or rewrite wheat plants to produce more grain."

Chimera responded with an amused sniff. "You see why the Solar Empire was a paradise. Under the rule of the Imperial family, the continent knew neither plague nor famine."

"How do you know this, Chimera?"

She produced a long hissing sigh. "I was the oldest and most malcontent goddess on the ancient continent. I wanted to do more with the original languages. I wanted to rewrite a new breed of humanity. I thought that the Empire's use of Language Prime to improve the life they knew, and not invent new life, would lead ultimately to stagnation. And when Los was born, I knew I was correct."

"You knew Los? The first demon?"

Again the sigh. "I knew him before he rebelled. I knew his plans for

Language Prime. That is why I fled the ancient continent. The Empire had forbidden me from textual experimentation. So I took my followers across the ocean to this new continent. Here I transformed my followers into the Chimerical peoples."

Something occurred to Nicodemus. "The Chthonics were once human?"

"They were. And so too were the Kobolds, the Goblins, the Lycanthropes, the Pelagics, the Incultans, and too many others. At first this continent was a paradise, but then my peoples began to fight each other. In hopes of governing them, I split my soul and impressed its parts into the many different Bestiaries. To each tribe I gave three books. But my efforts proved futile. The differences between the Chimerical peoples grew too great. When your ancestors crossed the ocean, they found my peoples divided."

She paused and made a low swishing sound. "At first, I hoped to repel your kind. Your deities were weak then. To escape the demonic host and cross the ocean, they had to slumber within their arks. This made them forget nearly everything they had known, including Language Prime. And your Imperial family was scattered. But my peoples, as divided as they were, were no match for humanity. Once your ancestors established a foothold on this continent, they slaughtered my peoples."

Nicodemus considered his words. "Chimera, why do you give me this knowledge? It is an extraordinary gift."

She did not answer for such a long time that Nicodemus began to worry that she had left. "I have given you the bitterest of knowledge. This marks the beginning of your suffering."

"What do you mean?"

"Think on the consequences of learning the original languages."

Nicodemus's brow furrowed. "I will see a glow around all living things. But . . . there's something I don't understand. Why haven't I or any other spellwright felt a synaesthetic reaction to Language Prime?"

"The runes of Language Prime are extremely weak. They can affect little outside a living body. No human synaesthetic reaction is sensitive enough to detect them." She paused. "But you're not considering what will happen now that you know the Creator's Language. Think harder. Your mind rewrites nearby eugraphic languages—that is how your childhood dreams wrote the night terrors that saved you from Fellwroth. But the original languages are not eugraphic. They are cacographic; their spellings are redundant and illogical. What happens when you touch text written in a cacographic language?"

The realization felt like a kick to the stomach. At first Nicodemus couldn't talk. His heart raced and his tongue felt as if made of leather. "I . . . misspell them."

When Chimera spoke again her voice was low and doleful. "Look at the moth." A sphere of soft white light appeared next to Nicodemus's hand.

He looked and cried out in terror.

She had once been a delicate creature with a furry body, wide black eyes, feathery antennae. Her gossamer wings had once been pale cream punctuated with iridescent eyelike markings of yellow and black.

But the animal on Nicodemus's finger was now a bulbous, blackened corpse. Tiny, angry cankers of necrotic black bulged across her body like nightmare parasites.

Nicodemus cried out again. With his new knowledge, he saw how his cacographic mind had rearranged the moth's Language Prime text, causing parts of her body to grow into the monstrous swellings.

He snapped his hand back and the dead moth fell. The light winked out and Nicodemus was again floating in total darkness.

"Those were canker curses, weren't they?" Nicodemus asked between frantic breaths. "That's what Fellwroth did to Magister, isn't it? The monster misspelled the Language Prime texts in Magister's gut, and they're growing out of control."

Chimera didn't answer. She didn't have to. He knew it was true.

"I will misspell any living creature I touch," he realized aloud. "My cacography will spawn error inside their bodies. I will spread cankers everywhere I go." He felt as if he might vomit.

Chimera made a low huffing sound. "Not all the changes you make will lead to cankers. Many of the changes you will impart to a living creature will have no effect. Some will even be beneficial. But now . . ." She stopped and made the huffing sound again. "Now you see the price I have exacted from you."

"I do," Nicodemus said, pressing his hands to his belly. "You said I might learn how Shannon's curse could be removed. You never said that I would be able to remove it."

"You still have hope. Presently the cankers are spread about his stomach like gauze. If you touch him and concentrate, you might aggregate the curse into a discrete mass—"

Nicodemus interrupted. "—which Deirdre's goddess might then remove." Shannon might yet be saved.

"I can't say that you've cheated me," he said after a moment. "This gives Magister a chance for life. I would have agreed to your terms even if I had known that it would make me into a monster."

A sudden idea made him start. "What if I recovered the Emerald of Arahest from Fellwroth?"

The darkness undulated. He could again feel her swimming around him. She said, "I would not want that."

"But if I regained my ability to spell, I wouldn't give the canker curse to everyone I touched. I could become a Language Prime spellwright like those of the Solar Empire. Chimera! Fellwroth said there is no Halcyon, but I might still use my Language Prime against the Disjunction."

The waves in the darkness stopped. "If you regain that part of yourself, you will be useless to the struggle against the demons."

"How can that be?"

She began to circle again. "Fellwroth wants to hide the full truth about prophecy from you."

"The golem said all the prophecies are false."

"All the human prophecies are false," she corrected. "And the golem spoke truly about that. The golem also told you that the members of your family are pawns to be played by humanity or the Disjunction. In that too, he spoke part of the truth."

"What, then, is the whole truth?"

"Humanity uses the word 'prophecy' as if it were synonymous with the word 'destiny.' Nothing is destined. Prophecy is like rain falling on a mountain. The water must flow down. It must find its course in creeks and streams and rivers. One might calculate where the water would flow in a static world. In an unchanging landscape, we might say that this drop is destined to flow into this lake, this river flow into this ocean. But the world is always changing."

She paused to take in a long, liquid breath. "More important, the powerful may throw dams across rivers, may dig canals, may build waterwheels. And that is exactly what I have done to you, Nicodemus. I have pushed you into the river that will oppose the demons of Los. I would see you become a river-king."

The sickening dread returned to Nicodemus. He was all too certain what she would say next. "And what metaphorical river are you speaking about?"

"You see this world as a battlefield between your kind and demonkind. But humans, gods, and demons are simply currents in a conflict of two larger forces: that of linguistic order and stasis, and that of linguistic error and change. The wizards worship order. They look to the forces that flow toward increasing order. They long for a Halcyon, a river-king of immutable language. They want everything made smooth and calm. And they fear the Petrel—a river-king of mutable language. The academy fears the storm and the change the Petrel will bring. The academy assumes that unchanging language will fend off the demons."

Nicodemus's hands were no longer trembling; they were clenched in anger. "And you've decided that it's chaos and error that will oppose the demons? You've made me into a champion of mutable language?"

Chimera growled, "Life is mutable language, language that grows through error. Without error in Language Prime we are doomed. This is what I showed James Berr: I showed him that he could become the avatar of change, of disruption, of originality."

"Originality?" Nicodemus asked through grinding teeth. "By making us into monsters?"

"That which is original creates a new origin. That which is original, by definition, must stray off the previously worn paths. It must wander; it must err. Because of me, Nicodemus, you will generate mutable language, you will become mutagenic."

Something hot pressed against Nicodemus's back. "ALL THAT IS CREATIVE COMES FROM ERROR!" Chimera's voice boomed in his ear.

He spun round and tried to grab hold of her. "Damn you!" he bawled. "Damn you! You've made me into the Storm Petrel! You've made me into the monster!" His arms flailed wildly but struck nothing.

"You call that which errs grotesque?" Chimera asked from a distance. "You call the original monstrous? Then know that you've always been the monster. You've always been a cacographer. This is your true nature. This was James Berr's true nature. He too railed against it, and it consumed him. Will you deny your own self?"

"I AM NO JAMES BERR!" Nicodemus bellowed. "I never will be. I am no force of error. I wasn't supposed to be this way; I was cursed. I'll recover the emerald. I'll complete myself and become the Halcyon."

Chimera's response came as a low hiss. "You might yet wrest the Emerald of Arahest from the demons. That would make your life a lie. You will never escape your past as a cacographer. The emerald would make you a partial Halcyon. But know that there already is a true Halcyon."

"Impossible!"

"Fellwroth told you of the Alliance of Divine Heretics? The renegade deities also trying to breed a true Imperial?"

Nicodemus clenched his jaw. "The monster told me."

"Then know the Alliance has given you a half sister, your mother's other child. She's only a child now, but she may one day become the Halcyon. You never will."

The rage burning in Nicodemus exploded. Summoning all his strength, he filled his body with miles of sharp Numinous sentences and lashed out in the direction of Chimera's voice.

He shrieked as the incandescent sentence uncoiled into the darkness. The words of anger burned with a dazzling golden light.

And for a moment, outlined against the mundane blackness, there shone a creature made of darkness tangible. Her endless body spread out, looping and bulging like a worm's. In places her skin shone slick with black slime, in others knobby branches covered in scales erupted from her serpentine flesh.

And then Nicodemus's misspelled sentences crumbled into a coruscation of golden sparks.

Chimera's next words hit Nicodemus like thunder. "GO THEN AND DENY YOUR NATURE! SEEK YOUR EMERALD, YOUR LAPIDARY LIE!"

SUDDENLY BACK IN his body, Nicodemus found himself falling away from the Bestiary. Tears filled his eyes and hot pain tore through his throat.

He was shouting wordlessly.

His tailbone struck ground and shot a jolt of agony up his spine. He fell backward and stared at the ceiling.

"Nico!" exclaimed John. Suddenly the big man was leaning over Nicodemus, bending down to grab his shoulder.

"Don't touch me!" Nicodemus bellowed, whipping his arm around to cast out a hasty sheet of Magnus.

The spell flashed out into a plate of silver light that smashed into John's hand. The misspelled text shattered but not before breaking the big man's ring finger back until it snapped.

John cried out as the spell sent him sprawling backward.

Nicodemus pushed himself away from John. "STAY BACK!" he yelled at Shannon and Deirdre as they stepped toward him.

Hot tears blinded his eyes. Mucus coated his upper lip.

"No one touch me!" he bawled. "No one touch me ever again!"

CHAPTER

Forty-one

Nicodemus let go of Shannon, who turned away to vomit Magnus bywords on the ground.

No one spoke as he retched. Azure reformed her textual connection to Shannon and then provided an image of Nicodemus squatting beside him. The firelight made the boy's green eyes seem darker, more haunted.

"Well?" The old wizard spat out a last bit of the diseased language.

"I consolidated the canker into a single mass at the top of your stomach," Nicodemus said quietly. "Since I dealt only with that text, I created no new curses. But my touch has made the canker more malicious."

Shannon looked down at his belly. Indeed, a small stream of silver prose was already leaking into his stomach.

Above them, the cold wind was blowing harder through the trees.

"We must get you to Boann," Nicodemus said flatly. "Now she can cut out the curse." He looked at Deirdre. She nodded.

"I still don't like it," Shannon grumbled. He thought again about how Nicodemus had come out of the Bestiary, weeping, terrified, and filled with revelations about the prophecies and Language Prime. "What if Fellwroth is waiting for us?"

"He might be," Nicodemus replied in an exhausted voice. "But it's our only option now. Chimera has made me the Storm Petrel, made me mutagenic."

He paused to close his eyes. "I would sooner die than stay this way. Alliance with Boann is my only hope. And she is your only hope, Magister. Only she can cut this canker out of you."

"He's right, Shannon," Deirdre said from the other side of the campfire.

Nicodemus stood. "John, are you all right?"

The big man was crouched beside the fire, gingerly holding his right hand. Shannon had splinted the broken finger with a Magnus passage. "Yes," John said slowly. "I am fine."

"John, I am sorry."

The big man laughed. "I'll say it again: I'm happier with a broken finger than I would be with a canker curse."

Through Azure's eyes, Shannon watched an ivy leaf shudder in the wind. "Very well, if we're determined to go dashing into danger, let's do it before it gets too late. I'm old and it's nearing my bedtime."

No one laughed.

BEFORE THEY LEFT the ruins, Nicodemus walked into the woods. Making water was his excuse. But as soon as he was away from the firelight, he collapsed.

No tears came. No expression of agony twisted his face. But his chest rose and fell, rose and fell until his fingers and forearms tingled. The world began to spin.

Regaining control, he slowed his breath until the tingling left his fingers. He felt hollow. He was the Storm Petrel, the monster.

The insistent wind rushed through the trees. Beyond their leaves shone the icy light of stars.

He stood and wandered until he found a creek. To his eyes, all living things now radiated Language Prime's soft cyan light. This allowed him to see the glow of several tiny fish swimming in the black water.

He wrote a net of simple Magnus sentences and used it to pull a fry from the water. With the silvery sentences, he held the tiny fish before his frowning face. He dropped it into his open palm.

The poor creature flopped about in his palm. Nicodemus could feel the thing's Language Prime text changing every time its cold scales touched his skin. He could feel the power of his spellwriting accelerating the changes.

In only a few moments a shiny black growth bulged out of the fry's gills. "It's true," he mumbled, and his eyes filled with tears.

He killed the fish with a quick, clinching paragraph and watched as its cyan glow began to fade. It took a long time.

At last he dropped the fry and buried his face in his hands.

Before him shone an image of the emerald—small, dark, perfectly lacriform. He tried to feel his fear and anger and self-loathing. But he could feel nothing. So he imagined the emotions becoming light.

He poured the light into the emerald and watched it begin to glow. More and more he poured into the gem until it shone with a brilliance that seemed to penetrate into his body.

When they recovered the gem he would no longer have to be afraid. He would no longer need to feel rage or self-hatred. When they recovered the missing part of himself, he would cease to be a monster.

THE FORESTED HILLS below Starhaven descended in slow undulations for five or six miles to end in the wide oak savanna.

On the border between foothills and grassland, the Westernmost Road stretched its dusty length from Dar in the north down to the City of Rain in the south.

By the time Nicodemus's party emerged from the forest to stand on the highway, all three moons had risen. The combined glow bathed the savanna in milky blue light.

As he hugged the Index to his chest, Nicodemus surveyed the few farms and oaks that dotted the landscape. Several trees had died and become wiry skeletons.

Save for the homesteads, waist-high savanna grass covered the earth from road's edge to distant horizon. Here the wind transformed the grassland into an ocean of rolling waves.

Deirdre took their only horse and galloped ahead to scout for danger.

The three men walked in a close huddle, the wind blowing color into their cheeks and tossing Nicodemus's long raven hair. Azure often ruffled her feathers and issued low, plaintive squawks.

Nicodemus's keloid began to burn. Shannon had wrapped the scars with distorting Numinous spells. Nevertheless, he watched as a sphere of Language Prime flew away from him in all directions. The broadcast was diffuse; it wouldn't reveal his precise location to Fellwroth. But it would tell the monster that he was on the move.

Thinking about this made Nicodemus's heart beat faster. He closed his eyes and focused on recovering the emerald—of transforming himself from Petrel to Halcyon—until his icy determination returned.

Just then Shannon had to pause to vomit silvery logorrhea bywords.

When they continued their trek, Shannon showed him how to write several common language sentences around the Index so that it would float in a slow circle around the younger man's waist.

"When wizards must fight," the old linguist said gravely, "we float our spellbooks like this."

A moment later, Deirdre returned with auspicious news: there was no sign of wizards in Gray's Crossing. She had learned from a town watchman that shortly after sundown all the black-robes had run up to Starhaven.

After another quarter hour walking, the town came into view around a bend. It was not much to look at: a huddle of round Lornish cottages clustered around two inns, a smithy, a fuller, and a small common. At the hamlet's center sat the intersection of the Westernmost Road and the smaller road that ran up to Starhaven. Most of the inhabitants were farmers or shopkeepers who sold to the wizards.

With Deirdre leading the way, the party hurried off the road and into the trees. Cautiously, they picked their way so as to emerge behind the stables of a dilapidated inn named the Wild Crabtree.

Deirdre hustled them into the back of the building and up a flight of rickety stairs. Shannon wrote a flamefly spell and scattered the incandescent paragraphs around the party so as to light the way.

"The inn's owner is a Highlander," Deirdre whispered. "He rents the top floor to Dralish smugglers who buy weapons in Spires and run them down to the Highland rebels. There's a secret compartment in the floor where they hide the blades."

She stopped before a door. "Be quiet now; I have to let the other devotees of Boann know we are friends." She knocked twice and then froze.

Her hand had pushed the door open slightly. Inside it was dark and silent.

"Careful," Shannon whispered, a spherical Magnus spell appearing in his hand.

Deirdre drew the greatsword from her back and then pushed the door wide to let the light from Shannon's flamefly spell fall into the dark room.

Peering past her shoulder, Nicodemus saw—sprawled across the floor—a motionless body.

THERE WERE EIGHT dead men, three women. Not a drop of blood on any of them.

Shannon found a slowly deconstructing Numinous paragraph lodged behind the ear of one victim. "Fellwroth," he said, inspecting the text. "Attacked maybe twenty hours ago."

The three connected rooms were spacious and sparsely furnished. Nicodemus walked into the farthest room and noticed a bowl of stew sitting on a table. "The monster took them by surprise," he noted, looking at the fat congealing at the bowl's edge. "No sign of struggle."

John went to each of the bodies and closed their staring eyes.

Meanwhile Nicodemus studied the ceiling. With his new knowledge of the original languages, he could see the cyan auras of rats as they scurried among the rafters.

Deirdre stood unmoving by the door. Her lips pressed white against each other. "It makes no sense," she said. "There's no way Fellwroth could have known the ark was here."

"Deirdre," Shannon said from across the room, "I am sorry for your loss. I don't know if you knew these souls well, but—"

"Boann's ark is missing," she interjected. "I must get it back!"

The grand wizard looked at her. "What does the ark look like? Could it have been hidden?"

"It is a standing stone, six feet tall, two wide, two deep. The edges are smooth. It is a water ark—most of the year it rests in one of the Highland rivers sacred to Boann. Three parallel lines flow down from its top; they symbolize her rivers."

Nicodemus looked at Deirdre. Something about the ark's description stirred his memory.

Deirdre began pacing around the room and looking down at the wooden floor. "There is a chance it was hidden. The tavern's owner built a secret compartment in the floor. The other devotees may have concealed the ark in it."

She bent down and knocked on the wooden planks. "We have to be quiet. But we can find the compartment by listening for an echoing knock. One of the druids told me so."

Again something pulled at Nicodemus's memory. His hands were wringing each other. He glared at the tattooed things and willed them to stop.

Both John and Shannon had joined Deirdre in rapping softly on the floor. "If we can't find the ark," Shannon said, "then we have no choice but to flee for Starfall Keep."

"I won't leave my goddess behind," Deirdre insisted.

Shannon shook his head. "But if Fellwroth has stolen the ark, it could be anywhere."

The avatar continued to knock on the floor. "Then I will make Fellwroth tell me where it is."

John was tapping the floor by the window.

Shannon grunted in annoyance. "Even if you captured a golem, the monster would simply disengage his spirit. And we haven't a clue where Fellwroth's true body might be."

"Then I will find the true body," Deirdre said while knocking again.

The old linguist grimaced. "Deirdre, we must get Nicodemus to safety."

"We go nowhere, Magister," Nicodemus said coldly, "unless it's to recover the emerald or disspell your curse."

Shannon folded his arms. "It's not enough that I must die? You two want to join me?"

Before Nicodemus could respond, one of John's knocks produced a hollow echo.

"Sweet heaven!" Nicodemus swore, taking a step backward. His cold focus was shattered. Now his frightened mind teemed with memories of his dreams: the dying nightmare turtles, the pale ivy, the body shrouded in white. He remembered walking on the Spindle Bridge with Shannon, their boot heels clacking unusually loudly on the bridge stone.

"Sweet heaven," he swore again and grabbed the Index from the sentences that had been floating it around his waist. He sat heavily in an empty chair.

The others went to John and helped him hoist up a trap door.

"It's empty," Nicodemus heard himself say as Deirdre, John, and Azure peered down into the secret compartment.

Deirdre stared at him. "How did you know?"

Memories flashed through Nicodemus's mind so quickly they made him dizzy.

"We'll need a distraction." His words were quick and anxious. He was trying to speak as fast as he was thinking. "With the signal text from my keloid diffused, he'll never realize we're so near. We can slay his living body. But the distraction will have to make him use a golem and . . . when the living body is dead, I can use the emerald to disspell Magister's canker. Or Boann might . . . but I'll have the emerald."

A wave of heat washed through his body. "I'll have the emerald." He stood and dropped the Index back into its floating orbit around his waist. "I'll be complete!"

All three of them were staring at him now. "What under heaven are you talking about?" Shannon asked.

Nicodemus went to the far window and removed its paper screen. The room looked out on the forest. High above the skyline, cutting a black silhouette against the stars, stood Starhaven's many towers.

"We can recover the emerald," he said, "because I know where to find Fellwroth's true, living body."

NICODEMUS PURSED HIS lips. "I should have known when I was replenishing the ghosts' book and saw through the young Chthonic's eyes. I knew the Chthonic's thoughts; I knew that the Chthonic people first emerged from the underworld up there."

He nodded out the window toward Starhaven. "They came out of a cave high up on the rockface. I learned that the Chthonics protected themselves from the attacks of an older race they called the blueskins by filling the cave mouth with powerful metaspells. And the blueskins filled the cave mouth with tortoise-like constructs."

"But we know this," Deirdre said. "You saw in a later vision that the Chthonics had collapsed the cave."

Nicodemus looked back at the avatar. "I saw that the cave was gone, but the Chthonic whose eyes I was seeing through never thought about the cave. His mind was preoccupied by the human army laying siege to Starhaven."

"The cave wasn't closed?" Shannon asked.

Nicodemus shook his head. "And Fellwroth's true body lies in that cave. In a dream I saw ivy—representing the Chthonic metaspell—and the turtles—representing the blueskin constructs—attacking Fellwroth's body.

They must represent the ancient spells still resisting Fellwroth's intrusion into the cave."

Shannon made a low, disapproving sound. "But we know that Starhaven's Chthonic metaspells prevent Fellwroth from creating a golem within the stronghold's walls."

Nicodemus clenched his fists. "But the cave isn't within Starhaven's walls. The cave is filled with metaspells much older than those in Starhaven."

He turned to Deirdre. "Boann's ark is also in that cave. I saw it in my dream standing behind Fellwroth's body in the second nightmare. I didn't know what it was at the time. But just now, Deirdre, when you described it to me, I realized what it must be."

"So the cave is hidden?" John asked slowly. "Some ancient spell opens the mountain?"

Nicodemus shook his head. "Think of the Spindle's shape. All other Chthonic bridges are thin and flat. The Spindle is as round as a tree bough. And when we walked on it, our footsteps echoed. Remember, Magister, the racket the sentinels made when marching toward us? And, Deirdre, what did it sound like when the war-weight gargoyle walked on the Spindle's landing?"

She nodded. "Like a drum . . . like the sound was moving down the bridge."

"Exactly," Nicodemus said. "And in one of my nightmares, I was moving through a tunnel that ended in the chamber with Fellwroth's body. When I was going down that tunnel, I heard my own voice talking to Magister about the Chthonic carvings. I heard that voice pass above me."

"So the Spindle Bridge—" Shannon started to say.

"Isn't a bridge at all," Nicodemus finished. "It's a tunnel. The wizards haven't found anything in the mountain face because they're searching only the rock in front of them. Don't you see? The tunnel covers the cave's mouth."

Deirdre was nodding, but Shannon and John still wore frowns.

"It makes perfect sense," Nicodemus insisted. "The Chthonic languages deconstruct in sunlight. And while the Chthonic people could tolerate sunlight, their blueskinned ancestors could not. The Spindle Tunnel must have been a diplomatic structure—a place where the Chthonics could meet the blueskins in darkness." He snatched the Index out of its orbit.

"Here, I'll find a mundane text that . . ." He began to undo the book's clasp.

"No, no," Shannon said. "I don't doubt your logic; I simply wonder what we do with the information."

Deirdre spoke quickly. "We do exactly what the boy suggested. We cut our way into the Spindle and tear Fellwroth's body to pieces while the fiend's mind is still in the golem."

"Is the Fool's Ladder still in place?" Nicodemus asked. "If we hike around to the back of Starhaven, could it take us up to the Spindle's landing?"

The grand wizard scowled. "It could, but this plan is too dangerous. What if Fellwroth is not in his golem?"

"Running wouldn't be safer," Nicodemus insisted. "Fellwroth can follow me because of my keloid scars. And, Magister, my dreams were sent to me by the emerald. It wants to be rescued."

Shannon shook his head. "Nicodemus, you and I are linguists, not sentinels."

Deirdre rested a hand on Shannon's shoulder. "Only this plan will rescue my goddess's ark. It is the only one I will accept."

Nicodemus closed his eyes. "It is the only plan that will recover the emerald." He opened his eyes and stared at Shannon. "And it is the only plan that will disspell your curse."

"And me," said John. "It is the only plan I will accept."

All eyes turned to the big man.

"For decades, I lived under the demon's curse. If I have a chance to end this monster, a chance for revenge, I will accept no other."

Shannon started to say something but then stopped.

"Besides," John said slowly, "I think I know how to reach Fellwroth."

Shannon drew in a long breath and let it out through his nose. "You know how to reach the monster?"

"It depends, Magister," John said with a solemn stare. "I need to know exactly what Fellwroth said when he set you free."

CHAPTER

Forty-two

In a new clay golem, Fellwroth stood on a balcony near the top of the Erasmine Spire.

A squat gargoyle with a monkey's body and goat's head sat on the railing. Fellwroth had rewritten the construct to siphon encrypted messages from the wizards' colaboris spells. The agents of the Disjunction had long ago learned how to tack their texts onto wizardly communications.

So far the goat-faced gargoyle had performed perfectly. In Fellwroth's hands glowed several golden passages from other important demon-worshipers. "When were these received?"

The gargoyle's reply was slow and monotone. "Two hours past the dawn bell."

There were several emerging situations that would sour without attention. Dar in particular was concerning; the demon-worshipers there were becoming increasingly unresponsive. Likely they were hiding something.

"Reply to Dar," Fellwroth commanded. "They are to expect my arrival within a twelve night. And they are—"

A rat gargoyle with a dog's ear growing from its back scurried up the railing. Fellwroth smiled. "My newest creation, what have you overheard?"

The stony canine ear flattened against the rat's back. "Three sentinels came to the gatehouse moments ago," the small construct squeaked. "They were patrolling the road to Gray's Crossing. They told the guards they have Nicodemus Weal."

Fellwroth's lips curled into a smile. This was expected. The emerald had known Nicodemus was on the move. "Did they say where they are taking him?"

"To the stasis spell in the stables," the rat replied. "Until a prison cell is chosen.

He nodded. "Very good. Now I want—"

Another of the stone rats scurried onto the ledge. "Noises in the Spindle," it squeaked.

"What kind of noises?"

The rat began to wash its whiskers. "Scraping noises. Grating noises. Like we make."

Fellwroth grunted in annoyance. "Remind me to edit your sensitivity. I don't want to be notified every time you overhear a rat's nest. But we can deal with that in a moment. For now, all of you back to your functions. I have a Language Prime spellwright to collect." With that Fellwroth let the clay golem deconstruct.

The world dissolved into blackness as his spirit—which had been animating the golem—leaped into the air and then shot down to Starhaven's Spirish Quarter. Though subtextualized, Fellwroth needed to avoid even the remotest chance of detection; without a body, a spirit was exceedingly vulnerable.

The spirit floated among the towers to descend into an abandoned alleyway. Earlier that day, Fellwroth had commanded a gargoyle to place a bag of sand there.

The spirit found the bag lying under several weather-worn boards. Inside the sack sat three golem scrolls. The spirit slipped its narrow sentences into the sand and pulled the spells free.

The new body began as a speck of pain that blossomed into a beating heart, a breathing chest, a head, two legs, two arms. The bag split and with a long sigh spilled its excess sand onto the cobblestones.

Fellwroth struggled to sit up in the new, brittle body. Vision was always the last sense a golem acquired. At first the world appeared only as fuzzy blotches.

For this reason Fellwroth always placed a white cloak or sheet near the incarnation site. It was vital to cover a golem with cloth while it was still fresh; otherwise bits of the body would rub off on the surrounding environment.

With some fumbling, Fellwroth found the white cloak. Old tattered boots sat under it.

Once his golem was dressed, Fellwroth trotted off toward the Spirish stables. There was no time to lose.

His vision had returned completely by the time the Spirish stables came into view. The black-robed fools were protecting the place with only four guards—all male, only one with a grand wizard's hood. In one of the stalls gleamed a silvery Magnus column. That would be the stasis spell holding Nicodemus.

Fellwroth wrote four quick, subtextualized censor spells. "Hold, druid," the hooded guard called upon seeing Fellwroth's white robes. "These stables are now out of bounds, we've—"

Fellwroth threw a censor spell into the man's face. The netlike text dug into the man's mind and set his eyes rolling back as he fainted.

The other three guards called out, but it was too late. Fellwroth caught them with the remaining censor spells.

"Nicodemus Weal," Fellwroth said with a laugh, and stepped into the stables. "You are not as foolish as I thought."

The stasis spell manifested itself as a column of slowly rising Magnus passages that entrapped a man as firmly as tree sap imprisoned a bug; something Nicodemus seemed to be discovering. The upward current of sticky words had lifted the boy four feet into the air and was slowly rotating him. Currently a black-robed back faced Fellwroth.

Fellwroth began to write a Numinous disspell down the sand golem's right leg. "I will edit you from the stasis, boy, so don't squirm—" He jerked back in shock. "You!"

Staring down with a lopsided smirk was the big male cacographer whose mind Typhon had distorted.

"What is meant by this?" Fellwroth growled.

The big man's mouth quivered. "Siii . . . Simple John show himself to north sentinels on road. T-th-they never have see Nico, so they believe John when he says he is Nico." The big man exhaled as if saying so much exhausted him.

Fellwroth resisted the urge to grind the golem's sandy teeth. "Don't waste my time, oaf. If the sentinels come before I have answers, I'll rip you in half."

The cacographer started to stutter and struggle, but the stasis text kept the oaf spellbound. Fellwroth waited impatiently for what felt like a quarter hour before speaking. "All right, calm down. I won't hurt you if you tell me what I need to know."

The big man swallowed. "Nnnn . . . Nico sends John as messenger. Nnnn . . . Nico wants to have proof that red-eyes man is . . . t-t-telling the truth. Then Nico submit to . . . submit-t-t . . . to red-eyes man." The oaf stopped to pant.

A soft crunch in his jaw filled the golem's mouth with sand. "Blood and damnation," he cursed and spat the sand out. He had been unconsciously grinding the golem's teeth. "So what does the boy want?"

The oaf took a few breaths. "Red-eyes man is to go t-t-to place in Gray's Town . . . no, Gray's Village . . . no, Gray's Crowing . . ."

"Gray's Crossing," Fellwroth snarled. "Hurry!"

The cacographer nodded. "Red-eyes-man is to find Mag-g-gister Shannon and is to fix broken person part of Shhhh . . . Shannon. Nico will be—"

A ratlike gargoyle scurried into the stable. "Fear! Fear! Took too long to reach you. Had to ask other gargoyles where to reach you."

Fellwroth glared at the construct. "What is it? What did you hear?"

"Fighting in the Spindle!" the thing yelped. "Our protections torn apart! Living body under threat!"

Suddenly the stables rang with loud, hearty laughter.

Fellwroth looked up at the big man's smiling face. "Fool! So willing to believe in my disability? You truly think I talk that slowly?"

A wordless, animal shriek escaped from Fellwroth's sandy throat. The monster lashed out with the half-written disspell. But the unfinished text was too dull. It bounced off the stasis spell. Worse, the force of the rebound snapped the sand arm off at the shoulder.

"WEAL!" Fellwroth shrieked, "I'LL TEAR YOUR THROAT OUT FOR THIS, WEAL!"

Fellwroth wrenched his spirit from the sand golem and sent it racing upward toward the Spindle Bridge.

FELLWROTH'S TRUE EYES snapped open to see Deirdre. Her rusted greatsword swung up above her head and then flashed downward with all her divine might.

Fellwroth flinched, but the blade came to a clanging halt as it struck the Magnus shield written above the black table.

Light from a hundred flamefly paragraphs illuminated the cavern. Previously Fellwroth had seen the place only in the dark.

The low ceiling sparkled with quartz chips. The cavern widened only a little way into the mountain. The floor was smooth and gray.

Boann's ark—encased in Numinous—stood at the head of the table. Farther into the mountain, the cavern descended into myriad kobold tunnels. In the other direction loomed the entrance to the Spindle's tunnel. A patch of starry sky shone through a hole the humans had torn into the tunnel's roof.

With another screech, Deirdre's greatsword crashed down onto the textual shield above Fellwroth. A plate-like paragraph buckled under the strain.

Suddenly the world flashed full of golden light, and Fellwroth realized that Shannon was standing beside Deirdre and dashing disspells against the shield. The blue parrot sat on the old linguist's shoulder.

More terrifying, Nicodemus—standing at the table's foot—was jamming his fingers into the shield. Blurry rings of misspelled prose radiated out from the whelp's touch.

Fellwroth bellowed out his rage and terror. The attack had almost worked. If the big oaf had distracted him for a few moments more, the three humans would have broken through his shield and slain his body.

But now his left hand closed around the Emerald of Arahest. With a flash of heat, the gem bestowed the ability to craft infinitely detailed prose without error. When touching the artifact, a spellwright did not fear misspelling even when extemporizing the most complex text.

With a savage yawp, he punched a fist of incendiary Magnus sentences against the protective shield. The spell exploded outward with enough force to knock the three humans onto their backs.

Fellwroth leaped off the table and turned.

The avatar was the first to attack. She launched herself across the stone table and thrust out her greatsword.

Extemporizing through the emerald, Fellwroth wrote a fine Magnus lace and cast it from floor to ceiling.

Deirdre's sword point stuck into the mesh. The blade snapped a single sentence but then turned. Shock widened the girl's eyes as a force invisible to her twisted the sword out of her hands. Her body crashed into the mesh. The spell stretched but did not break. She fell awkwardly onto her shoulder.

Fellwroth wrote a thick Magnus chain and tied it around her neck.

Gasping, the woman grabbed the spell and heaved against it. Only the divine strength in her arms kept the text from crushing her neck. But that strength would not last long.

The cave flashed brighter. Fellwroth looked up to see Shannon cast a many-bladed Numinous spell. The parrot on the linguist's shoulder screamed.

Though impressive for a human text, the spell posed no real threat. With a wave of his hand, Fellwroth extemporized a spray of Numinous disspells that ripped Shannon's attack into fragments.

Shannon kneeled and slammed his fist against the ground, casting a tundern spell. Like subterranean lightning, the silvery bolt shot through the stone floor. It was meant to erupt into a geyser of crushing sentences. But Fellwroth stamped his foot on the incoming spell and shattered the text as if it were made of glass.

With a short laugh, Fellwroth wrote a thin Magnus net and with a wrist flick cast the thing around Shannon's stomach. As the spell tightened, the wizard had to turn away to vomit out the logorrhea bywords that had filled his belly.

Through the emerald's power, Fellwroth could see that the canker curse in the wizard's stomach had consolidated. That would not do. Fellwroth cast a net of Language Prime that scattered twenty new cankers throughout the old man's gut.

With another flick, Fellwroth cast a Numinous censor spell around Shannon's brain. When the text dug into the wizard's mind, the old man collapsed and left his parrot to flap in short circles.

Something struck Fellwroth's head. The world spun for a moment but then stopped, leaving only a ringing in his left ear. Some kind of subtextualized censoring spell? Fellwroth turned to see Nicodemus's face twist with rage. The boy had written several white sentences around an ancient codex and was using them to float the open book beside him.

The whelp must have attempted a censoring spell in a language Fellwroth did not know. "So here you are in all your glory, Nicodemus. The heir to the Imperial family and you've got nothing to write but cacographic mush."

The boy pulled back his right fist as if to make a second attempt. Amused, Fellwroth raised his palm, ready to disspell the boy's text into nonsense.

But no spell formed in Nicodemus's hand. The boy lunged forward and slammed his knuckles into Fellwroth's jaw.

The brief contact with the Nicodemus's skin showed Fellwroth a glimpse of the boy's past—a beautiful woman with long brown hair, reading.

Not caring what private memory was now flashing through Nicodemus's mind, Fellwroth cast a voluminous Magnus wave that knocked the boy back onto the stone table. The boy's spellbook struck the tabletop and lay open by his hip.

"There shall be no more!" Fellwroth bellowed, and raised the emerald. "Today, Nicodemus Weal, your mind shall be splintered."

A wafer-thin Numinous paragraph grew from the emerald to become the thinnest of blades. Fellwroth stepped forward and swung the textual sword down.

Desperately, Nicodemus lurched backward but found his hands useless on the slick tabletop.

Fellwroth's arm flashed through the air, but when the blade was an inch from Nicodemus's brow, a blast of crimson light burst from Boann's ark and struck Fellwroth's hand.

The blow was not strong, but it was enough to pry the emerald from Fellwroth's pale fingers.

The gem dropped.

The instant Fellwroth lost contact with the emerald, the Numinous blade misspelled into dull sentence fragments that splashed harmlessly into Nicodemus's face.

"No!" Fellwroth bellowed.

The green stone fell quietly onto the boy's chest.

In that moment, Fellwroth recognized the emerald's betrayal: it had somehow told Boann's ark when and how to pull it free.

The boy's hand flew up to his chest and closed around the emerald.

AS AMADI AND Kale hurried to the stables in the Spirish Quarter, the secretary explained about Simple John's appearance and the golem attack.

To Amadi's profound relief, two of the provost's officers—the rector and the dean of libraries—followed close behind. They were coming from a closed meeting in which Amadi had tried to explain the events of the past two days to the provost. It had not gone well. Blessedly, Kale had saved her with urgent news.

By the time they reached the stables, two of her sentinels had edited John out of the stasis spell. Though they had censored the big man, they had also sat him down on a stool and brought him a cup of water.

"John," Amadi said when she stood before the cacographer. "Where are Shannon and Nicodemus?"

He pursed his lips and looked at her with narrowed eyes. "You wouldn't believe," he said slowly.

"I know about the golem," she said curtly. "Blood of Los, but I know about the golem! And I have a day, maybe two, to prove that the creature exists or the provost will censor magical literacy out of my mind."

The big man thought about this before nodding. "Nico and Magister have gone to attack the golem's author in the Spindle Bridge."

Amadi took a long breath. "That's a long way off. And forming a party will take time." She stopped. "You said 'in' the bridge?"

"Go there," said John. "You will see what I mean. Only . . ." He paused. "Only take all your spellwrights . . . and all your strongest words."

CHAPTER
forty-three

Nicodemus saw no dazzling flash, felt no rush of power. Everything seemed the same.

And yet, somehow, he knew exactly what to do. His right hand tightened around the emerald and his left landed on the opened page of the Index.

His mind flashed into the Index's starry sky to collide with tirade—an epic Numinous-Magnus spell possessing an aggressive and self-reflexive style.

A scriptorium of grand wizards would have needed a year to craft such a versatile text without error.

But when Nicodemus forged within the emerald, perfectly formed sentences exploded into his hand and spilled down his arm. In the next heartbeat, he blazed from toe to tongue with violent language.

The spell's dazzling glare illuminated Fellwroth's white-robed figure. The creature's hood had fallen during the fight, and Nicodemus looked on his enemy's face.

Limp white hair hung down to Fellwroth's thin shoulders. His pale skin shone with a dull sheen like maggot's flesh. His smooth jaw, hollow cheeks, and snub nose seemed human but strangely asexual.

Between the creature's pale lips opened a maw filled with a hundred quivering tendons. His eyes gleamed red. His forehead presented a golden rectangle of flowing Numinous sentences.

With a backhand slash, Fellwroth cast a spray of needle-like disspells.

But Nicodemus threw out both hands and cast his tirade. The spell produced a Numinous sheet that enveloped the disspells and then discharged a Magnus sphere. This latter passage smashed into Fellwroth's chest and knocked the monster to the ground.

Nicodemus leaped up from the table and cast a thousand filaments of intertwined Numinous and Magnus.

Though sprawled on the floor, Fellwroth thrust his right hand upward to produce another spray of disspells.

But Nicodemus's tirade was too cogent. The filaments darted through Fellwroth's disspells and unwound.

The Magnus tirade coiled around the creature's body, binding his arms to his side and wrapping his legs together. The Numinous tirade spun a web around the monster's mind, cutting him off from all magical language.

"Hold!" Fellwroth cried. "I yield!"

NICODEMUS STOOD OVER his spellbound foe expecting to feel triumphant. But the only emotion he felt was uncertainty.

Just what in the Creator's name happened now?

Though tirade's glow had faded, the remaining flamefly paragraphs provided ample light. Nicodemus looked around and saw Deirdre lying on the floor. She was struggling against the Magnus chains contracting around her neck.

Nicodemus caught the text between thumb and forefinger. Using the emerald, he gleaned the spell's structure and edited two passages. A link snapped, and Deirdre yanked the thing from her throat.

Across the cavern, Shannon was lying motionless on the ground. Azure stood beside him, trying to pluck Fellwroth's censoring text out of the old man's mind.

Nicodemus thought for a moment and then extemporized a vinelike Numinous disspell. He cast it onto Shannon with an underhand toss. The disspell grew up the old man's body and delicately removed the censoring text.

Groaning, Shannon began to stir.

A smile crept across Nicodemus's face as his self-doubt began to fade. Without the emerald, he would have misspelled such a text within moments. He was whole now, complete.

"You cannot kill me," a voice rasped. "Without me, Shannon will die."

Nicodemus turned back to see a spellbound Fellwroth glaring at him with baleful red eyes.

"Only I can disspell the old wizard's canker curses," the creature rasped. "I spread dozens more throughout his gut. You need me. Only I can teach you how to remove them. Only I can teach you the meaning of Language Prime. You will never understand that life is made of magical text and—"

Nicodemus flicked a Magnus gag across the monster's mouth.

He went to Shannon. The old man was on his hands and knees, vomiting another glowing pool of logorrhea bywords. Threads of blood now coiled within the silvery text.

It seemed that Fellwroth had told the truth about planting more curses in Shannon's body.

"No," the old linguist sputtered while trying to wave Nicodemus away. "Find out about the Disjunction. Question the monster."

Nicodemus scowled. "Magister, hold still. I have to disspell your curses."

"Later," Shannon grunted. "The sentinels will be here soon. We must get Fellwroth to—"

"Magister!" Nicodemus snapped. His voice was firm though his hands had gone cold with fear. "Be quiet and hold still!"

The wizard sat on his haunches. "Very well, but hurry. We don't have long."

Nicodemus had to touch the old man to disspell the curses. But as he reached for his teacher's cheek, his hand froze. It was shaking.

"I'm not the Storm Petrel anymore," he whispered to himself. "I won't curse him. I'm the Halcyon now."

It wasn't supposed to be like this. He had the emerald. His doubt and fear should have vanished with his disability.

"I am the Halcyon now," he assured himself and pressed his palm against his teacher's cheek. The old wizard drew in a sharp breath.

Suddenly Nicodemus was looking through Shannon's skin and sinew to the old man's stomach. It was not pink flesh he saw, but the cyan glow of the organ's Language Prime text. Five knobs stood out on the otherwise regular folds. They glowed brighter than the rest of the stomach.

Nicodemus set about disspelling the cankers. It was difficult work; Fellwroth had cruelly restructured Shannon's Language Prime prose. Worse, the old man flinched every time Nicodemus made a major textual change.

"Is it done?" Shannon asked when Nicodemus removed his hand. The pain had made his face shine with sweat.

"I disspelled the worse curses around your stomach, but I saw smaller cankers on other organs. They're not growing quickly. And I want to study them more before—"

"Disspell them later," Shannon said while restoring Azure to her perch on his shoulder. "We haven't long before Starhaven realizes we're here and comes for us."

Nicodemus helped his teacher stand. "Why do we need to worry about the other wizards?"

Shannon took a step on unsteady legs. "When the provost learns the truth about you, Nicodemus, we'll land in the largest embroilment in the history of academic politics. If we want to avoid becoming the provost's political prisoners, we must learn everything we can from that monster."

Nicodemus turned to look at Fellwroth, still spellbound and lying on the floor.

Deirdre had picked herself up and gone to Boann's ark. Fellwroth had written a Numinous shield around the object, but the avatar had forced her arms through the prose to lay her hands against the stone.

The contact seemed to be strengthening the ark; a red aura was growing around the stone and gradually deconstructing Fellwroth's Numinous shield.

"Monster, I'll have the truth from you." Shannon limped over to stand above Fellwroth. "What do you know about the Disjunction?"

The creature glared with bloody eyes. When Shannon disspelled the gag, the thing laughed. "With what do you threaten me, Magister? Torture? Death? Neither will work. You, old goat, will never have my obedience." The bloody eyes swiveled to Nicodemus. "But the boy might."

Nicodemus frowned. "What are you playing at?"

Fellwroth grinned. "You may not need me to disspell the old man's curses. But I command the forces of the Disjunction. Let me live and I will put all the resources of the demon-worshipers at your command. You can rule as a new emperor."

"Don't be stupid," Nicodemus snapped. "I'd rather rot in hell than be your ally."

The monster continued to stare at Nicodemus. "Think on it. You can't go to the wizards; they will never overcome their belief that you're the Storm Petrel. They will imprison and manipulate you. And you can't trust that girl dressed up like a druid; she betrayed me and will betray you."

Nicodemus's heart grew cold. "Deirdre betrayed you?" he asked, remembering his first encounter with Fellwroth in the Drum Tower. The monster had acted surprised when Deirdre had resisted.

Fellwroth ignored this. "We do not have to serve the demons, Nicodemus. You can use me to resist the Disjunction. Think of the opportunities. I can show you how to find the demon-worshiping cults. I can help you eliminate them or manipulate them. Nicodemus, if you want to protect humanity, you cannot afford to destroy me."

Nicodemus looked at Shannon.

The old linguist began to scratch Azure's neck. He took a long moment before nodding.

"Very well," Nicodemus said, turning back to the monster. "Tell me everything you know about the Disjunction."

"TALK FAST," SHANNON said. "The sentinels will be here soon. How did Typhon cross the ocean?"

Fellwroth's red eyes darted between teacher and student. "I am neither human nor a construct, something in between. By combining dust with demonic godspells, Los sought to create a new race to replace humanity. I was to be the first of the new men. He gave me life, but he never completed me. The Pandemonium was away at war on the coast, trying to stop the humans from escaping across the ocean. They had left Mount Calax empty but for Los and my unfinished self. A party of powerful human avatars surprised the arch-demon. Sacrificing their lives, they combined their godspells to drain Los of all strength until he became solid rock. I was left incomplete and forgotten in Los's mountain palace."

Fellwroth shifted uncomfortably beneath the restraining Magnus sentences. "Having no devotees, the demons could not pursue humanity across the ocean. And only Los knew how to break their bonds to the earth of the ancient continent. But I am part of the ancient land—a being made from godspells and dirt. So when—centuries after Los's demise—Typhoneus accidentally discovered me, he knew I could be his vessel to the new world. The demon implanted himself inside of me, made me his ark. We built a crude ship and sailed to this land."

"And why did you cross?" Shannon asked. "Were you going to ferry the demons across one by one?"

Fellwroth shook his head. "Only an Imperial's fluency in Language Prime can reanimate Los's frozen body, so we crossed the ocean to breed one. Typhon had reconstructed the genealogy charts of the Imperial bloodlines. That's how he created you, Nicodemus. And once we had your Language Prime fluency, we set about creating a dragon that could carry us back to the ancient continent."

Nicodemus frowned. "Why not simply sail back?"

"Can't be done," Fellwroth replied. "Being trapped on the ancient continent has driven the demons mad with bloodlust. Mindless, they stalk the southern shores and will destroy any approaching ship. Typhon and I escaped by sail only because the demons did not imagine it was possible. Now their fury is whetted; even Typhon would not have survived a landing by ship."

"So you need a dragon to fly over them?" Nicodemus asked.

The monster shook his head. "The flying helps, but it wouldn't be sufficient. The dragon I completed could fly, but the demons would have torn it into pieces. A true dragon is more than wings and scales. True dragons can change the nature of a mind; they make their victims think unthinkable thoughts."

Shannon exhaled. "A true dragon is a type of quaternary cognition spell?"

Fellwroth answered without taking his eyes from Nicodemus. "Precisely. Only a true dragon can travel past the demons to Mount Calax. There we could reanimate Los with your ability to spell in Language Prime. Los could then tame the feral demons and break their ties to the ancient continent. Then the War of Disjunction would begin at last."

"So then why send your dragon to burn in Trillinon?" Shannon asked before laughing dryly. "No, let me guess. You killed Typhon before the dragon was finished. When you tried to complete the wyrm on your own, you failed to make it powerful enough to get past the demons. So you sent the dragon against Trillinon to cause havoc."

Fellwroth bared his teeth at the grand wizard.

Shannon responded with a humorless smile. "So I am right. But tell me why you killed Typhon. Why sabotage your own plan?"

The monster hissed. "Typhon was a fool. The old goat was so bent upon reconstructing Los that he failed to see that I am Los's legacy. He jeopardized my life for trifling matters. So when the emerald showed me how to kill him in the river, I did so and stole part of the demonic godspell. That's how I learned to manipulate dreams."

"There are no more demons on this continent, then?" Nicodemus raised his eyebrows. "So to stop the Disjunction, all we need do is kill you?"

"Not quite, boy." Fellwroth produced a toothy smile. "Typhon and I established hidden cults in every human kingdom, each of which will continue trying to breed a true Imperial. If you want to prevent the War of Disjunction, you will need me. I can help you destroy the cults or rule them. You can choose to do either, but to have any hope of discovering them you must protect me from the wizards and from that vile woman." Fellwroth nodded to something behind Nicodemus. "I won't have a betrayer near me."

Deirdre approached. Her green eyes shone with a wild energy. She had recovered her goddess, her pure love. "How could I have betrayed you, monster?" she asked. "When from the beginning I sought nothing but your death?"

Something occurred to Nicodemus. "Fellwroth, how did you find Boann's ark? Why bring it here?"

The creature laughed and looked at Deirdre. "You mean she doesn't know? Her hussy of a goddess never told her?"

Deirdre stepped beside Nicodemus. "Hold your tongue." She leveled her greatsword at the monster's head. "Or I'll cut it out."

"Nicodemus, Boann is traitorous," Fellwroth replied hotly. "She wants to control you."

Shannon stepped forward and pulled Deirdre's sword arm down. "We need to handle this carefully," he muttered.

Fellwroth continued to glare at the woman. "Boann and I made an arrangement. The goddess agreed to serve the Disjunction if she could become a powerful demon."

"You lie!" Deirdre growled.

Shannon laid a hand on her shoulder. "Easy," he murmured.

Fellwroth laughed. "Stupid girl. You were the one who negotiated the agreement. You offered to capture Nicodemus for me because I did not then know his identity."

Deirdre looked at her two companions. "Don't listen. He's trying to trick you into distrusting Boann."

Nicodemus met her gaze. "Deirdre, how did he know where Boann's ark was?"

Fellwroth was the one who answered. "The girl begged for her life when I cornered her in that Chthonic tower. She told me where I could find the ark and how to surprise the druids protecting it. How else could I have gotten it here so quickly?"

Deirdre shook her head. "It's a lie."

Nicodemus's fingers tightened around the emerald. Something was wrong. "But why did you bring it here, Fellwroth? The spell that knocked the emerald from your hand came from the ark."

The creature sneered in disgust. "Boann suggested that I bring the ark here to reassure me of her allegiance. If I had her ark, she could not break her word and run away with you, Nicodemus."

The monster sniffed in disdain. "Even though I was foolish enough to agree, I took a precaution: I sealed the ark with protective text. It was a strong shield, but one short spell could slip through if the ark knew exactly how my prose was written. Somehow the emerald plucked that knowledge from my mind and fed it into the deity inside the stone. Somehow the emerald told the ark exactly when to strike so that I would drop the stone."

Nicodemus's brow furrowed. "But Boann shouldn't know about the emerald. Only you, Fellwroth, knew about the emerald. Well, you and . . ." He stopped himself from saying "Typhon."

Cold terror spread through Nicodemus.

"You see, neither the girl nor the goddess can be trusted." Fellwroth insisted.

"You can't believe him, Nicodemus," Deirdre insisted, her chest heaving. "It's been a year since I sinned against Boann, and we are so close to redeeming—"

"Deirdre, something's wrong," Nicodemus interrupted. "Listen, a year ago Fellwroth killed Typhon. You started having seizures just after that."

Deirdre shook her head again. "We knew that, Nicodemus. We knew that Boann saw Fellwroth killing the demon. That's how she learned of you. That's why she sent me to rescue you."

"No, Deirdre," Nicodemus said, taking a cautious step closer. "We don't know that for fact; that's what we suspected. But what if it isn't true? What if Typhon succeeded in infecting Boann when he was in her waters? You told us that Boann kept her ark in the Highland rivers."

Fellwroth's crimson eyes bulged. "Boann inhabited that river? Deirdre said the goddess was of the city. Nicodemus, quickly, we must get away from the ark. She's not Boann's avatar anymore!"

Deirdre's sword arm was trembling.

Nicodemus began composing restraining Magnus sentences.

Fellwroth kept talking. "Nicodemus, Shannon, we need to get away. There are fates worse than death! She's not Boann's avatar! We have to escape Typhon!"

"Deirdre . . ." Shannon started to say.

But Deirdre, moving with inhuman speed, slammed her elbow into Shannon's face and then thrust her blade into Fellwroth's skull.

The Numinous rectangle on the creature's forehead exploded and sent a wall of force careening through the cavern. When the shockwave hit Nicodemus, everything went black.

Then he was lying on his back staring at a torrent of blazing Numinous prose streaming from Fellwroth's corpse to the ark.

Nicodemus extemporized a disspell along his forearm and cast it at the textual stream.

But his text crumpled in the air and fell.

Numbing shock filled Nicodemus as he watched the disspell shatter on the floor. How could he have misspelled?

He looked down at his hands and found them empty.

The emerald was gone.

CHAPTER

Forty-four

A rumble shook the stairs under Amadi's feet.

Slowly the sentinels pushed open the giant iron doors that led onto the Spindle Bridge's landing. Before her stretched the moonlit bridge and the dark mountains beyond. "Secure the landing," she ordered.

The twelve sentinels who had volunteered for the expedition began to spread out. They were all excellent spellwrights: ten wizards and two grand wizards. Three bore caesura wands, another a tundern wand. The rest carried spellbooks full of wartexts.

The dean of libraries and the rector had accompanied the party to observe.

Simple John stepped beside her and pointed. "There!"

Amadi's gaze followed his finger to where the Spindle Bridge met the mountainside. A hole seemed to have been blasted in the Spindle. Out of it shone a golden blaze.

The sentinels muttered. Someone was casting a powerful Numinous spell from inside the mountain.

"Kale," Amadi ordered, "stay here with John and the provost's officers. The rest of you, advance slowly and keep closed ranks. Subdue anything dangerous, and kill anything nonhuman."

DEIRDRE STOOD FROZEN in her thrust—legs bent, arms extended, hands locked around the sword hilt. Fellwroth's unmoving body lay before her.

When Nicodemus said Deirdre's name, her eyes moved but her body remained as stiff as stone.

Shannon lay behind her, bleeding from his nose and a wound on his shoulder. Azure had disappeared.

Nicodemus went to the wizard and turned him over. He took care to touch only the old man's robes, never his skin. Without the emerald, he was once again the mutagenic Storm Petrel.

Shannon looked up at him with a dazed expression. "Fellwroth . . . is dead?"

"He is," Nicodemus croaked, crouching beside the old wizard.

"And Deirdre is . . . Typhon's avatar?"

"She didn't know." Nicodemus shoved his arm under the wizard's back.

"But how did you figure it out?" Shannon gasped as Nicodemus tried to lift him.

"Magister, now is not—"

"No . . ." the old man said between rapid breaths. "You have to tell me."

Nicodemus grimaced. "Fellwroth cut Typhon in Boann's river. After that Deirdre started having seizures and seeing visions of Fellwroth attacking Typhon. Something of the demon must have infected Boann's ark and later her avatar. Deirdre didn't recognize the change because she thought it was Boann's punishment for having an affair with Kyran."

Only four flamefly paragraphs remained; they hovered above Shannon, shedding a small pool of wan incandescence.

Shannon shook his head. "But how do you know that?"

"Fellwroth's words," Nicodemus answered. "The creature was terrified that Typhon was after us."

Shannon inhaled sharply as Nicodemus sat him up.

The younger man continued to explain as he draped the old man's arm over his shoulder. "Typhon knew Fellwroth would have to find me when the emerald needed replenishing. So he pretended to be Boann and sent Deirdre here. She was to bring me to the ark; that way Typhon could invest his soul into me and use me to defeat Fellwroth. But when Fellwroth caught Deirdre alone, the demon changed his plan. He tricked Fellwroth into bringing the ark up here, next to his real body, knowing that Fellwroth would bring me here."

The old wizard groaned as Nicodemus hoisted him to his feet. "But why," Shannon asked as Nicodemus wrapped his arm around the old man's waist, "did the demon want you in the same place as Fellwroth and the ark?"

Nicodemus was now half-walking, half-hauling the wizard toward the Spindle Tunnel. "The demon knew that if Fellwroth died near the ark, he could steal the creature's power. So Typhon waited for me to arrive, and then cast a spell to tear the emerald from Fellwroth's hand and give it to me. He knew I could defeat Fellwroth when the emerald completed my mind. But now he's taken the emerald back. I can't find it."

Nicodemus stumbled and nearly fell. Warmth spread across his cheeks. "All the things that've happened in the past few days, they've all been part of Typhon's plot to kill Fellwroth and recover the emerald."

A slow clapping sound echoed through the cavern. Nicodemus stopped.

In the darkness before the Spindle's entrance stood a man—seven feet tall with a silken mane of red hair and a beard to match.

Two amused all-white eyes stared down at Nicodemus. The newcomer's obsidian skin was black and glossy, making it hard to see his narrow nose and high cheeks. The broad muscles on his torso bulged as he clapped, and out from his back spread two long wings, checkered with red and black feathers. A loincloth covered his groin but not his thick, powerful legs.

When the demon spoke, his voice rumbled. "Impressive that you managed to understand so much." His calm laughter sounded like distant thunder. "Nicodemus Weal, you've grown."

THE DEMON WORE a friendly, almost avuncular, grin. "You've gleaned my plan almost exactly, save for one thing."

"Typhon," Nicodemus said breathlessly.

The demon nodded. "Set the old one down. I've censored him."

With a start Nicodemus realized that Shannon had gone slack in his arms. Careful not to touch the old man's skin, he laid the old linguist on the ground.

"Have you ever seen a deity before?" Typhon rumbled, his checkered wings fluttering.

Nicodemus shook his head.

The demon nodded sympathetically. "It is overwhelming for most mortals. But my boy, I want you to overcome this. I want you to think for me. Think of when Fellwroth discovered you and Deirdre in the Drum Tower. What should I have done?"

"You could have sent Deirdre into a fit," Nicodemus said automatically. "If she had given me to Fellwroth, the creature would have taken us here right away."

Typhon's crimson beard split into a smile. "Correct. After Fellwroth captured the ark, he enclosed it with a Numinous shield. I had not anticipated this. The spell almost completely blocked my control over Deirdre. That's why she continued to execute my previous instructions—which were to seduce you and bring you to Gray's Crossing."

The demon paused. "Nicodemus, it is the shame of the world we had to meet this way. I am your creator. I brought your parents together, and I ensured that you would end up as a Starhaven cacographer."

The demon's black lips grimaced. "It hasn't been the best home, I realize. For one of your talents, being a cacographer must have been difficult. But the alternative was to watch an Alliance assassin take you from me." He shivered. "And I couldn't watch another of my Imperial boys die."

Nicodemus blinked.

The demon was studying him. "Fellwroth told you of the Alliance of Heretics, yes? About the clandestine human deities also trying to breed a Language Prime spellwright? They have been murdering your cousins for centuries. And they will kill you in a heartbeat. That is why you must let me protect you."

Nicodemus stood paralyzed by shock. The demon's tone was one of genuine concern.

Typhon took a step closer. "We are so close to our goal now that we no longer need to hide you in wretched Starhaven. Join me now and you will help me compose a new dragon. With Fellwroth dead and the emerald restored to its full power, we will need only seven or eight years to write a new wyrm. Then you will become the first dragon lord, a new kind of being invulnerable to the attacks of the Alliance."

This last startled Nicodemus out of his paralysis. "In a dream I was your dragon. I'd rather cut my own throat than help you create such a monster."

Typhon shook his massive head. "You were not my dragon; you were Fellwroth's dragon. That slave turned my draft into a clichéd, fire-breathing lizard. Fellwroth never understood what a true dragon is. Nicodemus, they are texts more glorious than you can now imagine. I could give you the spells needed to understand how glorious dragons are and how glorious you and I shall become."

Rather than answer, Nicodemus looked around for an escape or a weapon. He saw only Deirdre, frozen still as a statue.

"She can't help you yet," Typhon rumbled. "She is my avatar now and possesses most of my soul. It will take time to win her over, but you and I will win her."

When Nicodemus took a step back, Typhon flicked his hand out as if casting a spell. Nicodemus flinched, but nothing happened.

The demon frowned. "Curious," he said. "The censoring text I just cast around your mind misspelled and deconstructed. Does your cacography influence language unknown to you?"

Nicodemus's mind filled with images of the night terrors that had hidden him from Fellwroth. He took another step back.

Typhon flapped his wings once. "I do not want to restrain you. We are not enemies."

He held out a massive obsidian hand, in the center of which sparkled the Emerald of Arahest. "When I trust you, you shall have this back. You shall survive the War of Disjunction and live with Deirdre. You two will become the first dragon lords. From your children shall come a race to replace humanity. Demonkind will reward—"

"You crippled John!" Nicodemus heard himself shout. "You crippled me! You and I shall only and ever be enemies!"

The demon sighed. "Fathers and sons, authors and texts, they often clash before reconciling. I am going to restrain you now. If you struggle—"

Typhon's next words were drowned out by an earsplitting thunderclap. A brilliant spray of Magnus flew up from the demon's back to splash against the ceiling. Someone had dashed a wartext against the malicious deity.

Nicodemus spun around and ran for the kobold caves at the back of the cavern. Behind him, Magistra Amadi Okeke's voice rang out. There was a brief silence, which was broken by a blast of sound so low and loud that it vibrated Nicodemus's chest like a drum.

He looked back. Typhon roared at a dozen sentinels as they came swarming down from the Spindle Bridge. A storm of silver and gold spells flew from the spellwrights. Typhon pulled back his wings and—

Nicodemus slammed into something and suddenly was on his back. Groaning, he sat up. In front of him, he could feel a solid but invisible barrier. His cheeks burned hot. Typhon must have cast some textual wall at the cavern's end, and Nicodemus must have run straight into it.

Dazed, Nicodemus wondered how his mind had unknowingly disspelled the censoring text Typhon had cast about him when his body had smashed so painfully into this text.

The barrier must have been written in a different language. One like the Chthonic languages, that used logical spellings. His mind quickly distorted those languages with illogical spellings. That would mean that he could misspell the barrier only slowly.

But slowly was better than not at all. He pushed his hand into the barrier and felt his cacography begin to corrupt the prose.

Another roar rolled through the cavern.

Nicodemus looked back to see Typhon lunge forward and grab a sentinel by the robes. With a one-handed heave, the demon flung the man upward, crushing his head into the low ceiling.

On the cavern's other side, a sentinel lifted a silver hammer—a tundern wand—and struck it against the ground. A subterranean lightning bolt flew out of the artifact and erupted beneath Typhon's feet into a spray of jagged Magnus sentences and rock fragments.

But neither words nor stone pierced the demon's obsidian skin. With a backhanded lash, Typhon cast a blade of red light that flew across the cavern and cut the tundern wielder in two.

The surviving sentinels, Magistra Okeke at their front, were retreating into the tunnel.

Nicodemus turned to the textual barrier before him. It continued to shift under his hands but felt no weaker. This was taking too long. He'd never break through in time.

"Nicodemus," Typhon bellowed behind him. "We must get you away from here. These humans will kill you. I've been imprisoned for too long, and too much of my soul is locked into Deirdre. I'm not strong enough to kill them all at once."

The five sentinels had fallen far back into the tunnel. Typhon raised a massive hand and struck the tunnel floor. A burst of glowing red streamers erupted from the demon's fist and then blasted down. The cavern trembled as part of the Spindle's floor fell into blackness.

With cries of shock, the sentinels ran deeper into the tunnel. Typhon cast an unseen spell that knocked free another bit of the floor. Through the growing hole Nicodemus could see the moonlit forest far below.

A sentinel who had not retreated fast enough shouted as the stones beneath him gave way. There was a silver flash as he tried to textually stop his fall—then nothing.

Typhon roared.

Nicodemus's head felt light. His lips were numb. He couldn't deconstruct the barrier fast enough.

One of the sentinels threw a Numinous spell that exploded against Typhon's shoulder. The flash briefly illuminated Shannon's unmoving form. "Magister!" Nicodemus exclaimed. He could not leave Shannon behind.

But how to retrieve the old man? Without the emerald he stood no chance of injuring the demon. If only he had time to write out a subtext to hide himself, he could . . .

"Fiery blood!" he swore and pulled back the sleeves of his robes. "Of course." He began to pinch the Chthonic sentences tattooed on his right hand.

At first the sentences were recalcitrant and kept inscribing themselves back into his skin. But with a fury of yanking, he managed to disengage the spell.

The Chthonic ghost had warned him that Wrixlan and Pithan sentences would score his skin. But even so, Nicodemus was shocked by the searing agony that consumed his arms as the sentences unwound.

Once free of his arm, the purple language spun itself into Garkex, the firetroll.

Previously the construct had been no bigger than a child. Now the three-horned spell stood six feet tall and possessed arms so muscular they bulged like flour sacks stuffed with river stones.

Initially Garkex wore a grumpy why-did-you-wake-me expression, but the instant the troll's eyes fell upon Typhon they bulged with fear. With a snort, the construct scooped up Nicodemus and began to tear the other Wrixlan constructs from his skin.

Every inch of Nicodemus's arms and forearms burned with pain as the purple prose was ripped from him. He fought the urge to cry out as Garkex rolled him over and over and peeled off more fantasies.

After what felt like an infinity of agony, the troll set Nicodemus down.

All of the night terrors now stood around them: Fael the lycanthrope, Tamelkan the eyeless dragon, Uro the nightmare insect, and many others. Because the constructs had absorbed some of Nicodemus's strength by storing themselves on his skin, each one had grown.

In the next instant the fantasies scooped up Nicodemus, placed him on Tamelkan's back, and surrounded him with their concealing dark blue skin.

Typhon tossed a last spell at the sentinels. The Spindle had not fallen, but for fifty feet the tunnel's bottom had been ripped out.

"Nicodemus, they are far enough back," the demon called. "They can't hurt you now. Nicodemus?" He had turned and was peering into the cavern.

"Magister Shannon," Nicodemus whispered to Garkex. "The body there. We need to retrieve the body and escape."

The troll nodded.

"Nicodemus, this is not the time to hide," Typhon rumbled. "Wizards are finicky authors." The demon began searching the cavern's northern edge.

The huddle of night terrors—Nicodemus suspended in the middle—crept away in the opposite direction.

"The wizards believe in a false prophecy and think you are the Petrel," Typhon said. "They'll censor and kill you."

The pack of invisible monsters approached Deirdre. Most of her body was still frozen, but she had managed to drop her sword. Her head hung forward and her chest heaved.

A sudden volley of Magnus spells filled the cave and smashed against Typhon's side. The sentinels hadn't given up. Roaring furiously, the demon ran to the cavern's mouth to return the attack.

Seizing the chance, Garkex darted out to grab Shannon and slung the old man over his shoulder. With the troll gone, Nicodemus's left shoulder had become visible. Typhon was still preoccupied by the sentinels, but Deirdre—standing not five feet away—turned her eyes on him.

Panic flashed hot in Nicodemus's mind. How complete was Typhon's control over her? For a moment he considered attacking her to keep her from raising the alarm. But the idea died almost as soon as it formed. Instead he pleaded with his eyes and brought a finger up to his lips. Garkex returned with Shannon and plopped the old man onto Tamelkan's back.

Slowly Deirdre's chest filled with air as if she might scream.

Nicodemus shook his head vehemently.

Her chest contracted. "Please," she croaked, "kill me."

"PLEASE," DEIRDRE WHISPERED. "I hold most of his soul."

Nicodemus felt his blood go cold. "I can't—"

"You must," she hissed. "If I die, so will he."

The cavern shook again with Typhon's roar. A red glow grew around the demon and then flashed. All was silent for a moment and then a distant sentinel screamed.

"Nicodemus," Typhon called in an anxious voice. "More wizards will come soon." The demon had turned around and was striding into the cavern. "We must . . ." his voice died as he looked down to where Shannon had once lain. "The old one," he rumbled.

"Please!" Deirdre whispered.

Suddenly Nicodemus had to look away from an intense white blaze. It was Typhon. The demon had held up his right hand to cast a spell that shed pure physical light. It glared brighter than sunshine.

All around Nicodemus the constructs screamed. Physical light deconstructed Wrixlan and Pithan, and each of the night terrors was written in purple prose.

Typhon turned toward Nicodemus. In the piercing blaze, the night terrors had become visible. The demon's all-white eyes opened wide.

Realizing that they could hide no longer, Garkex spouted flame from his horns and charged Typhon.

The other night terrors followed, shrieking out a caterwauling war cry.

Nicodemus grabbed hold of Shannon, just barely pulling the old man off Tamelkan before the eyeless dragon charged into battle.

Typhon meet Garkex with a blast of red light that deconstructed the construct's left arm. But with a brutal right-handed slash, the troll raked his claws across Typhon's cheek and knocked the demon's head to one side. The rest of the nightmares rushed forward in a tide of scales, tentacles, and talons. They bowled into the demon and knocked him onto his back.

"Kill me!" Deirdre cried. "His control over me lessens." Her arms had gone slack. She looked at Nicodemus with wide, pleading eyes.

"Deirdre, I c-can't possibly—"

"The blade," she said nodding to the greatsword she had dropped. "Pick it up."

The cavern blazed brighter with Typhon's white light. Garkex bellowed as Typhon crushed the troll's chest with a blazing fist. The other night terrors were deconstructing as the light frayed their exterior sentences.

Nicodemus picked up the sword and stepped toward the brawl; he would rather die with a weapon in hand than hide in a corner.

"For pity's sake!" Deirdre pleaded. "Typhon corrupted my goddess. He led me to endanger Kyran. Don't let me live to serve the demon." Tears filled her eyes. "He will twist my will. He will make me one of them!"

Nicodemus could not move.

Before him Typhon leaped to his feet with a deafening roar. The demon tore apart Fael, the night terror lycanthrope. Oily blood now seeped from small wounds across the demon's head and chest. Only Tamelkan, the eyeless dragon, remained.

"Now!" Deirdre pleaded. "Nicodemus, before it is too late!"

Typhon lunged forward and caught the small dragon's head. With a quick twist of the torso the demon snapped the wyrm's neck and threw it aside.

Nicodemus raised his sword.

Typhon turned to him. "Nicodemus, stop. You will only harm yourself."

"Nicodemus!" Deirdre cried. "I beg you!"

Typhon shook his head. "I have chosen the two of you to beget a new race after the War of Disjunction. You are to know unparalleled happiness. You must survive together!"

"Please," Deirdre whispered. Her tear-bright face shone with torment and longing. Her trembling hand drew back her cloak to reveal the dirty white cloth above her left breast. "Save me if you bear me any love."

"No!" Typhon bellowed as Nicodemus thrust the rusted blade through Deirdre's heart.

DEIRDRE CONVULSED. HER hands came up to grasp the sword.

Typhon howled, a torrent of crimson blood spewing from his left breast. The demon fell to his knees, wings flapping wildly, arms trembling.

Deirdre collapsed into Nicodemus's arms. They sank slowly to the floor. She looked up at him, struggling for breath. He could barely see through his own tears.

Without warning, a massive obsidian arm pulled them apart and tossed Nicodemus to the ground. Typhon lifted Deirdre up and pulled the sword from her chest. He hugged her close. "No!" she gasped. "No! Nicodemus, help! He's healing—"

The demon had dissolved into a dark cloud that was imbuing itself into Deirdre's body.

Confused relief flooded through Nicodemus. Deirdre wouldn't die after all. The demon's red and black wings now grew from her back. She held the greatsword in one hand.

Nicodemus struggled to his feet and grabbed her arm. Touching her sent a shock through his body and filled his mind with a vision of Deirdre as a girl running through a field of heather. He saw her holding a child. Then he was back in the present. She was holding him. Her once green eyes were now black as onyx.

She began to whisper, not with her own voice, but with Typhon's rumbling one. "Lord Severn, April, James Berr," she whispered. "You've always been mine. The next dragon will make you mine again."

Nicodemus opened his mouth but could not speak.

"Kill the beast!" a woman's voice bellowed as a Magnus wartext shot over Deirdre's head. Suddenly Magistra Okeke and two sentinels rushed into the cavern casting violent language at Deirdre.

The sentinels must have magically spanned the distance from the fractured Spindle Tunnel to the cavern.

With a shove, Deirdre sent Nicodemus flying to slam against the cavern wall. Everything disappeared for a moment. Then he was slouched on the floor.

Deirdre leveled her greatsword at the sentinels. With blinding speed, she dodged around the spells to charge the black-robes. The first she slashed across the chest, the second across the throat. But when she lunged for Magistra Okeke, the woman leaped back in time to avoid the blade.

Another silver spell flashed through the cavern and knocked the sword from Deirdre's hands. One of the sentinels remaining in the Spindle had renewed the attack.

With a cry, Deirdre ran for the cavern's entrance. Nicodemus struggled to his feet in time to see her leap out into the tunnel.

He ran forward and saw her drop out of the tunnel's decimated floor and spread her wings.

She was too heavy to fly, but by flapping hard she turned south and began a slow descent to the forest. Occasionally her arms swung out with the effort. Once, before she had fallen too far, Nicodemus glimpsed in her hand the small, glinting emerald.

CHAPTER

Forty-five

Nicodemus watched until Deirdre disappeared into the forest far below. The wind set his long black hair fluttering. The cold autumn night smelled of coming rain.

"She will survive the demon," a soft voice said behind him.

Nicodemus turned to see a short, transparent figure that at first seemed to be a ghost. She stared at him with lapis eyes and pressed her wide lips into a solemn line. Her hair was not hair at all but a slow, white torrent: a miniature white river that tumbled down her back to splash against her ankles. Thick green robes floated all about her as if underwater.

"Boann," Nicodemus said with a nod and a backward step.

"What is left of her," the figure said, returning the nod. "I have escaped the prison Typhon made for me in my own ark, but I am now too weak to manifest myself physically."

"Can you save Deirdre?" Nicodemus asked, taking another step away.

The goddess looked past him to the forest in which Deirdre had vanished.

"No." She studied Nicodemus. "But one day you might. I have watched you, Nicodemus Weal. And when Deirdre touched the ark, I learned all that she knew. I would swear on the Creator's name to protect and help you in your struggle against the demons. Do you know what that means? For a deity to swear on the Creator's name?"

Nicodemus had been backing away. Now he stopped. "It means you would be bound to your oath, that you could never break it."

The young goddess nodded and held out her transparent hand. "Will you exchange oaths? I will pledge myself to you if you pledge yourself to freeing Deirdre."

Nicodemus studied the goddess. Deities sometimes swore fealty to each other, but never to mortals. "Why would you offer such a thing? Being human, I could break my vow; you could not."

Boann's hand did not waver. "I am little more than a wraith now, unable to affect the physical world. I will remain so until reunited with Deirdre.

Unless you take me under your protection, Typhon's followers will find me and tear me apart."

Her voice grew urgent. "If you refuse, Deirdre will languish under the demon's control. It is only through you that I might regain her."

"Then I accept," Nicodemus said firmly. Together they kneeled and swore on the Creator's name—he to rescue Deirdre, she to protect and serve him.

Slowly they stood. She nodded and sent her waterfall-hair cascading over her shoulders. "The human deities resisting Typhon call themselves The Alliance of Divine Heretics. My mother, the rain goddess Sian, is a Heretic. Long ago I sought to join the Alliance, but they declined. They felt my political involvement in the Highlands made me too visible to the demon-worshipers."

The goddess sighed. "And it seems they were right. My scheming somehow alerted Typhon of my connection to the Alliance. He sought to infect me in hopes of gaining a spy among his enemies. But Fellwroth attacked him during the infection, and so the demon won control of my ark but never of me. In time, he learned to manipulate Deirdre, though she fought him with all her will."

Boann shook her head. "Because of Deirdre's strength, and yours, Fellwroth failed to replace Typhon as the leader of the Disjunction. But now the demon is free again. If you accept my guidance, Nicodemus, I will help you convince the Alliance that we can help fight the Disjunction. Will you accept my counsel?"

Nicodemus looked around the dark cavern. Nothing moved. In the other direction there was open air and distant Starhaven. Sparks of gold and silver glinted in the Spindle. Some of Magistra Okeke's sentinels had survived.

"Goddess, I will," he said. "I find myself without allies or direction."

A half-smile spread across Boann's lips.

Nicodemus's heart ached. For a moment, she seemed the very image of Deirdre.

The goddess nodded. "It won't be easy. The Alliance deities, even my own mother, will distrust me now that Typhon has invaded my ark. Worse, the Alliance has already bred a Language Prime spellwright, your half-sister. Now that Fellwroth has loosed a dragon on Trillinon, they know the Disjunction also has a Language Prime spellwright. Even now they are sending out hunting parties to assassinate you, Nicodemus. Our task is to convince them that you can aid the fight against the Disjunction despite your . . . cacography."

Nausea filled Nicodemus. He was again a Storm Petrel—a champion of error in language, unable to touch another living being without misspelling the living language inside it.

He closed his eyes and imagined the emerald. He pictured his determination to end his disability as light falling into the gem.

"Come, Nicodemus," Boann said, turning back toward the cavern. "We must see to your teacher."

"Shannon!" Nicodemus exclaimed. "Is he—"

"He lives." She pointed to the old man lying on his back. "I disspelled the text the demon put around his mind. And I hid his bird during the fight."

Azure was next to Shannon, nervously preening the old man's silvery dreadlocks. Boann reached down and pressed a transparent forefinger to the grand wizard's head. His white eyes opened. "Nicodemus?" he said.

"Here, Magister," Nicodemus said, kneeling beside him.

The wizard sat up and moved as if to take his pupil's hand.

Nicodemus flinched. "You can't touch me, Magister. I would misspell your Language Prime texts."

The old linguist pressed a hand to his temple. "What happened? My . . ." Azure climbed up the wizard's sleeve to perch on his shoulder.

Boann stood and spoke loudly, as if addressing an unseen audience. "Nicodemus Weal has defeated the creature Fellwroth. He has discovered his identity as a true heir of the ancient Imperial family. He has learned the truth about the prophecies. He may possess the powers of the Storm Petrel, but he is not predestined to serve the Disjunction. I, the river goddess Boann, have pledged myself to aid his struggle against the demon Typhon."

Though troubled by the goddess's sudden formality, Nicodemus was relieved to see that Shannon's nose and shoulder wounds had stopped bleeding. The old man was making cooing sounds to Azure as he struggled to his feet.

"Nicodemus," Boann whispered. "Behind you lies the Index."

Nicodemus retrieved the book.

The goddess faced the dark cavern. "How much of that did you overhear, sentinel?"

Out from the shadows stepped Magistra Amadi Okeke. A bruise was swelling up on her pale forehead. "All of it, goddess."

Boann glared at the woman with crystalline eyes. "Then you realize, Magistra, that Nicodemus is not a destroyer?"

Amadi's eyes widened. "Forgive me, goddess. My understanding of prophecy is imperfect. When I take Nicodemus back to Starhaven, I will explain all that I have seen."

Boann laughed. “Nicodemus cannot return; you kindled the fire of counter-prophecy. The wizards now fear him too much.” The goddess’s eyes shone brighter.

Amadi stepped backward. “But goddess, I—”

“You must undo the damage you have done. You will return to Starhaven and report all that has happened here. But you will not seek to correct the Erasmine Prophecy or the counter-prophecy. Rather, you will become our agent within the Numinous Order.”

Amadi took a deep breath. “Goddess, no one will believe me. I must have Nicodemus and you to confirm what I have seen.”

Boann tossed her long river-hair and sent a waterfall splashing down her back. “Fellwroth’s body will be your evidence. You will say nothing of Deirdre. But you will report that Nicodemus and Shannon died when fighting Typhon. Say the demon threw them out of the Spindle; that will explain why their bodies won’t be found. Hopefully that will stop the sentinels from pursuing us, at least for a while.”

Amadi looked back at Fellwroth’s body and then nodded. “As you say, goddess.”

“Magistra Okeke,” Nicodemus said slowly, “what can you tell me of the cacographer Simple John? Does he live?”

The sentinel frowned. “He does. He was the one who brought me here. We left him on the Spindle Bridge’s landing.”

Nicodemus let out a relieved breath. “The wizards must not know what Typhon did to him.”

Amadi narrowed her eyes. “And what was that?”

After describing how Typhon’s godspell had crippled John’s mind, Nicodemus looked into Amadi’s eyes and said, “If the wizards found out, they would suspect him of still being under the demon’s sway.”

“I understand, Nicodemus,” said Amadi, pushing a dreadlock from her pale face. “I honor what the man did to bring me here. I will keep his secret.”

Nicodemus considered her impassive expression, then nodded. “Thank you, Magistra.” He bowed his head. “Will you tell John I am sorry—”

“Nicodemus,” Boann interrupted gently. “John, like everyone else, must believe that you and Shannon have died.”

Nicodemus started to object, but then he saw Shannon. The old man stood just behind the goddess, holding Azure. The grand wizard was shaking his head.

“Very well,” said Nicodemus, and bowed again to Amadi. “Thank you, Magistra.”

The sentinel’s dour gaze softened. She pointed out into the night. “I can see more spellwriting. The other wizards will be here soon.”

Nicodemus saw golden light in the Spindle's remains. The sentinel was right.

"It is time to be gone," the goddess announced. "Nicodemus, you must carry what is left of my ark." She gestured farther into the mountain.

Nicodemus saw that the formerly massive standing stone had crumbled. Most of it had become dust, but a single chunk of rock, not bigger than a cat, remained. He went to the now miniature ark and lifted it into his arms. Three undulating lines were carved down its length.

When Boann spoke again her voice became soft, almost sing-song. "Come, Nicodemus, Shannon, we travel into the mountains, into the kobold caves. I know the way to a private haven. There we shall heal and make ready to rescue Deirdre and recover the emerald."

"But where can we go?" asked Nicodemus. "The wizards will search the caves regardless of what Magistra tells them."

The river goddess smiled. "Where else can we go," she asked, raising one eyebrow, "but to Heaven Tree Valley?"

CHAPTER

Forty-six

The party walked through most of the night. The labyrinthine kobold caverns stretched before them. Some were adorned with luminescent blue lichen. Others housed pools of water that reflected the light of Shannon's flamefly spells.

They stopped in a round cavern near the surface. A fissure in the ceiling revealed a sliver of starry sky. Thick moss made a bed for the weary spellwrights, but Nicodemus's sleep brought only nightmares of Deirdre convulsing as Typhon watched.

In the late morning, they pressed on. Nicodemus argued that they should chase after Deirdre as soon as possible.

At first his words met silence. Then Boann explained why they could not. She was weak and would not grow stronger until reunited with Deirdre. Shannon still suffered from their encounter with Fellwroth; there was no telling how his body would react to the cankers still seeded in his gut.

"And you, Nicodemus, are healthy but unprepared," the goddess explained. "We must heal and build our forces. You must train and study."

"But for how long?" he asked.

"As long as is needed," the goddess replied.

Shannon agreed. "Patience is necessary. Think of the emerald. By touching you, the gem regained its full strength. With it, Typhon would be powerful beyond our comprehension. But after four years away from you, the gem will lose its power. If we remain hidden long enough, we deprive Typhon of his most powerful weapon."

Nicodemus objected. "But he might start another dragon spell."

Shannon replied. "There's no 'might' about it. He will begin another dragon, but he won't complete the wyrm. As he said when trying to woo you, he needs seven or eight years with the replenished emerald. So long as we hide from him, he will only have four."

Sighing deeply, Nicodemus let himself be convinced.

Three more days of walking passed. They lived off spring water and mushrooms Boann showed them how to find. Twice the goddess led them up to the surface. Shannon cast Magnus traps to pull trout from the streams.

Boann and Nicodemus searched the sparse alpine forests for autumnal nuts and berries.

Each night they sat around a campfire, but they never found much to say. Nicodemus stole into the dark to study the magical languages of the Chthonics.

Using the Index, he taught himself Pithan. A powerful language, it produced luminous indigo runes that, like Magnus, could affect the physical world. Because of its logical grammar and spelling rules, Nicodemus's cacography did not impair his ability to spellwrite in Pithan. For that reason he began tattooing wartexts all across his body.

Most nights this work kept him up late, which suited him; his sleep was plagued by bad dreams of Deirdre or Devin.

Often he woke with a pain in his chest. It felt as if his beating heart were wrapped in stiff leather. At such times he closed his eyes and thought of the emerald. Determination and discipline, he decided, were the new guiding stars of his life; they would help him rescue the missing part of himself. Then he could free Deirdre, cure Shannon.

At the beginning of the fifth day, Nicodemus realized that his keloid scars had not cast a Language Prime text to the emerald since he encountered Typhon. When he mentioned this to Boann, she nodded. "When imprisoned by Typhon I learned that your scars seek to communicate with the emerald only when they are within fifty miles or so of each other. Fellwroth might have used that capability to track you, had you fled Starhaven. But now that that Typhon has taken the gem far away, you needn't worry about your scars betraying us while we are in the Pinnacle Mountains."

Nicodemus scowled. "But that means, when we pursue the demon, he will know I am coming."

Boann nodded.

"Might we cut out the scars?"

Boann shook her head sadly. "Not without killing you. When it was extracting your ability to spell, the emerald made the scars to extend down into your spine."

Nicodemus shivered and resisted the urge to touch the back of his neck. The party continued on in silence.

At the end of the seventh day, they camped in a small cavern with a sandy floor. That night, Boann woke them with loud but calm words: "Shannon, Nicodemus, rise quickly. Three kobolds have smelled our fire. They are a mile away and running fast. We don't have long before they attack."

Instantly, Shannon was on his feet, forming a textual connection with

Azure and extemporizing powerful Magnus spells. The campfire embers filled the place with a shifting red light.

Nicodemus cast a Shadowganger subtext on himself and was about to cast another on Shannon when three humanoids burst into the cavern.

Loping on all fours, the muscled creatures moved with shocking speed. Their skin was such a deep shade of blue it seemed darker than black. Their long blond ponytails matched their wide golden eyes. Their black claws matched their jagged black teeth.

Shannon cast a blaze of Magnus at each attacker. Two of his wartexts found their mark and detonated. The blasts tossed one kobold into the air and knocked the other flat. But the third monster produced an ax-like spell that shone with indigo light. With a quick swing, the creature burst Shannon's wartext into silver sentence fragments.

Nicodemus's heart went cold. The monster was a kobold spellwright.

Bellowing, the creature stood on his hind feet and rushed at Shannon. The old man tried to cast another Magnus spell but dropped it. Nicodemus threw himself forward and slammed his shoulder into the monster's hip. They tumbled to the ground. Then he was on the kobold, jamming his knee into the monster's throat. The kobold drew his arm back as if to strike with his claws, but Nicodemus pulled a dagger-like Pithan tattoo from his chest. The indigo spell illuminated the kobold's golden eyes now wide with terror. Nicodemus jammed the spell into the monster's shoulder and felt it pierce muscle and sinew.

Shrieking, the kobold thrashed violently enough to shove Nicodemus off. The world spun and then Nicodemus was lying on the sandy ground.

The cavern echoed with howls. Nicodemus pushed himself up to see the kobold spellwright clawing at his massive chest. Everywhere the monster had touched Nicodemus, his blue skin bulged with black cankers. Beside the terrified monster were his two companions. Shannon's Magnus spells had covered them with short lacerations, but not killed them.

Nicodemus stood and pulled a long tattooed wartext from his hip. The indigo sentences folded themselves into a jagged broad sword whose spikes danced like flames.

All three kobolds fell perfectly silent and still. The wrestling had dispelled part of Nicodemus's subtext, making him visible only from the waist up. He took a step toward the monsters and raised his textual sword.

The kobolds turned and sprinted away.

"Kobolds have prophecies as well," Boann observed when all was quiet again. "They will come back for you, Nicodemus. And when they do, I will have work for them."

But the monsters did not return that night or any other during their journey.

Three days later, toward midday, the party emerged from a tunnel to behold the Heaven Tree.

FIVE MILES IN diameter and almost perfectly circular, Heaven Tree Valley sat within a tight ring of mountains. Indeed the valley walls were so steep that in many places they became small cliffs. Atop these sudden drops stood grassy plateaus that were home to small herds of white goats.

On the valley's far side, a narrow stream tumbled down, pausing in places to form pools and short waterfalls. A lush covering of ferns grew on the surrounding rocks.

The stream flowed into a crescent lake that lay along the valley's northern edge.

Giant roots—each as thick around as a Starhaven tower—grew from the dark waters to stretch toward the valley's center. All across the valley floor the land heaved and bulged among the roots. Small stone walls wound across the valley, enclosing empty fields and ruined shade gardens.

Near the valley's perimeter, stone houses were clustered into homesteads. But the closer the buildings stood to the valley's center, the greater they became in number and size. Around the Heaven Tree's trunk stood a small abandoned city bristling with diminutive towers.

But it was the Heaven Tree itself that most impressed the eye.

From top leaf to taproot, it was easily as tall as most Starhaven towers. From the great trunk grew six limbs at varying heights, all of which hosted leafy canopies the size of rainclouds. Save for the two at its zenith, each massive bough reached out to rest its end on a plateau of the valley's steep walls. Around these landings stood the ruins of small villages.

Narrow bridges connected the plateau villages to the boughs. And along each massive limb ran a cobblestone road that tunneled into the trunk.

High above them, the cold autumn wind was blowing. It set the uppermost canopies to swaying and so filled the valley with a dappled wash of shifting shade and sunlight.

"So, Nicodemus Weal," Boann asked, "do you think this will make a sufficient home?"

"Home?" He laughed. "It's paradise."

They hiked onto the nearest bough, where exploration revealed that the tunnels carved into the trunk led down to the valley floor. There they found the overgrown gardens teeming with rabbits and the lake filled with trout. In the small city, they claimed a sturdy building as their new home.

The next day brought a thunderstorm that swelled the stream and filled the lake with muddy mountain runoff. For days afterward, the Heaven Tree's leaves continued dripping fat raindrops across the valley.

Most mornings Nicodemus spent with Boann. She lectured on history, theology, and politics. Afternoons were for spelling drills in the wizardly languages with Shannon. After dark, he studied the Chthonic languages alone.

Two fortnights passed slowly, and then autumn descended upon them with a bout of freezing rain. The cold painted scarlet onto the Heaven Tree's topmost leaves.

Shannon had not once needed to vomit logorrhea bywords. It seemed that Nicodemus had subdued the old man's cankers with the emerald.

As the days grew colder, the leaves farther and farther down the Heaven Tree blushed red. But few ever fell.

It was a time of talking and reflection. After the evening meal, Nicodemus and Shannon often sat before the fire, recounting Simple John's bravery or grieving for Devin.

With only three occupants, the valley could be a lonely place. Lectures and conversations had a way of exhausting themselves into silence.

So on some autumn afternoons, Nicodemus wandered. He scaled every inch of the Heaven Tree and the valley walls, discovering private grottoes and coves. He learned to hunt rabbits and goats, learned to fish the lake's dark waters. But he never learned to cook. Those meals he prepared drew Shannon's increasingly graphic but good-natured ridicule.

Sometimes after evening study, Nicodemus wandered the green valley floor. He would think of Devin or Kyran and grow glum, or of Deirdre and grow impatient. Time passed as before, slowly.

Then, one chill night, Nicodemus woke to hear Boann calling his name. Outside their house, he found the goddess standing in the middle of the cobbled street.

The three moons were full. Their glow filtered through the great boughs to fill the valley in a diffuse light.

"Walk with me down to the lake," the goddess said in her calm, sing-song voice. Nicodemus followed her out of the small Chthonic city and into a field of waist-high grass. "Tonight," she said, as they walked, "you begin an education that neither Shannon nor I could give you."

Nicodemus said nothing. They reached a raised, grassy bank that overlooked the lake. In the moonlight, the usually limpid pool was purest black. Boann turned to him and said, "When we leave this place, you will be in the greatest danger that—"

"Goddess," Nicodemus hissed and sank into a crouch. "Hold very still. Up ahead, on that rock, there's a subtextualized kobold spellwright. His prose style is shoddy." He crouched lower in the tall grass. The figure he could make out shone with dim violet sentences. The kobold was crouched atop a boulder that overlooked the water and, judging by his silhouette, was looking the other direction. "I don't think he's seen us," Nicodemus whispered.

Boann did not move. "They call it warplay," she said calmly. "It teaches young kobolds how to survive their constant tribal wars. I'm telling you this because they believe you are the human prophesied to restore kobolds to the glory they knew before the Neosolar Empire destroyed their kingdoms."

"Keep your voice down," Nicodemus whispered and pulled the tattooed attack spell from his hip. Holding it low in the grass to hide its shine, he let the text fold into a flickering broadsword.

"Each night, they will teach you a new lesson. Tonight's lesson, I believe, is the tactical importance of a decoy."

Nicodemus froze and then looked up at the goddess. "A deco—"

The charging kobold hit him from behind and wrapped two cloth-covered arms around his chest. The force of the tackle knocked the indigo sword from Nicodemus's hands and launched both of them into the air. There was a horrible moment of falling as the kobold bellowed out victory. Then they struck lake water with a jarring splash. Twisting violently, Nicodemus slammed his fist into what he assumed was the monster's face and reached for a blasting spell he had tattooed down his back.

BOANN WATCHED NICODEMUS and the kobold splash into the lake. Beside her Shannon and an ancient kobold chieftain deconstructed their subtexts. Shannon cleared his throat. "Was it truly necessary to deceive the boy? At least we could have told him that you had spoken with the kobold tribe."

Boann shook her head. "Now he will never forget this lesson."

Shannon frowned as his parrot eyed the water under which Nicodemus had disappeared. "You are sure this warplay won't kill him?"

Just then a blast of what looked like indigo fire erupted from the lake's surface. Because she was a goddess, Boann could see all magical languages. Presently, she watched the shockwave of Nicodemus's spell blow water and the kobold attacker high into the air. The yelling humanoid landed on the muddy bank with a thud. An instant later, a sputtering Nicodemus emerged in the shallows. He was stripped to the waist and peeling a wartext from his side.

"Yes, Magister, quite sure it won't kill him," Boann said dryly. "I'm more concerned he will kill one of his instructors."

The chieftain sniffed in disdain. "Any kobold who could be killed by a human new to skinwriting, savior or no, deserves to die."

Boann smiled tightly. "And how good is Nicodemus in your languages?"

The gnarled kobold scratched his beardless chin. "Considering he has been skinwriting for only a season, he is the best I have seen."

Shannon spoke up. "And that troubles me. His disability in the wizardly languages is growing worse. He cannot control even simple spells now."

"Magister! Boann!" Nicodemus yelled from the water. "There are kobolds all around!" Two more subtextualized kobolds were stalking the shore. The monster he had thrown off with the blast spell had regained his feet.

Boann called down to Nicodemus. "Tonight, your task is to avoid capture. If you can make it to sunrise without being tied up or killed you are doing well."

The boy had covered himself with plates of violet light, textual armor, she guessed. He seemed about to answer her when the kobolds charged.

The chieftain nodded at the blast and counter-blast of textual battle. "This is excellent. Now we shall teach him evasion and stealth. In late autumn we shall put warriors under his charge and teach him to lead. He will compete in this year's New Moon War. Then other tribes will witness his power and know that we have found our savior at last."

Shannon was scowling. "That would slow his training in the wizardly languages and delay his attempt to learn more about his new Language Prime fluency."

Boann waved this comment away. "Those can wait. After so much loss, he will benefit from a taste of success and a chance to become a leader." She looked at Shannon. "Besides, if he is to survive outside of this valley, he will need time for the lessons of warplay to become instinct."

Shannon narrowed his white eyes. "So let us teach him to survive, but why turn him into some kind of warlord?"

"Not a warlord," Boann corrected, "but a commander. His half-sister is presently being tutored by Trillinonish generals and Ixonian admirals. She is the one who will lead humanity's forces in the War of Disjunction. But before she does that, she must track down and kill the Language Prime spellwright who enabled Typhon to write the dragon that attacked Trillinon. I doubt she knows that she is training to kill her half-brother."

Just then the kobolds yelped as Nicodemus cast an indigo shockwave that knocked them over. Wasting no time, the boy sprinted away down the lake shore. The kobolds struggled to their feet and hallooed a hunting call as they ran in pursuit.

"Compared to her agents, these kobolds will seem mild as kittens. And don't forget that Typhon will have a half-completed dragon at his command," Boann said to Shannon. "We must do this to keep him alive long enough to fight in the War of Disjunction."

Shannon pulled a silvery dreadlock from his face. "Perhaps this training will keep his body alive, but what will it do to his soul?"

Boann looked back to the lake and thought about this. "Shannon, my new friend," she said after a moment, "I don't know."

A DARK MOOD came over Shannon as life in the Heaven Tree Valley took on a new, more urgent rhythm. Each morning, Nicodemus came stumbling in, often bleeding and always chattering about what he had learned in warplay. One night it was how to scale a city wall with Chthonic spells. Another night it was how to outflank a hostile force or how to attack an enemy camp or some other blood-minded action.

The boy also talked about his discovery that kobolds could briefly touch him. Their blue skins were remarkably resilient to the cankers his touch produced. The monsters could simply rip them off without consequences other than minor bleeding. Though such contact came only during fighting, the boy was relieved to touch another living creature without killing it.

After describing the night's warplay, Nicodemus would sleep until late afternoon and then study the wizardly languages with Shannon.

But the boy's cacography was indeed getting worse. The spelling drills had no effect. Worse, when asked to compose an original spell, the boy would write a tattooed draft on his forearm before attempting a wizardly version.

Some days Shannon despaired of teaching and took Nicodemus for long walks around the valley. He told the boy about his childhood, of his diplomatic service during the Spirish Civil War, of his disastrous love and the loss of his wife.

Nicodemus listened carefully. At times, to Shannon's surprise, he found himself being consoled by his student. It gave him a hollow feeling.

Worse, Shannon's old body began to suffer from bouts of severe fatigue. Often his stomach hurt after meals and sometimes he had difficulty in the privy. As the days got colder, he spent more and more time sleeping before the fire.

One day, he felt too weak even to walk with Nicodemus. The result was an argument: Nicodemus insisted that he would soon be strong enough to pursue Typhon. Shannon had refused to listen and pointed out that Nicodemus's precious Chthonic language functioned only in the dark and neither Typhon nor his half-sister's agents would do him the favor of attacking only at night.

Shannon tried to emphasize the importance of learning to harness his new Language Prime fluency and using the Index to research Typhon. But Nicodemus had only stormed out of the house, yelling that he would not watch Shannon die when there was a chance he could recover the emerald.

That evening, both student and teacher apologized. But nothing was resolved.

Shannon did know moments of happiness when he saw flashes of the boy he had known back in Starhaven. Toward late autumn, during one chill afternoon, snow sifted down through the Heaven Tree's boughs.

Shannon and Nicodemus set out to wage a snowball fight. Azure acted as Shannon's eyes, and Boann—not being tangible enough to pick up a snowball—judged the contest. But so few flakes made it to the valley floor that Nicodemus and Shannon soon resorted to the traditional Jejunus cursing match. Shannon, having a linguist's trove of dirty words, easily won.

But the flashes of boyish Nicodemus grew rarer as his warplay training grew more intense. He was befriending the kobolds, coming to trust them in the way that soldiers came to trust one another. It was a bond that Shannon had never known.

Nicodemus talked incessantly of the New Moon War: a ceremonial gathering of all the kobold tribes. On the night when the three moons were dark, they would emerge from the underground to occupy a plateau deep in the Pinnacle Mountains. The plateau had held the kobold capital city before the Neosolar Empire destroyed it.

Each tribe would send a party of ten warriors into the ruins to hunt for a golden bough that a kobold priest had hidden. The party that returned with the bough won their tribe the right to protect for the year the crown of the last kobold queen.

When the winter solstice approached, and the Heaven Tree's scarlet leaves began to fall, Nicodemus left with his kobold warriors for the New Moon War. Boann went with them, but Shannon had to stay behind. It would be hard enough, claimed the kobold chieftain, to bring one human to the gathering. Two would be impossible.

Left alone, Shannon found his days passed slowly. His appetite and energy had improved, but he slept poorly and spent most hours nervously walking the valley.

After the longest fortnight of Shannon's life, the kobold party returned with Nicodemus on their shoulders. He wore a jagged gash on his jaw, a large bandage around his chest, and an ancient band of steel on his head.

He had won the New Moon War and had brought home fifty more kobold followers.

As luck would have it, Nicodemus returned the night before Midwinter's Day. The kobolds held a feast around the bonfire. Shannon sat next to the boy during dinner. He wanted to hear everything about the New Moon War, but the kobolds kept up such a racket with their singing and dancing and boasting that no communication was possible. Two of the blueskins started to fight before Nicodemus stopped them with a barked command.

Later that night it began to snow. Again few flakes made it to the valley floor, but it was enough to end the feast. The kobolds all bowed to Nicodemus and retreated to their caverns.

Shannon took his student back into their house, checked on his wounds, which were not worrisome, and fell into a deep sleep of relief.

He awoke to a bitterly cold and dark morning with an inch of snow on the valley floor. While they ate, Nicodemus recounted the war among the kobold ruins. One kobold tribe had disbelieved that Nicodemus was the prophesied savior. Their party had ambushed his during the New Moon War. At first Nicodemus bragged of how his warriors had rebuffed the attack, then he grew solemn as he remembered the enemy kobolds he had killed. Shannon made him retell everything twice.

After they ate, Nicodemus went back to sleep. He awoke when it stopped snowing in the afternoon. "It's Midwinter's Day," he said, looking out a window to the clearing sky beyond the Heaven Tree. "They'll be celebrating back in Starhaven."

Shannon agreed that they would be. "Doesn't seem right that there's so little snow on this holiday."

Nicodemus was silent for a moment. "Maybe I'll hike up to the topmost canopy and see the snow. There's a small Chthonic fortress among the boughs. Its watchtower has a splendid view."

Shannon had never been up that high, but he did not think he could keep up with the younger man. He told Nicodemus to go alone.

WHEN NICODEMUS REACHED the watchtower at the top of the Heaven Tree, he took in the vast panorama of snowy mountains. Far to the north stood the slim black silhouette of the Eversong Spire.

The Chthonic watchtower had long ago lost its roof and now a foot of snow covered the place. He cleared off what had once been a table and settled in to watch what was left of the year's shortest day melt into dark.

When the setting sun bathed the world in a burgundy light, Shannon's loud breaths sounded from the stairs.

Nicodemus ran to help the old man with the last few steps. "Magister," he scolded, "you should have told me you were coming up. I would have walked with you."

"Then you would have wasted your time walking with an old man," the wizard huffed. Nicodemus helped him sit.

"Fiery blood, but I'm tired," Shannon said, putting Azure in his lap and surrounding her with his cloak. The parrot stuck her head out of her new cloth nest so she could continue seeing for them both. "What a wonderful view!" the old man said with a wrinkled smile.

Far ahead of them, the Erasmine Spire shone with the sunset's glow. Gradually Shannon's breathing slowed.

A colaboris spell erupted from the Spire and flew over the eastern horizon and into the coming night.

"A boy is trapped in an academy," Nicodemus said softly. "He learns he is incomplete. He sees those around him suffer. For a moment he glimpses himself entirely before he escapes. But no matter where he goes, no matter what he becomes, he will cause or witness suffering. Still, he wants nothing more than to try to end the suffering."

Shannon said nothing for a while. "You know that I have begun to ghostwrite?" he asked.

"An impressing matrix shines about your head when you sleep," Nicodemus said without looking over. "It shines in Azure's mind as well. I think it has something to do with dreaming. Have the cankers grown worse?"

To see them with his Language Prime fluency, Nicodemus would have had to touch the old man. He dared not.

Shannon took a long breath. "No. In fact, I've been feeling better. I suppose this improvement is temporary. There's no way of telling. I believe we will recover the emerald in time to cure the thing growing in my gut. But . . . I don't want to be caught unawares. I'm ghostwriting . . . as a precaution."

Nicodemus nodded. "It is a race, then, between my training and your disease. If I lose, you die."

Shannon sighed. "There is no race, Nicodemus. To help fight the Disjunction, you must learn to control your Language Prime fluency. You must do that alone; I cannot teach it to you. And now that the Index is misspelled, only you can use it to learn about Typhon. Those tasks will take years if not decades. Leave this valley before then and you won't be able to oppose the demons. You won't even be able to survive."

"Magister, the kobolds say I am the most powerful spellwright they have ever known. And I command a small army of their warriors."

The old man shook his head. "Kobolds rarely leave their underworld. A kobold army would be helpless on the war field. And, Nicodemus, your spells only function in the dark. You must continue to train in the wizardly languages. If you run after Deirdre and the emerald before then, it won't take Typhon or your half-sister long before they realize you're powerless in daylight."

"I won't watch you die!" Nicodemus replied hotly. "I know what I must do now."

Shannon opened his mouth as if to object but then shook his head. They both fell silent.

Gradually the sun sank below the horizon and the stars made their slow debut. A wind picked up and began to sing its whistling song among the bare branches.

"Nicodemus, you haven't escaped Starhaven," Shannon said. "You think you're out here. You think your strength lies in your Chthonic texts or in your skill as a commander. You think you're incomplete without the emerald. You can't see that your true strength is already inside of you. And that means you're still in that academy." He nodded toward the spire. "You're still running from golems."

Nicodemus pursed his lips but said nothing.

"You must realize that you are complete now."

The young man shook his head. "You are dying. Deirdre is enslaved. The purpose of my life is to regain the emerald and end my disability. Nothing will be right until then."

Shannon began to protest but then stopped.

They sat together, in silence.

AN ICY WIND curled around Nicodemus and Shannon and flew away north.

It blustered about on the white mountains and then split itself among Starhaven's many towers. It howled over the bridges and sprayed dry snow into the gargoyles as they pushed drifts from eaves and cleared ice from the gutters.

The wind circled the Drum Tower and rattled its paper window screens. Simple John—now Lesser Wizard John of Starhaven—removed a screen and looked into the night. He took a long tremulous breath and again thought about his dead friends: Devin, Nicodemus, Magister Shannon.

Behind John someone knocked, likely a young cacographer. As the new Master of the Drum Tower, John replaced the screen and turned away from his sadness to see to the little one.

Outside, the wind swirled away from the Drum Tower before dropping into the Spirish stable yard to ruffle Amadi's thick cloak. She was overseeing her sentinels as they prepared for the long journey back to the North.

Though her expression was calm, her heart teemed with fear and anticipation. Colaboris spells had carried reports of Fellwroth and Typhon to the other academies. Not everyone believed the news, but no one denied its effect. Thoughts of prophesy were now on every wizard's mind, political speculations on every wizard's lips. And now she was returning to Astrophell, where the game of factions was being played with murderous intensity.

Inside the stable, she put politics and prophesy aside long enough to inspect every pack, saddle, and horse her party would take on their journey. Then she dismissed the sentinels and walked alone into the snowy stable yard to look up at the stars.

Once back in Astrophell, she would owe loyalty to no faction. Alone, she would have to navigate the infighting and gather information useful to Shannon and Nicodemus once they emerged. Doing so would undoubtedly incur the distrust of every major faction. The slightest mistake could kill her.

Amadi smiled. In her soul she loved nothing so much as great purpose. Now she certainly had that.

The icy wind grew stronger. Pulling her cloak more tightly around her shoulders, Amadi started off to find her bed and dream of Astrophell under the hot Northern sun.

Above her, the wind rushed out of Starhaven and rolled down the foothills. It passed over the ruined Chthonic village and made the ghosts look up with wide, amber eyes. They could not feel cold, but they shivered nonetheless. They knew that the world was about to change.

Onward the wind tumbled, down the foothills to the Westernmost Road. Then to the north it flew, traveling to warmer lands. Slowly the landscape shed snowy white for lush green. Now the wind turned westward, blowing long waves through the tall savannah grass until it crossed a narrow caravan road and crested a ridge. Here stood a tall sandstone watchtower.

Beside this fortification crouched Deirdre, her red-and-black wings fluttering in the wind. Before her, the road ran straight for five miles before meeting the tan walls of a Spirish city. Even in the dim starlight, she could see the city's many tiled roofs and the wide octahedral dome of its temple.

Slowly, Deirdre stood. Tears streamed down her face, and blood ran down her arms. At her feet lay four dead city guards. Typhon had compelled her to kill them; he wanted the city to receive no warning of his approach.

The wind blew harder, scooping under Deirdre's wings and lifting her a few inches off the ground. Involuntarily, she tightened her fist around the Emerald of Arahest. She had been through the deep savanna and fought the beasts that lived there. She had seen the unspeakable things Typhon had done to those beasts with Language Prime.

The wind lessened and she sank until her boots touched ground. Then she started walking. A fresh surge of tears coursed down her face. She was already grieving for what Typhon would force her to do in the city.

From her contact with the demon's mind, she had learned about the newest Language Prime spell he had begun to write. That is why she prayed that neither Boann nor Nicodemus nor Shannon tried to rescue her. If any of them did, they would face a spell that none of them could truly comprehend or even see.

They would face a true dragon.

Epilog

The linguist felt as if he were choking on his own words.

They were short, commonplace words originating from his old heart, making it beat faster. He took Azure out from under his cloak.

She had been sleeping in the warmth and sent him a testy sentence.

Seeing through her eyes, the wizard stood and made his way back toward the steps. "I'll start down now," he said to his pupil. "Come help me when you're ready."

Nicodemus nodded.

By the stairs, Shannon found Boann watching him. "Did you convince him?" the goddess asked.

Shannon smiled sadly and cast a few flamefly paragraphs for light. "He's too impressed by his new abilities." He paused. "He needs time to see that he hasn't escaped his limitations." Through Azure, he watched Nicodemus close his eyes and lean into the wind.

"But his progress is unexpectedly quick," the goddess said. "Perhaps he might be right? Perhaps there is a chance he will be ready in time to save you?"

Shannon exhaled. "There's no telling, but I certainly hope . . ." The strange choking sensation filled his chest again. "Nicodemus," he called, to keep the feelings at bay. "I need your help after all."

The young man sprang up and came running, concern painted across his dark face.

"Besides, there's a pot of stew waiting at home," Shannon said through a smile. "And you didn't cook it, so this time it won't taste like boiled horse sweat."

Nicodemus laughed and then took Shannon's arm, careful to prevent his skin from touching the old man's.

Suddenly the old linguist had to draw a sharp breath and look away.

"What is it, Magister? Does it hurt?"

"No, no," Shannon said as firmly as he could. "There's a . . ." His hand came up to his neck. "A sensation here . . . I can't . . . I don't know if there's a word for . . ."

Again he tried to name the feeling. But the words in his heart mashed themselves into a small, spiny ball and jammed themselves into his throat.

He was choking on a jagged mass of the words "loss" and "gratitude," "desperation" and "relief," "fear" and "awe."

He was choking on the sharp knowledge that he was slowly dying.

"Maybe it's heartburn from drinking my horse sweat stew," said Nicodemus.

Shannon laughed and decided that the best word for the strange emotion in his chest was "love."

He looked at his student. The boy had become a man, and in him Shannon saw a flickering potential that just might grow strong enough to give the world hope.

Nicodemus looked back at Shannon. His young face was lit by several incandescent paragraphs. The bright words had illuminated his smile with soft white light and, by contrast, filled his dark eyes with a joyful, sparkling black.

ABOUT THE AUTHOR

Blake Charlton first overcame severe dyslexia in the sixth grade when he began sneaking fantasy and science fiction books into special-ed study hall. Inspired, he went on to graduate summa cum laude and Phi Beta Kappa from Yale University. After college, he worked as an English teacher, a medical writer for UCSF and Stanford, a tutor for the learning disabled, and a junior varsity football coach. Blake is currently a third-year medical student at Stanford Medical School, where he teaches creative writing for medical students and has received a fellowship to write fiction. *Spellwright* is his first novel. His hobbies include cycling, swimming, backpacking, and collecting jokes about dyslexia and premature baldness.